The Dancehall Years

Joan Haggerty

A NOVEL

Mother Tongue Publishing Limited
Salt Spring Island, BC
Canada

MOTHER TONGUE PUBLISHING LIMITED
290 Fulford-Ganges Road, Salt Spring Island, B.C. V8K 2K6 Canada
www.mothertonguepublishing.com
Represented in North America by Heritage Group Distribution.

The Dancehall Years is a work of fiction.
Names, characters, places, and incidents are the products of the author's imagination
or are used fictitiously. Any resemblance to actual events, locales, or persons,
living or dead, is entirely coincidental.

Book Design by Mark Hand
Front cover photo: Bowen Island Inn, circa 1930s, Vancouver Archives AM75-S1-: CVA 374-327.
Back cover photo: Lady Alexandra docked at Bowen Island, circa 1940s, Vancouver Archives
AM1184-S1-: CVA 1184-3499, Photographer: Jack Lindsay.
Printed on Enviro Cream, 100% recycled
Printed and bound in Canada.

Mother Tongue Publishing gratefully acknowledges the assistance of the Province of British
Columbia through the B.C. Arts Council and we acknowledge the support of the Canada Council
for the Arts, which last year invested $157 million in writing and publishing throughout Canada.
Nous remercions de son soutien le Conseil des Arts du Canada, qui a investi 157$ millions de
dollars l'an dernier dans les lettres et l'édition à travers le Canada.

LIBRARY AND ARCHIVES CANADA CATALOGUING IN PUBLICATION

Haggerty, Joan, author
      The dancehall years / Joan Haggerty.

ISBN 978-1-896949-54-3 (paperback)

      I. Title.

PS8565.A35D36 2016   C813'.54   C2016-901040-6

FSC logo

For Ray Cournoyer
who built the space

FENNS   KILLAMS AND GALLAGHERS   YOSHITOS

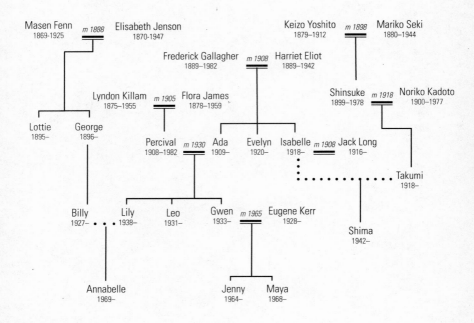

Masen Fenn
1869-1925
m 1888
Elisabeth Jenson
1870-1947

Frederick Gallagher
1889–1982
m 1908
Harriet Eliot
1889–1942

Keizo Yoshito
1879–1912
m 1898
Mariko Seki
1880–1944

Lyndon Killam
1875–1955
m 1905
Flora James
1878–1959

Shinsuke
1899–1978
m 1918
Noriko Kadoto
1900–1977

Lottie
1895–

George
1896–

Percival
1908–1982
m 1930
Ada
1909–

Evelyn
1920–

Isabelle
1918–
m 1908
Jack Long
1916–

Takumi
1918–

Billy
1927–

Lily
1938–

Leo
1931–

Gwen
1933–
m 1965
Eugene Kerr
1928–

Shima
1942–

Annabelle
1969–

Jenny
1964–

Maya
1968–

THE DANCEHALL YEARS

BOOK I

BOOK II

BOOK III

BOOK IV

BOOK I

DANCEHALL

1.

June, 1939.

Next to Christmas, this is the best day of the year. The end of June, school's out and they're on their way to Bowen Island. I'm a leg man myself, Gwen's dad says winking when he drops a suitcase on the Sannie wharf in Horseshoe Bay. Her mother's skirt rides up her calves as she climbs back up the steep runged side of the gangplank. The flats ooze mud with clam breathing holes and barnacled mussel shells ring the ankles of the wharf pilings. We have enough stuff for a month of Sundays, he says. What do we think, we're going to feed an army? He piles three hats on his head to make them laugh.

The captain holds the painter of the small passenger launch like the reins of a horse, white hair glinting in the sun. Small green waves lap the sides of the boat; the deck gives a little when you step on it. Coming up for good, are you, Gwen? he says which means he knows you're arriving for the whole summer and are not just a day tripper like the picnickers. He wears everything in matching navy like an old man going to private school. It's easy to rest your hand in his palm and step gracefully on board if your parents aren't looking.

Which they aren't because her brother, Leo, is standing at the top of the gangplank taking one foot on and off a rung like he's trying to get on the escalator at the Bay. He'll wait there until the cows come home if someone doesn't go up and get him. Percy you go, their mother says, tucking baby Lily higher on her hip. Their dad smiles as he lopes back up to walk down with his son.

Next thing you know they're facing each other on the side seats of the *Sannie*, canvas flaps rolled down over the glassless windows in case it's rough. Parcels and suitcases strapped to the roof. Once out of Horseshoe Bay, sections of sun glint through the clouds. Cedar and fir covered slopes smooth and darken. Near Passage Island, small sailboats tack back and forth across the channel. All Gwen's doing is reaching out to test the temperature of the water but her mother grabs the tail of her blouse, neck jerking forward like a grouse crossing the road.

Do you mind, Mom? I can swim.

All *right*.

When they arrive at the Cove, the launch tucks itself under the wing of the tree feathered point. The black line of the high tide marks a bathtub ring around the stony bay. Here's the moment the card promised when the postman tromped up their laurel lined Blenheim St. path in Vancouver to deliver a hand-coloured photo of the Lady Alexandra sailing to Bowen Island. Lipstick red funnels, turquoise sea. Picnic crowds getting on and off. *Dear Gwen, The salmon berries are ripe so I start marking off the days. It won't be summer until you get here. Love, Auntie Isabelle.* All next month and then for another, the two of them will swing in the hammock strung between the two dogwood trees, white flowers blooming like outsized stars in the green sky. The sun coming along on an invisible leash. New alders will nudge under the canvassed bulge of their bodies like small animals. They'll hold buttercups under each others' chins to see if they like butter.

As soon as they're close enough to see the ochre rockweed on the beach, Auntie has to start from their cottage on the south side of the end of the Point and make her way down to the wharf, the sun casting shadows in the shapes of thimbleberry leaves onto the trail below her. There she is standing exactly where she's supposed to be—hurrah—the one who comes up first to open the camp now a waving speck on the verandah. Gwen waves back, her hand a small flap that won't stop. Last summer she and Auntie found a leaky dinghy which they rowed into the Cove and sank at the exact moment the *Sannie* passed so the passengers would wonder how on earth those two could be sitting upright in the water with nothing underneath them.

Auntie Isabelle's always shy when she comes to meet the *Sannie*, narrowing her eyes as if to make sure they're really family. Even when her eyes are shut, there's a faint blue light shining through the lids as if she's gazing through porcelain. At twenty one, she's tall, like their dad, with pale, even skin, and a long oval face. Her dress has a flounce over the seat. Her socks are rolled over her running shoes like sausages. Light cast through a canopy of maple leaves flickers over her as she comes down the tearoom hill. Mother says Auntie makes such a fuss over them because she's looking forward to having children of her own.

Here, Ada, let me take the baby, Auntie says, lifting Lily from her sister's arms. She holds her close and pats her back. There's a good girl, she says. Let's go to the tearoom and get ice cream.

Strawberry?

Strawberry.

Leo always has Neopolitan.

When you're rowing under the wharf, people don't know you're the Billy Goat Gruff until you call up to them. More light flings itself on the water between the planks in strips. Just so you all remember, everyone's on duty until everything's done. Their mother always says that. It's her job. Every last item has to be carried from the wharf up past the dancehall and over the hill to the end of the Point where their cottage is located. After that, they're up for good and only the dads go down. The dads have to work all week and stay with grandparents at night because their houses in town are rented for the summer which is too bad because renters let houses go to rack and ruin.

They shouldn't be getting ice cream on the first trip but no one cares. It doesn't matter. It's summer. The dancehall sits like a giant music box above the wharf. Ivy and wisteria climb the sides of the octagonal building and along the roof to the central cupola where the summer kids climb to lie on their stomachs and spy on the dancers inside the circle of white mock Corinthian columns. You're only allowed to dance inside the columns if you're in love or if you're spectacular dancers. The floor is lined with horsehair. The grownups say it and the Commodore are the best dance floors in the Lower Mainland. A single leaf blows along the powdery floor. The place smells of beer, cigarettes, perfume and disinfectant from the bathrooms.

Auntie turns a salmonberry on its back, checking for worms before she pops it in Gwen's mouth. Opened salmonberries make perfect fairies' blankets. The places she passes through have more light after she leaves than when she steps in. When you're alone with Auntie, she stops being shy, and acts as if life is a parade and she knows all the elephants. The fork they don't take leads to Sandy Beach where even now you can hear the shouts of kids going down the slide double, the thighs of the one behind fastened tight around the one in front. You get a skin burn if you don't pour a can of water on the chute before you slide down. The cool water beckons paradise, paradise.

The next stop is the resting rock, a stone shaped like a miniature North America on the hill down to the cottage. Auntie's skin is pale—she never goes out in the heat of the day—her arm smells like the sea and the sun. The air around her is chartreuse green. The resting rock is where you cool your feet at the beginning of the summer when you haven't broken them in yet. It's where you sit with your face in your hands when you're It for kick-the-can. It's where you watch the Lady Alex coming through the cedars: black prow, trees, brass portholes, trees, red funnel, trees, red funnel, trees. It's completely still and then it's all boat, a huge bulk massing out of nowhere. Fairy chariots set off between the Douglas firs in the yard of Miss Fenn's cottage, the closest one to the dancehall on the north side of the point separating Snug Cove from Deep Bay. Because Gwen's family cottage is on the very tip of the point, they sometimes they call it the Point Point.

Crowds of people come up on the steamer (some people call it the Lady Alex, some people call it the Lady Alec, it doesn't matter). They sing we're heere because we're heeere because we're heeeere because we're heeeeeere. On Saturday nights when it's the booze cruise they change it to we're heeeere because there's beeeeere. Ha ha. The ship seems to press against their point of land the way a tall dog leans against you and doesn't care about budging. Triangular flags on the rigging flutter like bright fall leaves between the dashing cedars. Ivy twists up the corked fir bark like veins on the back of a giant hand. On the boat, the cheering people rest their elbows on the deck railings and laugh. When the sun finds a gap in the boughs, a swath of forest lights up without a sound.

When you come up for the summer, it takes a few nights to sort out which noises are which. *Chip dee do. Chip dee do dee doo.* It's only an owl. Go back to sleep. The resting rock is where you take a magazine with a picture on the cover of a lady in a polka dot bathing suit tanning herself on a blanket, reading a copy of the magazine she's pictured on. That idea would go on forever if you could see far enough. In the morning, the billowing ghost leaning against the dogwood turns out to be the drying mosquito net Mother used to strain the coffee because she forgot the percolator.

The iron cots that Mother, and her younger sisters, Isabelle and Evvie, slept in when they were children still line the attic. Wooden fruit crates are nailed to the wall where you put away your shorts and t-shirts. On the verandah, a bathing cap hangs by its strap from the knob of a chair. When Gwen lies on a stool kicking her feet in the air practising the front crawl, her dad passes by with a raised hand and says what a chance.

When she sits on the verandah stairs eating a left over jam and bacon sandwich that Auntie saved from breakfast—her favourite—her hair flickers in a spotlight of sun so she can't tell the difference between hair shadows and the feathery branches. The firs are nearly three times as tall as the house. Lily is put down for her nap in a cot under the Douglas fir. A crow splits its beak wide enough for a coin to slip in and caws. Funny Auntie Charlestons around the corner, wet sheets draped over her arm, a clothespin on the end of her nose. She takes more clothespins out of her mouth and marches them along the clothesline like wooden soldiers.

Name one other place, Gwen, one other location you're cognizant of where people hang up their wash to wetten, she says.

It doesn't take much to make the children laugh, does it? Mother says.

The Alex gets it in its mind to leave exactly the moment you've forgotten it's in; the whistle makes you jump and the steamer rushes the pram, the fan-tailed chickadees, the washing, the baby and all out in its wake as it reverses out of the Cove.

One of these weekends please will Percy get a saw and cut a few lower branches from the fir nearest the house so they can have *some* sun. Percy says he will, but he might not get around to it; the dads work so hard during the week they get to do exactly what they like on the weekends which is mostly fish from the *Adabelle* and sit on the verandah shaking ice cubes in their rum and Coca-Cola glasses. When the dads go down on Sunday nights, the mothers laugh more. They smoke Lucky Strikes and drink coffee from cups with lipstick on them. You can jump up and down as long as you want on the living room couch. Stay on the beach until the sun goes down, watch slips of turquoise in the sea turn silver, no they're green, no they're silver. Logs float in the bay you can swim out to and claim, paddling flat with your alligator hands. Crabs scuttle under new rocks when you lift up their houses. Leo takes the wheel on the ship log. Blue forget-me-nots grow in the crannies. Take us to Bowyer. Take us to Anvil. No, take us to Passage.

High tide in the morning is way different from high tide at night. When it's high tide at night, the water feels like it's going to stay in while you sleep; in the morning, when it's in, you know it's going to turn around and go straight back out. Waiting for a grown-up to take you to the beach must be the way their springer spaniel, Molly, feels when no one wants to go for a walk and she's left pawing at the air. One sec, Auntie says, while I water these azaleas. There are no miniature people behind the lit fabric on the radio. Leo says only babies think that. Past where the sword ferns tuck into rock crannies, sunlit gold coins shimmer between the waving boughs. The next tree turns off the switch. If you furrow your fingers into purple foxglove blossoms, crouch below the cottage window ledge, stick up gloved fingers one after the other and bend them down again, Auntie will look up and laugh. If you do it faster and faster, it will be funny enough for her to come over to see who's masterminding the show. By then, you'll have ducked so far down she'll think it was the fairies.

After she's watered the azaleas, she says she won't be long, she's just got the petunias to put in. Who cares about the petunias? When Mother takes her to the beach, all she does is sit in the shade, only coming into the water to breast stroke a few yards, lifting her chin to keep her head above water so her hair won't get wet. What kind of a life is that?

In the end, there's nothing to do but go to Sandy on her own, *hang her clothes on a hickory limb* and not go near the water. Sit on the concrete stairs and wait. If she can make everything hold perfectly still, grasp her wishing self tightly enough, the longer she doesn't let herself look, the more likely it'll be that, when she does look, her swimming teacher, Takumi Yoshito, will be standing on Sandy as if he's always been on the beach and summer can begin at last. The cork ropes that should outline the swimming area will be coiled by the racing wall ready to be pulled to the wharf in the rowboat. The door to the lifeguard shack will be open, the blankets tucked firmly into the cot. The first-aid kit and pith helmet hanging in their places on the wall. Charts posted showing rescuers pressing the backs of drowned people so water can pour out their mouths. The huge beach thermometer that's hopelessly exposed when there's no tide to measure will be decently covered with water and Takumi will be raking sea lettuce along the high tide line, his tender smile wandering more to one side of his face than the other. Even this far away you know that when he catches sight of you heel toeing along the narrow board that tops the backrest down the length of the beach, you'll be able to swing on a star. His sweatshirt slopes down to his narrow hips and his eyelids fasten flat against their sockets, not like her dad's which fold back like an accordion. Takumi acts as if teaching children to swim is how he always imagined grown-up life. As if he lives to shape their keels and set them afloat like boats.

There he is standing in the water up to his thighs, the deep note of his voice ready to sink soft and low in the back of her head. Her neck turns as if it's been oiled when her head drops into the silky sea. If you believe in the sea and pretend you're in your own bed at home, he says, the water will want to hold you up. There's nothing else for it to do. Lying below him, the current streams through her hair the way it did the time she was allowed to have it out in ringlets that dropped from her mother's fingers like laburnum blossoms. When Takumi slides his hands from under her back, the magician in the shiny blue suit at the vaudeville show spreads a cloth over the girl lying on a table and she disappears. One of his hands strokes the air above the cloth from her waist to her feet, the other from her waist to her head. She has to grab his upraised wrist so he can yard her straight out of the water, flashing her up with the spray until she's flying like a fish.

You were swimming, he said. You were swimming.

2.

June, 1941.

This summer nothing's like it's supposed to be. Not one thing. Their mother's parents, Grandpa and Grandma Gallagher are at the cottage already which means they have to mind their Ps and Qs in no uncertain terms. Meals will have to be on time, no ifs, ands, or buts. It's their house, their mother says. Who else built the fireplace? I ask you. At the wharf no one's making bets about the number of trips it's going to take from the wharf to the cottage. Nothing about ice cream at the tea room and what flavour it's going to be. The only thing to do is tuck yourself into the adult formation and let them take you along willy nilly, even if it seems like what Auntie wants is for everyone to keep walking to the end of the Point, wade into the water and keep going so not even their heads re-appear.

When they get to the cottage the grown-ups line up on the verandah and stare down at the beach. The tide's so far out the distant rocks encrusted with barnacles look burned. No one says, *If you kids are going to eat watermelon, go and lean over the verandah*. No one asks for anyone to come and look at what she's been doing in the garden. Someone's hand on the table, someone else's on top, then another, top to bottom faster and faster until you don't know whose hands are whose? Not this year. All you've got are a bunch of umber ponds in the intertidal zone that will have disappeared by suppertime. It's as if they've passed their own stop on the tram and don't have a chance of finding their way back, like the time before their dad was married when he fell asleep coming home from dancing downtown and the conductor had to wake him at the end of the line. He fell asleep again and ended up going from one end of the city to the other all night long!

On Sunday mornings before Lily was born, she and Leo used to walk to the store holding their mother's hands. Paths furrowed along Salmonberry trail that weren't there the night before. The grey mass of beach at Sandy was carried over as ballast in the Lady Alexandra when it came from Scotland. A freighter is built to carry freight. If you don't have any freight to bring from Scotland, you put sand in the hold. Crushed ferns, rum bottles in the grass. Drunk people who missed the boat asleep in the woods. Clothes on thank goodness, their mother said. What they're supposed to remember in cases like this is to walk along as quickly as they can and pretend not to see. A lady always knows when to leave the party. A lady can always pretend not to see.

That night after the moonlight cruise steamer has docked and the music from the pavilion is drifting down the hill, Gwen lies in bed in the attic listening to the adult voices drift up the gap by the chimney. Grandpa Gallagher is holding forth in no uncertain terms that Auntie Isabelle shouldn't be gallivanting around by herself on dance nights and where on earth could she have got herself to?

She's a big girl, dad, says Mother. She can take care of herself.

She's not as level headed as you are, Ada.

The trouble is that it's the war now and not one of those summers when it's easy to remember that when the sun comes up, it's really the earth curving away and not the other way around. That it's the tram on the track beside you pulling away even though it seems you're the one doing the moving. If she'd been able to hold that fact in her mind a bit longer, maybe she'd remember whether or not the moon rotates as it's going around the earth. If she climbed down the fire escape ladder nailed to the side of the house, it would only be a ten minute walk through the woods to the small meadow beside the dancehall where she could chin herself on the window and see what the dancers are up to. She can't go to sleep anyway without Auntie on the other side of the partition calling out sweet dreams. Sleep tight, don't let the bed bugs bite. She pulls up Lily's blanket on the cot beside her, makes sure she's sound asleep, puts her underwear back on so she can tuck in her nightie and not trip climbing down the ladder rungs. The full moon lights her way along the path to the edge of the small meadow where she's about to start up the grassy hill to the pavilion but, ahead of her, she almost trips and has to back away from the forms of two people lying in the grass. Grandpa's footsteps pad along the nearby trail. Fear spreads below her diaphragm like water oozing under stones on the beach when you pick them up and the crabs have to run away to find new houses. People from the dancehall pass by hollering it seems like to nobody. She can see that it's Auntie alright but whoever it is she's holding in her arms has his back turned. The wharf lanterns corkscrew their beams into the dark oily water.

The next morning Grandpa slaps down magazines with pictures of soldiers kissing their girlfriends. All people have to know is how to behave! he shouts. Later, after Auntie snuck back in, he'd pounded up the attic stairs and slammed her door so that it whapped hard against her bed. Don't think I didn't see you over in the shadows, Isabelle. What if you don't get your period? Why would he be getting mad at her for forgetting what's at the end of a sentence? At breakfast, Auntie winces his hand off her shoulder and he hits the table for no reason. I'm going to work, she says. Gwen's coming with me. I need her. *She needs me.* She runs to the shed, stuffing pots of red geraniums into cardboard boxes. Take these, Gwen, and these. My wretched father. He darn well could say anything to anybody. Of course Lily wants to come with them but Auntie tells her to stay here this time because she's a tag along. The two of them march over the causeway bridge that separates the lagoon from the salt chuck, along the trail past the honeysuckle and wild rose arbours. At the greenhouse behind the hotel, they stop in front of the head gardener, Mr. Yoshito, who's sitting at his garden desk peering over the tops of his glasses. A few seed envelopes are stuck in his hat band. A picture of Takumi rowing his lifeguard boat has pride of place on the desk.

Flower pots are stacked inside each other behind him. Mr. Yoshito is famous for collecting rare plants from all over the world. Smell this, he'll say and slide a magnolia grandiflora under your nose. Grandpa Gallagher is the gardener of the family and says he doesn't know what he would do without Mr. Yoshito's top soil. Very - nice - soil - you - have here, he says breaking up his words which makes Auntie frown. Once, when Gwen was sent to the store to buy a tin of Old Dutch cleanser, she was so busy looking at the nun with Dutch shoes on the label she tripped on an uneven wharf board and scraped her knee. Mr. Yoshito came out from behind his vegetable stall, told her to straighten her leg, and smeared balsam pitch on the cut. She kept staring at her knee all the way home because she was used to getting bawled out if she got pitch on her skirt or shorts. Maybe it was okay on her knee though. Up at the hotel, Mr. Yoshito takes flower bulbs from his pockets and fastens them in the ground like doorknobs.

Now, at the hotel greenhouse, Shinsuke Yoshito doesn't say a word about the geraniums; instead jumps to his feet and strides up and down the spicy aisles, picking suckers from the tomato plants. He takes in all of you at once glance, and doesn't suffer fools gladly.

I was thinking maybe we should plant water lilies in the lagoon, Auntie says following him.

Water lilies spread way too fast. You know Beaver Lake in Stanley Park? A few decades from now they'll be dredging it at exorbitant expense because some idiot got it in his mind that water lilies are picturesque.

You have to remember, Isabelle. You and Takumi aren't children anymore. He shoves a box of cherry tomatoes along the counter. I told your father I'd send these over. If you want to help me, do what I tell you, Isabelle. Just do what I tell you.

So he has said something, I can't believe it, she mutters on the way out the door. How early did he get over here? He must have got up before the sun. Bloody hell.

Auntie.

Sorry, Gwen. Excuse my French.

Walking from the greenhouse down to the hotel, it's like a

cube of glass forms around Auntie's head and balances on her shoulders like a pot. What ho, Gwendolyn, calls Miss Fenn from over the fence at the lawn bowling green, dipping her knee in a curtsey as she lets go the ball on the manicured lawn. Miss Fenn is their neighbour and the school teacher; it's strange to think but she stays in her cottage all winter with only her cats for company. She wears white ankle socks and Cuban heels, lots of pale powder on her face shaded by a veiled hat that dangles a long white chiffon scarf. At the lawn bowling green, they have to wear all white. When you see her coming across the causeway, Auntie says you can tell she thinks she's in the Easter Parade. Miss Fenn always calls Gwen Gwendolyn the way their dad's mother, Grandma Killam, does when she writes her a letter from the Prairies. Grandma Killam always calls her father Percival, too, but everyone else calls him Percy. People say it isn't summer until Mrs. Yoshito and Miss Fenn have delivered every last flower basket to every single solitary resort cottage. Double geraniums for the First Aid Station, double geraniums and extra lobelia for the deluxe cottages at the back of the hotel. That's what makes them deluxe, Miss Fenn laughs. When you press your hands on the lawn bowling green, the surface rises back up as if it's never been touched. Plum trees grow on three sides of the surrounding bank. The bowlers whisper to each other as if they're in church when the balls hush themselves along the grass. The honk of a trumpeter swan expands over the bay, flattens and dies.

Guests come through the hotel's glassed in porch and stroll down on the lawn. Lovely day. Isn't it? they say, congratulating each other on the weather. The hotel manager, Mr. McConnecky's skin, moustache and hair are all the same kind of fleshy pink. He leans over Isabelle's typewriter as she types the new brochure.

Salty coves and rushing waterfalls. Sunny spots and where to find them. The salt coast Riviera? Is that what you want me to say? Auntie asks. Her brown hair is braided in a crown above her worried forehead. I thought the sun coast Riviera, says the manager. But leave it in, dear. The dining room has tables with white tablecloths and folded serviettes like party hats. At lunch— Gwen's allowed to pass out the menus—the general manager who's over from town for the day says he'll take the cold salmon mayonnaise. He hands off his menu to Auntie, turns to the man beside him who's what they call a silent partner visiting from England and is tucked beside him like the dormouse.

The northern steamship runs are all different now, of course, with the tourist industry down, the general manager says. It's a good thing they've got Bowen here to concentrate on. No gasoline money so it's a nice short excursion for people. Moving servicemen around they're not having to haul as much cargo north the way they were before. It's a nightmare travelling with only navigation lights though. No two ways about it, they're going to have to switch some of the longshoremen to the local runs.

I've never seen mauve roses before, says the general manager's wife who is very pretty.

When Mr. Yoshito passes under the front window, his glasses mirror the blue hydrangeas. Auntie looks frightened as if a small furred animal has leapt under her dress and crawled up her calf. The general manager's wife says she does want to see the gardens.

We'd better join the ladies. Otherwise, it'll look....

I guess it will. Is it still raining?

After lunch, Mr. McConnecky, the dormouse and the general manager take their seats in wooden deck chairs under the monkey tree. Garter snakes which Leo says winter underground in circular clusters slither in the grass. It's because Leo's always thinking about science and how things work that he gets stuck places like on the gangplank to the *Sannie* wharf. Mr. McConnecky waves as Auntie passes. Gwen xylophones a stick along the slats of the honeysuckle arbour where Mrs. General Manager and Mrs. Dormouse emerge blinking under their hats. Some people's children, they say. Tennis balls splat on the courts.

At the end of the lagoon, the wives from the luncheon party hike their dresses up so they can wade in the brown water. Maybe they would like to hear the man in the tuxedo who plays the spoons at the afternoon concert in the vaudeville bowl. At the lagoon, Auntie is concentrating on chucking tomatoes into the water when a red haired man with freckles all over his back dashes up the causeway and asks her if she'd go in the three-legged race with him.

They're holding the start for us, he says.

Oh, I'm not on the picnic, she says as the haze along the Sound blends the horizon of the sea and the mountain to a dusky blue. Then. What the heck. Why not? She pushes herself off the wide cement railing and strides beside him to the starting line at number one grounds by Sandy beach where they drag each other the first few yards, the skirt of the flowered sunsuit she changed into after work flies as their joined middle legs pump together and their outside legs kick in. After they cross the finish line, she unties the knot pulled tight around their ankles. Would she like to come over to the Longshoremens picnic at number two grounds, have some potato salad? Oh I can't, she says, I have to get home. But thanks for the race. Draping the man's tie over his shoulder, she turns up the trail leaving him empty-handed like a dancer in the dancehall when his partner walks away.

When they get home from the race, Grandpa is lifting the heads of creamy snowball plants so waterlogged from all the rain their stems bend to the ground. He lets Lily shake them but she's getting herself all wet. If you let morning glory climb the hydrangea, it chokes the whole plant.

Have you noticed how carnations smell like cloves when they're wet, Dad? Auntie says, smelling the ragged magenta blossoms as if it's dangerous to even look up. Cloves? Grandpa asks, standing there in his lawn bowling whites, the white and shade of him the wrong way around like on a picture negative. The way his mouth is high above his chin makes him look like a picture in a book where you have one of those old-fashioned adult heads on a child's body. His forehead slopes up to the low part in his hair. Grandma Gallagher comes up the path from the beach carrying a pile of sheets with stained corners where the clothespins have mildewed. When she bends over a pail to deposit cigarette butts people have thrown off the porch, you can see blue veins on the backs of her legs. Only impatiens can bloom at their cottage because it's all shade.

Nobody's irreplaceable, Isabelle, Grandpa says. Remember that.

Auntie jerks back as if she's been lassoed, tries to get her foot on the stair and misses. On the beach, gulls perch one after the other down the line of boulders. Brittle tips of rockweed mark the tide line. The rusty frayed end of a loop of cable is caught under a rock. After the race, the red haired man looked down at

Auntie's ankles as if he wanted to pull up the backs of her socks so they wouldn't slide down inside her running shoes.

When they've finished supper, Auntie takes a bowl into the back bedroom and smudges soap in her armpits with a thick brush, pulling the razor down hard so her skin stretches like a chicken's spread out thighs. This must work if it's what men do every day, she says scraping bits of hair into the basin. The mirror has a jagged flaw. She thumbs up her eyebrows to pluck under them, yanks out a few nostril hairs, nose going one way, mouth the other. Drops a white pleated skirt over her head, ties a matching headband around her forehead until not one piece of hair shows. Tucks her tennis racket under her arm. The arbutus trees roll back their auburn bark like stockings. When she walks up the hill, she picks her feet up higher than she needs to. One arm swings at the joint as if it's loose. At the corner of the dance-hall and tearoom, the ground is scuffed with tiny pine cones.

The verandah of the tearoom is so wide people could dance on it. Sometimes they do. Customers inside drinking milk-shakes tie their dogs to the balcony railing but the dogs bark and the owners have to bring their milkshakes with them and take the dogs for walks. Isabelle arranges herself on the wide railing, droops for a moment as if she has no bones, gently curls the back of her hand against her mouth. She lifts one knee with both hands as if it's broken and her palms set it in place. Her face flutters when she looks away before it settles into a new position. She arches her hands on top of each other and puts them on her knee. (She sleeps with her arms crossed over her chest, hands cupped like tulips.) Inside the tearoom, two girls are standing at the counter buying toffee in a package with a pretend plaid bow. That saxophone player? The one with the sandy hair? He's really good.

Maybe he heard you, they giggle as the red-haired man from the three-legged race comes up the stairs. All of him is there to see Auntie, not just his face.

I didn't know you were in the band, she says.

Oh, you know. Keeps me off the streets. He picks up her tennis racket, leans the mesh on his palm. These cat gut?

I don't think so. Are they supposed to be?

I don't know. I thought they were some kind of cat gut.

She takes the racket from him, pretends to swat a ball. He turns and pretends to see it rolling along the ground.

You work at the hotel, eh?

How'd you know?

Oh you know, asked around.

It's pretty hectic right now. Management, managements' wives, trustees, silent partners from England, you name it. Talking about re re-scheduling steamer runs, thinking of cancelling some, so on and so on. She takes the racket back, sweeps her arm in a wide arc, wrist turning like in an arm wrestle match. Look at my stupid forehand. I darn well always do it like this. She serves as if her arm has been lifted straight up on a string attached to her wrist. Then it collapses.

Oh well. His smile seems to move his face before it actually moves. The way his muscles fill up his clothes, it's like his pants and shirt would keep their shape even after he's taken them off.

Mostly I go up to the top court, says Isabelle. It's not really a court.

The grass up there grows through the clay and the marking strip's come unstapled. No net. Only a backboard with a line painted at net level so people can practise alone. Jack, right? she says.

Jack Long.

Isabelle Gallagher. This is my niece, Gwen.

Hello, Gwen.

When Auntie puts the racket down, Jack Long covers her hand with his so the two of them could be on the top of a cane. He looks as if he wants to carry her arm somewhere and set it free.

She passes him her cream soda. Want some? He frowns at the bottle and hands it back without a word. Maybe he's a rum and coke man. He mostly works in the grain holds on the ships, he says, where you get buried alive if you stop to blow your nose. When the band starts up, he tells Auntie to come over to the pavilion and listen to the last set.

No, she says. I like listening from here.

She does, too.

The next weekend when Auntie comes down the hotel stairs eating cherries, Jack Long's waiting for her in the deck chair under the monkey tree.

Life's the pits, eh? he says.

It's not too bad. She looks up. Oh.

Don't choke on it.

I'm liable to.

He looks as if he wants people to see him walking across the causeway with Isabelle on his arm the way her dad does when he and her mom get dressed up to go out dancing. Her parents don't go to the dances up here, just places in town like the Royal Vancouver Yacht Club. Mr. McConnecky's standing in the lobby window. Auntie takes Jack Long's arm to walk across the causeway like someone putting on her lifejacket in a rowboat because her parents are watching.

Does the kid have to come with us?

She does, yes.

They take the Bridal Falls Trail the tennis court way. The water from Killarney Lake races under the white picket bridge, gathers speed to foam over the ledge. A dead tree lies on its side at the edge of the lagoon below the falls, limbs curved like thin ribs. A small oak lifts its leaves and lets them down again. A piece of water splashes up below the second white picket bridge.

Laburnum St.? That's where you live? Jack Long says unfastening a cigarette package from the twist in the sleeve of his shirt. My dad used to fish steelhead in a stream that ran down Blenheim to the Fraser. Folks would see the fish coming, use clubs or hoes or what have you, drag them ashore. He picks up a stick, reaches down from the bridge and drags it in the water. Beautiful fish he said they were. Lucky for us longshoremen the sockeye keep running, eh?

He climbs down the ferned rocks at the side of the falls as if he doesn't care two hoots that Auntie's taller than he is. Takes a box of matches from his pocket, checks a piece of paper inside, excuses himself and heads up a side trail. When he comes back, he has a bulge in his pocket. The sun does its famous trick, lighting up for an instant before it turns off, then switching on as a surprise in the blackberry. The chartreuse light in the shade is a joke; it's in the laurel behind the cedar, no, it's come out in the salmonberry behind the hemlock. When Isabelle steps into the shade, she hugs her own arms as if she needs to have her cardigan on as much as she wanted it off a moment before when she was in the sun. The blackberries heat up when the day heats up. Someone should lift her chignon and pin it higher on her neck so it won't be heavy on her shoulders. Her high loose knees and elbows fling up softly when she walks as if she knows exactly what she's doing and couldn't care less whether anyone likes it or not.

A leaf swirls under the second bridge. Thick ivy trunks grow so many leaves and twist so many times around the host fir you can't see the bark. The maples let a net of sun down onto the road. Jack Long ducks under a cedar branch.

Work's better now, he says, but, before the war, way too many days, I was over on Dunleavy St. in Vancouver watching my dad playing horseshoes waiting for a dispatch to come up. This one time, the dispatcher, he's the guy who hands out them chips, right? If you get a chip that means you're going to work. One day he took a handful and threw them on the ground. I was just a kid, new on the job. One of the older men told us not to go down for them, said it was degrading. So I didn't.

A duck clicks its bill in its underwing, puffs and settles. The whistle sounds in the Cove like a horn. Another time? The dispatcher put out his hand like he was going to give my dad a chip but when my dad reached out to take it, the sonofabitch snatched his hand back and gave it to the next guy in line. You don't forget a thing like that.

I don't suppose you do. Do you like being a longshoreman?

You bet. I love the long northern runs the best.

A few loose dog footprints are sunk into the muddy patches of Skunk Cabbage Trail that never get the sun. Jack Long keeps talking at Auntie the way Molly won't leave you alone when she's trying to get you to throw a stick. If you leave without it, she picks up the stick and follows you. Isabelle looks flatter and flatter as she tries to keep him talking all the way home.

The Vancouver waterfront? Oh he's always known the Vancouver waterfront. Way before he was a longshoreman, they used to play ship on the streetcar on the way down to the docks, bunch of them lurching down the aisle pretending they were on a boat. You know those clear windy days when the sea is that kind of dark blue…?

Cobalt?

That's it, cobalt. Those days, aren't they something? Even the days when the port lay shrouded in rain, he'd be hanging around the sheds watching the boxes get loaded. Everything had to be balanced before being lifted into the hold.

Back at the lagoon, a group of red-eyed pigeons ripple pink and green down their backs. The swan on the nest closest to the viaduct coils its neck into a loop and goes to sleep.

I wonder what it's like being them, Auntie says, pulling the hair band down around her neck like a necklace, shaking out her hair.

Mostly I guess you're looking around making sure there's nothing close by that wants to eat you.

Guess so.

Jack Long smiles and tries to jerk Gwen's hand into his own so she'll be between the two of them, but his freckles, bristly red hair, and the anchor tattoo on his hand make her drop his rough hand and walk by herself.

At home on the verandah, Auntie hands him the binoculars and watches him watch a great blue heron stand on one foot, then the other. Closer, beside the wading rock, a small browner version raises both wings on what look like broken sticks and lowers them again.

What birds are those? If that's the heron, is that a different kind of heron?

They're the juveniles.

Oh.

Gulls stand beating their wings to dry them off. Flying away, they leave quick white streaks in the sky. A group of crows cuts the other way. Foxgloves wave their bulby fingers. Once, Auntie tells him, she brought some friends from her sorority over here but they ran out of beds and some girls had to sleep on the floor and in the bathtub! She goes into the house to get photographs to show him the gang in their short skirts and long blouses. Two kneeling, one kneeling on the back of the two kneelers sort of thing. The ones on either side stretch their arms to the ground.

A couple of summers ago she'd worked in the Empress Jam factory in town with her friend, Frances Sinclair, but there was no way she could keep up with blapping huge blobs of jam into cans at the pace they wanted, so they put her on folding cartons. They needed thirty every half hour. Couldn't he just see her? He could. A hummingbird quivers with the need to put its beak somewhere.

As the tide goes out, the dark grey rocks lighten. Clouds let themselves down to rest on the shoulders of the mountains.

You know how you play a trick on someone and it falls flat? Auntie says. Once, on April Fool's Day, I took a glassful of soapy water from the dishpan and told my dad it was a milkshake. He pretended he thought it was.

How old were you?

Five. Maybe four.

Oh well, then he had to.

Grandpa Gallagher comes up the verandah stairs, smiling broadly when he sees Jack. He shakes his hand, then excuses himself, gently shutting the door from the verandah to the house as if he doesn't want to wake the baby. When they go in a few minutes later, he's sitting in his easy chair by the fireplace. See that stone on the hearth there, Jack, he says. Pick it up. Mother comes to the kitchen door. She and Auntie and Grandma Gallagher wag their heads back and forth, silently mouthing the refrain. That's where we were going to keep the family jewels only there never were any family jewels, ha ha.

At lunch, Jack Long is asked to stay. Grandpa hands him the jug of lemonade, the bowl of raspberries, the plate of sandwiches, watches him pour the cream.

These are good. Where'd you get these?

From the Japs down on the wharf, Grandpa says. They can grow berries, you can say that for them. Never mind that they've taken over all the best fishing.

Get my shawl, will you dear? Grandma says to Auntie, frowning at the open back door. Grandma Gallagher's a small woman, thin as a wren. No one makes a move to close it. Auntie leaps up, leans her hand on the hot stove, snatches it back.

Oh for heaven's sake, Isabelle. What's the big idea? Grandpa says. You've almost dragged the whole lunch on the floor.

Jack pulls his chair closer to Grandpa's, dishes himself more berries, pours cream. It's true what your father's saying, Isabelle. Even on the docks, you know, they work for a lot less than white guys. It causes hard feelings.

Excuse me?

Japan's made a lot of trouble in the Pacific. Look at China, look at Manchuria. You can be a bleeding heart liberal until you come up against it, Isabelle, but from the way you've been talking all afternoon I don't think you've even come close.

Down on the beach, a duck lifts one orange leg and paddles away. A salmon jumps and dark seed pods from the broom plants rattle in Auntie's hand. The incoming tide softens the rockweed tips and the kelp relaxes. Gravel shell fragments swish around as if they have more room than they actually do.

Later that night, Auntie has her hand stamped at the dancehall wicket, waits at the edge of the dance floor facing the bandstand. On stage, Jack Long is looking intently at the sheet music in front of him. Maybe he's only pretending not to notice her because, at the waterfalls, he told her he didn't know how to read music. One of the men who'd eaten salmon at the hotel comes up to the stage; Jack puts down his saxophone and steps out onto the back porch with him. Someone comes up and asks Auntie to dance. When the song ends and her partner returns her to her place, the bench hits the backs of her knees which makes her sit down hard. When Jack comes in from the back porch, it's intermission and he drags her out on the dance floor as if the music's still playing. She holds his wrist with both hands as he pulls her between the pillars across the empty floor to a spot below the special window where she stands with her fist curled against her mouth.

What's the big idea, Isabelle? You knew the whole time, didn't you? You heard the big managers at that lunch you told me about.

I'm sorry, Jack. But I came to talk about something else.

You knew, didn't you?

I didn't mean to lead you on—

I'm losing my northern run job. I can't stay in the city, only working the one dock. You already knew a northern run would be cancelled when I started talking about my job and you didn't say nothing.

One of the band members taps on the air with his fist. Knock knock. We're on.

Jack holds himself still for another second, juts out his chin, turns and heads for the stage.

I'll see you around, Isabelle. Don't take any wooden nickels, eh? That's all I ask. Just don't take any wooden nickels.

WOODEN NICKELS

3.

October, 1941.

Come and play Mother May I with us, Auntie. Come and play Go Go Stop. Of course she'll play Mother May I. Of course she'll play Go Go Stop. Since the night her father smashed her bedroom door against her bed, Isabelle will do anything to keep him at arm's length. Hide herself behind whatever game the children want.

Back in Vancouver at Laburnum St., she and her father press her mother's wet sick clothes through the washing machine rollers in the basement. Careful you don't catch your hand in there, he says. Your mother's too weak to sit up, too restless to lie down. Her bed jacket doesn't fit her properly if it's up on her shoulders like that. Never been well since Evvie was born has she? he says. Some balance device gone haywire. Weeks when she continually feels as if she's falling. Isabelle bruised her mother's forearm once with a finger imprint, offended her by asking whether she was handling the pie dough too much. Sometimes she's so frail and unstable you'd think there was a wind in the house.

What's Isabelle's bad back from having to bend over the sick bed compared to her mother's suffering? Her father needs her to be there with him. We have to turn her, Isabelle. You take one side of this undersheet. I'll take the other. Now shift. You heard what the doctor said. We have to keep moving her position if we don't want her in hospital.

She does want her in hospital. She hates the standing tray cuffed over her bed. The bedside table with its amber bottles and spoons. The way her father pretends not to understand that it's bizarre for him to be stretched diagonally on her own bed, holding up a new brand of applesauce that might help his wife's constipation for heaven's sake. Her mother's mouth pulls thin at the edges and collapses, forehead and eyelids smooth as marble. Lavender and vomit. Apple juice through a straw.

I might as well say it now, Isabelle says, feeding a nightie to the wringer. I'm thinking of going back to the cottage to be by myself for a while, Dad.

What are you talking about? The water's turned off. It's not winterized. It's not ours in the winter, anyway. He drags a piece of scum from his hot milk, dangles it from the spoon. What'll I do with this, he asks in an overly intimate voice. If Isabelle holds the bottle of applesauce up to the light to admire the colour, the worried look fades from his face.

I could apply for the postmaster's job, she says. I heard what's-his-name has signed up to go overseas.

He stabs the milk scum into the sink. It's out of the question, Isabelle. I don't want to hear another word about it.

I'll come in to see mother. You know I will. There are boats, dad, there are boats.

I told you. The water's turned off.

I'll get George Fenn to help me turn it on.

It's better if people stay with their own kind, that's all I'm saying. Whatever happened to that nice Jack fellow?

I'm going over to be by *myself*, dad.

Run interference between you and the hotel manager if you want to know the truth is what she doesn't say. Be close to the man I care about most even if I can't see him.

She leaves the next morning when her father's at work downtown managing the Woodward's food floor. Takes a bus along the lower levels road past West Van and Whytecliff, to Horseshoe Bay and the Sannie depot. When she gets to Bowen she makes her way down to their place at the end of the point, unlocks the back door and leans against it. Dark branches cross and uncross against the front bedroom window. The walls have never felt thinner. It's much colder than she thought it would be; the skin on the edges of her fingernails starts to split and she has to dab sheep lanolin on the tips. *They're summer cottages, Isabelle. What do you expect?*

The thick firs that offer shade in the summer gloom and drip in the rain. It must be lovely and cool at your cottage people say. You have all that shade. She props salty cushions and damp bedding on the hearth, hangs a thick comforter from the beam in the living room for protection from the north wind blasting down the channel. She'll have to get an oil light of some kind; the generator's turned off in the winter. At least the cedar splits easily for kindling and the fir bark burns in the woodstove wet or dry. Somehow she has to stop her father saying anything more so the Yoshitos won't lose their jobs supplying the hotel with produce. She doesn't know what but something. The hotel is closed in the winter, but Mr. McConnecky keeps his office open and comes up on the weekends. Surprised as he is to see her, he agrees to talk to the higher-ups to see if she might replace what's his name who really has left his post office job to go overseas. He'll see what he can do about arranging for her to stay in her own cottage.

Sure you won't be too cold over there?

Hope not.

When she opens the mail wicket the first day at work, she finds the *Sannie* captain at the front of the line, Lottie Fenn in a pink cloche hat with a rhinestone brooch waiting behind him. The war's in Europe, he mutters. It's thousands of miles that way. Why are we bothering with this lights out palaver? If Takumi weren't sleeping in the government shed on the wharf guiding me in with a lantern, I don't know what I'd do.

When the customers in the queue step up to the wicket, they look at Isabelle as if it's her fault when they don't receive the letters they want. After work, she walks home the beach way along Sandy past Miss Fenn's Rocky beach with its patch of higher ground in the bay that becomes an island when the tide's coming up. Then around the Point to their place at the tip. When she looks up from the beach, whether her father's there or not, she always sees him standing with his hands on his hips, white flannel trousers belted high on his waist. Isabelle, please will you go down to the beach and bring me a rock the size of your foot? No cottage in those days; he'd built the fireplace first, easier that way, then the Union could build the cottage around it. She'd measured one stone with her right foot, another with her left, again and again until she found a flawless one that curved along her instep. Her sister, Evvie, had to go down next, find a thin flat rock that would fit in the hearth as a stone lid: if they were going to make an indentation to hide the family jewels, they'd need a lid. This size, he'd said, fingers and thumbs joined to make a lopsided square. Evvie put two feet on each stair before stepping down to the next, mouth pursed and intent, coarse yellow and brown curls massed all over her head. Back up at the cottage, she presented her father with a slip of flat stone like a piece of outsized money. He slid the lid over the indentation and it rested there, glueless. He'd held Isabelle's rock like a shoebrush over its spot before mortaring it into the hearth.

Isabelle'd been carrying her father's bowling bag to the lawn bowling green for him when she saw Takumi Yoshito for the first time. Haunched on the lagoon shore in front of the swans, he held his hands a foot apart as if someone were rolling a ball of wool from them. He looked up, nodded rapidly for her to come and pick up the top and bottom bulrush strands of the cat's cradle he was making and turn it inside out. When she darted over, picked up the two strands and rotated her wrists to present the woven length, they both smiled that she knew exactly what to do.

The next day she and Takumi swam together at Sandy for the first time, walked along the dusty Government Road hitting each other's knees with their towels. Mrs. Yoshito pulled up in the only truck on the island. Noriko Yoshito was so small that, when she leaned over to open the door for them, she had a hard time keeping her foot on the brake pedal and unfastening the lock at the same time. Strange, isn't it, the way a person runs out of things at the worst possible moments? she said, looking embarrassed to be in her apron as if they'd caught her in a *négligée*. All the way to the store when all I needed was a last bit of paraffin for the canning. She patted the seat next to her for Isabelle to sit down, the cushion warm and ready.

Come and have lunch with us, she said as Takumi climbed into the truck bed and made funny faces through the back window.

Like when you run out of thread the last inch hemming something, Isabelle chirruped back, wanting to be on a par with this mother who has not been lying in a sick bed with a wet cloth over her eyes off and on for years, who could push a floor gear stick into position with her wiry arm, straining her neat face up over the steering wheel.

They drove up the Government road, turned onto the Miller Road, and around the Miller's Landing corner to Scarborough beach where the Yoshitos lived. When they clattered down the rutted driveway to the large handsome white tongue and groove house on the sea, a trumpeting morning glory spread wildly over the seashell path. Geese flapped out of the way, the peak of the house split the light and waving sword ferns beckoned them in. Mrs. Yoshito jumped briskly out of the truck, hurried into the kitchen, grabbed her oven gloves to pick up the canner as if she'd never been gone, carried it to the sink to drain the salt from the piccalilli. Picked up tongs to lift hot jars from the steaming water bath. Six hands she said she needed this time of year. A small wooden man and woman announced the time one after the other from a Dutch cuckoo clock.

Before Mrs. Yoshito went into the dining room, she stopped in front of a stand and rang a small bell. Carefully placed it back on its tray, lit small candles, and strange smelling sticks. Poured water into a tiny dish, propped flowers in another and offered huckleberries in a third. With one hand on Isabelle's arm, she stopped her gently, took a long slow breath and pushed the swinging door open with her shoulder. When she stood leaning against the door so Isabelle could pass, she smiled as if the offerings themselves had turned on the glow in the shining wood table. A huge plant with leaves like soft green moose antlers hung from a layered papery bulb. Birds of paradise decorated the porcelain cups in the china cabinet. Stained glass windows and a scroll of writing with the moon in it hung above two clay urns placed either end of the oak sideboard. Mrs. Yoshito went out again, returned and presented the soup. Her hair was shorter on the back of her neck than along her cheeks. Rainbow patterns wavered over the surface of the urns.

This is kombu, she said. The seaweed you kids know from the beach.

She ladled the soup slowly, as if this was the only meal she'd ever prepared, placing the gleaming bowls in carefully chosen positions, as if the polished table were the background to her creation. Isabelle looked with delight at the birds on the cups, high enough in the china cabinet to sing to her from their branches, slid her chair down to the corner of the table where the etched grain of the wood surface swirled into a pattern of wings. Cupped her palms over the spot where the grain coalesced into the pattern of the eye of a bird. Mrs. Yoshito picked up her hand, gently turned it over as if she were going to tell her fortune, then threaded two chopsticks between her fingers and showed her how to open and close them like a beak. The three of them bowed their heads over the soup, said ita daki mas as if each time the family came to the table to eat, they gave thanks for the warmth of its presence and each other.

After lunch they walked up to the fields where the berries ripened: the strawberries first, the blueberries, then the high hedge of blackberries in the west. Throwing in boards to break a path, Mrs. Yoshito fingered the bushes so fast it was as if she were milking them. Later, they walked the path to Bridal Veil Falls to start the pump which started the generator so that, over in Deep Bay, people at the hotel and in the cottages could listen to the news.

After that first day, Isabelle and Takumi played together all the time, running around the Point and the Cove, in and out of peoples' cottages as if they owned the place. Sang for his baby sister who got born dead by mistake which is why his family had to divide her ashes into two urns in case one went missing. That way, she could eat in the dining room with the family every day whether she was alive or not. Singing in the treehouse that Isabelle's father built for Miss Fenn in the curve of the cedar that leaned out over her rocky beach, they watched the tide come in until only one piece of high ground was left in the middle of Deep Bay. Then only a bright green patch of sea grass on that island, which flourished because it was hardly ever under water. When the tide was at its highest, even the grass was covered

Once the Gallaher's cottage was built at the end of the Point (and the family moved out of the tents under a real live roof), the two of them conducted sing-songs in the attic, pulling sheets between their legs to coil into birds' nests. Burst into Zip-a-Dee-Doo-Dah each time Takumi's sister got born in the dead baby shiners they squeezed from the mother fish down at the pier and dabbed one by one along the boards.

Until one day in the treehouse their hands changed from pretend crabs scuttling over each other's faces into palms moving to each other's mouths to be kissed. When Isabelle's father whistled loudly for her to come up and help him with her mother, the pirate ship they were riding sank into the sea. The chariot clattering through the meadow lost a wheel. *I always know where you are, Isabelle. Sometimes I don't like it, but I know.*

I don't know what I'd do without you Isabelle, he said at the top of Miss Fenn's trail to Rocky. We have to go home. Your mother has to lie down. She needs a facecloth on her headache.

Back on the island now, gumboots sinking into mud with every step, Isabelle re-stacks last summer's wood and hurls chunks of wet alder under the verandah to dry. One afternoon after work she smashes her father's old fedora on her head and goes down to pick clams to make chowder for supper. Get back in your shells, you little suckers. In the pail with you. Up at their cottage, a shadow that's probably a piece of furniture shifts on the window pane. When she looks up again, she sees that it's Ada and the children of all people. Gwen, Leo and Lily are standing on the *gumshuwa* at the bottom of the trail.

We're here to see you, Auntie! And it's not even summer.

Up in the kitchen, she finds Ada fussing around saying she doesn't mean to sound put upon but Isabelle knows perfectly well this is the last thing she needs, coming all the way over to Bowen in the winter when Percy's so busy in Vancouver making engines for the war effort, and their father's rattling around Laburnum St. all by himself. Their mother has to be visited in hospital every day, as if Isabelle doesn't know. Ada's thickened at the waist, has to lift her gabardine skirt a touch at the thighs to sit at the kitchen table.

This place is a freezing cold box, she says.

What are you doing dressed like that, Ada? You look like you're going downtown. Don't you hate it when you leave a cupboard door open and bang your head on it?

Working the tablecloth between her fingers, Ada keeps frowning at the wonky blanket stitching around the edge. This looks a bit worse for wear, she says. Put that bucket down, Isabelle. What have you got in there?

Clams. I'll make chowder for lunch. Cut up some celery, will you?

The children don't like clam chowder.

I'll open a can of chicken noodle for them. She forgets the stove is hot *again*, puts her hands on it, grabs them away.

No sugar, I guess.

What's that bird, Ada? For heaven's sake, it's the heron up in the tree. Isabelle points the spoon. What's it doing there? A spider in the chowder pot has to be shaken out the window. That's good. They eat aphids. Do you ever think what it must have been like for mother when there was only a tent here? Wasn't it the doctor who said she had to get away and have a holiday? What kind of holiday would it have been with three children? Ada's knuckles move back with the celery; she forgets to stop at the edge of the board and cuts at the air before she fiddles the bits into the bowl.

It was nice of them to leave you some clams, I must say.

Pardon?

The Japs. At least they haven't cleaned out the whole beach. They eat everything you know, all the fish guts.

Are you doing this on purpose, Ada?

I mean it as a compliment. You don't have to look at me like that. I guess you haven't heard. The Japanese are being put away in camps. It's the only safe thing to do.

What did you say?

The Japs are being sent to the interior. Because of Pearl Harbour. You haven't heard about Pearl Harbour?

I don't have a radio. You took it down.

The Japanese attacked Pearl Harbor. They're in the war.

But it's only the people in Vancouver?

I don't think so.

What did Dad say to you?

Just come home, Isabelle. This is no place for you in the winter. Dad's worried about you.

How can we be talking about Dad after what you just said? says Isabelle. When did this order come out?

Are you going to come back on your own or am I going to have to send Percy over to get you?

You wouldn't do that.

I would you know.

In the mail queue the next day, pent up slurs are given voice as if permission and credibility have been granted now that the news of the internment is official. Last week they were all saying as to how Shinsuke Yoshito was the best gardener in the Lower Mainland; the Stanley Park gardens didn't hold a candle to his beds, but now phones are lighting up of their own accord. The day my son came home from school saying Takumi Yoshito got his best marbles off him in the recess game? Won them fair and square was what I thought at the time but maybe I was wrong not to side with my son. What's Yoshito senior been doing over there sitting on his verandah with those high-powered binoculars of his, eh?

Down on Miss Fenn's Rocky getting more clams, Isabelle looks over at the causeway bridge and sees Takumi running toward her along the low tide flats. He's almost there, then not there yet, then closer and closer until he's falling into her arms, his mouth opening and closing with no sound. She loves him so much she'd lift his folded length and carry him anywhere he wants to go. Anywhere.

I'm not afraid, Isabelle. Where do I go to enlist? I want to sign up.

I heard about the evacuation order, she says. Ada came up to tell me. It's only the people in Vancouver, right?

No. It's everyone. I'm not going.

Of course not you're not going.

She places one hand either side of his face. Come tonight and we'll talk. *Don't leave me. Don't ever leave me.*

I can't come tonight.

Soon then.

When she looks up a few evenings later and sees him standing in the doorway of her cottage, he steps toward her as slowly and surely as the tide below them would find its way to the winter high mark under the house. Each of his footsteps contains all the footsteps he's taken in the years they've known each other. They wrap their fingers in each other's hands as the winter sea below them tries to soften the stones. Woodpeckers fly diagonally in front of the beach, wings flung backward. A long caw from the fir branches, then silence. When he pulls her to him by the small of her back, her vertebrae mount on top of each other like the small stairs in the woods by the falls they'd climbed the first day they met. In bed, she nervously folds her nightie up from the hem in small pleats, raising her eyes over the horizon of her breasts to watch him unfasten the buttons on her nightie, then start on her cells. *Not hearing from you is a desert. There are no houses, no trees, no people.* He is her brother, he is her child, he is her beloved.

A loon tucks his head and bloops into the water, the way he slips out of her afterwards. She lies with him in her arms, his head on her breast. *Never stop looking at me like that. Never stop telling me what you're going to do next. Talk to me.* He smiles in his sleep as if he has as much confidence in the covering and uncovering of the life between their bodies as he does in the emptying and filling of the bay below them. If he leaves a trail of crumbs behind him on the way to her house, she'll go out at night and pick them up. In the city, people pull their blinds down and seal them with tape. Black eye patches with slits cover their car headlights. If he pretends to be concealed by her, the announcement will never have been made. He's sleeping where he said he would be sleeping, in the shed on the wharf with his lantern dutifully guiding in the *Sannie.*

That night Isabelle dreams she has to pack her father's bin-oculars, bowling balls, and white flannel trousers. There's going to be a terrible flood. She's not supposed to have his things, only her own. What's she doing with his binoculars? Where did she get that dollar?

In the early morning, Takumi sits up in bed drinking the coffee she brings him as if he'd been shipwrecked and barely made it to shore. A faraway light on the horizon shines through the trees. The moon is in shards on the sea. The embers in the fireplace coals flash on and off: the last log glows underneath. Night will gather at the start of the day, massing at the horizon to bring them cover as their limbs move together, fluid as coho. The light from the last log in the fire softens lines between their bodies they don't know about yet.

Except that there's a knock on the back door and both of them startle up. Pulling on her dressing gown, Isabelle opens the door to find Noriko standing there in her hat and coat. She looks three inches shorter as if gravity has doubled its pull since she last saw her.

Some people had to leave so fast they left food on their plates.

They're taking us away, she says. The officer said I could come and give you the key to the house. Take care of everything. We won't be gone long. She turns and looks up the hill.

Of course you won't be gone long, says Isabelle. It's all a mistake. It's just this awful war.

It's just this awful war. Where's Takumi, Isabelle? Do you know where he is?

I do, yes.

Tell him they're be looking for him. Take care of him, do you understand me?

I will. Look after yourselves. Please. Isabelle reaches for her but there's nothing there. Back in the bedroom, Takumi's sitting on the edge of the bed with a look of collapsed loneliness she'll never forget.

That was my parents, he says. I have to go.

No, you don't have to go. We have to stay calm and think this through. We'll figure out something.

He pushes her hands away, grabs his shirt off the floor, rushes up the hill after his mother who holds him tightly, then pushes him away.

Get away from here right now.

I can't let you go without me. .

They said we have to be *detained*, Takumi. Try to sell the house. It doesn't have to be for a lot. Sell it to someone who'll sell it back to us after the war. Get it in writing. Dad and I will be counting on you.

I'll find out where you are and get you out somehow. Tell Dad I'll look after everything. It won't be for long.

A quick embrace and she's gone.

That evening, palming their flashlights, Takumi and Isabelle meet at the Yoshitos' Scarborough house, pack all the warm clothes and dried food they can fit into a knapsack. She stuffs in more rolled socks, hangs her swagger tweed coat in the bedroom closet to protect the place when she's not there. They leave silently and he turns up the trail to Killarney Lake where he'll spend the night.

Where could you go, even if you do get away? she asks.

North.

They're going to find you. They'll be watching the coast.

Inland then.

I can't let you go.

You have to let me go. I'm not going to any camp. I'd die first.

Promise you'll come and tell me where you're going.

I can't promise you anything. All I'm asking is that you look after the house.

I'll do my best.

Not your best. You'll do it. Let go of me Isabelle.

In bed, back at her cottage, every cell in her body on alert, she matches her palms flat together and winnows them between her thighs like a child in shock. Searches for the notes in her fingertips that will let her know he's still with her, that the spider legs of her fingers have been left behind for her to use. *I have a lover. I feel like a piano.* She holds her hands where his shoulders should be, his head should be. She's self sealing. The darkness is everywhere. If she can see him clearly enough, smell him deeply enough, press herself on his mouth at exactly the right angle, he'll be with her forever.

The next day getting supplies out to him is all that matters. Already she feels people are watching her. Miss Fenn, say, the only other person on the Point in the winter, but quiet as Takumi was, she might have seen him come in. The Yoshitos lost their jobs anyway, no matter what Isabelle did.

It's so cold and rainy the next day when she heads back to the Scarborough house to get more dry clothes for Takumi, she automatically pulls more straw and moss over the strawberry fields for mulch the way Mrs. Yoshito would. The varnished ball supporting the sweet peas has rolled off its pedestal. The fields are trodden over and wet spoked maple leaves heeled into the ground. The white rose bushes Mr. Yoshito planted on the other side of the fence so anyone looking out the window would see cascading blossoms rather than roots and stems are pulled up and tossed out to die. The padlock she and Takumi hooked on the front door is sawn through with a hacksaw. Inside, everything has been taken from the china cabinet and thrown on the floor. The windows in the dining room alcove are broken, the upstairs mattresses slashed. DIRTY JAPS scrawled on the upstairs wall. KEEP THE JAPS LOCKED UP. Their precious table is heaved on its side in a corner. She walks from room to room crying, picks up a ripped kimono and hangs it up. The good porcelain is gone, the family pictures in the alcove shredded. The sofa slashed. Someone has even taken sections of the oak floor. Splinters of window glass crack like shattered ice, the smaller bits powdering into dangerous sand. Jagged sections stick in the frames.

Still crying, she scoops the heap of ash into one of the fallen urns that's miraculously not broken and takes it with her for safe keeping. Can't find the other one anywhere. Covering the gaping window frames with plywood, she goes to the store to buy a sturdier padlock.

That night as she's sitting numbly by the fire she sees Takumi coming up the verandah steps of her cottage under the stealth of the moonless night and the cedars.

You shouldn't be here, she says. It's too dangerous.

I'll only stay a minute. How's the house?

Fine.

What's a house like Scarborough going to do empty Isabelle? It'll start rotting in months. We should have seen this coming. Why do you think we had to register everything we owned with the custodian months ago, get cards with identity numbers and all the rest of it?

I don't know.

You didn't want to know.

All I want is for us to be left alone.

It's not enough though, is it?

They look at each other realizing that everything that might have been theirs is out of reach. No matter how many words they reel out, they'll almost have each other and one of them would slide through the other's hands.

The only thing I can think to do is get you to buy the place from us, he says. You can sell it back to us after the war. Borrow the money from Percy Killam. Pay it back to him a bit at a time. You could take over the market garden until we get back. We're loaning you our jobs, our business.

You're loaning me your jobs.

Yes.

Maybe you could sell it to me for a dollar. Buy it back later for a dollar.

I can't do that.

You don't trust me.

It's not that. It's my parents. What are they going to do for money? There's no one else I can ask.

Will they need any?

Of course they will. It's my responsibility. I'll find out where they've been sent and get it to them somehow.

It's too dangerous, you being out there at the lake.

We've had a post office box in Blaine for a long time. My father didn't trust the local post office. All you have to do is fill in your name on this deed, get someone to do the conveyancing and send the cheque. My parents will send a forwarding address. Four hundred dollars, it's not much. All I wanted to do was sign up. Be a Canadian soldier. He goes out and leans over the verandah railing.

She follows and stands behind him. I'll try, Takumi, but it might not be until the summer. It'll only be when the others come up that things will be settled enough to talk.

When she sets out for the lake the next night, mist slides behind the trees on the hill on the other side of Deep Bay. All along the Government Road, she keeps looking behind herself to make sure no one is following. Switches off the flashlight when she turns onto the Killarney trail in case someone inching their way in the pitch black happens to spot her departure from the main road. Once the tree branches close behind her, she turns the light back on so she won't trip on a root, lifts her palm on and off the beam when she stops to listen. When she reaches the lake clearing, she shines the light into the bushes to locate the beginning of a trail he might have bushwhacked, checking a few yards past where he likely would have camouflaged his entrance. At last she finds it, parts the wet bush and steps onto the new trail still stopping to listen every few minutes as she goes. When she finds him sitting on the ground in his cold dark camp, he turns away as if his back hurts: a slight tender man, his hair is long enough to scoop into her palm and lift to kiss the back of his neck.

You shouldn't have come here, Isabelle.

Wordlessly, she slides her hand along his shoulder blades until all she hears is the rush of two rivers meeting on the far side of a distant mountain. When they lie on the ground and pull the sleeping bag over themselves, the tops of the firs click and creak in the wind. I'll stay at Scarborough as much as I can, she murmurs. Sleep there. *Touch everything you've ever touched.* Stones ricochet from a far away ridge as he gropes toward her breast as if it's his last chance at thirst. His longing springs from a place so far inside himself the rush of the river is a hum in her thighs. It's so damp she feels her hair turn as blue as the far side of the mountain. Then he's inside her trying to listen for danger and keep his edge at the same time. He raises himself on his elbows listening for sounds that might become the enemy on the other side of any man's ears. *I'll listen for a while. Can you do that?* The rush of him then on the hard sleeping bag when he disappears into her as if he's finally arrived at a private place in the forest where he'll hunt for an animal he's never met. They're close to breaking out into an open meadow full of their own light when there's a stomping through the bush and two officers push into the clearing where they stand determined and miserable. Takumi's on his feet in one leap, hair flying, buckling his belt, throwing the blanket over Isabelle.

We're sorry, Takumi. We have to take you.

I'm not going.

When they grab him and twist his hands behind his back, Isabelle pushes her way between them, fierce and naked.

If you take him, I'm going too.

Don't put those on me. I'll come on my own.

The officer picks up the blanket, tries to put it around her, but she pushes it off.

I'm coming with you.

You're not, Isabelle. You know you're not.

Takumi's baffled angry look throws her as much as the shock. She tries to hold his face, but he shakes his head, as if to say did they see you, did they follow you? I told you not to come. He tries to bolt between the trees but the officers grab his arms and drag him through the woods away from the only house they'll ever have.

NARROWS INLET

4.

It's so good to hear the children playing, Lottie Fenn'd said to her neighbour Frederick Gallagher that summer of '41 when he'd come down from his place the end of the point to build new window boxes for her. He'd offered to build her a fence as well: no, no, no it certainly was not an imposition, more like a god given opportunity for him to practise the technique he'd learned from the Japanese up at the hotel. This right way? he'd ask Mr. Yoshito as he reached up to help him arch an alder under a fence railing as if he'd never learned his definite articles. Painstakingly humble when he wanted something, but when Shinsuke Yoshito came to sell vegetables at the Woodward's Food Floor, the master gardener would be received at the back door and Frederick Gallagher wouldn't even pretend to be on familiar terms.

If only there were a way to get Frederick to finagle an arrangement with the Union, to put a light at the end of the island that forms off her rocky beach as the tide comes in. The situation is dangerous as all get-out, especially in the summer when picnickers keep their put-put rentals out till all hours. It's when, not if, a boat is going to run aground on the rocks. The other night she'd had to go over to the Gallagher place in her dressing gown—a tailored plaid—knock on the bedroom window and ask Frederick to come over and row out to rescue a group of stranded drunks. Looking down from his window, his smile seemed a long way down from his nose on his large oval face.

The two of them were good enough neighbours that he'd be comfortably deadheading her azaleas (or her his) while they chatted. He had so much alder lying around his yard, making window boxes for her was doing *him* a favour, he'd say. When he arrived at her back door with his tools on that sunny, shady morning, she'd been glad she'd put on her new crepe blouse. Fastened a sequined comb in her platinum hair. While she talked to him, she twisted cups of brown paper on what looked like a wooden darning heel, turned up the vessels and filled them with seeds. Was aiming, she said extending her hand, for a *sweep* of nasturtium right the way down the window boxes.

Once the Gallaghers were up (especially Frederick, let's face it) she found herself thinking twice about hanging her underwear on the line and didn't even consider wearing a sleeveless blouse without a cardigan. Batwing sleeves on a sweater are one thing—seed

pearls stitched along a sweetheart neckline say—but the fleshy version pouching under your arms when you're hanging the wash, not on your life. A veiled hat to keep away the bugs, her prettiest gardening gloves—roses hand painted on the knuckles – Frederick coming along the path, panama hat dappled with the pattern of the overhead alder leaves. Who could ask for a better morning?

He'd ended his work by asking if, when his family went back to the city after Labour Day, she'd mind keeping her eye on their place over the winter. Of course she wouldn't mind. All the long time renters seemed to think of the cottages as their own, never mind that they belonged to the Union Steamship

Company and it was only by the company's good graces that the reservations were kept from summer to summer.

Hitching the conversation back to their earlier remarks as if trying to find the membrane that would slip the shell from a boiled egg, she'd been reduced to picking the bits off one after the other, not wanting to say, but she'd disliked the way he'd said *the Japanese* like that, flattening people she spent complicated winters with into one dismissive silhouette. Saying nothing is best with the summer people who seemed to think that, after they went back to the city, the residents put their lives on hold and the cottages sat perched like inert pieces on a board game waiting for the seasonal occupants to return.

Well, they don't. The hotel was closed, certainly: the blankets folded and put away, the concession stands boarded up. Shutters pulled over the windows of the dancehall. Her brother, George, went round and turned off the water in the cottages. The Yoshitos put the hotel gardens to bed and concentrated on their Scarborough farm harvest. And she herself got ready to teach school.

They don't even ask, though, that's the odd thing. When George informed the summer tenants that the water would be turned off after Labour Day, he was perceived as that burly fellow who lived year round with his son, Billy, in a cabin at September Morn Beach, named after a calendar on his wall that pictured a naked lady dipping her toe in the water. You'd think people like the Gallaghers would be interested in what makes the place tick when they're not there, and be curious as to why this man George Fenn with the booming voice who looked as if he should be in trade, as they say in the old country, had such a proprietorial air about him as if he were indulging their unwelcome presence for a few sunny weeks each summer out of a sense of *noblesse oblige.*

There are those who live on the island who are of the opinion that the situation should be reversed: that the Yoshitos were the ones who belonged in a cabin and the Fenns ought to be ensconced in the Scarborough house maintaining a nice standard of living.

Still. Sit Shinsuke Yoshito down next time you're by the hotel greenhouse and ask him to tell you how his family came to live on Bowen Island. Miss Fenn, not wanting to harp endlessly on about parsing sentences, preferred her students to grow up with a sense of the island's past and invited Shinsuke to come to her classroom to tell the story.

The day Keizo Yoshito, Shinsuke's father, saw the island for the first time, it was dampened and blanketed by fog, a shroud that deluded Keizo and his crew into thinking they were alone on the high seas. When the overcast lifted, he realized it'd been blue and sunny inches away the whole time. The coho run was so good they were winding the nets back out as quickly as they could pull them in. An unexpected trawler loomed beside them, and called out that they were pulling alongside. Keizo thought they must be in trouble; otherwise, why would they haul over and throw a rope? He cut the motor and welcomed the men aboard. The visitors leapt over the gunnels, tied the crew's hands behind their backs, lashed the two boats together and hoisted their captives into the second ship. They'd had it with the Japs selling fish to the canneries for nothing. We've told you and told you, but do you listen? No.

Keizo's seeing his boat cut adrift and sent idling off to goodness knows was like having his heart cut out of his body.

Everything he owned was tied up in that boat. He and his two crew members were rowed ashore and forced up a gravel beach at gunpoint into a camp near Scarborough beach where a group of tents stood in a circle. They were to be guarded there until the fishing season was over—while his wife remained worried sick back in Steveston with their new son, Shinsuke.

One day, one of the guards needed a diversion and escorted Keizo out to pick blackberries. Through the leaves, past patches of dazzling sea, the forest was thrown into silhouette by the brightness of the sun, and Keizo saw the bay windows and wide verandah of the Scarborough house for the first time. Orchards at the back, a cart and horse hauling a load of kelp up from the beach. Maybe because he saw the clearing on such a beautiful day, or maybe because he was being held against his will, or maybe because he had no idea how he would make a living with his boat cut adrift, to his longing eye, the place seemed so desirable that at the end of the fishing season when he was set free, he returned to the island to approach the owner of the house, Mr. Masen Fenn. Yes, their teacher's father.

Mr. Fenn was sitting with his son, George, on a stoop at the side of the house he'd arranged to have built while he worked on the other side of the island managing a logging camp which was divesting the south shore of its virgin timber in order to feed the mill across the Strait. He'd hoped to stay on indefinitely with his wife and family, but new house or no new house, that very morning his wife, Elizabeth, had begged him to let the family move to the city for the winter. The rain would not spare them, the winter darkness was closing in; they could stand it no longer.

When Keizo asked if there might be work, Masen Fenn took him on a tour of the property and promised they'd talk further.

In the end, Shinsuke's father moved his family to the island as caretakers of Scarborough and the Fenns retreated to the city.

At the time, cleared areas on the island were weighted down with stumps, Shinsuke told the students. But a few years later, his father started work in the new explosives factory on the west side of the island, where swaths of forest had been harvested into ties for the Vancouver Island railway. Keizo's job was dangerous. Until the highly poisonous liquid, nitroglycerin, was combined with some form of dope, the substance was inclined to destabilization—they were not to shake it or impact it in any way; the simplest movement could cause it to explode. Luckily there were sufficient quantities of sawdust left from the massive tree cutting to use as absorber and, once the oil was neutralized and the sticks wrapped in paper and paraffin, they were safer to handle. Because the "mixer" was the worker with the most dangerous position and received a few more cents each day, Keizo volunteered for the job, hoping to put the bonus aside. The day he met Mr. Fenn, he asked that he be considered first if the place was ever for sale. He planned to bury any money he saved; that way none of them would be tempted to spend it.

You're my witness, he said to the listening boy, George Fenn.

Except that the Yoshito family needed every penny they could lay their hands on to survive. Miserable insect invasions took most of the fruit blossoms. Many years they had no fruit at all. You try working soil that's as rocky as the ground around here, Keizo would say. Without the heaps of fish and kelp he and Shinsuke hauled up from the beach, they wouldn't have been able to grow a turnip. There he'd be; Shinsuke couldn't remember whose idea it was first, but it must have been someone who didn't mind the stench who'd necklaced a line festooned with fishhooks on Rocky beach so they could catch dogfish. They lit fires under pots so the oil from the livers would rise to the surface, then sold it as lubricant for the planks on the skid roads so the felled trees could slide down to the sea. Shinsuke would pass that bit of money to his mother and she'd tuck it in her pocket as if she'd scratched it out of the earth herself.

After Keizo died, you wouldn't think his wife and son would have been able to survive on the place, but they did. Young as he was, Shinsuke had to go to work in the logging camp. Then he was hired by the Union to help build the bridges, trails and summer cottages around the lagoon. When he was eighteen he arranged to have a bride brought from Japan. Maybe his resourceful young wife, Noriko, was inspired by watching Shinsuke and the others fell a huge tree by opening the crevice with a long saw, stuffing coals into the opening, lighting them and burning the trunk, because she immediately found a solution for her lack of preserving bottles: trailing a piece of cord through a saucer of coal oil, she tied the dampened string around the top of an old liquor bottle, let it burn right round and then banged it on the table so the top would break with a clean edge. Then she submerged a piece of paper in the white of an egg and laid it across the mouth of what was now a jar.

For years, the Masen Fenns came back in the summer and the Yoshitos had to move to the bunkhouse. Masen's attraction to Noriko began as he watched her slice coho at the fish cutting table in the summer kitchen on the beach, his desire for her coalescing in the bend of her shoulders and the exposed back of her neck as her little boy, Takumi, carefully handed her the clean jars. She stayed winter month after winter month in his house, polishing the newel post until it glowed as if for him alone. In the summer, she grew fragrant sweet peas up the south wall. But she wouldn't turn around the day he reached for her with one hand, holding the other over her mouth to stop her crying out. Please, he said, trying to turn her to say it was because she'd become everything he missed in the place, he hadn't meant to hurt her. When the will to force her was spent, she walked away from him dripping semen and didn't look back.

Noriko made sure never to be in the same room alone with him after that. She no longer met anyone's eyes. Masen eyed her shame-facedly and was mortified on her behalf when his wife, preparing to entertain guests who were coming from town, protested—she could see the advantage of having a Japanese family working for them if they knew how to keep their places—there was no reason on God's green earth why the Yoshito man's wife couldn't put on this nice maid's uniform and make herself presentable. Masen noticed that Noriko's straight tunic was pulled taut where her abdomen had grown and hardened; the uniform laid out on the ironing board had a narrow waist and apron sashes meant to be pulled tight. Leave it, he said. It's bad enough we're in Noriko's kitchen.

Noriko's kitchen? Noriko's kitchen is down on the *beach*.

That winter, Masen Fenn suffered a heart attack and died in his Hastings Street butcher shop where rows of torsos hung in layers from the ceiling. In his will, Elizabeth Fenn found that her husband had given away Lottie and George's inheritance; he'd bequeathed the Scarborough house and property to Shinsuke Yoshito,. His attached letter explained that, considering the years of work the Yoshitos had put into the place, he hoped his family would understand his desire to protect them.

When she realized she was pregnant, Noriko took quantities of penny royal and black cohosh, praying the herbs would work; if they didn't, the child was likely to be damaged by the infusions. One night when she and her son were harvesting cabbage, a pain sliced through her and the foetus slid onto the ground. Takumi rushed it up to the house on the palm of his hand. If he could get her there fast enough she'd start mewing. His mother managed to get upstairs to bed where his father pressed folded rags between her legs as she cried as if she were grieving. When the tiny one refused to start breathing, Takumi sat at the dining room table with the foetus in a jar, its large misshapen head gathered at the front of the skull above the buds of its beginning arms. We have to burn that right away, Shinsuke said when he came downstairs. Takumi dropped his cheek to the table, resting it on the pattern of the eye of the bird that Isabelle would stroke the first day she came to Scarborough. At the death ceremony, he and his parents passed the tiny bones to each other with chopsticks. They'd keep her ashes with them always, they promised, in two urns in case one got lost.

Later, when Takumi sat mixing blue-flesh tones of foetal skin, his father jabbed his arm. This paper is to record the flora and fauna on the farm, he said. That's what I bought it for. We need you to do that. Only that.

One evening at parents' night, after the other mothers left the classroom, Noriko sat as if stranded in her son's desk—Lottie had asked her to stay—while her son's teacher opened a drawer in her desk and took out Takumi's drawings. When she'd told him to work as large as he wanted, he'd swept and smudged the charcoal with his thumb, pushing a series of shaded mollusks from long thin lines. Only one touch of colour, a dabbing of soft blue shadowed a blobbed foetus floating in a mucous sac. She handed Noriko each page as if it were an illuminated manuscript. Why would my son be allowed to draw something like this at school? Noriko stood furiously at her son's desk, her grimace exposing a blue line along the top of her gums like an implanted string.

He's very talented. To do work like this so young. It's extraordinary.

He's to learn reading and arithmetic and that's all, Noriko said firmly, leaving the room with the drawings under her arm.

Never trust anybody around here, Noriko said to her son later when they were pushing the heavy roller over the lawn bowling green. People can turn against you when you're least expecting it.

Even Isabelle? Takumi asked because she'd just eaten lunch with them.

Even Isabelle, his mother replied sadly, and was silent. A forlorn note faded away like a loon's call.

5.

March, 1942.

George Fenn pulls his truck up way too close to his sister's back porch and it squeals to a stop. He tornadoes his way through the house, shouting at her in the garden. The bloody government's finally got it right. The Japs are gone. The Yoshitos were taken away without the kid. They got him in the end, but he slipped off the wharf for christsake. Couldn't find his body when they dragged the Cove. He's either drowned or he's half way to Horseshoe Bay by now.

Can he hear himself, Lottie thinks, pulling herself into her cottage on the rope of his sentences. She'd been out planting nasturtiums in the boxes Frederick Gallagher made her last summer, thinking how the kinked stems reminded her of his daughter, Evvie's, hair. If things had been different, she thought sometimes.

I'll start clearing out the place, see what I can find, George says.

You'll do nothing of the kind, Lottie says. You'll have some respect and leave things as they are, she says. What's happened is bad enough without you behaving like a vulture. Sometimes his blustering seems to her to be compensation for having such pale skin and hair he could almost be an albino. Billy too; he'd picked up only his father's looks, at fifteen the oldest child in her classroom and a constant bully. His mother died having him, and no wonder, keeping her out in the September Morn shack until it was too late to get her across the Sound.

That's not it, Lottie. That old Jap told me they'd never intended to accept the Scarborough place as a gift. We'll repay your family some day he told me. Had a bit of a search going on when I seen that Isabelle Gallagher lurking at the top of their driveway. Should have figured the way she was always hanging around with those Japs, eh? Wants her head shaved I guess. Never did know what was good for her, that one. Leave her be for now I says to Billy. Let her cry over spilt milk, one of these days she's not going to know what hit her. Maybe they've left money behind the Yoshito senior buried somewhere, I heard him say he was going to. It's an ill wind... eh, Lot?

Nothing to do but let him go on until he runs out of steam, dwindles out and sits there deflated. She makes tea for him without serving him anything along the lines of the date squares she'd offered Frederick. Her brother doesn't know the first thing about the Yoshitos. Never did. Thankfully has no idea the moon had been behind a cloud the night Takumi escaped; that, when the officer turned his head, the prisoner shot feet first into the sea. Swam underwater between the piles so fast you'd think he was wearing fins. Traversed below the surface up the north side of the Cove where the tide was so high there was no beach on which the police could track him. Voices shouted, then stopped as if they'd been turned off by a switch. Give it up. That kid's probably drowned, she'd heard them yell.

Wouldn't have a clue she'd followed him down the slope where he was hiding on her beach beside Gwen and Leo's tarp-covered rowboat she kept there off season to protect it from the winter tides. She'd helped him pull off his soaking clothes and change into old rain pants; given him sweaters, a blanket and flashlight; an oiled duffle bag filled with beef jerky, apples, rubber boots, matches, and a knife.

The moon sailed out from behind a cloud, too bright for him to take a chance on setting out until it slid behind another. How many days and nights to Jervis Inlet? he asked. Egmont first; he'd have hide the rowboat every night, a lot of days to be on the exposed shoreline. I want you to take this key to our post office box in Blaine, Miss Fenn, he'd said desperately. We've had it for a long time. If you could get down there in a month or so, please hold on to anything you find in the box.

As he pulled away, Lottie heard everything in exaggerated detail: the clunk of the oarlock, the seagull squawking from the rocks. Facing the bow, using an oar as a paddle, she saw him prop the flashlight between his legs as he felt his way into the bay. White caps slapped against Millers Point; outside the Cove, a westerly ploughed down the mile wide stretch of Queen Charlotte Channel, at least blowing in the direction he was heading.

6.

Night closed in as Takumi rounded the Millers headland, pulling hard on the oars that deposited paisley scoops behind him. The dinghy lifted into the next trough, a southwester pushing him away from the concave curve of Passage Island lowering over the horizon. As the sky and channel opened wider and the Point Atkinson beam and the far lights of Vancouver dimmed, a stretch of sky lightened under a line of dark low clouds above the mountains. He passed Hood Point and started into the open stretch of Howe Sound.

He keeps rowing as if he'd always be rowing so numb with shock he hardly feels the cold night; the current and wind push the swelling sea with him as he's pulled away from Isabelle's body again and again. *Never trust anybody around here.* How could she have let herself be seen? How could she? Already he's living his life in reverse, shunning rather than welcoming the approaching day: rounding Hood Point, the chop from a northerly Squamish in the middle of a tide change like this, a williwaw whipping down off the mountains and he's rowing as hard as he can but not getting anywhere. As the approaching dawn buffs the rocks out of the dark, the design on the sea weaves into a pattern dense as the lines on an elephant's hide.

When the off flow gathers more strength, signals of hope like the clouds that shielded the moon and the westerly being on his side collapse as light returns to find him rowing uselessly in place the way magical elements in old sea tales are withdrawn at dawn. Even the wind that normally dies down before dark and picks up before light is reversed.

Cutting diagonally into the grim shade and overhanging rock face of the north end of the island, a small bay cuts so narrowly between two cliffs nobody would think to look there even if they did suspect he hadn't drowned. The water turns cornflower blue to starboard, gunmetal green to port. A cracked fallen fir slants into the water. Dawn will expose him to any patrolling boat. He hitches the boat to a branch, twists boughs over the hull to camouflage it, and balances his gear up the beach.

Trying to lean driftwood poles together above the high tide line, he has to stop and warm one hand after the other. Climbs along another fallen giant of a tree to a stretch of trunk that's crumbled into red powder where he stabs enough bits of resined wood to start a fire. Dry twigs from the underside of a spruce, a few pieces of driftwood, a plank stuck sideways to direct the wind into the flame. If the fire is small and peaty, the smoke will get lost curling through the overhanging mist and canopy of branches. All those times on the beach when he wanted to skip rocks in the water and his father would call him over to the fire, to show him where to stick the plank. You might need to know these things some day, he'd say. He digs a few clams, smashes them open with a stone. A few swordfern fiddleheads for greens. Turns up crab shells to collect rain water, piles hot stones around his blanket, lies down on the beach and falls asleep exhausted.

In the morning he pulls the flap of the tarp over his head,

the absence of the people he loves a song he once knew and can't remember the words to. *Didn't she look behind herself? Didn't she hear anything?* The sound of his mother's knife on the cutting board, the soy smell, the radish between his teeth, a bowl of soup between his palms. Instead, only the black perforation of the high tide line ready to peel along the rocks. If a south-easterly comes up, he could be stalled in place until tomorrow night. Nothing to do but dig a long cedar root the way his dad showed him, circle it into a hoop, slash grommet holes in the tarp, and thread the fabric with a long piece of kelp stipe to make a drogue, a curved sail sunk under water in front of the bow to use the pull of the tide to help row. When a southeast-erly blows up, his legs cramp, his fingers blister, but he manages to make Keats Island before dawn where he passes a cold stiff second day's sleep in the woods back of a deserted beach.

The next night as he's rowing toward the Sechelt peninsula, the dawn is so misty he has no idea how close he might be to the beach. Row in too close, he'll scrape the rocks, stay out too far he'll miss a landing spot. When the wind changes with the tide, he can't hold the boat to port any longer. He lifts his hands off the oars to lick his blisters, checking over his shoulder to see if he's still pointed at the next headland and a massive wave crunches the boat against the barnacled rocks. Water pours through a hole smashed in the side; the drogue splodges like a collapsed parachute. He struggles out hurling his precious pos-sessions on the rocks, so wet and cold and alone he almost gives up and swims out to drown with the dinghy, but the storm stops as suddenly as it started. When the sun starts to rise, he realizes he's directly across the isthmus from the inlet, the bush so thick and dark maybe no one would see him bushwhack through the narrow neck of land. He takes two trips—the tarp on the second so it can dry in the sun. When he finally pushes up and over a slope of massed ferns, he sees a few boats tied to a dock in the inlet. Switching a canoe around so the bow seat is in the stern and he can kneel on the floor in the middle, he points what's now the bow into the wind and turns his stroke to a j. If he were allowed a day—he can almost remember day—the sun would burnish the arbutus trees on the bluff between thrusts of land sloping into the sea. When the inlet widens, he lucks into a quiet calm, staying close to shore then drawing sideways into a beach where a moss covered ledge towers above him. At least the canoe's easier than a rowboat to portage into the tree cover.

At moonrise the next night he passes between the slopes of Tzoomie Narrows, a natural barrier a third of the way up the inlet. When he lifts his paddle to mark his arrival, the cliffs seem to close behind him like a gate. In a nearby bay, he knocks a lot of mussels off the rocks and fills the canoe with enough oysters to keep him going for a few days; with the peninsula between him and the outer coast, he'll be able to gather seafood on the beach when the tide's going out. Any boats entering the Skookumchuck would come in on the flood; he could be back in the hills by then. Gliding into an area where an unlikely slope gradually rolls into gentle hills, he's drawn almost without stroking into a creek where his boat is lifted as if into a series of canal locks that usher him under a grove of huge moss trunked maples whose leaves let themselves down in such a convincing front he's shocked when he goes in behind and sees that the timber on the hillside has been logged off. Beaching the canoe, he hacks his way through the alder scrub, stopping short at the edge of a bluff where the logged trees would have catapulted into the sea. The remaining fir stumps are so large his encircling arms only half embrace them. In an area back from the edge, several rock faces have broken off and there's a lot of chit chit chit from birds he doesn't know. A small bluff gives way to large pieces of more broken rock as if from a slide, the pieces so settled the thick fir roots provide edges for natural dirt stairs. He'll be able to climb high enough to keep an eye on the Narrows; if anyone does see his fire, they'll think it's someone up hunting goats. Back down at the stream edge, he makes camp for the night—raw clams, young nettles and miner's lettuce for supper. When the rain wakes him, he realizes that, in his relief and exhaustion at finding a safe camp, he'd grown careless and left the canoe floating in the creek. It's filling up with rain water. At least it's a boatful of good drinking water, he thinks half asleep. Wait a minute, it'll sink if he doesn't get up. He staggers over to bail it, props it over his lair of moss and goes back to sleep.

He'd hung his tarp, but, in the morning he wakes up soaking wet, rain from the edges of the overhang had dripped straight onto his blanket. He split long kelp stalks to dry in the sun to use as cupped gutters for the eaves of his burrow roof. Later, back in the scrub, he finds the remains of an old logging cook shed, its shake roof doused in moss. The floor planks are rotted away, the sink matted with slime. The door comes off in his hand. A cast iron stove and frying pan have been left behind, and a sharpening stone. Miraculously, an axe.

An iron range is hooked up to a barrel of oil, a bit still sloshing in the bottom. Chewed through sacks of rotten flour, rice peppered with mouse droppings and the sweet smell of death from the packrats skittering in the crawl space. An old bottle out back magnifies the last of the sun's rays into a fire, the first since the day his matches got soaked. He finds a large round stone with a flat bottom; thinking of his mother, he makes a stupa to connect himself to the place that has received him. When he puts rounded, thick sticks of driftwood to dry on the stove they look to his hungry eyes like loaves of bread. The chain he hangs to drip rain funnels a multitude of excited drops into his bucket.

When he meets a deer in what he already thinks of as his field, he goes back for a length of cable he'd seen at the camp. Traveling the trail the next day, he realizes she'd have her head lower than the day before when she spotted him, so he hangs his snare close to the ground. Careful and exacting as he's been, he's still astonished the next morning when he rounds the bend and sees his kill heaved on the ground in front of him. Using his whole body to shift the carcass, he lifts her hooves onto his shoulders, the way he and his father did with their deer every fall. Lets her down on her back, pressing her chest until she's splayed wide enough for him to slice through her skin from windpipe to anus. Cross strokes across her breast from armpit to armpit; the skin tightly furled with one hand, he takes small strokes at the connecting membranes with the other. Draws the knife under the skin pulling it under her to protect the meat from getting soiled on the ground. Her small muscled body heaps over itself until it rests on its own skin blanket. When he slices through the pelvis, heat, blood, and intestines spill in a rush into a puddled heap on the mossy rock. Freeing the diaphragm from the ribcage, he runs the blade under her muscle sheet and up her neck, lifts the windpipe into his other hand and feels around his own shoulder to find the line between the blade and ribcage he'd look for had the kill been himself. When he pushes back the deer's thigh, it gives like a dog opening her body to be petted. He packs the torso on his back, one leg over his shoulder, another under his arm until a multi-limbed creature covered with blood and slime finds itself struggling back to camp.

The next day he paddles a half-mile further up the inlet and carries back large stones to pile across the entrance to a stream. When the tide comes in, salt water would rise into the creek. If it recedes fast enough, the cod and shiners will be trapped. He'd twist a reel of inner bark from a cedar, lash his knife to a stick and nip them onto the bank. That summer, he'll learn to fish like a bear, lying by the side of the creek reaching out to grab the sluggish chum floating dead in the water.

BOOK II

TAKE LEO

7.

March, 1942.

The days without Takumi go on and on. *I think about you all the time in case you don't know.* When the first crocuses come up, the telephone operator from the Union office sends a message to the post office that Isabelle's to call her sister.

Mother's very bad, Issie, says Ada. You'd better come to town.

In town it's pouring so hard peoples' breath steams the insides of the windows of the streetcar. Isabelle gets off, trudges up Willow St. to the General Hospital. Here's Isabelle, Harriet, her father says, trying to insert a sponge on a stick between his wife's lips. Yesterday your mother was asking for sips of water, now she won't even open her mouth. Harriet pulls off the sheet, presents mottled purple patches coalescing around her knee caps. Her feet are twisted as if they've been wrenched by her pulled apart toes.

What's happened to your feet? Isabelle cries. A starched white arm reaches in the door, perches a lunch tray on the sink. Why are we feeding her if she doesn't want to eat, Dad?

Is that my Evvie? Harriet asks as Isabelle bends over her. I have to know whose hand this. Is this Evvie's hand? Please someone is this Evvie's hand?

Back at the cottage, crouching on the toilet, Isabelle stretches the crotch of her panties between her fingers, searching, smelling for a stain that isn't there. Magazine cartoons her father pasted on the bathroom walls stare down at her. *This is Watchbird watching you sweep dirt under the carpet instead of into the dustpan. This is a Watchbird watching you reading the paper when you're supposed to be using it to light the fire.* She climbs the attic stairs, sits on the cot where she and Takumi played birdsong, turns over the mattress and pounds out the dust. Under it, a yellowed magazine that the Varsity girls passed around the time they were up (in another life) featuring an article about an evil butcher who lives down a back lane and spends his time sharpening knives to scrape babies from the insides of unsuspecting teen-agers. They'd laughed *they'd laughed*, gossiping about a girl who was supposed to come up for the pajama party but couldn't because she was up the spout. She had to go some place in White Rock and have the baby alone.

If only her period would come, she'd clean the cottage, wash all the curtains, even the ones in the attic, chop enough wood to get them through next year. He'd gone, when? March. Okay, April, May, June… counting on her fingers. Dear god, it would be December. It can't be December. What would happen if her mother died, she was in White Rock having a baby and couldn't come back for the funeral? What about Christmas?

She'd take hot baths. Or was it cold baths? She steps into the galvanized tub with the enema hose draped over her arm. If she could flush herself out, maybe *her little friend* would let go the shore and swim out like an obliging fry. The second month passes with no period. She begins to be sick in the mornings. Her breasts hurt when the first salmonberry blossoms come out.

She could go to town and ask a doctor to give her a pregnancy test, instead lies in bed in the back bedroom and watches an occasional bit of sunlight dapple the wall.

She'll have to leave before she shows but she needs to cover her tracks until then, devise some ploy so nobody suspects. Still, she has to get up. She has to. The Sannie will be here any minute, the children here for the summer

At work the next day, the last thing she expects is a letter to herself. Standing behind the unopened wicket, she turns the foreign looking envelope over and over as if cooling it.

Later that night she sits in bed, thigh bones socketed high in her hips. Who's writing to her as if he knows her like this? No return address. She skips to the last page. Oh *him*.

S. S. Inverness
September, 1941.

Dear Isabelle,
I'm writing to apologize. I should never have taken my problems out on you that night in the pavilion, but the news about my job loss threw me for a loop. I'm not one who can stay stuck in the city. The obvious thing would have been for me to sign up, I know that, and that's one reason I was on such a short fuse. I'll take any other job but I don't want to go to war.

The long and short of it is, I've managed to land a job as a purser, working my way across the Pacific at least as far as Singapore. They told me I might find work in Malaysia. So that's where I'm heading, in the opposite direction from where I want to be going. But at least

this way, I'm away from conscription if it should come along. If it wasn't for that possibility, I'd head on up to the captain's bridge and turn the wheel back toward your island, where I imagine you standing under the monkey tree in that blue dress of yours looking like a million dollars.

I have to tell you this, Isabelle. I love you. The way you move, the way you talk, the set of your mouth, your stubbornness. The way you wanted to listen to the music from outside the pavilion. I know there's no place I belong except at your side. I could pick you out of a crowd of a thousand if I had to. All you'd have to do is move. Don't ever forget that.

Your loving,
Jack.

She holds the envelope by the corner and taps it on the side table. Somehow, it's taken nearly a year for this letter to get here. Imagine him going way over there to get away from the war and then Pearl Harbour coming along. The way he'd run up to her on the causeway bridge, she knew he was the kind of man who'd trot from picnic ground to picnic ground splitting cords of wood when all anyone needed was enough hot water for tea. In any case, it will be a long time before he gets back to this side of the Pacific.

The next day she takes the *Sannie* to Horseshoe Bay, then the bus to town where she gets off in the pawn shop area at Hastings and Princess and, in a store window by the bus stop, sees what she's looking for: a silver engagement ring that takes all her savings to buy. On the street she pushes the ring grimly onto her engagement finger, stuffs her thin wrists deep into her pockets. Back at work, she makes a point of handing out all the letters with her left hand.

I didn't know you were engaged, Isabelle.

Well, I am. I met him at the dance. You know. That saxophone player. He's overseas now, but he managed to send me this ring. He'll be home when the war's over.

Aren't you the lucky one?

I certainly am.

8.

July, 1942.

Gwen sits at the kitchen table in their cottage watching her mother wrap a small disk. How could anyone in her right mind be wrapping wax paper around a stupid nickel when it's not even anyone's birthday? The next time they send her for ice cream so the grown-ups can have their coffee in peace, she'll fling the ice cream container in the bushes and sleep under the dancehall porch. Stuff lambswool into the points of her toe shoes, prop them legless in the corner of the dancehall. It's not worth it, though, because her mother will pull that blind down over her face that stays fastened all week. It'll be days before she even looks at you let alone likes you. Nothing else for this mother-may-I girl to do but sit endlessly on the concrete staircase above Sandy *again*.

I'm bored. I've got nothing to do.

Don't tell me you're bored, Gwen. I'll give you a job.

Can't I swim by myself if the lifeguard is standing right there?

No, you cannot. Not until you get your Intermediates.

In two minutes flat, her mother's going to find herself changed into a shriveled woodbug crawling out of the rotting log under the dogwood tree. She flicks a towel at her legs.

All right for you, Gwen. You're beyond the pale. Wait until your father gets here.

She'd rather not. Percy and Grandpa Gallagher patrol this place day and night, arms raised waiting to give you something to really cry about. Her mother's the one who's beyond the pail. I have had it up to here, she says. Wonders will never cease, though, because here's Aunt Evvie and her gang from the ship building plant marching down the resting rock hill in squadron formation singing It's a Long Way to Tipperary even if it's a song from a different war. People came up. People went down. They sang through the brass trimmed portholes on the steamer. One thing about the war, it sure brought people together.

Standing so straight her shoulders bend back, keeping her chin steady no matter who's teasing her, Aunt Evvie poses by the sink in her pleated tennis dress. No, Leo you're not going out, says mother. You have to stay in the house until that fever's down. Get back to bed and I don't mean perhaps. It sounds stupid her saying that. Only dads and granddads say that so you have to do what you're told.

Now when Gwen slips the foxglove blossoms on her fingers and crouches down outside the window of the kitchen nook, Auntie Isabelle sees the hoochey coochey puppets all right but all they make her do is squeeze her thin mouth in and out as if trying to get it around a straw and lean toward the radio as if it's telling her what to do with the rest of her life.

Last winter, when they came up in the winter that time by mistake a tufted toilet seat cover lay on the floor in the bathroom instead of a rug. A curl of black pubic hair on the bathtub. A leaf scrap stuck in a spider web. What are spiders supposed to hang onto if their web are flicked away? The toilet wouldn't flush.

For heaven's sake, you haven't gone and let the pipes freeze, have you, Isabelle?

I'll go get a bucket of sea water, Auntie'd said, so sadly that Gwen had wanted to run after her. What's wrong? What's wrong?

Why were they having to sit around on the beach, shifting dead crabs in their palms like hopscotches? The ovoids within ovoids that switched from green to blue in the summer weren't there, only a staccato shimmer where a bandaged crescent pulled a leftover goose up by the throat. It'd been so awkward getting her snow pants down in the pretend bathroom in her cave on the beach, she'd had to go up to the real bathroom on the back porch and listen to her mother's voice hammering away at her beloved aunt as if Isabelle had turned wild like a cat that'd been left on its own too long after it was born.

You can't stay here by yourself all winter, Issie. You know that as well as I do.

I'm all right.

You're not all right.

She sure didn't sound all right.

Later that afternoon it'd been so cold and rainy Leo was commandeered to keep his sisters entertained in the attic. His idea of entertainment was to make extra boards for monopoly so they had to go around New York, Montreal and Vancouver before they got back to the original Go square. His concentration doling out the starter money and rolling the dice was so serious and grown-up, you couldn't help wanting to bug him. She held up a magazine with a picture of a horrible looking man with a small black moustache and eyes like hot coals, yelling his head off on the cover.

Who's *he* when he's at home?

Hitler. He's the head of the German army. He's coming over here to kill us.

No, he's not, she said. The captain wouldn't let him on the boat.

At least on Sunday mornings, it's her nice dad who pokes his head up the attic stairwell to let her know it's time to shimmy into her still wet bathing suit so they can walk to Sandy and swim together in the sweet early morning. Her nice dad is the one kids visit to get their baby teeth pulled out. It's almost ready, he'll say, wiggling it gently. Come back in a few days. When they do come back and their teeth appear on his hand, he pretends to be as surprised as they are. At the beach, he climbs to the high board, dives off, bends in half to touch his toes, shoots his legs behind him, then swims back to the beach as if he hasn't done a thing. Puts his shoes on without socks. On weekends, dads don't have to wear socks. Once, he says, he dove from a cliff that was higher than the funnel on the Lady Alex. It was so high he had to take a breath on the way down. If it weren't for you kids, he says, I'd start walking. Start with Siberia, cross the Russian steppes. He doesn't mean he wishes he didn't have kids. That's just what he'd do.

At the concrete stairs the tide is on its way in so Takumi's rowboat has to be pulled way further up the beach than that!

Otherwise, he's going to be down there yarding it up every five minutes. If you're a beach monitor and have to go home for lunch, someone else can take your place, but if *that* person forgets to keep their eyes on the boat and it comes adrift, everyone has to push and pull until the boat sucks itself out of the sand and practically carries itself back up the beach.

Takumi isn't allowed to talk to people in the afternoon when the beach is busy. He has to be out in the rowboat making sure that every single person's head that goes down comes back up. But he's not there today. Instead, outside his shack, there's a sturdy looking woman wearing a nubbly red bathing suit with a tiny girl in an identical bathing suit diving down her hip bone. Standing in Takumi's place raking sea lettuce around the incinerator drum, the edge of her bathing suit sits along her thighs at the exact place that would peel back at her tan mark. Whoever she is, what does she think she's doing letting the smoke from the fire chase her around the pit? A gull that was invisible a moment ago flashes into a feathered white streak against the Millers hill. Her thick short hair is greased up from behind in a point. The distance from the corner of her eye to her ear is wider than most peoples'.

Fist in her beach jacket pocket, Gwen heel toes along the top of the beach backboard, knuckles stopping up against a small hard disc the size of a quarter. It's her Juniors swimming pin. So that's what her mother was wrapping. She offers it to the new lady on the flat of her hand.

You have your Juniors, do you?

Is this Takumi's day off?

Takumi? Oh, my predecessor. Takumi won't be with us this year I'm afraid. I'm Francis Sinclair. Don't worry. We'll still have swimming lessons. People with their Juniors are allowed in the boat. Can you row?

Of course she can row, but she's not allowed in the boats of people she doesn't know. The teacher said. Taking off in the substitute lifeguard's boat (their own rowboat is gone—Isabelle says not to tell their father, lucky he doesn't often go down to Miss Fenn's Rocky) is like flapping a towel at a wasp until it finds an open door. The oar keeps turning flat. If this Frances person is supposed to be a lifeguard, what's she doing standing up in the boat? The sun burns a flash in the hotel window that she can't stop looking at; the bow almost collides with the pier and suddenly the substitute lifeguard is out of the boat walking up the slope to the hotel so fast there's nothing for Gwen to do but row back across the bay.

9.

Playing Redeemers, everyone has to put their forfeited objects in a pile in front of the It person who kneels with her eyes on the ground. One player holds an item over her head and the others chant *Heavy heavy hangs over thy head, what shall the owner do to redeem it?* What the owner has to do is knock on the kitchen window, tell whoever's listening to the war there's a boat with a man in it stuck on Miss Fenn's island. Then say April Fool. That's crying wolf. They're not allowed. Yesterday, when Auntie's redeemers were to swim from their side of the beach around the Point Point to Miss Fenn's Rocky and back, what did she go and do but swim the old-fashioned overarm side-stroke, elbowing her arm above her head over and over like an orca fin. Now it's Auntie's turn to be It and she announces that the owner of the forfeit has to go down to Sandy and borrow the new lifeguard's whistle. (If you haven't done your redeemers yet, your shoe is kept in a pile in the back bedroom until next time they play. The only reason they have shoes in the first place is because their father works his fingers to the bone for them.)

Down at Sandy, the new lifeguard lies on her beach blanket turning her head slowly from side to side like the beacon on a lighthouse. As the tide laps the shore, she picks up handfuls of sand and lets them run between her fingers like an hourglass. When the sand's finished running, she shuts her lazy iguana eyes, turns the hourglass over so the sand can stream the other way. Sits perfectly still to stop the newest coat of tan on her legs from marring. Her heavy gaze stretches further each day until it's as if she can see which swimmers are above water and which below. On hot days, she smears a triangle of white Noxzema on her nose. In the afternoons when she's out in her boat, she pulls Takumi's pith helmet over her forehead and leans on the oars. The kids hang onto the sides. Take us to Bowyer. Take us to Anvil. No, take us to Jericho. Back on the beach, when she's lying on her stomach with her chin propped on her hands, you could climb all over her and she wouldn't notice.

After work, Frances says that what she really wants to do is swim home to the hotel float instead of walk. (She boards with the waitresses up in the Girls' Dorm back of the apple orchard.) But even if everyone's gone home and there's no one left to guard, she's still not allowed to swim alone. But if Gwen, say, walked along the shore beside her, and Frances swam in close where it wasn't over her head, she wouldn't be swimming alone. As soon as she hears the idea, the new lifeguard smiles as if that's what she'd been thinking all along. Before you can say

Jack Robinson, she's handed over the pith helmet, pooled the whistle and chain into Gwen's hands, pulled on her bathing cap, adjusted her goggles, rotated her powerful shoulders and begun her masterful crawl toward the hotel.

The cuffs on the adult sweatshirt are so heavy they hang like paws from a skin. The pith helmet bounces; the stubby whistle dangles and the sweatshirt band drags. When Gwen nears the honeysuckle arbour on the trail above the golden loaf of the hotel sand bar, Frances is already down on the hotel wharf climbing the ladder between the two tire bumpers. She gazes at the hotel dining room window, her body glistening, her hand waving Gwen away as if to say don't bother coming the rest of the way.

Gwen's heavy heavy game redeemers are in her hand before she even noticed. It's more fun to be lucky than smart, her dad says. Even. When she gets home, Auntie and her mother and father stop talking when she comes in the way mother says some friends of hers did once when they were planning a surprise birthday party for her and the confusion wasn't worth it. Auntie's pretty ears flatten against the sides of her head. Small girls dance the Highland fling on the oilcloth tablecloth.

What do you need that kind of money for, Isabelle? We're just getting on our feet. Are you in trouble? Maybe this is something you ladies want to talk about alone.

Of course I'm not in trouble, Auntie says. As I said, I want to buy the Yoshitos' house from them for four hundred dollars. They made me an offer before they were taken away. That way, we can hang onto it and they'll buy it back after the war. Then I can pay you back. I'll find a way to send them the money wherever they are.

When Gwen splats the whistle in front of her, Auntie looks at it like a dead mouse a cat brought in.

What's that for?

My redeemers.

Oh right, she says, scything the whistle and chain into her lap like a round of jacks.

You still have my shoe, says Gwen.

I do?

Of course she does. Why's she pretending she doesn't?

They're bending over some kind of new ring Auntie's wearing, a sharp edge of questioning in the air, as if the ring were one of the forfeits. Of course they remember Isabelle's fiancé, that nice longshoreman who came to lunch? He's overseas but he's managed to send her this ring, and when the war's over, she's going to marry him.

Well, congratulations, Isabelle.

Thank you, she says.

10.

Gwen is prancing her knees up and down, pointing her toes like a pony. Someone has to come with me to Sandy, she says. When can you, Auntie? I need to give Frances back her whistle.

Don't worry about that, Gwen. I'll talk to her about the whistle. What's Frances doing here anyway? Isabelle says to Ada who's washing dishes. I thought she was going to waitress at Britannia Beach for the summer. They've got all those miners to feed up there.

Not after I told her the lifeguard job was free. You can wait until one of us is good and ready, Gwen. Do you have to go to the bathroom?

You told her that?

Why wouldn't I? She has to make a living same as everyone else. She must be doing something right. Gwen can't get enough of her. Those beach rats, people say, they'd sleep down there if you let them.

The next night Isabelle crosses the porch of the Girls' Dorm up behind the hotel, passes through the lounge and down the long corridor perpendicular to the living room where she finds Frances in her room gazing longingly at her friend, Jeanette, sitting on the cot opposite, head so far down on her chest all you can see is the part in her hair. When Isabelle comes to the door, Jeanette widens her eyes above her receding chin, opens and closes the fork and spoon she's holding between the fingers of one hand. Want to see how to serve a mashed potato? she asks, twirling the fork, then pushing the prong tips along the belly of the spoon to scrape the pretend spud off the plate.

Ha! says Isabelle.

This is Jeanette, Frances announces proudly as if the object of her affections is a chickadee with a frosted tiara and necklace because she's blown cold air into her feathers all night. When Jeanette has to go back to her own room to get ready to go to work, so much of her admirer goes down the hall she doesn't notice Isabelle's bewilderment and misery.

I have to talk to you Fran, says Isabelle. It's to do with the man whose job you took.

I didn't take anyone's job. Frances drags herself back to the room. He was Japanese. They've all been sent away.

Isabelle sits down where Jeanette had been sitting which is maybe why she's finally noticed. I love him, she says. I spent the winter here and we were together. I'm in trouble.

How do you mean, trouble?

What it sounds like, I'm afraid.

The fear in their eyes says it all.

Nobody knows?

Nobody. Ada said you had a waitressing job lined up in Brittania Beach.

I did. But lifeguarding is what I'm trained for.

Has anyone else taken it yet?

I don't think so.

Maybe I could pretend to take that job. Better money than the post office I could say. Do you think your cousin would mail my letters to my father if I sent them there so they'd have a Brittania Beach postmark? I read about a place in White Rock I could go to have the baby.

Then what will you do?

I don't know.

I think she'd do it, considering…. But aren't you scared?

I'm terrified.

What are you going to do for money?

I pawned Takumi's whistle for a start. You'd better tell Gwen it's okay.

Oh, right. Will that be enough? I'll loan you some.

I'll pay you back, Frances. I really will.

11.

G wen stands at Auntie's bedroom door watching her lay five and ten dollar bills on the bedspread like a solitaire hand. Ten, fifteen, twenty, she counts. Not enough. Not nearly enough. You'd think a solid silver whistle would be worth more than that.

Maybe Auntie wants to buy the Yoshitos' house so the two of *them* can go live there and be alone all summer long. In the magazine ads for Community Silver, the model only gets to lie in the grass and have stars painted in her eyes when she has an engagement ring on her finger. So it must have been that man, Jack Long, who was lying with Isabelle in the meadow below the dancehall that night, but it couldn't be because Takumi's the only one she lets stroke her arms from the sockets to the tips of her fingers when she stretches them above her head on the horseneck tree platform on Miss Fenn's Rocky.

Here's our girl, Takumi and Auntie always said, reaching their hands down from the tree platform to help her up. *The water wants to hold you up, there's nothing else for it to do.* Teaching Gwen to float, Takumi always smiled back at Auntie on the beach as if he wanted to lift her dress up over her head so mother-may-I would let her go out to swim. When he slides his hand from under her own back, she holds her arch for all she's worth so she can stay floating. Being with the two of them is like when you have a new friend and decide to walk her home. I'll walk you back, one person says but, when you get to the other person's house, that person says now I'll walk you back so it's like the polite twins who never got born because one kept saying to the other *after you.* Later, she's a bridge between Auntie and Takumi's hands as they walk home down the resting rock hill.

Good floating, they'd say laughing, swinging her between them.

Gwen's supposed to laugh too, so she does.

She'll cry, too, if that's what they want, because even if Isabelle's sitting in her room counting out her money like the king in his counting house so they can run away together, she obviously doesn't have enough. In her cave down on her beach Gwen checks to make sure the special quarter which she can never spend because it belongs to the boy who sings for the open air interurban at 41st and Dunbar is still there. The passengers throw money at him. It's okay to help him pick it up, but once she slipped a quarter into her own pocket when he wasn't looking, and one of the dark quiet people from the Reserve who sits at the back of Mr. Pyatt's store saw her. His hat was narrow and had an Air Force crest of wings on it.

That night, the glow shines under the door of Leo's partition which means her brother's reading with a flashlight. *Go back to sleep. It's only the dance.* It's a great life if you don't weaken, their mother says. But of course you do. Grown-ups act as if, when night comes, they'll have a better life without the children there.

Her dad's words steam up through the gap around the chimney. Does anyone know where the dinghy's gone? It happens, says Isabelle. An especially high winter tide, I guess. Have you noticed how good Gwen's swimming is getting? When grown-ups say things that let children know they like them, they grow in their sleep.

When she sneaks into his room, Leo wants to talk about the man in the story he's reading who escaped the German army and became part of the Resistance, whatever that is. If you're part of the Resistance and speak German, evidently they take you to a hotel somewhere in England where they brainwash you which must be like having your mouth washed out with soap. After they empty you of whoever you were before you came to Allied territory, they fill you up with everything they know about some German person who's dead. Then they wake you up in the middle of the night and ask you questions.

Say you're him, Gwen. What's your name? Where do you live? What are the dates of your children's birthdays?

Is that rain or leaves? Rain. The toilet flushes. The silence shifts.

The amount of equipment that's going out of here by train, her dad says up through the chimney, all Gerry has to do if he's got any brains is land a couple of plainclothesmen on the coast. Get them on the train to Lytton, assign them to blow up those two bridges that crisscross the Fraser. That'll hold up things for a while.

You're not supposed to say things like that, Perce. Jugs have ears.

These children of yours are jugs? Raising kids is impossible. Whatever you do is wrong. You say too much, you're interfering. You don't say enough, you're irresponsible. I give up.

You don't mean that, Percy.

I do, yes I do.

12.

Take Leo. That is, if you can find him. It's supper time and Gwen's supposed to be fetching her brother from the tea room as usual but the *Alex* is coming in; someone who's catching the boat has given Leo a bunch of free pinball games, and there he is up at the helm pulling levers and yanking side arms smashing silver balls against miniature lighthouses till the cows come home.

It's supper, Leo, she says. You have to come home. Two shakes of a lamb's tail, he says, flipping another lever. Get the ice cream and wait for me on the verandah. She does—it has to be vanilla—she sits on a bench holding the folded box by its wire purse handles. Miss Fenn could learn a thing or two about makeup from the chickadees here, the way the shadows on their eyes sweep deftly back at the sides, black fading to white. They jump around on their stiff legs pecking crumbs from leftover hamburger buns.

Drat, says a man in the phone booth when his change falls between the slats in the floorboards. There goes my nickel.

The ice cream's starting to melt, Leo. Come on.

All *right*.

They start for home, but, wouldn't you know it, at the bottom of the bluff the big boys, Billy Fenn and them land in a whoosh, career in front of Leo like dogs that don't know how to go straight on the road.

Hey Professor Snodgrass, got anything for us today? Billy's face is flat and pale like his father, George Fenn's, and his sticking up hair is so blonde it's almost white. A couple of nights ago Billy let Leo join his softball team and Leo traded him a Captain Marvel comic for only a Captain Marvel Junior so you'd think maybe they'd go easy, but no.

My brother is smarter than all of you put together so blow it out your ear, why don't you? she says.

Don't say anything Gwen. They'll get you.

They will too. You have to stay clear. They're supposed to make allowances for Billy because his mother died but why should they when he waits until you have the very last grain of sand in place on your sand castle before he kicks in the turret.

Keep walking, keep looking straight ahead, says Leo.

Don't think we don't have our eyes on you, Professor Snodgrass. You too, Gwenny-Henny.

In the summer they're not supposed to get up before the big hand is on twelve and the little hand is on seven but even Lily's way past telling the time that baby way. *Early one morning just as the sun is rising, I heard a maid singing in the valley below.* Why can't I ever come with you? she says. Shhhh. Go back to sleep. The way Gwen's thinking, if one of the dancers ended up having to call home in the middle of the night to say he missed the boat, he'd likely be reeling around and might end up dropping change between the floorboards in the tearoom phone booth. From watching boys play war, she knows how to worm her way into the crawl space under the verandah below the phone booth, scrabble her nails in the dirt to unearth the shiny edge of a nickel, and then two dimes and a penny. Not bad for starters. She's not the only person out this early though; when she crawls out, there's Mr. Fenn wandering around in the bush, combing through the salal with a stick.

From the platform on wheels down on the wharf used to boost the gangplank to the steamer when the tide is low, there's a good view of the blackboard on the shed that announces the day's picnics. Today is Eatons; great, they're a good picnic. Crowds troop from the wharf along the Government Road to number two grounds behind the post office where the concession stand man is supposed to tear the picnickers' tickets in half before he throws them on the ground, but lots of times he's so busy prying caps off pop bottles and passing Dixie cups over the counter he forgets to tear them. They're using purple today. Good, they've got lots of purple. When the picnics go down, she and Leo pick the untorn ones off the floor, go home and bottle them in jars in the attic. Hudson's Bay, 1940. Longshoremen, 1941.

Once they know the colour, they race down the hill, tag the resting rock, rush into the kitchen and up the stairs. One of these weekends please will Percy make a railing for the attic stairs. Lily almost fell down them the other day. Back at the dancehall, Gwen and Leo set up a booth on the porch where they sell the purple tickets to the other camp kids. Three for a penny. Seven for two pennies.

Gwen's got her swimming lesson after the picnic and she has to go even if it is raining. She won't melt. She's not butter. On Sundays, when they go to Sandy for their morning swim, her dad says he'd rather be heading for a nice clean lake on the Prairies where he wouldn't be obliged to swim in salt soup but beggars can't be choosers. Billy and his boys are down at the hot bench on Sandy pushing each other on and off as usual. Leo's thin top lip pushes forward when he sees Billy and his gang; he stands tilted forward, eyes fixed on the ground, concentrating on the farthest star he can find in his mind. Billy lands in front of him, lurches into his walk like a held out coat. He holds up his hand and looks at his nails. Only a day late. That's not too bad, Leo. Not by all accounts. The rest of his gang hurls boxes of hot ice over the racing wall. The steaming bubbles come back up as the boxes sink. What do we do to poor sports, eh boys? Get over here, Leo, we have to take your fingerprints. Think if it was your tongue. Another time they shoved her brother under the cobwebby back dancehall stairs and stuffed *poisonous* mushrooms in his mouth. After they left, she had to coax him out like a scared puppy, his mouth full of guck like cotton batten sticks the dentist forgot to take out. He spit and crawled along the ground. The whole day he kept spitting. Are you sick? Have you got earache again? they said at lunch. I'll take him to the wharf, her Dad says. He can help me put the boat up on the ways. Stop spitting, Leo. You think it looks tough or something?

Billy marches Leo over to the bluff, lifting his knees one after the other from behind with his own. If he touches hot ice, Leo's fingers will stick together forever. *You don't get fingerprints on hot ice, you get finger skin.* Get his bag off him. Twist his arms behind his back. We'll take him prisoner. Skin burn him. Butt him up the bluff. They prod him with their sticks and march him up the rock, the back of his jacket pulled over his head. They've done this so many times Leo knows the way blindfolded.

We'd better make sure this kid knows we mean business, says Billy. We're still in business, right Leo? Got any of those pellets left there, lieutenant? When you've got rats you don't want escape holes. This prisoner has got five on his head alone. When they twist his head, Leo concentrates on another star, trying to get high enough to see himself down on the bluff where the front of one of his torturers' pants has stretched hard. They push his head to the other side. All right, prisoner. Let's have the secret admission papers.

They're in my paper bag, says Leo. He looks over his blindfolded shoulder even if he can't see.

These are coded correctly, are they soldier? You're not leading us on a wild goose chase. Otherwise, it'll be double or nothing.

The tickets will get you past the enemy line, says Leo. They're all disguised today as Eatons' employees.

That was kind and considerate of you, soldier. Wasn't that kind and considerate, boys? Hand over that filthy paper bag of yours. Keep this deal under that twerpy Boy Cubs cap of yours, Leo. You too, Gwenny-Henny. If you say anything to anybody, we'll get you worse than ever.

They leave Leo flat on his back, panting, ankle noosed to a tree. He can't breathe through his nose because his nostrils are stuffed with pussy willows. She has to help him turn on his stomach so she can get his leg free and help him home.

At Sandy, there's a sign on the First Aid station bulletin board announcing a sand castle contest. First prize twenty dollars, and all you can eat for dessert at the Shack Café. A chance to blow the whistle on the Lady Alex. Good, Gwen thinks. She'll win and find a way to talk to the captain and tell him to make sure Hitler isn't trying to get on the boat. And she'll be able to save the money to give to Auntie.

She has to get on with finding building materials to go with the curved stick for the main sand house beam she found on Miss Fenn's Rocky. Smaller versions to fasten into the beam for rafters. A piece of tin painted green, scooped scallops around the edge to mark the roof, wet sand walls that drop straight to the ground. From above, the house would look like a giant alder leaf resting on the forest floor.

She'll use the blue plastic bowl from the cupboard for a swimming pool, sprinkle rose petals in it when she sees the judges coming. The blossoms will have to be cupped and floating, not water logged and sunk. Gentle laps below the house turn schools of minnows back on themselves; the green strokes of water fade to slate, change to pale blue shimmers. The amber light on the roof of Lily's doll buggy pops into red into orange into pale circled yellow as the lily-of-the-valley peals in the shade.

The sandcastle contest judges are Frances and that waitress she's so crazy about, Jeanette Ann somebody. The two of them, dressed in white skirts and navy blue blazers, are bent over some stupid half baked Lady Alex sogging along the sandbar looking more like a lump of dough than a boat. As they zigzag from one side of the sand bar to the other, Gwen keeps a close eye on them, waiting to strip the petals from the stems at the last possible moment. But, instead of crossing the sandbar back to her side like they're supposed to, what do they go and do but continue along the same side toward an even worse Lady Alex so it's going to end up like in school when the teacher calls questions up and down the rows, you've counted ahead and figured out the answer to your question, but then she changes her mind and starts working the room lengthways instead of across. By the time the judges get to her, all the petals have sunk.

For heaven's sake, Gwen, says her mother when she comes to pick her up. It's not the end of the world. You learn from what you did wrong and do better next time. Is it part of sand castle contests that you use mostly sand?

SECOND CHILDHOOD, MY EYE

13.

What many on the island know but pretend not to is that, like many others during the Depression, George Fenn had been determined to find a ruse to get by and you had to say he latched onto a good one. He first got the idea on one of his excursions over Scarborough way when he'd watched Shinsuke Yoshito hauling sack after sack of potatoes up from his field.

Give you a dollar for a few of those? George said. Shinsuke knew he couldn't have too many vegetables in his root cellar for the winter, but was canny enough to take the opportunity to begin to pay off the Fenns so they'd have doubly earned Scarborough and nobody could have a case to look twice at them.

You take as many as you want, he replied, resignedly watching George load the sacks into his truck.

The implication was lost on George who was already planning his whiskey still. He went home, got his first batch of potatoes cooking, added the barley. Had to experiment to get the proportions right, cheered when the concoction settled down to saccharificate. On Sunday mornings the woods around the dancehall were filled with empty bottles for his product. He collected them in the empty potato sacks and began to save match boxes.

Someone who sells matches, where's the harm in that? What they don't know won't hurt them, eh? Can't buy a drink for love or money in the dancehall, so what are the moonlight cruisers supposed to do when they've downed their hooch by the time they get to the island? Open the matchbox they've bought from George, and find the map to the hidden bottle with an X marking the spot, what else? Two dollars for a box of matches? Well, who was counting?

Only thing was, he didn't want his sister to know about his sideline. Lottie was a stickler for the rule of law, picky picky about anything she thought remotely shady. Downright prissy half the time, being a teacher and all. When he visited her, he kept his bootlegging franchise under the table, ha ha, instead tried to impress her with his business like grasp of their family situation, sitting in her kitchen matter-of-factly suggesting that, if their dad had a bee in his bonnet about the amount of work the Yoshitos had put in, why couldn't he have left Scarborough in trust to the Japs and arranged to have it passed back to his own family when he died?

Give it a rest, George, Lottie said. Dad was just trying to do the right thing.

You don't care where his decision left me. It's all very well for you, being in with the Union and all.

The Union has been good to you, too, George. They're not offering anyone else your winter job.

That's true.

14.

Huddled against the rain streaked window of the bus to White Rock—windshield wipers slapping back and forth – Isabelle tries to knit an infant's dress but the lurching ride keeps jolting the yarn off the needles. When she folds what she's managed to knit so far and nods off, she dreams she's lost her skirt: the only way she can make herself presentable is by tying the sleeves of her jacket around her waist and wearing it like an apron. That way, her behind is exposed but, if she wore it as seat padding, the sleeves wouldn't be long enough to cover her vagina. The bus driver feels so sorry for her he gives her the fare. The one seat that looked vacant from the front of the bus turns out to have a baby in it.

The residence for unwed mothers is a large gaunt house that smells of artificial pine floor cleaner cut with fried fat; the paint on the halls and stairways seems scrubbed with antiseptic. Old triangle patterned linoleum on the wide stairs. A spare woman in a tweed skirt leads her down a corridor to a room with a narrow bed, the reading lamp tied to the corner post with string. The matron, if that's what you'd call her, looks at her askance the way the bus driver did in the dream.

When Isabelle reaches up to put her few things in the cupboard, her arm drops like a piece of clothing from a line. She lies down still in her coat. This is how Takumi must have felt, alone and hauled away from everything and everyone he knew. Hard to believe it was only a week ago Gwen'd turned her change purse upside down and emptied dimes and nickels on the cottage bed. This is to help buy your friends' house, Auntie. I saved it for you.

It's not enough, sweetheart. Thank you though. Oh Gwen, don't cry. I'll make it up to you some day. I promise.

For the last few weeks she's done nothing but fall asleep but now, in a half dream before they're called down to supper like girls in a boarding school, she finds herself giving birth to a curved log swaddled in leaves. Downstairs, the cook in the institutional kitchen bangs her pans of instant scrambled eggs and powdered potatoes. It's not her fault, her tired glance says, that Isabelle has to load a tin tray to feed the life inside her that's never going to belong to her. What excuse has her family made? She visiting a maiden aunt like the rest of them?

It's the saddest, most sullen time she'll ever remember. She can't bear being there with the donated furniture and sidelined girls, pretending they're hidden when they couldn't be more visible. When the baby moves inside her for the first time, she thinks of shiners eddying back and forth at low tide. She spends most of her time lying in bed, occasionally managing to comfort herself by touching the part of her beloved deep inside her body. This baby is staying with her, no matter what

(A leaf falls. A mouse drowns in one of Takumi's rain buckets so that one's not for drinking. Small reflections of sun flash on patches of dark water as shadows pick out the cedar and hemlock on the ridge across the inlet. A spotlight lifts the tone on the opposite bank to a vivid sage as the background overcast darkens. He dreams about a baby he's never met who lets go his hand and is sucked into a narrow viscous tube in the sea. He isn't worried because there's a shallow beach at the other end where she'll be able to wade. Later, diving down the tube himself, he discovers it's a dead end and she didn't manage to get born. Swimming back, he explains to the people questioning her death that no one told him there was no opening at the other end.)

15.

December, 1942.

In the summer it's all Grandma and Grandpa Gallagher but, back in Vancouver in the winter, it's Grandma and Grandpa Killam who've moved to Vancouver from Saskatchewan because life is too hard on the prairies. Grandma Killam's over at Blenheim St. to help because it's so close to Christmas. She sits on a stool at the ironing board in a stiff suit holding herself straight like the first person to salute the platformed general in a marching parade. Coming out on the train, Grandpa Killam lay on the bunk craning back his neck trying to see the tops of the Rockies as they rounded the bends. Now they live in an apartment at 43rd and Larch; wonderful to be so near the grandchildren, but they can't get used to living up off the ground.

Grandma Killam folds a pillowcase in half, irons it, folds it in half again. They did have a time on the train. Kind of a holiday. People don't get much in the way of holidays in their neck of the woods. Not like being able to go to a cottage with your children every summer and sit on the beach all day, Ada.

Dear knows they'd only been here a few weeks before Lyndon started pacing up and down the apartment lawn looking for his cows. Holding a shirt up at the cuff and armpit as if measuring it, Grandma sticks the sleeve over a narrow board that folds down from the ironing board cupboard. Second childhood, my eye, she says. He plain misses his livestock. As for her, she misses her sister Eleanor. Ada would understand. She has sisters. Eleanor. The loveliest name in the world when you come right down to it. Loveliest person in the world for that matter. Grandma Killam stops ironing, her face softening as if she's hearing Silent Night crooning from a music box. When Grandma and Grandpa Killam arrived in Vancouver, Great Aunt Eleanor's flower water colours had to be brought up from the basement. Bevies of wrinkled roses weakly capsized in a grey wash now hang in a row on the dining room wall.

Eleanor's the one who insisted on living in a room above the barn because she wanted to paint. Oh she sounds exactly like Eleanor, their dad said scathingly at the dinner table when mother mentioned as to how, at camp, Isabelle liked to use the coffee grounds to mulch the azaleas. Not *exactly* you could tell she wanted to say. Isabelle's not asking to live in anyone's barn. Funny how you can get away with saying something mean about someone in your own family but let an outsider make a remark and it's a different kettle of fish.

How about a big smacker, Gwendolyn? says Grandma Killam. Lines crinkle the edge of her eyes, her cheek is dry and papery. The look on her face when she's ironing is like someone in school who has to colour when she wants to be learning to read. Mother tucks a collar of brown paper inside the tin before she pours the light fruit batter. Arranges tree sugar cookies in a box decorated with Christmas soldiers. Change your dress, dear, before you go out to play. The house will become even more special when she's out, as if it's marinating in nutmeg.

Coated in grey stucco, the Killam house on Blenheim St.

near the lane behind Crofton House School has leaded glass windows, a square entrance hall and a spacious upstairs. Outside, a few kids are playing double Dutch even if the sky's darkening. Swaps of dead maple leaves flatten on the driveway. Gwen's jittery beside the person who's turning the rope. Trying to get the nerve to skip into fast pepper to keep the kettle boiling, her foot hesitates in and out the way Leo's does on the *Sannie* gangplank. Miss the rope you're out.

At her ninth birthday a week before Christmas (and not fair) her mother hangs streamers from the ceiling lamp to the corners of the new pedestaled dining room table her dad's brought in as an early Christmas present. They had to carry the old one down to the basement. At the party, she turns the chairs opposite each other in a row so the kids can prowl in a circle until the music stops and everyone grabs a seat. Then a chair is taken away. There has to be one less chair than the number of guests, so someone's out every time. Finally there's only Gwen and Leo running around the last one. When the front door opens, their mother's hand suspends above the gramophone arm ready to nip it back onto the stand to stop the music. She lifts the arm. Leo grabs the seat. Losing makes Gwen feel sick and she has to go lie down on her own birthday.

Aunt Evvie comes in, smashes a bag of groceries on the counter and the party's punctured like a balloon. Her hair's piled on top of her head but the ends have sprung from their bobby pins. She's gone, Ada, she cries. Mother's gone. She looked so alone, I couldn't bear it. The two of them stare into the sink as if Grandma Gallagher's blood is pouring down the drain. They never touch but now they reach for each other awkwardly as if they don't know what else to do with their arms. Mother pulls away first. Someone's got to get in touch with Isabelle, she says. They must have a phone in that café in Brittania Beach. She's said she's staying there for Christmas.

The children are sent to bed early. Gwen sits at the top of the stairs and listens to her mother hang up the phone.

For goodness sake, they've never heard of an Isabelle Gallagher, she says. I'm going to

call Frances. She's the only one who might know. Frances's phone rings and rings but there's no answer. Where could Isabelle be? Where could she possibly be?

16.

December, 1942.

Every week Isabelle's marched belly first to visit a thin, hurried obstetrician who rushes into the cubicle eyes on his clipboard, then reaches over to heave her belly back and forth as if kneading bread. The baby's positioned feet first, he tells her. If it doesn't turn soon, they'll have to do a caesarian. He tries to roll the baby into a head first position, but it stays stubbornly pointed the wrong way.

She, Isabelle says. It's a girl.

Even if she hasn't managed to look after the house the way she said she would, at least she'll have a granddaughter to present to Shinsuke and Noriko when they come back. A daughter to make up for the sister Takumi lost. At least there's that, but what's she going to do about her family? She can't be in Brittania Beach forever. Back at the home, she uses her own hands to try to turn the child head first into the birth canal, but the baby's narrow feet stay downward like small hooves.

One afternoon, there's a knock on the door she assumes is the matron's, but it's not, it's Ada of all people. She turns her face to the window, angry and relieved. What are you doing here, Ada? I want you to leave. How did you find me?

Ada sits down as if she'll never move again. I was at that pajama party too when we talked about that girl.

What happened to her baby?

I have no idea. You poor thing. You look as if you're almost due. Let's get you through this, Issie. Then we can talk about what to do.

How's Gwen?

Gwen's fine. She'll be expecting you at Christmas.

Well, I won't be there. I'm up the spout.

Isabelle, promise me you'll call when you feel the first sign of contractions. First babies can take a long time. So the minute you feel anything....

What do they feel like?

A kind of gentle tugging.

Until the contractions begin, Isabelle's certain she'll want to be on her own. But when she finds herself breathing slowly trying to leave her body and get up high so she can look down at the tops of trees, she's terrified. The part of herself that was in control disappears. Ada's done this; she must know something. How could she have known she'd need her this badly?

She calls. Can you come?

I'll be there.

And so in the end it's her sister who's holding her hand in the delivery room listening to the doctor say that the cervix may not be dilating because the baby hasn't presented its head properly. It will be best for mother and baby if they settle for that caesarian.

It's a she, Isabelle murmurs as she loses consciousness and knows nothing more until somehow—is it possible—she finds herself waking up in her old bedroom at Laburnum St., the cut down her belly aching and subsiding with post delivery contractions like aftershocks. Bruised with abrasions as if she's been scraped off a highway, pain pulling the stitches down her belly, she tries to sit up, vaguely remembering Ada's arm around her shoulders half-carrying her up the front stairs.

What are we doing here? she says when her sister comes in the room. Where's the baby?

Don't try to get up, Ada says, unpacking a bag of Isabelle's stuff she'd grabbed on the way out of the hospital room. She quickly put the half knit baby dress back in the bag so Isabelle wouldn't see it. I don't know how to tell you this, Isabelle, but I have to. The cord tightened around the baby's neck as she was being born. They didn't get her in time. I'm so sorry, but she died. I wanted you to be somewhere you felt safe before you found out. I was lucky enough to find an orderly who was willing to help me take you out a side door when I explained....

What, that the baby was Japanese?

Never mind that. We had to take a taxi back from Blaine and it cost a fortune. Dad thinks you've had a collapse because you've been working too hard.

Isabelle's eyes hood like her mother's, as if she's taking her place in the sick bed. How could you have taken me away without letting me see her? She's all I had left.

She was dead.

She was inside me; I knew everything she was doing and I

never even got to hold her! She can't stop crying.

I'm so sorry, Isabelle. Ada tries to hold her, but her sister pulls away. And it's terrible, that I have to tell you now. Mother's passed away.

Oh no. That too. It's too much for anyone, your daughter and mother dying at the same time.

For two days, Isabelle lies facing the wall. Her sister bandages her breasts to stop the milk, drapes a bed jacket over her chest as camouflage. You and dad should come and have Christmas at Blenheim St., Ada says. It'll do you good.

I'd rather see it in from here, says Isabelle. He's got me where he wants me, she thinks. My father's got me back where he wants me.

After she's been at Laburnum St. a week, she manages to make her way downstairs where she finds her father hunched at the table, his face swollen with grief and loss as if a layer of air has been pumped under his skin. Upstairs she'd seen him walking through the hall carrying articles of Harriet's clothing as if searching for an altar to lay them on. He looks so lost she covers him with one of the crocheted blankets her mother'd picked at, hooking stitch after stitch with nails that pecked like sparrows' claws. It's all right, she says, I'm back now. He throws off the blanket and falls heavily in his daughter's arms, leaning his large white head against her bandaged breasts. She winces but he doesn't notice, instead clutches her, sobbing as she lowers him to his chair. You have to eat something, dad, she says to the refrigerator. As she gets up, he grabs her ring finger and pulls it close to his face. This, he says, is the only good news we've had in months. A little scrap of hope at Christmas, that's all I ask.

17.

W hat's wrong with this tree, this tree is *fine*. This tree is not fine, Percy, and you know it. When the air's this tense, Percy's liable to reach out and whap something and it could be one of his daughters. So no, Gwen does not want to go with the family to get the tree: all they do is tramp mile after mile through the bush until every tree looks like every other tree. Smiles are at least supposed to be *trying* to get onto their faces but no, it's life or death whether it's the be all and end all perfect tree her father's holding by the neck as if he wants to throttle it.

At least, after the others leave, the air surrounding her fits better. The trim around the grey front door could use some lettering: words written equidistant around three sides of the white rectangle frame like the words around a Christmas card border. *This,* turn the card, *is Killams,* apostrophe before the s or after, over and down the other side, *House.* With the car lights turned off for the war, the lettering will make it easier for people to know they're at the right house because everyone's welcome at Christmas. Auntie too. She's at Laburnum St. but she's not feeling well. On the Killam family Christmas card, Lily's perched on the lowest stair, Gwen face-front on the next, Leo in profile on the landing, candles held high like Jack be Nimble, Jack be Quick. The girls in white flannel nightgowns, the boy in a white nightshirt. The worst story Gwen's ever heard is the one about Peter Pan who finally makes it home to his own window only to find another boy in his bed. He has to go back and stand on the blue stone in Kensington Gardens forever.

At school, she's one of the ones picked to take the white food drive cans down to the Reserve. You have to bring tins from home wrapped in white tissue paper. It turns out to be as awful as she thought it would be because the woman who comes to the door of the dilapidated house is one of the ones who sit silently in the back of Mr. Pyatt's store. Once, her potatoes fell out of her bag and she had to chase them down the Dunbar Street hill. The woman closed the door on the hamper, so there was nothing to do but leave it on the porch. Back on the dirt road, Gwen comes face to face with a thrashing cat that's been run over by a car. The man who'd seen her pick up the quarter stands beside it. Die, he says to the cat. He's still wearing the hat with the wing crest on the side.

She's stretching up as high as she can painting the last letters on the door frame when the Dodge drives up with its captured tree on top, her dad's angry eyes flashing over the dashboard. Her mother lifts her feet over the dirty whitewall tires. Where's Jean next door? She's supposed to be watching Gwen for heaven's sake. If Gwen thinks she's too big for her father to pull down her pants, turn her over his knee and spank her, she's got another thing coming. The hits ring out with the type of sting he'll tell you is par for the course but isn't. Once he took her aside and asked how she'd feel if he went and lived in a hotel for a while. She said it wasn't a good idea. He should ask her again.

Christmas Eve, Ada's still got a million things to do. Maraschino cherries to cut up for the holly on the shortbread for one thing. All that sewing. Christmas Eve wouldn't be Christmas Eve without Percy banging on the floor at 2 a.m. calling his wife to come upstairs. How's Santa Claus going to come until everyone's in bed?

Ada's re-arranging pine cones around the holly centrepiece

Percy's office sent as if she spent too much money on a hairdo, didn't like it and brushed it out when she got home. The phone rings. Will the children please do what they're told for once? I can't talk now, Ev. I'm way behind. Leo, take your boots off before you track in all that snow. Percy *deserves* his once a year office party. I'm not going to be mad at Percy. Why would I be mad at Percy?

It seems only yesterday Gwen was riding her trike around the house reciting The Night Before Christmas and now it's Lily's turn. Just settled down for a long winter's. Long winter's...? Winter's...? Stop now. You'll get dizzy. Or go the other way. Ready to peddle to the ends of the earth and for what? Once, when she was talking to Evvie and heard the car, she told her sister she'd read in a magazine that if you've been lollygagging and hear your husband drive up, you're supposed to leap up and start frying an onion. Something sure smells good, he'll say. I'm going to try it. The next day she called her back to tell her it worked and they laughed like anything.

Do you think the centrepiece looks too stiff, Gwen? You're the artistic one around here. All right, go on acting like you don't care. But don't think that attitude is going to get you anywhere.

One thing Gwen knows for sure is that her mother's dearest wish is for her children to be dressed in perfectly ironed blouses, posed gracefully around the piano when their father comes in, carol books open to Hark the Herald. Snow, definitely snow falling past the bulbless light fixture on the front porch. The second you hear tires on the driveway, plug in the tree. Chuck the bike on the landing to the cellar. Whoever heard of riding a bike on the hardwood floors? At least this year the tree doesn't have to be tied to hooks on the wall to keep it upright. When their dad opens the door, takes off his fedora, and wipes his steamy glasses, their mother reaches up to kiss his cheek. The car waits outside in the yard like the horse at the cabin in the blue painting above the piano he stares at from his chair when he's had a bad day. That man has everything he needs, he says. The cabin is on the Prairies, somewhere with open skies and a wide horizon. Gwen points a pulsing finger behind her mother's back to make sure he sees the mistletoe above him which is nice of her considering. *Oh well, she'd thought when he said about walking across the Russian steppes. I'll do it for him.* He winks and kisses her mother's cheek back so she can have her perfect moment.

On Christmas morning, when they head down the stairs in procession youngest to oldest in their slippers and dressing gowns, the holy lights dazzle on the be all and end all perfect tree. Storybook dolls dressed in fur trimmed coats lead a decorated elephant past a gingerbread house. Figurines in silver skates whirl on a pool behind a miniature town on the tree skirt. Someone on a corner is singing Silver Bells. Why can't it always be Christmas?

Gwen gets a powder blue corduroy skating dress and cap trimmed with white angora blanket stitching. Lily gets the same outfit in rose and a doll *with skates* dressed in the same ensemble. Made by Mrs. Santa Claus. Lunch is pick-up which means they don't sit down at the table. At five sharp, their dad leaves for Laburnum St. to collect his parents. Is the bird done? Will someone wiggle the arms and see if the juices run clear? The vegetables and turkey aren't ready at the same time but what can you do?

After dessert, mother folds the wrapping paper so they can

use it again next year, arranges the towels and sweaters back into their boxes for display. Their dad's present to his parents is to be saved until after dinner, but they have to give mother one sec to make sure Lily's down. She's completely overtired. Too much Christmas.

He waits patiently in the living room to present his *pièce de résistance*, not that dinner wasn't. The only trouble with dinner is that it's over, he says. Lily takes so long to go off they've already started on the *pièce de résistance* without mother. When she comes in, they're passing around a glossy photograph of a large white farmhouse with gingerbread trim, puffs of apple blossom and pearly everlasting in the background. Dad pushes his glasses back up his nose as if Christmas is only an excuse for what's he's got up his sleeve. Grandma Killam holds the photograph carefully by the edges. She's not to worry because things have been worked out fair and square for everyone. Mother slides into her chair as if she's late for church and they've started the first hymn without her. What's been worked out fair and square for everybody? she asks.

I've been over the details with the advisory committee, their dad explains. The money's going to the soldiers' relocation fund for the boys' education when they get back so our contribution will be to a good cause.

Mother picks up the photograph as if it's someone's unfortunate x-ray. The three people sitting in front of her are from back east and have no idea how things are done here.

You can't do this, Percy.

Of course he can, says Grandma. We'll manage a small place like this. We still have *some* pep.

Would you excuse us for a moment? Mother takes dad's arm

into the kitchen. What on earth are you doing with pictures of the Yoshito farm? Whatever committee you're talking about it's not theirs to sell. We're looking after the place for them.

What do you mean, we're looking after the place? Since when?

Well, I'm not exactly but you know perfectly well Isabelle's been.

Oh Isabelle.

You didn't think to discuss this with me?

Ada, my parents can't live in an apartment, Percy says. Scarborough's a hobby farm compared to what they're used to. It'll give dad a new lease on life. All mother can say is how badly she feels that she took dad away from the farm. If I hadn't picked it up, someone else would have. It was going for a song. Let's talk about it tomorrow, Ada. We don't want to spoil Christmas. At least it's still in the family.

18.

January, 1943.

What I want to know is how the *hell* Percy found out about these properties I was going to say up for sale but they're obviously up for grabs. Your in-laws, I can understand them turning a blind eye, but Percy, well now, Percy. I thought he said you didn't have any money. Why do you think I'm here trying to keep things up for them? Auntie stands above a pair of old gloves in a wheelbarrow at Scarborough; rakes and trowels lie on their backs beside a pair of open hinges. She looks weak and shaky as she tries to yank dead pea vines from a net trellis but they get even more tangled up.

Maybe she didn't get any presents this year over here, that's her trouble. Where did she have Christmas dinner? In a ditch? The ground is littered with fir branches.

It was nothing to do with me, mother says. I didn't know anything about the sale.

You never do, Ada. That's your trouble. That's what you get for marrying a man from back east.

You're alone too much, Isabelle. You should come back to town.

What's town got to do with anything? Who the hell sold it to them?

Percy bought it from the custodian.

Percy did, did he? Christ almighty.

Isabelle, the children. Your language. I know it's upsetting. I didn't know anything about this until Christmas day.

Do you do this on purpose, Ada, or are you really that obtuse?

I'm really that obtuse.

They can't have the place, whatever Percy thinks. What am I supposed to tell the Yoshitos?

I don't know, says Ada. Do you know where they are?

I wish to hell I did. I'll have to come to town and look at the documentation. Percy can't do this. Property deeds are property deeds.

Not in war time apparently.

Auntie walks over to a stump to change out of her gumboots, smashes her hat on her head. I have to go to work, she says. Walk with me if you want. At least they've given me my job back.

It's not your responsibility, Issie. I don't think there's anything you can do about it.

It certainly *is* my responsibility. They left me in charge. How could it not be my responsibility? And don't think you're going to get out of it that easily. He's *your* husband.

The store with the post office in it looks like a railway station—it's supposed to, the dancehall is like the roundhouse where the train gets turned back in the other direction. There's a picture of it in the hotel lobby. They pass through the meat alcove where a weighing machine hangs from a hook. Once she's behind the wicket, Auntie looks even worse. Her cheeks are hollow and her eyes so dark it's as if the pupils and irises are one large pupil. The whites are the irises. The dark circles outside the whites are like a raccoon's. No blue light through her eyelids now. The light from the bulb makes her skin look as if she's growing in the mail wicket like a mushroom.

Children aren't allowed to go to funerals when they're open casket so they weren't allowed to go to Grandma Gallagher's but, after the service, because their dad is an engineer he had to go back to the crematorium to fix the burner which wasn't working properly. Maybe he should take this scallywag with him. Oh for Pete's sake, Percy, do what you like. Neither of you gives two hoots how I feel, mother'd said.

It's too bad Grandma Gallagher died, but it still felt like one of her and her dad's special Sunday morning when they drove along 41st to Victoria Drive, turned up a driveway past mounds of sloping grass with gravestones propped like place cards. A burly man in overalls stood outside the crematorium which looked like the witch's cottage in Hansel and Gretel.

Something's haywire with the installation, he said which made her dad roll up his sleeves and crouch by the burner. Her dad says he doesn't mean to prevail upon the good offices of this fine establishment here, but if it's all the same to them, he'd like to give his daughter a little education.

When he finished the repair, he went over to the corner and flipped open the lids of a bunch of coffins lying against the wall like bass cases. Whoever was in those boxes had nothing to do with people. They were more like huge dolls that'd been left in the sun to dry. One fellow looked like he tried to be a man once but got so discouraged his stiff grey hair turned into a bird's nest. Another wore a pinstriped suit like the man at the corner who wanted to show them *his* dolls in a suitcase, but when they told their mother about him, he wasn't there any more. Another might once have been Grandma Gallagher but all that was left of her was a sucked up face, a satin blouse and a cameo brooch over a few sticks. When her dad started up the burner—the attendant said he knew he would get it going—they slid the coffins into it one by one like logs into a sawmill. Gwen was to sit on a stool by a peephole so she could peer into the burner like someone checking a jail cell. You watch, her dad said. The spine contracts as the body burns and the corpse sits up. It did too, as if it'd forgotten to tell somebody something. There was a shelf lined with urns over against the wall. If they didn't clean the bottom after each burning—and they didn't—how would they tell whose ashes are whose? That's all there is to it, her dad said on the way home. You get born, you live and you die. It happens to everyone and it's just about as ordinary as you can get.

19.

July, 1943.

For heaven's sake, Gwen, Isabelle's moved to the hotel and there's nothing anybody can do about it. I plain need you to go to Scarborough and get some corn for supper. What do you mean the place looks like a half erased drawing with the one underneath showing through? What kind of a thing to say is that? Get cracking.

Down at Sandy, Frances is still cluelessly pulling up the rowboat half a dozen feet at a time and leaving it stranded. Horseshoes clang in the pit beside the number one tables. After the lagoon causeway, she stays on the path in front of the hotel that heads down to Pebbley beach, hits the trail that slants diagonally up the south bank of Deep Bay. Hardly any houses on the way so maybe no one will see she's visiting the Killam grandparents who are not only the other side of the family from Isabelle's but are living in a house that's not even theirs. Past the cornfield, she picks up the driveway down to the Scarborough house where she stands tapping at the kitchen window to alert Grandma Killam who says she wants to be called Grandma Flora now that she's moved to the farm. She's standing by the sink peering at her thumb, so tall that her tiny navy blue hat and bibbed apron look like they're on the wrong person. Glad you're here, Gwendolyn, she says. See if there's a sliver in there, would you, dear? Poke it with the needle, it won't hurt. Over a bit to the side there. That's it. One thing I hate about living alone, you have a heck of a time taking out your own slivers.

But she isn't living alone. Where's Grandpa Lyndon?

The amount of cleaning we've had to do around here, we could have used an army. Someone left behind a perfectly good table saw. You'd think you'd be able to count on a day or two for the weather to stay fine enough for the hay to set but no. Couple more days of this mucky palaver and you might as well make haykraut out of it.

Moving to the kitchen table, she clinks and rattles a bunch of preserve bottles she's brought up from the basement. These are last year's labels but dear knows who made them.

Mrs. Yoshito I expect.

Who's that?

The people who used to live here. They were the hotel gardeners but they had to go to another camp. Takumi was my swimming teacher.

Is that so? Grandma Flora picks up an urn from the floor where it's fallen behind the table. She opens the lid and peers inside. What's this, Gwendolyn? A bunch of old ash. Pour it in the garden for me, will you dear?

I can't do that, Grandma. That's a dead person. I saw some urns like that at a place where my dad took me to fix a burner.

What was he doing taking you to a place like that?

Teaching me.

I see. Well put it on a shelf back in the shed then.

When Gwen comes back, Grandma Flora goes into the dining room, takes off her hat and lays it on the table. Her head is almost bald on top. So that's why she keeps it on all the time. A small handleless porcelain cup waits for its tea, part of a set with strange hieroglyphics written on it. The table is a piece of plywood on sawhorses.

Were they Japanese, the people who lived here?

Yes.

Why didn't anyone tell me that?

I don't know.

Grandma Flora's face turns serious. So this is what Percival's been talking about. The funds being set aside for the boys' education. He means when the soldiers return. I don't know what we've got ourselves into here, Gwendolyn. Poor people, no wonder nothing's been cleared up. If Lyndon would come in from the field, maybe we could make sense of this. All's fair in love and war. That doesn't seem like much of a saying, does it?

I'm supposed to get some corn for supper, Grandma.

We can do that. Do you suppose, what did you call her?

Mrs. Yoshito.

Do you suppose Mrs. Yoshito would mind if we used her canner? It's not the sort of thing I'd haul out on the train. The corn isn't doing badly considering the amount of sun around here. They knew soil, I guess, these people.

They knew everything about gardening.

Did they? Well, how fresh do you think fresh corn should be?

The same day?

Grandpa Lyndon comes down the slope like he's on skis and the snow's so rotten each step might take him through to his knee. His chest seems to have shrunk; his pants come halfway to his chin and the braces only have a short way to go over his shoulders to get to the other side. Flora takes a pot from the cupboard, says she'll get the water going.

Take Gwendolyn with you, Lyndon, let her pick a few ears. Make sure the tassels are dark brown.

When they get to the field, the corn is not as high as an

elephant's eye but it's getting there. Grandpa Lyndon stands behind the row as if he's trying to camouflage himself, the way Leo holds himself if he thinks Billy might be around the corner. What are we waiting for, Grandpa? says Gwen.

For the water to boil.

When the window opens, Grandma Flora calls out. Now! Grandpa Lyndon waves to her and starts peeling the ears, nodding at Gwen to do the same. They run back to the kitchen tossing husks as they go.

Now *that's* fresh, Grandma Flora says, popping the cobs in the boiling water. Four minutes is all these babies are going to need. She tosses the colour pouch to Gwen to mix into the margarine before they scrape it onto the edges of their plates, sprinkle the salt and pepper and spread it on the corn. They hold the ears up to their mouths like mouth organs, fasten onto each others' eyes and nibble fast to see who can get to the end of the row first. Their rabbit teeth remind Gwen of the way Isabelle bared hers when she was standing in front of this very house, so upset her ears looked like they might start growing out of her hat like a horse's.

Eat up, Gwendolyn. What's the matter? Isn't it fresh enough? says Grandma Flora and winks.

Now what's she supposed to do? She likes being with these Killam grandparents. They're funny and nice. Where's Molly? Down on the beach apparently—barking to beat the band. Grandma Flora pushes back her chair, grabs Gwen's hand and the two of them charge down the path hollering at the dog who's swimming overtop a struggling deer. Hauling up over its backside, she pushes her prey underwater as the antlers circle and disappear. *Get up here Molly!* Molly goes on hulking, slowly sinking the deer, intent on nothing she knows. She swims back slowly, not caring when Grandma Flora swats her. Hope nobody saw, she says. The dog shakes water everywhere. You'd better leash your dog up, Gwendolyn. Expect they send the RCMP round to shoot dogs for less than this.

So now Molly's her dog the way her mother tells her father to do something about *his* children when she's mad at them. Molly's come over to the farm for a while because they wanted a dog around the place. Sitting at the outside table, at least there's enough space between her and the cedars to think properly. You're a bad dog. You'd better learn to behave. Maybe money *is* a tool the way her dad says it is, otherwise, why's the idea popping into her head now? Suppose, just suppose, she's not saying she's going to, but *suppose* instead of spending the money she saved to help Isabelle on that new Hawaiian top on sale at the store—perfect for the end of the summer masquerade because of the bulrush grasses down on Miss Fenn's Rocky that she could use to make a hula skirt—she uses her savings to make a deal with Billy instead so he'd stop bothering Leo. Stay Molly, I told you to lie down and stay. Maybe then it would be okay to like being over here with her grandparents once in a while. From where she sits, she can see that the wooden lady's come out of the Dutch cuckoo clock in the kitchen to chime the hour. Wait a minute, look at her hat. Maybe that wasn't a nun on the Old Dutch Cleanser can. They had Holland in Socials this year, and the girl in the book was wearing one of those white hats. Maybe the one on the cleaning can was just Dutch.

When she gets back to the cottage, it turns out Leo's had one of his nosebleeds so she and Aunt Evvie have to take him to the First Aid station by number two grounds, a regular cottage with hanging flower baskets except that it has a red cross on the door. People picnic even harder during the war. There's always a sprain or fracture in the corner waiting to get bandaged up. Dr. Stan, the new First Aid man, does everything with his right arm so it takes a while to notice he never does anything with his left. He tries to distract Leo with questions about his comic book collection—how'd he know about his comic book collection? This boy's to go home and rest in bed for an hour, in case, he says. In case, what? says Leo. Never mind our Leo, she insists. I'll never forget the time. He couldn't have been more than four. Come on, Leo, I said. It's time for bed. But I went to bed *last* night, he said. Isn't that...?

Maybe the reason Dr. Stan is in such a hurry to get rid of Aunt Evvie is because, when he looked out the window, he saw Jeanette climbing up the stairs, shoulders sloped like a coat hanger. The two of them look like they're going to fall out of their faces. They say hello like people who know each other but are pretending they don't. The next morning Leo has earache *again*, so Dr. Stan has to come over, his whole warm height rising up the attic stairs as if he's coming up an elevator from a mine. All ready to knock 'em dead tomorrow, kiddo? he says to Aunt Evvie who looks like she's about to tuck one knee into the other, cock one hand on her hip, and the other behind her head hubba hubba ding ding. We all know you're the glamour girl of the family, Evelyn, you can tell mother's thinking. Wouldn't lift a hand to wash a dish if she could help it. Aunt Evvie'd come back from the First Aid Station announcing she'd made up her mind to ask Dr. Stan to be her doubles partner. Do you suppose he can play tennis with that hand? mother'd asked. What hand? Evvie hadn't noticed any particular hand. Now she looks at his carved fingers fastened on the wooden branch railing to the attic as if she'd accepted a dance with a man when he was sitting down and only realized when he stood up that he had a wooden leg. Maybe the only thing he'd need his left hand for was throwing up tennis balls before he hit them. Maybe the two handed backhand slam once in a while. Maybe separate fingers would have cost more.

Dr. Stan's face is sad when he looks around as if he has no idea where he is. Then he shakes his head and his face clears up. His hair rises straight off his head for an inch and kinks into the air. The smell of a good looking man coming fresh from the outside makes mother turn her chest up to him like an offered tray. The dentist gives you a plaster turtle after he's finished your filling, but, when Dr. Stan's looking after you and you feel like you're going to cry, he stops whatever he's doing, makes a poker face, raises two arms straight to one side, and breaks into a tap dance. His legs hang loose like a puppet's. At supper when *he's* asked to stay, he does something secret to the ketchup bottle. Gives it a twist, a flick of the wrist, that's what the showman said. Halfway through supper the lid pops off. Fairies, I guess, he says and winks.

In the attic, Leo's hunched against the sloped ceiling of his room. When Dr. Stan takes the book from the chair so he can sit on it, Leo's eyes follow the book so he won't lose his place. The doctor looms above him like the giant with his hen. Asks for a soup spoon to warm baby oil over a lit candle. Before we do this drill with the spoon, son, I'd like you to stand up, lean over and kick your opposite foot. Harder. Is it out?

I don't have water in my ear, it just aches, Leo says.

Dr. Stan's head pushes against the ceiling and beans grow from his ears. Back in bed then,

he says. Down on your side. He holds the warmed silver spoon carefully like he's in the egg and spoon race.

Is it like cod liver oil? I don't like cod liver oil.

I'm going to put it in your ear, son, not your mouth. A warm rush and it's in. Sleep on that side, he says. Things will seem better in the morning.

But they don't. They never do any more. Maybe if she'd won that sand castle prize *which she should have,* Auntie would have had enough money and the two of them would be having a lovely time over at Scarborough waiting for her friends to come back from whatever other camp it is they've gone to. Probably somewhere near Sechelt or Squamish.

In the city at school in P.E., the boys form a circle on the outside, girls on the inside and the two circles move in opposite directions. Miss Helliwell curves her torso over the gramophone, raises the thick twisted arm, and drops the needle on the record. Girls one way, boys the other. Right two three, left two three, all of them shuffling along in a line. The principal lifts Miss Helliwell's hand from the gramophone and starts dipping and gliding her around the room like a jib on a sailboat. Her big thrill for the day. *Feel* the music boys and girls two three. The other kids are keeping their arms at their sides, and following the line of dance the way they're supposed to, but Gwen can't because her hands keep lifting one after the other, fingers hanging loose and floating off her wrists. Her body streams into the sky like the lady in the striped wooden dress in the library book who soars above a deep blue field with cows and flowers, moons and suns swirling behind her. Leaving her sisters and cousins and aunts with no kisses to build dreams on. Next thing you know Mr. Calderwood's handed Miss Helliwell off to the gramophone, passed Gwen on the inside of the circle, turned back to reach for her hand like a runner passing a baton in a relay race. He leads her to the centre, puts his right hand on her waist and extends his left, palm turned upward. Lifts his chin to indicate that, if she puts her left hand on his shoulder, he can step into the dance exactly the right way. From now on all the king's horses and all the king's men can run away with whoever they like because, even if she's never been in this wide open place before, this is where she's been trying to get back to the whole time. If she keeps her chest pressed against his, her feet will follow and take care of themselves. Everyone else can go on with whatever it is they're doing; whatever they're doing is fine with her.

What's fair got to do with it? Since when is life fair? If I've told you once, Ada, I've told you a thousand times. They're going to have Evelyn in one boat, Dr. Stanley in the other, and somebody else's sister or cousin or aunt in a third. For heaven's sake, the kids are fine. They're having a wonderful time. What are summers for?

Anchors aweigh, Aunt Evvie says, lifting the sailor hat off Dr. Stan's head and putting it on her own. Loading the children into the put-puts at the motorboat rental, the two of them act like they have to know what other people are going to say before they say it so they can go on laughing. What is it with you two, did you see a stranger across a crowded tennis court? Love at first dribble? Stupid engine. Give her a harder yank. You've gone and flooded it. The next inboard is off, motor ticking hardity har har. No fooling around back there. Gwenny-Henny can come in our boat, Billy Fenn says pushing her down on the bow seat. Nothing to do but try Leo's trick of finding a distant star that might be like their own sun with a planet that has a girl like herself on a put-put heading into a dark lonely sea. You tell us if there are any logs coming up, Gwenny-Henny, Billy says pushing his hair back. *My Bonnie Lies over the Ocean, my Bonnie lies over the sea.* We don't want to mess up the ocean so someone please bring me a pail. They pass the spot where she swam her Juniors test, the wave in front of her so high it was like swimming over a wall, the sea so rough her teacher let her dog paddle the last few yards instead of crawl. When she climbed onto the hotel wharf, her mother dried her as if she'd never seen her before in her life. I couldn't believe they didn't cancel, she heard her say up through the chimney gap. She was so brave out there.

At least when she swam the Juniors test she was in charge of her own body, not like now with Billy thumbing the lever to make the put-put slow the boat down, then pushing one of the oars between his legs. What we're going to do now, Gwenny-Henny, is tell rude jokes. Boy, are you ever going to like what we've got to show you. In case you don't know, this is how you got born. Your dad put his long one into your mother's hairy one and spurted and you got born from it. Yep, they got fooling around when no one was looking, and next thing you know, you popped out of your mother's pea hole. Gwen huddles on the put-put floor, arms around her knees. At least the things he says are so dumb you don't have to even pretend to listen. As if her parents would do something like that. It would be out of their range, like a foreign language.

If your date's ever driving badly, her dad will say later, or misbehaving in any way whatsoever, you say stop the car. Get out and use your mad money to phone me to come and get you. In the middle of Deep Bay? Watch out for Miss Fenn's island! The tide's so high Billy might not see the rocks. Nothing to do but make herself as tiny as possible, fly down the inlet on the back of that wooden lady from the library book, zero in from the north shore mountains, dive bomb through the wide doors of the boat building plant and fly around until she can find Auntie Evvie, face flickered and shadowed by lights from the welding torches. Lengths of sheet iron smash like cymbals as a crane lifts its neck over a group of people breaking ranks, pulling others back from the track. Shouting. Excuse us. Pardon us for living, eh?

When the put-put rounds the Millers Landing corner, the waves slap the pebbles so hard the bow scrapes the edge of the rasping beach. After they land and climb out, Dr. Stan holds up his hand to stop them so they'll turn around and go back along the beach the way they came. Don't look back, he says and the kids obey. Except Gwen who looks anyway and sees Grandpa Lyndon and Grandma Flora crouched beside the bloated deer carcass with its face is all nibbled away. Sea wrack twists in its antlers; its legs are so stiff it should be carried upside down, hooves lashed by thongs to a stick. If she were safe at school, she could put up her hand and it was her dog who drowned the deer, the way when someone throws a rock through the gym window, Mr. Calderwood announces at assembly he knows in no uncertain terms that whoever committed the crime will come forward and take responsibility. They do too.

When the bonfire's lit, the kids are told to peel sticks for the wiener roast. Dr. Stan's supposed to be organizing the sing-song, but instead of giving them a note like he's supposed to, he decides to walk down to the water and stare hard at the shore line. None of the other grown-ups are doing what they're meant to either; they're back in the shadows acting as if they're going to start yowling like the cats you hear but don't want to hear in the bushes on dance nights. *Go back to sleep, it's only the dance.* A couple of them lurch over each other as if they want to turn themselves inside out. When Evvie and Dr. Stan come back to the fire, Evvie's got her arm around Dr. Stan instead of his arm around her; his head is down on her shoulder as well, so things are the other way around from the way they're supposed to be *again*. Buckling over with dry heaving, he leans over like he's trying to throw up but nothing comes out. Parts of his body look stiff in the firelight as if he'd been put into an ice box by mistake, taken out barely in time and they had to stick the frozen parts of his body back together. The wind comes up and pebbles scrape the steep beach as he clings grimly to Evvie who tries to unfasten him limb by limb, but every time she removes a hand, he gloms it back on. When his fake hand starts clawing at her, she looks alarmed as if she's afraid people will see her trying to unfasten a large crab stuck on her chest. Finally, she manages to drape a blanket around his shoulders and get a thermos into his hand.

It's the gravel, he says. I can still hear that scraping. There were parts of bodies all over the water. It was Dieppe. Trying to find my own hand. I couldn't find my own hand.

A couple of other grown-ups try to get the singing going but nobody believes in it; it sounds hollow the way it does at school when you don't have a good music teacher but have to try any-way. Stuck out in the middle of the night with nobody's marshmallows turning golden, people poke their branches into the fire, torch the white puffs until the black mash fastens onto the sticks. Waves grate the beach, scrunching into the black ocean as the kids break into small groups and huddle together, talking only to each other.

Billy disappears up the pathway, comes back to the fire looking tired. Maybe he's only mean during the day. Maybe he's nicer at night the way the toys in the attic might wake up and speak softly when it's dark and the children are asleep. Nobody's supposed to be in that goddam house, he mutters in a deep voice as he hunkers in the sand, his face swelling like a potato in a bonfire. When he takes off his shirt, he's bright in the moonless night. Firelight picks out red cuts on his thin back. How am I supposed to find that money, he says. With those new people living there, eh? Can you figure it out, Gwenny-Henny? He drinks a gulp of pop, heads up the path toward the farmhouse.

No point saying you're going to be brave unless you are, so she follows him. She watches his arm whip out from behind a cedar to hurl a rock. What's the big idea out there? Grandma Flora hollers. Come out where I can see you. Grandpa Lyndon's huddled in a chair in the open doorway, looking so helpless he could be in diapers. Someone should tell Grandma Flora that no one here wears those worn out print dresses; men don't wear worn out suits and shirts with frayed collars either.

In the cedar grove, she finds Billy sitting on the ground leaning against a tree. That's supposed to be my dad's house, he says, jerking his thumb. My grandfather gave the farm away and now my father has nothing. The Jap who got it was saving money to make it up to my dad, but he got taken away before he could tell him where it is. My dad says I have to find it. What've you got there, Gwenny-Henny?

It's some money, Billy, she says rushing the idea out so it won't get away from her. I'll give it to you, (and she will, except for the elk head quarter) if you'll stop bothering my brother. I'll look for the hiding spot when I'm over here. I'll do that for you Billy, I promise.

You'll be getting more?

He counts the coins. Okay, Gwenny-Henny. It'll do for starters but I'll be watching you.

Back at the beach, she wants to wrap her arms around Aunt Evvie's waist and tell her what she's got herself into, but she knows enough to stay quiet the way Mr. Yoshito says that there has to be quiet around seeds once they're planted so they'll grow.

No, Gwen, you can't come back in our boat, Aunt Evvie says. I'm counting on you to be a hundred percent grown up tonight and help look after the younger kids. There's not a single thing to worry about. Every boy in that boat has his Seniors.

IN KIND

20.

August, 1943.

The next day, the people in the mail queue wait for the wicket to open, and a desperately pale Isabelle stands slotting letters into peoples' mailboxes as if there's no tomorrow. In so thick with them Japs, George Fenn thinks, he wouldn't put it past her to slip a few care packages up to the Slocan Valley or wherever it is they've got them penned. Couldn't be getting enough sleep with those dark circles under her eyes. Come to think of it, maybe *she* knows where that money's hidden. If they told anyone it would've been her. The least he can do is offer her a ride to the hotel. Plain woman like her, she'll be flattered to have his escort service. Crying shame the hotel flower gardens are going downhill, he'll say to get things started. The place isn't the same without what's their names. What *is* their name anyway? It's gone out of his mind.

He's started using his truck as a taxi. When Isabelle rushes past him without acknowledging his signal, he notices Lyndon Killam sitting on the bench outside the store, staring blankly down the side of his beaky nose. He pulls out his wallet, and hands George the new address card Percy'd written for him.

Doesn't see, doesn't hear, that one, George says to Lyndon, nodding in Isabelle's direction. He's growing a paunch, has to lower his extra chin to read the Scarborough address. Six of one half a dozen of the other, he thinks, taking Lyndon's arm around to the passenger side of his truck.

At Scarborough, Flora's on the back porch staring in dismay at the overgrown yard. Her anxious look is so much like George's mother's when they came back after a winter in town, the years disappear and, for a moment, he feels she *is* his mother, the way her hand pushes her hair back as if wanting to clear a view to the ocean. She bends over a box, stands straight again.

He seems to be *shrinking* Flora thinks, eyeing Lyndon in the cab. Thank you for bringing my husband home, Mr.…?

Fenn, says George. George Fenn. I'm the Union caretaker.

We're still trying to get settled, she says, opening her hand at the pile of boxes in the kitchen. The people who lived here before us left everything. I've learned they had no choice but I've had to pack their things before I could even start unpacking ours. They used to work for the hotel, I understand. Do you know where all this could be stored until they collect it?

I have a shed, George says. I'm over September Morn way. It's a beach, do you know it?

Can't say as I do. Come in. I'll give you the tour.

I know the place pretty well, he says. I grew up here.

Did you? she says. He might well have, everyone else seems to have. It's so rainy her visitor has to stand on the porch edge and pour rain from the brim of his fedora. Inside, they hear a chortling in the basement. What *is* that? she says. It's been irritating me all morning.

That'll be the sump pump. Them things give up when they have a mind to and then you have a flooded basement.

It'd been churning all night like an intermittent waterfall.

Did they have one back home? She can't remember. How can she be forgetting things in her own house? Does it ever stop raining here? She doesn't want this stranger to know that her husband thought the noise was a longed for rain for his wheat crop. The two of them sleep in twin beds, reach out in the night to take each other's hands. Sounds as if it's raining at last, he'd said radiantly. The stalks will green up, you'll see. He'd turned over and gone back to sleep, content for the first time since they arrived. Let him remember the good years before the drought and dust storms ruined their lives.

It was so hot and dry that fateful day Percival took their creeping daughter down to play in the cellar where it was cooler, the wind even layered dust in the basement. Dust on the vegetables if they'd been lying on the plates for five minutes. When the scarlet fever came and they had to burn the furniture, every stick went up in flames except for the one rug Lyndon threw down the cellar stairs. When their daughter caught the fever and died, Lyndon left for the fields. When she went out to comfort him, he was sitting in his smashed wheat field, face in his hands. She left, it was too private. Never speak of her, he said when he came in. Or we won't manage to go on. We simply won't manage.

She'd been looking for her photograph albums all morning and when Mr. Fenn—she'll make a point of calling him Mr. Fenn, that way everything will be above board—came back from loading the boxes in his truck, darned if they weren't sitting on the kitchen table in front of her. Whole sections where the pictures had been torn from their triangular corners. Who'd do a thing like that? She's almost managed to keep the child out of her mind, announcing to Lyndon on the train that the mountains would be a wall between themselves and her grave. They'd buried her on the prairies and on the prairies she would stay.

So why's she having to walk around the kitchen shaking the album by its spine, pages flapping like wings, hoping the snapshots might be loose and fall out on the floor? Whoever would have taken them, she mourns to Mr. Fenn as if he should know, forgetting that in her grief she'd torn the images out herself. Maybe it was that young man who comes over here and throws rocks, she says.

Lyndon's sitting at the table turning a dinner plate in his hands like a steering wheel. Will you stay for lunch, Mr. Fenn? asks Flora. It's just scrambled eggs but they're fresh. Flora reaches for a napkin and wipes the corners of her husband's mouth.

Another time, George says. But thank you.

People say you shouldn't retire to an unfamiliar place when you're getting old because it might be difficult to make new friends. Maybe they should have thought about that possibility more seriously before they left the prairies. It's terrible here. You can't walk anywhere without some branch poking you in the ear. You can't tell clouds from sky. There's no decent distance for the eye to travel and where has the horizon got itself to? When they arrived, Lyndon'd angled his face up at Percy. Is there a barn? he'd asked. There's a barn. Are there cows?

You could buy one.

That'd be sufficient, he said with dignity. Terminal City alright. She wants to go home, drought or no drought. And that mail clerk, Percy's sister in law, the one who looks like a widow even though she's engaged? She's tried to be friendly with her. Nothing for you, Mrs. Killam, she'd said coldly as if the name meant nothing to her. Well, they're not here for the social life.

Most mornings Lyndon gets up before her and takes off down the Government Road stopping at fern infested cottages to ask how their cows are getting along. Sits forlornly on the bench outside the post office watching people go in and out. The loneliest place in this world is where the person you thought loved you doesn't recognize you but still expects to be fed. She can't let any of them know his condition or they'll take him away. Best if she doesn't encourage Gwendolyn to come over either, she's far too observant.

If Eleanor were here, they'd know what to do. When Mr. Fenn leaves, she goes upstairs and immediately spots the photograph of her sister stuck in her dresser mirror. Smack up in the front of the snapshot as if asking for someone to take her hand and help her out. Head down so people could see the appliqué roses stitched on top of her pillbox hat. If you're short and people are obliged to look down on you, Eleanor liked to say, they might as well have something attractive to see. If she hadn't wanted to leave the nursing home, why would she have stepped up so close to the camera? There's supposed to be a decent residence at the end of the pathway behind her but there's only a shack. Cold wind blows between the wooden wall slats. No insulation. An iced over pail of water hauled from a tap. People bent double tending to sugar beets in the yard.

What kind of shape's the linoleum in the spare room in? Worn but clean. When she passes that bedroom above the kitchen, she always closes the door as if a baby's sleeping in there. Downstairs, crossing the well trodden piece of floor from the stove to the sink, she suddenly feels as if she's in the body of a much shorter woman hunched over in a sleeveless tunic. The feeling is gone by the time she turns on the kitchen light.

Nothing to do but phone Percival again. Is it too much to ask, the occasional lift to the boat terminal? Eleanor's not *in* a shack, Mother, he says. She's in a nursing home in Regina with a starched nurse at her beck and call around the clock. Watercress sandwiches for lunch. I most certainly will not arrange to have her put on the train, pick her up and help her on the steamship. We are *not* having her come out. Hold on a minute, mother. I know it's your nickel. It was a mistake having you move over there. I'll call you back. Don't go anywhere.

As if she could. She's been holding the phone at arm's length for most of the conversation so she doesn't have to listen to the parts she doesn't want to hear. They have their lives, she'll grant you, but how long do you have to wait before it's not too soon and call them again? Only ask about them. Otherwise you'll sound like you're pleading and they'll never call back.

All she has to count on is some strange young fellow who throws stones from behind trees. And here's Gwendolyn over for more corn. The other day she'd caught her turning the clock over and shaking it like a piggy bank. Now she's rooting under the sink, holding up a tin of cleaning powder.

I wasn't a nun after all, Grandma, she says. At the masquerade last year. I was just Dutch. (Aunt Evvie had been beside herself trying to find her a costume and had sent her over to Miss Fenn's to ask if she could borrow one of her dark dresses.)

Were you now? You'll break that clock, Gwendolyn.

This is a Dutch hat on this lady, right? Nothing to do with a nun's habit?

That's right.

Wooden shoes?

Wooden shoes.

If only Eleanor were here coming down to the house from her loft in the barn as usual. That room is supposed to be for the *hired man*, Lyndon would say when Eleanor came to the kitchen door asking for a bit of flour to use as white paint. Do you know what she used for black?! Percy'd thundered at his children at the dinner table, waving the carving knife. Prairie dirt! She started giving music lessons and let the children paint pansies on the dining room walls. *Pansies on the walls, think of it.*

In the middle of the night Flora goes downstairs and writes herself a note. *The Tuesday Alex, 10 a.m.* By morning, she's forgotten her wishful thinking guess, hears steps downstairs, thinks she's at home and Lyndon's on his way out to do chores but he's in the bed beside her. When she goes down again she thinks well, no it must have been Percy because the writing on the note is backhand, same as hers the way she taught him. He probably didn't want to wake her. Tuesday, the morning *Alex*. Which means he's changed his mind and will pick Eleanor up and put her on the boat. He must have realized it's only fair that she have her sister. His wife has her sisters. Once Eleanor's there, they'll have the place sorted in no time. If the tide is low, the captain will hand her down the gangplank to the raised platform and she herself will help her down the rest of the way. Candied violets in their salads at lunch time. Feet up, rest on their laurels. They deserve it. If it's too hot upstairs in the summer, they'll make a bedroom for Eleanor in the basement. There's a lot to be said for basements; you feel tucked into the earth without being dead, and they're cool. When Thursday comes and Flora makes her way to the wharf, she's thrilled to see Eleanor coming down the gangplank on the captain's arm, but when her sister lifts her chin, it's not Eleanor at all. It's a woman with marcelled red hair she's never seen before in her life.

21.

When Isabelle hears her name called across the lobby, her face blanks out as if recognizing the name of someone she knows but can't remember from where. A squat woman with gold-rimmed teeth, freckles and neatly waved red hair insists her way over to the desk, a crooked pencil line stitching the contours of her non-existent eyebrows as if with black thread. Isabelle Gallagher, says the lipstick on her teeth. You're Isabelle. I'm not Pinocchio, thinks Isabelle, arch as always under pressure. When something's supposed to be funny these days, she stretches her neck back and laughs her face down in a bray. Checking the day's guest list, she blanches when she reads the name Mrs. Martha Long remembering Jack Long telling her his mother comes to the Bowen Inn every year. Thumbing the tiny diamond on her silver ring around to her palm as if locking a diary, she pulls a clean smile out of her face like fresh Kleenex. Mrs. Long, your usual room is taken, I'm afraid. The person is staying over so we've upgraded you to a deluxe cottage. They're getting it ready now.

O God, is he back? He can't be back. He'd be with her. He's got to still be overseas, he has to be. Mrs. Martha Long takes her by the hands. I'm pleased to meet you, Isabelle. Jack's told me all about you. He told me he would marry you if it was the last thing he ever did. Now I know he didn't give you that ring before he left so he must have sent it to you from over there? So my son's alive.

He is, Isabelle says, hoping she's right. Stalling for time, she parks Jack's mother by the hostess station, the woman's legs so short her feet don't meet the ground although she's wearing built-up pumps.

A narrow green carpet stretches the length of the large sunny dining room famous for the tomatoes Mr. Yoshito grew in the bay windows that'd been a trademark of the hotel: guests were able to choose their own and the waitress took them to the kitchen to be sliced and presented. Outside, the striped awnings quiver in the breeze; sweet honeysuckle and the smell of sea salt strike high and low notes through the open windows. Taking a second job to save money, Isabelle tried to keep up the tomato tradition but the plants came up all legs, so the lot of them had to be pulled up. The cucumbers she put in as a replacement turned bitter—the south window exposure's may be too hot—but she's done well with Shinsuke's gorgeous purple bougainvillea in the lobby. Hibiscus and orchids thrive in the upstairs glassed-in balconies. Mr. McConnecky doesn't like to say because his employee verges on panic if the plants are threatened, but he isn't sure the best possible use of his desk clerk's time is running around adjusting venetian blinds. Testing the moss for moisture gives Isabelle an excuse to turn her back on this brash woman who's arrived to demand well, what?

Where's your hairnet, Jeanette? Isabelle asks the waitress at the end of the inspection line-up.

In my pocket.

What's it doing in your pocket?

Jeanette would say if she were asked—she's not—that Isabelle Gallagher is impossible to work for, the way she goes berserk if there's a melted piece of ice in the dish presenting the shrimp appetizer. It's Isabelle's fault in the first place that she was off work last week with a sprained ankle because who else but her boss forgot to have the maintenance man fix the loose stair down from the staff eatery which sent her collapsing over on one leg as if her foot were a paper doll tag? Passing the bench on her way to the Ladies, Jeanette comes face to face with Mrs. Long, a large short toad of a woman who's wearing, could it be a red wig, and is parked smugly on the reception bench. That hostess over there is going to be my daughter-in-law, she says.

Is that so? says Jeanette. My alarm clock didn't go off again and now she's given me the worst station in the dining room, can you believe it? Behind the ferns where all the old ladies who don't tip sit. Frances is at the hotel collecting her pay check when Jeanette comes into the lobby; she takes her chin between her thumb and finger and plants a lingering kiss on her friend's forehead. Every time she bends a half grapefruit in her palm, she thinks about what it would be like to make love to this woman.

They'll tip you, she says. Nobody could resist tipping you.

Oh yes they could and they will.

At the hostess stand, Isabelle spills a few drops of water on an orchid leaf by mistake, wipes it carefully with a napkin. Down the hall, when she sees Frances bestow an intimate kiss on Jeanette's forehead, she can hardly breathe for realizing. Frances's frightened look not only acknowledges that she knows Isabelle's seen and understood, but also sends a message that she knows her friend will have concluded she's the only person who could have told Ada about White Rock. Frances lobs back a look that says *I had to tell her. Ada was desperate.* Isabelle returns the shot. Now that I see what's between you and Jeanette, if you even *think* of telling anyone else about my pregnancy, one word from me to your boss at the community centre in town and you'll be fired. Up here as well. Frances returns with yes, but there's not a chance of your telling. If you expose my secret, I have a card to play that will ruin *your* life. Mrs. Long looks back and forth between the two of them as if watching a tennis match.

I'll have my lunch now, she says to Isabelle. At that table over there.

It's a choice one, in a window corner. Once she's sitting down, Mrs. Long takes her hostess's hand as if she's behind a counter about to fit her for gloves and turns the ring back to the front. That belongs over there, she says.

(Up Narrows, Takumi is trying to thrash his food platform into place so he can dry meat; the small fire he's made to speed the process flares and has to be banked down. The food needs to be dried, not cooked. It's the first day with no rain he's had in weeks and not likely to hold off much longer. The clouds are piling up, the far banks have misted over; his bark pyramid hat drips around the edge. If only he could get dry. One warm week to bake the damp out of everything. The wettest August he can remember. Is that mould coating the last few blackberries or frost? The weather teases him with an occasional slit of blue. Then the overcast flattens and the clouds seal off. It couldn't pour any harder. Then it does. Ends suddenly in a paused silence. Then another downpour.

He's made it through the winter by re-building the old logging cookhouse and laying flat pieces of driftwood for the roof. Only lit the fire in the battered oil drum on foggy days so the smoke would blend with the mist. Even managed an extra bit of light by building a traditional two tier shingled overhang using twisted kelp rope. Fishing before dawn it's unlikely any boats will be coming through the Narrows, but even so, there's something about bringing in yet another left eyed flounder and turning it to its blind side that appalls him. Worse, when he casts his line again, the last of the wire hooks he fashioned from what was left of a coil he found falls off. Gutting the rock fish cuts his hands to shreds.

Getting the fire going at least cheers him into an idea for dealing with the canoe when the maple and alder leaves fall. He's exhausted from carrying the boat down the hill to fish and then back up to hide. He attaches a line of knotted kelp rope to a pulley from the camp, then to the canoe as a painter to secure the boat; that way, he can sit behind one of the few remaining cedars and reel in the canoe as the tide comes in. Why didn't he think of this in his lifeguarding days?

Still so lonely and angry in the fitful night he expects the tin pan alley crowd to routinely file in as soon as he's closed his eyes, keep up their usual hour of drumming fingers before they let him sleep. Let it be the wind tonight, not the ocean spirits he's continually trying to placate. The meat's too wet to dry. He's infused enough kelp to make dashi and more dashi, but can't bear the thought of another bowl of seaweed soup. If only he had a dog who could nail an occasional hare. Return with it splayed in his mouth. Tonight, it's the faint hum of an unseen presence in a language he still doesn't understand; when he's learned enough, will he be allowed to sleep well for once? Down on the beach at dawn, he nicks off two-inch lengths of kelp stem and stuffs them with small lengths of cedar sticks. Plugs the ends of the kelp with stones and buries them in the ashes of the fire, hoping the tubes will inhibit any burning but allow the wood to become soft enough to bend into fish hooks. Another trick he'd been made to rehearse years ago.

The next day he carves a series of small molds in a planked log, lays the curved warm pliable sticks in them like in vitro specimens. Once they're cool, he shaves a few barbs of grouse bone with the knife Miss Fenn gave him, lashes them to the hooks with spruce root, carries the line carefully to the canoe holding it at either end like a necklace. *Stretching a thread of his semen far enough that it would spin before it broke, she smiled and cut it with her finger like a spider web.*

She'll be back with her family now; his mother was right, Isabelle would never know what it was like to feel your people were unseen and taken for granted. She's never had to feel that her every move has to be guarded. Knew enough to say that it was dangerous for him to be at Killarney but not enough to make sure she wasn't being followed. When he's tired, and he's very tired, it seems the rain even obliterates their precious traces back at the lake camp where he'd pulled out of her so fast it felt like her skin ripped with him. They'll think he's drowned. Would they drag the cove for him?. He brings out the extra sweater Miss Fenn gave him and saved to put under the still wearable rubber jacket and pants. *Listen to the spirits in the rocks and branches and sea, son. They're better company.* A few re-constituted dried meadow mushrooms from last spring for breakfast. Out in the canoe he finds the hooks are too light and float uselessly back to the surface. Clouds drift around the ridge on the other side of the inlet as if steaming up from underground. A huge jellyfish hovers like a poached egg in the water over by the bluff. When he hears a boat coming through the Narrows, he pulleys up the canoe, hides it, and climbs back to his winter lair. The next day he ties a small rock into his line as a sinker, but it keeps slipping out. Sitting on a log, discouraged, he finds himself tracing a small with his finger, *oh that*, carves a short length of the denser gnarl; after it cools overnight in its kelp tube, the new hook sinks and stays.)

That evening, Isabelle takes the road northeast from the Girls Dorm up past the disintegrating greenhouse. Weeds have taken over Shinsuke's beautiful raised beds. No one's picked the plums which hang black and useless on the branches. Passing the horse stables, she turns onto the trail around the back of Killarney Lake, hacking branches as she goes. Throwing down pieces of log to bridge the boggy areas, finally, behind the forest of stripped trunks as if staked in the water when they dammed the lake, she manages to stamp her way through the overgrowth into the small clearing where Takumi's tent still stands. A mouse has made a nest in the pocket of one his shirts. She straightens the poles, smashes the tent pegs in with a rock, spreads out her sleeping bag. Empties the pocket, holds the shirt to the side of her face like a pillow. Our baby died, my love, I'm so sorry, she whispers. Wherever he is, she knows his days and nights are so dank and dark they close in before they even start. If only he's found shelter; if only he has wood. If only he still loves her. When they dragged him off, she staggered back along the trail throwing up as she went. Maybe if she spends a night here where he was so wretched and unravels her own moves back to the first stitch she dropped, catches up the threads back there and starts again, coming to terms with her own past might help him in some way she doesn't understand now.

22.

Only half as many kids as expected show up for the Killarney Lake hike. Glad you're here, son, Dr. Stan says to Leo staring at Billy and his henchmen astride their two-wheelers beside the First Aid Station. Leo chucks his bike against the fence like the rind of something he doesn't need. One look at Leo's stricken face and Dr. Stan says maybe the lad could stay and help him batten down the hatches while they wait for the other kids. Battening down the hatches is closing the shutters, watering the hanging moss baskets until the water drips out the bottoms even if the lobelia has faded and the alyssum is brown and scraggy.

Once they start hiking, the minute they even *think* they might hear the enemy coming, they should fling themselves flat into the ditch at the side of the trail, he says. Something's scratching on a tree. Is that Gerry? No, the small purple shadow curving over the ditch is a squirrel. Gerry hasn't come up behind them yet but he might be around the next bend. Billy and the other boys whip by on their bikes so fast you don't even know they were there.

From above, Killarney Lake looks like an ordinary lake but come closer now. Green lily pads lap over each other like giant artichoke sepals; spearmint grows along the shores beside the dam. Beetles bend their legs on the rocks and quiver their delicate antennae. A band of silver streaks across the lake underlining the penciled dead trees at the other end. A scum of algae surrounds the lily pads, thick skinned as a green carpet. Yellow-balled lilies cup on their shocked stems. If you reach out your hand, a chickadee with stiff knees and feet like black wire might hop on and settle its plump feathered body into your palm. When the wind comes in from the west, the stronger laps on the distant shore sound like someone running softly. The cement dam stretches from shore to shore holding back the lake the coho no longer inhabit.

When Billy stands astride his bike against the edge of the lake, his shadow looks like an elongated insect with wheels. Swatches of grass grow in brush strokes across the road. A butterfly noiselessly claps its wings together; crates of glistening dark bottles built in glass rounds like stacked translucent coins cool in the lake. No see-ums churn off each other several inches before they collide. Dr. Stan wipes each bottle on his sleeve, rolls the glistening spine between his palms and tosses it to a drinker. Gwen raises her bottle to her mouth like a trumpet as Dr. Stan starts to tell them about the people who used to camp at the other end of the lake before it was dammed, how there was a summer when they were so feverish and sick they lay moaning on bulrush mats while crows dropped clam shells to break on the rocks. Up the Sound and down a jagged inlet, some inland people discovered something soft and tender called salmon and that salmon passed through the bodies of bears and fertilized the trees which protected the streambeds. The sick people at the lake sent their spirits up through a channel they could only navigate when the tide was high. A bank sloped to a gentle landing where the chief of the inlet people asked some of the children on the beach if they'd mind stepping into the water for a few minutes. The children began to swim and play in the shallows until slowly, very slowly, they began to turn into salmon. The inlet people caught them and ate them, but every... single... solitary... bone had to be put back in the water until the bones formed again as children. But one day, one of the inland people kept back a single bone and, when the children came out of the water, one of them was missing a nose.

Suddenly, Dr. Stan sits up as if hearkening to a sound none of them can hear. He leaps up with the same alarmed look he had when Jeanette came up the stairs of the First Aid station. Hold the fort, Billy, he says. I'll be right back. No one is allowed out on the dam. They all know the rule but Billy heads straight for the barrier. Time's up Saturday, he hisses to Gwen before he steps onto the cement border. When he jumps the gap in the cement designed to drain excess water if the lake's high in the spring, a large piece cracks off and rolls into the stream bed. Far more water than before pours through the enlarged opening now too large for him to jump back. His face drains as if he's on the ledge of a tall building and wild air is blowing beneath him. No trail on the other side of the lake where the dam wall ends. Leo's down at the lake edge; when he sees Billy silently beseeching him not to tell how scared he is, it's like an age gap between brothers that seems large when they're young diminishing as they get older.

Leo runs up through the meadow to alert Dr. Stan, staying out of sight when he sees him reach into a hollow stump for a dark liquor bottle that he stuffs in his knapsack. Dr. Stan takes a booklet from his inside shirt pocket, hunkers down, and lights it with a match. When he hears shouts back at the lake, he stomps the half burned pages and smothers the flames with gravel. Once he's gone, Leo rakes the half burned army I.D. papers from the smoldering heap, waits for them to cool and opens the booklet to see a photograph of Dr. Stanley but the name underneath reads Murray Alderson.

Isabelle knows she's late for work; she hardly slept at the lake and comes down the road past the lawn bowling green to the hotel to find Mrs. Long sitting on her own stool behind the desk filing reservation cards. Pinch hitting until you got here, she says proudly. Oh, and I've taken care of the upstairs watering, dear.

That night in the attic, Leo sits on Gwen's cot and shines his flashlight on the half burned pages. Dr. Stan must be a spy, he says. They change their names. He knows all about Gerry be- cause he *is* Gerry.

I don't think so, says Gwen.

The tin around the chimney flashes. Do heaven and hell turn with the earth so heaven can stay above people's heads? Or what? The silence shifts and Lily cries out from her bed.

Go back to sleep, Gwen says. It's only the dance.

Downstairs the grown-ups are so quiet, you can tell their dad wants to tell mother something but is holding back because she goes by the saying if you can't say something nice about some- body, don't say anything at all which is what the Wise Old Owl said to Thumper. Leaning his knees together, he slants his long legs one way then the other, trying to get them under the table. If Ada wants to know what he's thinking, all right he'll say it, there's something about this Dr. Stan character who's turned up from goodness knows where that doesn't quite meet the eye. Why would a bona fide doctor pick up bits of left over food from the sink with a spoon, the way he did the night they had him to supper? No real doctor would be so squeamish.

He's a first aid attendant, says their mother. We just call him a doctor. A first aid attendant who's turned up and helped out

every single solitary mother whose children have ear aches and
are up here on their own she might add.

Don't pay any attention to me. I'm probably talking through
my hat.

You probably are.

23.

At Scarborough, the man in the clock has made his appearance so it must be time for Flora to be making supper.
Maybe that pot roast she's got in the icebox. Where'd these coho
come from? What if her sister made it all the way to Vancouver
only to find herself wandering around Cordova St.? She's got to
talk to Percy again, but her phone is on the blink. The tearoom
phone will be working; she'll take a walk over there.

Nightie on instead of a slip. How'd that happen? Well, it'll
do as a slip. Why's this dress so tight? She hasn't been eating
that much. It's not the lack of people making her lonely; it's the
shadows behind the bushes and trees that refuse to come out. It
won't be long before the thousands of picnickers will be ghosts
and there'll be no more steamers whistling up the inlet.

It's too early for the sun to be going down; the sun's always
on her right in the evening when she walks over to the Cove.
Now, when she makes sure it's on her right, the hotel's on her
left. What's the monkey tree doing over there? Not supposed
to be a hill so soon. The sun's supposed to be setting on the
west side of the planet so people on the other side of the earth
can have themselves a day so what's it doing over there on the
wrong side of the bay, gaining inches into the sky above the
north shore mountains? Something's turned the whole ball of

wax the wrong way around. The latticed arbour beside the hotel is covered with honeysuckle the way it's meant to be, but that short red haired woman who was supposed to have been Eleanor is inside, her face patterned by the sketches of leaves and light. Strange to see a grown-up person whose feet don't touch the ground.

What day is it? Flora asks.

Monday. Do you know Isabelle Gallagher? I'm going to be her mother-in-law. I'm Jack Long's mother. This used to be his stomping ground before he went overseas.

Is that so? says Flora. I'm looking for the tearoom. I seem to have gotten turned around.

It's that way.

Oh, of course.

Another block or so further down the trail she sees Isabelle inside the second ivy covered arbor, sitting so still on the bench it's as if she's turned to wood. Flora leans into the shadows. There's a woman in the other arbour who's looking for you, she says.

I know, says Isabelle.

At last, there's a sunny day up Narrows Inlet and Takumi can make progress in his plan to move out of the dank shed. If he builds a structure higher up so he's facing south he'll get the sun and might not come down with that racking cough again. The maple leaves will fall soon, the forest floor softer on the deer leather binding his feet. An inner tide has turned in the night; the firs seem more anchored, the bottoms of the trunks wider. His hands feel strong again. Up and over the slope in the small meadow he's cleared, he paces out what he guesses would be the floor measurements of the Scarborough house. Marks what would be the corners with rocks, ties the chain he'd used to direct rainwater from the gutters of his first lean-to onto a propped log and pulls another log into place to mark the house corner that's appeared in his drawings since the day Isabelle's father whistled when they were hiding in the tree platform. Now, softening alder into flesh with an old chisel from the shed, he, remembers her pulling away, running up the stairs to Miss Fenn's cottage where her father was scything foxgloves. Scooping the swing seat under her, Mr. Gallagher weighed her lap with a mass of foxgloves as Takumi sidled by them up the hill, a paradise inside him so intense it was a relief to be going home to his own bed above the kitchen.

In the life guarding boat, he'd let go an oar and thrust his hand back like a speed skater to delineate the thrust of her shoulder if her scapula were bent into a wing. In the tree platform he'd lift her knee to see if her skin turned bluer when it stretched. Now, walking the beach, feeling the forest settle within him, he sees what will be her pelvic bone arc in a piece of beached fir, one end anchored, the other skimming the ground.

As autumn moves in and it's safer to be on the shore, he begins to move comfortably between large pieces of driftwood as if they've become his furniture. Accenting a line of whiskers in an upended butt of a weathered fir evokes a family of seals. Tracing his palm along a peeled log flank, a sweep of giant snail hunkers to meet him. His hands are so cold he alternates them in and out of a disintegrating pocket, shaking the one he's working with to keep it warm.

Eaarly one morrrning, I heeaard a maiid siinnging, I heeard a maiid siinnging, in the vaallley below. Percival, Flora says to the receiver on the phone in the tearoom booth. I saw your note. I went to meet Eleanor, but she wasn't on the boat. I'm worried she might have missed you. You didn't leave a note? Well, who did? I don't know, Percival. It's too much for me. I don't mean that. She hangs up. You have to be careful what you say to them or next thing you know they'll be putting you out to pasture.

When Flora starts down the tearoom stairs, Gwen crawls out from under the verandah. You're out early, Grandma. Three different dress sleeves emerge at Grandma's wrist like layers of re-done wallpaper.

So are you, she says. It's exciting to be up when everyone's still asleep, isn't it?

All right, fine, pretend she knew all along they were in the a.m., not p.m. If anyone asks, they always have roast beef for breakfast. Guess she already had a dress on when she put another one on this morning. Later, at home, Lyndon's upstairs in bed listening to Flora ingratiate herself with that yokel handyman who's here to talk about the drains.

When I opened my icebox this morning there were these lovely salmon, Flora says. I have no idea who put them there.

George smiles. That'd be me.

It was *you* came early this morning, was it?

Odd that she doesn't feel offended by the way he must have walked in unannounced, and now clearly intends to help her with the canning. He moves casually to the sink where he starts washing jars in steaming water. Can't have a speck on these here, he says, or they'll spoil. I'll have the heads and fins cut off and the insides scooped out in no time.

(The way Lyndon figures it, if he pretends to be too feeble to make it home from the store on his own and gets George to drive him, he might find a sabotaging clue in the glove compartment of Fenn's truck. Why does the fellow have so many matchboxes that don't rattle when you shake them? He opens one, copies the x-marked maps he finds while his nibs is in for the mail. Let them think he's wandering aimlessly down the Government Road. Morning Lyndon. Morning Ada. On your way to the Pie Shop?

Wish I could say so, Lyndon, but I'm delivering Leo's newspapers. He has earache again.

I'm sorry to hear that.)

24.

W hat are you looking for, Gwen? Every time I come into a room you're holding up a pillow. Her granddaughter can hardly say tomorrow's the Labour Day masquerade and her deadline. Not that she's going. It'll only be the kid part she'll be missing so who cares.

At the beach, it's so cold and rainy they have to keep their sweatshirts on for water ballet dry practice. Bracket their hip bones, scull figure eights in the air at their sides with cupped fingers. In the water on her back, arms above her head, she feet-first propellers toward shore until Frances grabs her solid feet in one hand and pushes her away straight-legged like a drifting log.

Later, the lifeguard drapes each girl over her arm like dough to check their back bends. When she gets to the end of the line, Jeanette inserts her thumb under her own bathing suit edge and snaps it on her thigh. The quick glimpse of pale flesh makes Frances button her jacket onto her shirt instead of onto its proper buttons. She leans over and hisses. I'm teaching now for heaven's sake.

Okay.

After lunch, the tide's out so Gwen takes the beach way home, the patch of bulrush grass growing brightly on Miss Fenn's Rocky. Wonder why she isn't here this summer flinging her window open, flapping her hand back and forth conducting them on her swing between the Douglas firs? *O how I love to go up in a swing. Up in the air so blue.* Definitely enough grass on good old Miss Fenn's Rocky for a hula skirt. Her beige one-piece bathing suit would do the trick if she made a couple of leis to cover her chest. Maybe she could go after all. Over at the hotel, dozens of orchids in the upstairs hotel window press their faces to the panes like orphans. Dotting her fingers in a semi-circle around her chest, she heads into the lobby to talk to Auntie even if their mother said not to bother her. Since her aunt's been gone, foxglove blossoms are only foxglove blossoms. They're nobody's hats. If you plant your milk teeth roots down, lady slippers don't grow from them any more.

The lobby is cool and smells of honeysuckle and furniture polish. Auntie's not at the desk, not in the dining room, not out with Mr. McConnecky planting croquet wickets on the grass by the monkey tree.

I'm looking for my aunt, Gwen says coming back down the stairs.

Her day off, Gwen. Not sure where she is.

Mr. McConnecky shakes his fleshy head so the skin wobbles around his jaw. She heads out back along the side of the lawn bowling green; she'll go on up to the falls and practise dancing lovely hula hands so she can be ready for Saturday. Passing the corner deluxe, she sees Auntie sitting in a chair on the verandah so completely still as if she's turned to wood. Her eyes stare straight ahead as if they'll never blink again. A short lady with red hair sits beside her. Not now, the lady says as Gwen starts up the stairs. Auntie stares over her niece's head and says nothing.

At the falls, sitting miserably on the ledge above the spot where the water flows hardest, her feet hit up against something hard. She reaches down and pulls up a wine bottle. When her mother finds liquor bottles in the bush, she makes a big show of pouring out the liquor saying she will not touch a drop of alcohol as long as she lives, and it's not funny years later when Uncle Jack gives her a key chain with a gin bottle charm on it for Christmas. When Gwen twists off the wire and pulls the knobbed cork, there's a bang like a firework and the bottle shoots a geyser onto the rocks.

Frances is out in the rowboat backhanding the oars to stay in place so she can teach and watch the beach at the same time. Ada's lying in her spot over by the boat rental pier offering her haltered breasts to the sky. Small flat stones balance on her closed eyes to darken the sun.

Frances beaches the boat and goes to sit beside her. Gwen's working awfully hard at this water ballet, she says pointing her sun visor.

She's like that.

Too hard, do you think?

Oh, I don't know.

How's Isabelle? I haven't had a visit with her for ages. She hasn't been eating in the staff dining room. Maybe she eats in her room.

I doubt that, says Ada, fine tuning the stones.

Does she know I told you about White Rock?

Ada nods.

I guess that's why she's not speaking to me.

You know the baby died.

I didn't know that. That's terrible.

Yes, it is.

I assumed it'd been… taken care of.

It was.

They're quiet then, as if hoping the tide would come straight back in and cover the slimy raft resting akimbo on the muddy bottom. It's so hot even Leo's in the water, his white stomach like a skate fish as he flaps his hands to propel himself out to the small float joined by logs to the diving tower to create a rectangular pool. Billy and the boys on the Intermediate team are horsing around on the tower end. Gwen does her lengths, swims in and walks up the beach slope to join her mother and Frances.

Will you teach me to do a Catalina? she asks Frances, pulling off her bathing cap and shaking out her hair. She's almost forgiven her the sand castle contest disaster because the other night her swimming teacher'd taken her to a movie at the Laundry Tub cinema where a line of girls in dazzling gold bathing suits swung onto the screen and dove in unison into a pool below. Someone pulleyed a solo swing up way too high for Esther Williams to dive into the pool, but she did it anyway. When she surfaced in shimmering platinum, her smiling teeth gleamed and water flashed around her head like a halo.

It's tricky, Frances says when they're out on the water. Like rubbing your head and patting your stomach at the same time. Gwen strokes her crawl beside the boat, head raised above the water so she can hear the instructions. She's going to have to figure out something to protect Leo, since she can't find any money to pay off Billy. Scull hard, says Frances. Deep breath, ballet leg. Point your leg in the air, rotate your torso. Dive straight over your shoulder. Executing a wide leg split upside down, Gwen raises her left leg smartly to meet the right, heads for the bottom. If she can keep her body straight enough to execute four Catalinas across the pool like stakes pushed into the sea bed, shift from woof to warp and shuttle back and forth across the pool, she could weave an invisible net to block Billy and the boys swimming down to Leo's end where he's sprawled on the float like a walrus. They'd come a cropper and hit against the underwater net as if their bed had been apple-pied. Not the kind where you stuff in sticks and stones like they're going to do to Evvie's bed as a joke, but the kind where you take one sheet and fold it so it looks like two and, blam, when the person sticks her feet in the covers, she pops back out like a jack-in-the-box.

What's Frances doing out there, training seals? I'm not sure I want my daughter turned into a seal, Percy says from the blanket where he's joined Ada. She *is* husky, isn't she?

They have to be, dear. People get violent when they're drowning.

Crack, the boys are off, thrashing down the swimming lanes. Halfway down, Frances fires the starter pistol; the racers stop on a dime and turn back. False start, she says. A few more inches and the boys would have smashed up against Gwen's net. For the rest of the class they have to practise not jumping the gun.

25.

Matches, George, Frances says at the wharf. I need matches.

I bet you're after the romantic ones, eh? he says. The life-guard's probably set her cap at Dr. Stan, the way the two of them always have their heads together planning some swimming regatta or other. Never mind that the first aid attendant only has eyes for Evvie Gallagher. George spreads his assortment of small boxes of the hood of his truck and, yes, the one she wants is labeled with a rock and a waterfall.

Frances lies on her beach blanket dreaming of Jeannie *with the light brown hair.* Her Jeanette's is blonde but never mind. Isabelle saw you kiss me the other day, I know she did, the way she looks at me funny. If anyone found out how we feel about each other, I don't know what I'd do, Jeanette'd said. Even so, they're going to spend the afternoon together at the falls eating strawberries and drinking wine.

When Frances sees George over at the tennis court office that afternoon, she
goes in to talk to him.
It's there, is it? It's in place? she asks.
You're not supposed to talk to me about that, Frances.
Yes, but is it?
It is.

Carefully drawing the strands of his plan together, Lyndon gathers up the ledgers he found in the old Scarborough desk, makes sure his copy of the hand sketched Bridal Falls map in his pocket. Once the authorities know what the new *handyman* has been up to, it'll be off to town to jail for him, away from Flora once and for all. Trust me, he says to the RCMP officer sitting in the café. I have something important to show you up at the falls. No it can't wait.

So now it's his turn to head down the trail along the waterfall rocks below the white picket bridge. Turning around every few minutes to make sure the officer is following him, he unfolds the duplicated map on the ledge of the stone balcony and shows him the x. The running water drapes over his ropey hand and comes up empty.

That's odd, he says. This is supposed to be the spot. You know Fenn's a bootlegger, do you? George Fenn? He hides his bottles all over the Cove.

The officer could have his thumbs in his belt he's that blasé. I haven't seen George selling liquor to anyone, he says. I know he sells matches. Pretty harmless way to make a living, I'd say. As for you, sir, I'm not sure it's above board for you to be rifling through the glove compartments of peoples' trucks.

Now look here, says Lyndon. I haven't brought you on a wild goose chase. All you need to do is visit Fenn and see what kind of distilling equipment he's got over at his place. See here in these ledgers—he spreads Shinsuke's account books on the balcony—it must have started way back when the Yoshitos gave him bushels of potatoes for practically nothing. Bet your bottom dollar he knew what to do with them. And likely blackberry wine too, the way he's got that son of his picking pounds of the stuff. We're always having to chase him off our property.

The officer looks away. I'd have to get a search warrant for that.

Well, get a search warrant.

As I said, this is our busiest weekend of the year, Mr. Killam. I'd have to go to town and no can do. The way the officer looks indifferently off in the distance, he could have been about to charge Lyndon for wasting police time. He probably owes George Fenn for something.

Lyndon's started wetting his bed and the washing machine's conked out. Flora has to stand her husband up like a child to pull on his underwear. Soon she'll have to clean his bottom, lifting his pale hairless legs as he stares expressionless past her shoulder. Yesterday, he came down to breakfast dressed in two shirts, the collar of the first folded over the second. He no longer creases the top of his fedora before he pulls down the brim. One of the family's going to turn up any minute and no one, she means no one, is going to know how bad things are. When she has him dressed and propped at the kitchen table, he tries to feed himself and misses his mouth. When she takes the spoon and inserts it, he seals his lips so she can't pull it out. Worse, his speech is jumbled up and runs together like a speeded up record.

When Flora goes outside these days, it seems as if the wrong plants are growing from the wrong bushes. String beans dangle from the raspberry canes, corn sprouts from the squash. The long shoots of blackberries arc ahead, root, send out more shoots: when her back is turned, they leap further. She makes pies with the harried look of a reluctant volunteer having to feed a large crowd the way she did when the threshers were at

the farm. Remember when we saw her at Ada's nonchalantly ironing in her hat? You'd never see her like that any more.
Sometimes she sleeps in her apron.

That afternoon, when Percy arrives on the Daddy boat, he finds
George Fenn sitting at their kitchen table. George Fenn has
never sat at their kitchen table before but there he is briskly stirring sugar into his coffee. You'd think a weekend dad would be
able to pour himself a drink before being accosted with socially
ingratiating remarks, but no.

Expect you two are worried about the old people over there?
George says in an overly familiar tone, lifting his cup with both
hands. Once the hotel is closed, he goes on, I'm at loose ends for
the winter. Wouldn't mind stopping by on a regular basis to see
what needs doing. Mrs. Killam is having a heck of a time trying
to get Mr. Killam into his bath.

Since when is this?

Oh, for a while now.

Thank you for coming, Mr. Fenn. I'll talk the idea over with
my parents. Percy stands by the door to see him out. Mr. Fenn
was just getting comfortable, but Mr. Fenn sees he's expected
to leave.

Percy turns to Ada furiously. Why am I being told about my
parents by George Fenn of all people? Aren't you looking out
for them while I'm at work? This is a *family* matter. It's not for
outsiders.

Ada's trying to lift a poached egg from its simmering water,
but the egg slits yellow blood and slithers back into the pan.

Mom's really *busy*, dad, says Gwen.

That's not why Mr. Fenn wants to go over to Scarborough, she wants to say. Why does she have to be the only one who knows what Billy's up against? If he doesn't come up with the money, he'll be like the princess who couldn't guess Rumplestiltskin's name.

Thank you, Gwen, Ada says.

The door opens and Mr. Fenn pokes his head back in. Oh, I should have told you. Isabelle's been fired. Hasn't been able to concentrate on her work apparently. Can't manage the waitresses anymore.

Fired! Gwen rushes across the room and lays her hands flat on the table. Grandma Gallagher sits bolt upright in her flaming coffin. They can't fire her. She's not kindling!

It's all right, Gwen, Ada says. Firing means when somebody loses their job.

Apparently, she's left the island, says George.

We're going to have to find a home in town for dad, says Percy sadly. This can't go on. George Fenn waltzing in here with news about *Isabelle* as well? Can't you keep track of your own sister, Ada? He pours himself a rum and coke and heads out to the verandah to shake his glass.

26.

It's all the shadow people, Flora says when Percy comes in. Most of them have suitcases. They queue up for food and water, but nothing I feed them satisfies them.

It was a mistake bringing you here, mother. I didn't mean to isolate you like this.

Lyndon, catching Flora's imploring look, manages brightly, We'refine. Werereallyjustfine.

I'd be better if Eleanor were here, says Flora.

Nobody thinks that's a good idea, mother, Percy says. (His father couldn't be drunk but what then?) If you can't get dad out of the bath, how're you going to manage? There's a nice place I've looked at in east Vancouver, over on Grant St. Maybe... we could at least think about it.

How do you know I can't get him in and out of the bath? Flora says. They are never nice places. Lyndon stays with me. I'll get a lawyer if it comes right down to it.

She would, too.

What do you think of the idea of George Fenn coming by to help? Percy asks.

She looks up, relieved. That'd be fine with us.

Lyndon is shaking his head. Notim. Anybodybutim.

What's wrong with your voice, dad?

What if we tried it for now, Dad, says Flora. I could pay him whatever the going rate is.

She's never called him Dad before.

He's a good worker, she says. Now you get on, Percival, that eldest daughter of yours could use some attention.

George helps Flora move Lyndon's bed to the living room so he doesn't have to climb the stairs. He's fixed the washing machine and repaired the eavestroughs. When it comes to the bath, Lyndon pushes the door shut from inside and locks it. Crashes on the floor trying to get himself into the tub. George has to climb through the open window. Lyndon's bruised but nothing's broken – after that, he takes to sitting at the kitchen table with his eye on the door.

On masquerade day, when George has finished his moonlighting chores, he pulls the truck up to the Scarborough kitchen door where buckets of early apples are stacked on the back porch. When Flora asks him to get her more canning jars from the basement, he notices some boxes on a corner shelf. Reads the labels as he's carrying them upstairs. FOR GEORGE FENN AS PAYMENT FOR WHAT WE OWE HIM. Bottles of preserves: plums, carrots, blackberries, turnips. There's a note. *This should be a start in settling our account. We never intended to accept this place as a gift. Please find enclosed our partial payment in kind. We will provide you with the equivalent every year as long as we live. Sincerely, Shinsuke and Noriko Yoshito.*

Oh, for heaven's sake. George starts unfolding lids on other boxes. I can't believe this.

Flora holds a jar of plums up to the window. Someone's way of getting through the depression, I guess, she says admiring the ruby light. Think there'll be enough here to last you a while?

I think there'll be enough here to last me a while, he says.

You have to say this for George Fenn. At least he laughs. Life, eh? Isn't it something? he says. He'd better let up on Billy. He'll take him on that fishing trip he's promised over on the mainland up Gambier way.

27.

Now it's Frances and Jeanette's turn to clamber down the waterfall rocks below the white picket bridge and onto the balcony. Tablecloth on the rocks, yes. Strawberries, yes. The falls sparkling in the background, yes. When Frances reaches into the waterfall for the wine, she comes up empty-handed.

Where's the wine? It was supposed to be here keeping cool.

What're we celebrating?

Us.

I don't need wine, Frances. You're beautiful as you are.

And on this beguiling night, when people can be whoever they want, it's Jeanette who leans over to kiss Frances's neck, then each of her eyes. She takes her hand and leads her up the accordion pleated stairs to a private slope of their own on the other side of the firs.

Later, on the way to her shift at the beach, Frances sits on the causeway railing, tenderly stroking her own legs with baby oil.

I want my money back, George. You led me on a wild goose chase.

Her voice is so content he hardly hears her. How do you mean?

The wine wasn't there.

Well, I put it there.

Why are you laughing?

I don't know, he says. Strange bottles have been appearing and disappearing all day today.

The dancehall is in the same spot it occupied when the earth rotated around the sun last year. The doors will open and a new crew will take their places like a change of shift. New arrivals come by boat; some might fall from the sky.

Gwen lies awake listening to the music from the moonlight cruise Lady Alex as it steams into the Cove. Time's up, but she has nothing to show for it. If she'd been able to pick a few orchids, at least she'd have had a costume. Maybe she can go and watch the dancers through the window like she usually does.

She throws her shoes out the window, tucks her nightie into her slacks and climbs down the fire escape ladder. Has to heel in a starting line and take a run at the stairs to chin herself on the high back dancehall window ledge. Last time she did that, the dancers were all in windbreakers and slacks pulling each other in and out. Where were the dresses?

Thick branches swirl and separate. Clouds blow across the moon that stands out like a coin you could swallow. The stars are orchids. At home in bed, the trees don't sound as if the bough will break and down will come baby. Three chin-ups and re-treats, but she still can't get high enough to see if Billy's in there. She's back in the bushes getting ready for a fourth try when the door smashes open and Dr. Stan crashes out, a cravat tucked into his white lab coat. Dark air blows through him. His good hand misses the railing and he topples over the edge, hollering and lurching. What's the matter with this place? Can't a fellow get a decent drink around here? Nothing in this goddam hollow log either, he says before he falls down beside it.

Next thing you know it's Frances's Jeanette who's sitting on the railing, blowing smoke rings and sticking her finger through them. As if that's something I would make up, she says to one of the men who came up with Aunt Evvie's crowd. You should have seen his face when I went by the First Aid station. I was the last person he wanted to see, I can tell you. She stubs out her cigarette.

What's she going to do? he says. He and Evvie are finalists for the Northwest Tennis Doubles Championships.

I don't care if they're Siamese twins. I know his wife. He's from Quesnel same as me. She thinks he's missing in action. The best thing that can happen to Evvie is if he plain disappears.

More people appear in animal heads, princess hats, paper cups in their hands. They smash the weighted door open, congregate on the back porch. Hey, you back in the bushes. Come and have a dance. Gwen backs up the trail, turns and runs. Terrible things happen if she sneaks out when she's not supposed to. If she can get back to bed quickly enough, no one will know she's been gone. If she hadn't snuck out, she wouldn't have heard. If she hadn't heard, it wouldn't be true about Dr. Stan.

One morning a few days later, her parents sit holding their teabags gingerly by the corners, dunking and re-dunking them in their cups. Whatever's happened is so bad they haven't even made tea in the teapot. The picture of Evvie and Dr. Stan on the mantel above Grandpa Gallagher's fireplace is gone. Her arm linked into his, curly hair cut short up the sides and raised on top like bread. His smile lifts a touch above his teeth so his gums show.

Evvie's at the door. What's happened? she asks. Who's died?

It's about Dr. Stan, Evelyn.

What about him? I put him on the boat. He had to go down.

Evvie, we have to tell you this. He's married.

He's not. He couldn't be.

Why do you say that?

He would have told me.

Well, he didn't. And he is.

She sits down.

Now it's Aunt Evvie who's beside herself. One part has burrs and leaves tangled in its hair; the other stands erect and shocked, tightening its stomach muscles. Life's kind pairing that turned her into a grown-up because she had a boyfriend has withdrawn its kind favour. All it takes is one mistake to shame your entire family. When they stop the music, she has to pretend she likes the next man down the line from her real love and dance with him anyway.

The next morning, Gwen and Leo sit on the ship log and sing their private song. Good-bye, I see you last time. They're still so upset up at the cottage—they're always upset up at the cottage—the two of them could drive the ship log all the way to Vancouver before anyone noticed. Part of Gwen has never been out to the dancehall in the middle of the night. A giant hand set the dancehall going like a top and the roof flung off. Everyone scattered like crabs when you lift their stone houses.

Out in the new rowboat, Leo says that when the war is over, maybe they'll find out that Dr. Stan really *was* a spy. That's not it, says Gwen. He had to go away because he's married to someone else.

Is that why he took a different name?

I think so.

And someone blew his cover?

I guess so.

He could still be a spy, says Leo. One good thing. Billy hasn't bothered me any more since I stared him down that day he was out on the Killarney dam.

That's good, says Gwen.

If she says nothing about the deal she made with Billy, maybe she won't be to blame for everything.

Maybe the war is going on around the other side of Dorman Point. They row over to see, but when they arrive, the war isn't there. Maybe it's around the other side of Cowan's but Cowan's is too far to row. When they go down for the winter, Gwen leaves part of herself running around the perimeter of the dancehall, one foot in the dance floor, the other scootering the raised walkway. If she'd known, she would have waved at herself.

BOOK III

COMING HOME

28.

August, 1945.

Wracked with phlegmy coughs, Takumi lies awake in the night listening to the cries of a cougar that so far has escaped his traps. The shriek of what sounds like a terrified marten ripped apart in the dark. In the morning he finds the print of a raking claw and a chewed deer carcass piled over with alder branches. It must be a cougar: the front paw marks splay wider than the back ones; in the mud, a longer streak where its back foot dragged. The sweep of a curved fifth mark that would be a tail. He's heard large cats won't attack you from the front so he's carved a mask to wear on the back of his head: humanoid with lidless eyes and smooth skin. That way, the cat would be confused; if it does get around the front and charge, he's hoping its weight would impale itself on his knife lashed to a stick. It's a long shot: he's never hunted a mountain lion before let alone without a gun.

His hair is long now, his skin leathery. His muscled limbs press forward into the hunt as he sets out, back to back with his mask. A faraway drone of a plane behind a bank of fog, probably on the other side of the peninsula. A scrimmage in the woods ahead, maybe the cougar slipped in front without his knowing. Screams any second that would be his own. He begins to twitch like a dog dreaming about a chase. A ricocheted crash as he thrusts his knife forward praying the animal would die in a mass of heaving fur and flesh. Instead, a man in a torn Air Force uniform projects himself through the trees and lurches down the hill holding a badly injured side. Takumi reaches out to stop him from falling, supports him down the trail hidden along the hillside.

Back at the shack, although nothing seems to be broken, the man's in so much pain Takumi gives him his bed. It's been so long since he's seen another person, he cups his hand above his nose when he's sleeping to feel the miracle of his breathing. He sits by the bed, turning one of the pilot's wide strong-fingered hands palm up and lifts it into his own as if weighing it. When the bruised man wakes for a few minutes, he manages to spoon a few mouthfuls of mushroom soup into him.

The stranger finally stays awake long enough to turn his head. How long have you been here? he asks.

Some years, Takumi says, offering him another spoonful of soup. You were flying pretty low, he says, his voice hollow and scratchy.

Too low. I was looking for you. The people in Sechelt figured they'd got rid of the loggers and then there you were stealing canoes and camping on the territory. They waited for a pretty long time for you to leave before they contacted the Gumboot Navy....

Someone's going to know where you crashed. They'll be out looking for you.

I don't think so. I didn't file a flight plan.

Best to say nothing and keep his eye on the stranger's every move. Would he turn him in if he owes his life to him? Every meal is building up credit. Still, it's difficult to measure how much the debt is weighing on his visitor's honour and he can't take a chance. He'll have to hide the canoe, sneak away at night and leave everything again. At least he's camouflaged his trail inland.

Later, when Takumi is winding the canoe slowly up the stream with the pulley, he's surprised to see yet another stranger coming up the trail. There's a sailboat anchored in the bay.

So this is the trick you're using, the new arrival, a man in a captain's hat, says. I couldn't figure out why the canoe was heading up the stream by itself. Figured maybe it was a ghost canoe. I barely made it through the Skookumchuck. Had about a ten-minute window. It'll be good to have some gas now that the war is over.

It is? says Takumi. The pilot comes walking down the trail, out of bed for the first time. The visitor looks at the two of them. I guess you two are from the same tribe, eh?

Pretty much, says Takumi and laughs.

When the sailboater offers the two of them a lift back down the coast, Takumi packs up in a flash, burying items that had meant the world to him the day before. Leaves a cache in the woods he intends to come back for, and the carvings. Returns the canoe to the dock at the head of Sechelt inlet before the trip down the Sound.

He'd always seen himself coming home in the winter. The tide would be high, their house surer of itself because he's longed for it every day. When he's dropped at the wharf in the Cove, the sky clears and a low sun emerges behind a row of firs lighting the raindrops on each branch. As he crosses the lagoon causeway, he runs his hand over an exposed cement crack he and his father fixed years ago. The hotel gardens are a shambles. Taking the path down to Pebbley, he cuts up the side trail to Millers, finally turns onto his own road and heads down his own driveway. Smoke from the chimney sets his heart beating high in his ribs; his mother likes to get the fire going early in the season. Maybe they're back already. He must look terrible; the yachter gave him another sweater and a pair of old trousers but they're hanging off his frame. When he opens the door and calls in, an elderly gaunt woman with iron coloured hair is standing in front of the sink.

Yes? says Flora.

Are my parents here?

Your parents?

This is their house, ma'am.

George Fenn comes up behind Flora, looks at Takumi as if he'd personally buried his sea bleached bones and whoever's standing in front of him has wired them back together and set them moving.

Your kind are not allowed back on the coast, he says.

Excuse me, Mr. Fenn. Flora steps in front of George, extending her hand to Takumi. She might have been saying the other day she didn't know how she'd ever repay George Fenn; she would have been lost the day Lyndon collapsed and ended up having to go to the place in town, but nobody talks to anyone like that in her house. Even if she had allowed that the place sometimes felt as if it was becoming as much George Fenn's as it was hers.

I'm Flora Killam, she says, wiping her hands on her apron. You'd better come in. You're…?

I'm Takumi Yoshito.

Oh. Mr. Yoshito. I'm so sorry but this house was put up for sale by the government. My son bought it for us.

And your son is Percival Killam.

That's right, she says. It was so long ago now.

Was it?

Everyone thought you'd drowned. I believe someone tried to get a message to your parents.

He looks around at the new wallpaper, the familiar canner. Where are our things?

In storage at September Morn, says Flora.

I see.

The next day, he manages to catch a ride on a fishing boat out of Coal Harbour, crossing the border far enough from the coastline they don't have to bother with explanations. At the end of the pier in the small town of Blaine, the closest place he can be to Vancouver, he swings his duffle bag over his shoulder and heads down the line of canneries, turning onto the main street paralleling the low horizon of distant island mountains. On the other side of Drayton Harbor, flocks of swarming dunlins move as one over the sea, exhausting themselves trying to stay out of reach of lurking falcons. The tall Peace Arch rises north of the town and the trees of Semi-ah-Moo Point outline the thrust of land across the bay. He presses his hand against the brick stores to feel the solidity of real buildings; that people can sit inside dark bars and casually take themselves for granted astonishes him. Large Victorian houses on expansive lots on long leafy streets. At the corner of Peace Portal Way and Boblett, there's a Rooms Available sign on a gabled house that overlooks the railroad tracks and the beach. He's afraid any door that opens to him will be closed in his face, so he goes around to the back. The landlord nods distantly, accepts the money Takumi took away years ago and hasn't needed until now. The rooms feel as if no one's lived in them before. Lonelier than he ever was in camp—at least the earth he lay on there felt like his own—he stays in bed for days not caring if he ever gets up again. Isabelle's part of the family who took over their house and no amount of lonely rationalization in camp will change that.

When he's hungry enough, he forces himself to go down to the docks to look for a job. Even manages to check the post office on the off chance their box might still be in service, but of course it's not. Climbing over the decks of two gill netters to reach a third, he sloshes around in the muddy layer of plankton on the floor of the stern and talks himself into being hired. When the boat heads to the mouth of the Columbia, the sun is an orange ball above the horizon and the sea a mild chop. Again and again the net gets spooled out; again and again it gets spooled in, slotted with so many sockeye the hold is filled to capacity in a few settings and they have to wait for the packer to pick up the catch before they set the nets again. Those first days he's assigned to crawl around with a spiked stick stabbing fish that have slipped from reach. He learns how to lift the net between the uprights so it spreads evenly back over the roller. In the late afternoon they rest for half an hour while the tide changes. At night he sleeps in a small shelf lined with carpet behind an electrical panel that smells of diesel and bilge and to him is luxury.

The hard work on board leaves him so tired he sleeps long hours when he comes ashore. When he wakes up, he sits on the porch reaching endlessly for where he belongs the way a tongue searches for a missing tooth. The houses of White Rock slope up the eastern hill on the other side of the border and low mountains far away on Vancouver Island band the sky. Occasional trains pass along a ridge below him. When he writes to the Bird Commission trying to find information about his parents, the return letter tells him they may have gone back to Japan after the war; he would need to know where his parents had been detained in order for the authorities to begin a search. Why hadn't he paid more attention when his mother talked about her village in the old country; he can't remember its name or he'd inquire there.

He's been in Blaine nearly a month and must be lonelier than he thought because, in the general store one day, he sees a woman on her way out the door who, from the back, reminds him of Lottie Fenn.

He spends one of his days off walking up the streets in the small town admiring the cupolas and turrets on the houses. Inside the front door of a gabled house on an oak-treed lot, he hears a light popping as if someone's making popcorn. Then a voice. You want to step forward with the bat, Shima. Take a step forward dear, not back. I have to stop now.

It's Miss Fenn's voice. He'd know it anywhere. A little girl with a ping-pong bat in her hand opens the door. This is the red side, she says holding it in front of her face. Turns it over. Green. Inside, dinner plates line up along the wainscoting ledge of the living room.

She's always looking for someone to play with, Lottie says softly as if she knows he feels he's been sleepwalking from the time he rowed away from the island until now. How wonderful to see you, Takumi.

You too. I made it, thanks to you, he says.

Come in. What happened to you? How did you get here?

Well, I rowed. And rowed. Ended up settling way up an inlet. Lucky for me the guys who made those early logging camps left a lot of gear behind. But, coming back.... Did you know our house was sold? The Killams bought it. *The Killams bought it!* Mr. Killam's mother is living there.

I didn't know. I've been here a while. I'm so sorry.

All the time Takumi's talking, he keeps glancing at Shima. I'm fishing out of this town, Miss Fenn. It's the closest place I can be to my own city these days.

Lottie takes his face in her hands. I'm so glad to see you, Takumi. He sits on the edge of the sofa while Shima, Lottie says her name is, drops a ring of pick-up sticks straight from her fist. When she looks up, her smile is like his and Isabelle's combined in the cracked looking glass in the cottage when they played circus mirrors. When Lottie asks Shima to go out and play, she climbs on the swing between the oaks, straightening her legs and bending them again.

Is she...?

Lottie nods. She is.

Did Isabelle come here to have her?

Yes, but it wasn't like you think.

Right. An unmarried mother with a Jap kid, he says bitterly. Have you seen her?

Apparently, she's married, Lottie says gently. There was an announcement in the paper. I did what you asked. The first time I came to Blaine to enquire about the mailbox, they gave me the bum's rush. It being war and no payment arriving, they'd closed the boxes. At Christmas it seemed such a misery I'd have nothing to report to you, I came back to try again. Had they saved the contents, I asked, stored them somewhere? Not the faintest idea where any of it was, they told her. Likely it was kaput.

The returning bus stopped in White Rock. She hadn't thought to get off—felt too disappointed to move actually— but, when she looked out the window, she'd seen Ada Killam huddled over a cup of coffee in one of the café booths, looking so miserable and out of place she decided to get off.

Miss Fenn. You're a sight for sore eyes, Ada'd said. I'm completely beside myself. I can't tell anyone in the family, and I don't know what to do. It's Isabelle. She's at a home down here. She's having a baby.

And it's due quite soon?

How would you know that?

I was the only one on the Point last winter.

No one can know this has happened to Isabelle, Ada'd said. The baby will have to be adopted. *I've come to ask you if you'll keep an eye on things at our place over the winter.*

I'll do what I can about adoption arrangements, Ada. I'll be in touch. You take care of Isabelle.

I'll do that.

In the end, Lottie'd left her job, collected what she needed from her cottage at Bowen and returned to Blaine where she began volunteering at the local hospital. Was there the morning after Shima was born and the nurses were calling the phone number that didn't connect anywhere. Was there when the staff came to the realization the baby had been abandoned. Was the one who offered to look after the little girl until her mother could be found.

But it being war..., she says.

And the baby being a Jap..., says Takumi.

Right. The paperwork didn't get done. The authorities were prepared to look the other way if I was willing to provide foster care. To wait for you is what I didn't say. Your mother once told me if she ever had a daughter she'd call her Shima.... I've felt that she's too young to understand that her parents are....

Dead, he says. Well, I'm not.

I'm so glad.

When he's leaving, she stands at the door and takes his hand. You'll give her a while to get used to you before you tell her you're her father?

Of course I will.

Back in his room, he lies on his bed and stares at the ceiling. Maybe you go on paying for your chance at love for the rest of your life. But here, when he thought nothing would ever belong to him, is this child.

The next day he finds a warehouse for rent in a side street that would double as a studio. He moves in and, after a few weeks of visiting, makes a bunk for Shima. On the beach, he picks up a sea urchin to show her how it rotates off his hand on its spikes. They dig up clams and periwinkles. Back in the studio, she shapes clay into an urchin shell and inserts her pick-up sticks.

The first night she sleeps over there's an eclipse of the moon. The disc rises unsuspecting above the sea only to be blotted out an hour later.

Shima sits up straight in the bunk. I can't see, she calls out.

That's because it's the middle of the night, he says. Go to sleep now.

The next day she sits on a stool and says, You're my daddy.

I am, Shima. Yes, I am.

She smiles and goes on working. Neither of them can know that it will be another half decade before legislation passes that will allow him to take Shima home to his own province.

29.

August, 1945.

At Bowen, Leo and Gwen are sitting on the bench in the honeysuckle arbour holding out their legs comparing tans (Gwen's is darker) when all of a sudden the bay is filled with bells. Someone up on the bluff is ringing the school bell. The church bell at Collins clangs behind the hotel. Mr. McConnecky steps onto the hotel porch and chimes the dinner gong. Bells would ring when the war's over, their mother said. *Monkey tree no pinches back.* Leo and Gwen are on their feet racing over the lagoon causeway, bags of corn suddenly weightless, stopping only once for a chin-up at the back of the dancehall where a single curled maple leaf whisks along the floor.

They ignore the resting rock, rush through the back porch tunnel, across the living room, and onto the verandah where their mother is ringing a white china bell.

The war's over, she says, laughing and crying at the same time.

Who won? says Leo.

Astonishingly, there's a young man they've never seen before standing beside their mother. They'd heard about him: Frances'd brought a letter that his parents had written to Mr.

McConnecky from England. Their name was Sycamore; they'd visited the hotel years ago before the war—they'd never forgotten the island. Their son had been sent to Canada for the duration and his foster home—you couldn't call it a billet, could you—anyway, his foster home wasn't working out and Mr. McConnecky thought that since we... well I'm... living across the street from Lord Kitchener Elementary, this boy, Derek Sycamore is his name, might be able to stay with... me. He was so shy when he came I took him to stay at a camp on Anvil Island so he could be with other kids. I can't have visitors stay at the dorm so I was thinking, when he comes back, maybe I could send him over to meet your three. Frances sticks her fingers in the corners of her mouth to whistle at some boys fooling around on the diving wharf. No pushing on the slide, she yells out.

Ada hasn't wanted to say but she's been worrying about the masculine set of Frances's shoulders, the way she moves her left shoulder and leg together, then her right shoulder and leg. And the way Gwen wants to be with her all the time. What if she picks up odd ideas?

By all means, Ada said. You send him on over.

So now, it's all very well that Derek Sycamore is here (Ada says he reminds her of a young Rupert Brooke, whoever that is) except that he's going to sleep in the attic with them and Gwen has her *little friend*.

What are they supposed to do with this thin young man, blonde hair parted on the side and slanted up the back like Christopher Robin's? Take him to the tree fort? Offer him a comic? When mother puts him in their dad's place in the kitchen nook and tells him that lunch is green pea soup, he says jolly good, I love green pea soup. So do I, says Gwen and mother pulls her chin back and raises her eyebrows because she knows Gwen hates green pea soup.

The war's over, says Gwen.

For me it was over on in May on VE day, Derek says sadly. *Why hasn't he gone home then? Does he miss his mother?* It's raining so hard after lunch mother says they should go up and play in the attic. Not until she's been up ahead of the boys they're not. She has to rescue her paper dolls from the baseboard where they're lined up waiting to get asked to dance. She's way too old for paper dolls but it's rained all summer and, except for synchronized, there's been nothing to do except make cocktail outfits and formals for the cardboard girls to wear while they wait. It's so damp they've slid down the wall on their cardboard backs and rolled themselves up like wood shavings. When Derek and her brother come upstairs, she's backed into her dresser pressing them into the drawers like leaves.

Leo pours a jar of pickled tickets into Derek's hands as if rewarding him for single-handedly winning every Allied Victory in the war.

Are these ration coupons? asks Derek.

No, they're tickets for the treats they'll be giving away at races they have in the dancehall. Because it's raining.

Derek pulls a parcel from his knapsack. I'm supposed to give you this, Gwen.

When she unwraps the package, it's a bathing suit with silver stars on a black modesty panel, the back and sides black stars on a silver background. Frances told her—what did Jeanette say meanly, her *protégé*—that she's ready to go in the solos at the Canadian Championships at Crystal in town in the winter.

Frances's the only one who's listened when she said she wants to swim to *Stardust*.

At the dancehall, Derek jumps sadly around the dance floor with his burlap sack pulled up to his chin. When they hand him fifty cents as a prize, he says he'll have it changed to English money to take home.

At home in the attic, when she should be in bed, Gwen sits in the moonlight repairing the hem on the starry bathing suit. Derek comes out of her brother's sectioned-off room to go down to the bathroom. Use sticky tape instead, Derek says and she laughs like anything. After he goes back to bed, she strokes her own soft neck; when she slips her fingers down her side touching herself down there to see if there's still blood, she feels a rush of pleasure that she knows is something she's supposed to wait for her husband to give her on their marriage night of nights o holy.

The next day at dry practice, Frances draws an arched stick woman in the sand. If you keep your back arched in the feet first layout position, scoop upwards with your cupped hands and hold your feet steady, you'll arch your way around feet first until your toes break the surface. Change to your propeller stroke with your arms above your head and swim your body out flat. When Gwen arches too much and finishes a few inches below the surface, Frances has to lean over from the wharf, reach under her waist and haul her up. The second time she propels as hard as she can, still comes up feet first under the surface, opens her eyes underwater to see a wavering Frances who must be demonstrating the front neck rescue they learned at bronze medallion class because Jeanette's arms are up around her neck as if

Frances is about to turn her backwards by the chin and frog kick her to shore, except that from under the water it looks like she's kissing her on the mouth. It must be the water making, what do they call it, an optical illusion?

At least Leo's pesky earache is better and he's allowed out on the small wharf where he's lolling around with Derek. Bye bye, I see you last time, she says when she swims her lengths and comes up to his end. He's been a different person since he won that face-off with Billy at the Killarney damn. And Billy has stopped bothering her as well even if she didn't find the money or trip him up in an invisible net. Best let sleeping dogs lie as Grandma Flora would say. Right now Leo's going on about some spider who only understands length and width. If you put that spider on a line that circumnavigates a balloon, if the spider only understands two dimensions the way we only understand three, it'd think it was going in a straight line and be astonished when it came back to the original dot. Which just shows that we probably don't understand the fourth dimension which might be time. Derek looks baffled.

The chartreuse water glows under the pier as Derek leaps up and dives in. He's a fast swimmer, could zap through her Catalina weavings like a lion through a paper hoop, but half way to the diving tower end, he jerks to a stop as if hitting up against something which must be the net she'd shuttled. He knows. Amazing. He stopped there because he felt its existence. Later, when she starts her breast stroke lengths, there he is on his back under water below her, swimming elementary backstroke to mirror her breaststroke. She loves it when he comes up, throwing the water off his hair.

What were you doing down there? she says.

How can I see your breast stroke if I don't go under water? *Her big thrill for the day.*

At home, a plain wedding announcement card arrives with a note from Auntie informing them that Jack Long is home from overseas and they've been married by a justice of the peace in Point Roberts where they've decided to open a grocery store.

A grocery store? In Point Roberts? says mother in alarmed tones. Isn't that right across the border from Blaine?

I believe it is, says dad.

Back on the beach the next day, Gwen leans back on her elbows the way Frances does, the brim of her visor tilted at the same angle as the lifeguard's safari helmet. Jeanette arrives beside their blanket giving out the same grim smile that ladies do in the dancehall when they don't want people to see their real smiles. She has a new kinked hairdo widening in a wedge along her chin line.

I've never been so humiliated in my life, she says. All I was doing was practicing my synchronized at the hotel wharf like you told us to. I forgot my nose plugs and when I came back to serve lunch, I leaned over to give a guest his soup, I still had water up my nose and it poured straight into his *bowl.* You poor thing, says Frances, standing up and leading her into the lifeguard shack. Will you watch the beach for me for a minute, Gwen? Yell if anyone's in trouble.

Will she watch the beach? She's been waiting for months for someone to ask her to watch the beach. And Derek's looking at her from her parents' blanket, yay. The tide's too low for anyone much to be in the water, but Leo's still splayed out on the small float like a sea lion. The helmet Frances left on the blanket is still too big for her, but this time she finds a headband inside that tightens. Once she puts it on, she scans her head slowly from left to right and back again the way she's supposed to, but the next time her head swings back, Leo isn't there. She clutches at her chest but there's no whistle. Leaps up and races to the water's edge, but Percy's already on his way out to the spot where Leo's disappeared. He dives down and pulls him up sputtering.

What kind of lifeguard would let a twelve-year-old watch the beach? Who am I supposed to report this to?

Don't, Dad. It was just for a few minutes. She won't let me watch the beach again.

Good. What on earth were you doing, Leo?

The water was over my head so I thought the best thing to do would be to stand on the bottom and wait for my dad.

After they're all asleep that night, a bat gets into the attic and causes such a flap Gwen's afraid it'll fly under her nightie and start a ruckus like something unborn. Her mother gets up and hands up a tea towel for Derek to wrap the bat in before he lets it out the window.

30.

January, 1946.

Turn off that music, Gwen. Enough is enough. Her mother's shaking so much the knives and forks she's washing start rattling in her hand. She's started grinding her teeth at night too; the dentist is making her wear a plastic biting pad at night.

Her dad takes her gently by the shoulders and sits her down.

I don't understand what's wrong, Ada. You have three wonderful children. You have the house you always wanted. We're doing well at the plant. What *is* it?

Gwen's dry practising around the living room trying to extend her back strokes far enough to cover the full area of Crystal Pool. Turning the music up enough to drown her parents' argument, she spreads newspaper on the dining room table and glues tin foil stars onto a tiara she's cut from cardboard.

Is that girl responsible enough for us to be sending Gwen to train with her? I mean. It's one thing at Bowen when she's ten minutes away from home. As long as you pick her up on your way home after work, Percy.

No matter how shot her mother's nerves are, her dad's shirt still has to be pressed every night, the Peter Pan collars of her and Lily's blouses curved and smoothed. On his way home from the plant, her dad has to stop by the nursing home to see Grandpa Lyndon before coming to the west end to get her at Crystal. Three afternoons a week, she turns in her locker key and climbs in her dad's Dodge.

Wonder what Mom's made for supper, he says.

Porcupine meatballs, maybe.

Maybe. Gwen, your mother's going to St. Paul's hospital for a few days. For a bit of a rest.

She needs a rest from us?

It's not you, dear. She has trouble sleeping.

But she won't stay there for long?

No.

I can make porcupine meatballs, says Gwen. You mix ground round with rice and simmer them in tomato soup.

I'll look forward to that.

Rain slants across the car windshield the one night Frances is to drive her home – Percy's got an extra stop now at the hospital so maybe it won't hurt to trust Frances this one time. Frances's chipmunk cheek turns up so she can read the street signs lit by the traffic lights. Do you mind if we go a bit out of the way, Gwen? It won't take a sec. Instead of turning right over Burrard Bridge, she swings the car north. On east Hastings, discouraged looking people sit on curbs holding bottles inside paper bags, slop through multi coloured puddles from the neon signs. The rain pelts down and bounces off the sidewalk. Frances parks, leaves the motor running. I'll only be a sec, Gwen. Just wait here.

It's way more than a sec. Sitting by herself in the car doesn't seem like a good idea so she gets out, ducks into a vestibule, pulls open the door that she saw Frances go through. But it must be the wrong place because it's all men in there drinking and talking. But there's Frances alright in her synchronized sweatshirt with the crest on the back leaning into the face of a short slim man in a jacket and tie with one foot on the bar railing. Closer up, she can see that the faces at the tables are women's faces. As soon as you stop looking at the clothes, they're women. The barman, barwoman she should say, is drying a glass. This little lady might be a touch under age, she says touching Gwen's sleeve. The person Frances is talking to is wearing a hat and tie but when the man turns around it's Jeanette.

There's nothing to talk about, Frances. I don't want to swim any more. It's as simple as that. I only came to class in the first place because of you. I can't always do things your way.

Who are you meeting here? asks Frances.

Jeanette turns away. No one. I love you, Fran, but I have to have to be on my own for a while.

So I see. You're not supposed to be in here, Gwen. Let's go.

Nothing for Gwen to do but fold up what she's seen in the back of her mind, take it out later and see what she can make of it. They're a ways up Burrard when she sees her dad's Dodge in the hospital parking lot.

I can get out here, Frances. My mom's in there. My dad's visiting her. I can go home with him.

I should have taken you home first.

It's not that. It's… he's going that way.

I didn't know your Mom was in the hospital.

She's just tired.

When Gwen takes the elevator to her mother's floor, she finds the door closed. *Your mother doesn't like being touched. What were you doing then kneeling with your face between her legs when I opened the door by mistake that time?* Now when she knocks and hears her dad say come in, he's stretched out on the bed stroking her mother's cheek. I had no idea how difficult your job is, Ada. Lily can't find her shoes. I haven't made the sandwiches. Gwen's got that *Stardust* on for the hundredth time. Leo's slept through the alarm and I'm trying to get to work *all at the same time.*

Thank you, Percy. That helps. They sent a psychiatrist in this morning. He had the nerve to say I'm depressed because I think you're having an affair.

The intimacy of their laugh then; she'll remember the trust in their voices until the day she dies. So that's what marriage is like, she thinks. That's what you get. Their seeing but not seeing her gaze makes her feel safe. She's glad they have each other. Her dad gets up, tries to turn the knob on the balcony door. It's locked, he says forlornly as if that's the worst part of his wife being in the hospital.

How are you, dear?

Fine. How are you, Mom?

Her mother reaches for her hand and pulls her close to the bed. Much better. The rest is doing me good.

Will you be coming to the championships?

Of course I'll be coming to the championships.

She will too. She's the mother who makes satin hunter and huntress outfits for figure skating shows, ices pink cookies for the whole class on Valentine's Day. Nobody's Christmases compare to theirs. Maybe her mother takes on too much like her teachers say she does herself.

How did you get here, Gwen? she asks. Did you walk?

No, Frances drove me.

Her parents look at each other as if to say: oh her.

Well, you'll be able to drive home with dad.

Vancouver's Crystal Pool is built out into the sea; a balcony with potted palms lines three sides of the rectangle. In the locker room, Frances leads Gwen past an array of elaborate bathing suits, bras, and Mardi Gras headdresses. Satin capes with the swimmers' names scripted in sequins. Peacock feathers. Someone's hosing down the floor. She marches her through a gauntlet of professional looking swimmers to a cubicle at the far end of the dressing room.

Never mind them, Frances says, holding up the starry bathing suit by the straps so her protégé can step into it

I didn't know it was going to be like this. I'm scared.

Of course you're scared. That's what gets the adrenaline going. It's when you're not nervous before a competition you have to worry.

Her mother would say later that Frances should have made sure Gwen had more chances to practise under water with the music. As it is, the tinfoil stars on her bathing cap fall off as soon as they get wet. The pool seems way bigger than it's supposed to; her routine doesn't cover half the area. But it doesn't matter because her parents are up there watching—no Leo, no Lily, just the three of them alone together. Me and my mom and my dad. It doesn't matter if she doesn't come up smiling. Or if she comes last, which she does in no uncertain terms.

In fact, what's the point of contorting your body over and under the surface of the water, trying to stick your leg up and take it down again? If the audience could see under water from the side of a large tank the way they do at aquariums, it might be different. Maybe one day they'll have that—or screens mounted beside the pool that show what's going on underneath—but they don't now.

Driving home, her mother turns to her in the back seat, shame-faced. I had no idea what kind of scale this was on, Gwen. I would have made you a costume.

It's okay, Mom, she says. I learned a lot.

She did too.

TIDE IN MY EAR

31.

September, 1951.

Halfway down the seedy block of Hastings east of Woodward's, Lottie Fenn picks her way between scraps of crumpled newspaper and empty cigarette cartons. In the window of a pawn shop next door to some kind of *outré* nightclub, she spots the unmistakable silver whistle with its odd marking like a crying mouth in a cocoon that Noriko'd given Takumi years ago when he started his lifeguarding work.

That whistle? Lottie says to the proprietor who lifts it from its dusty velvet backing.

It's been here a long time, he says. Odd how no one's asked for it. Don't often see a solid silver whistle. A woman came in years ago and pawned it.

Lottie tucks the talisman in her purse, continues her walk down to Woodwards where she finds Evvie Gallagher checking out groceries, masses of brown blonde hair still kinking over her forehead like nasturtium stems.

Miss Fenn. Long time no see.

Hello, Evvie. Helping your father, are you?

I had a job at the boat-building yard, but the war ended, eh?

It did that.

Lottie! Frederick Gallagher buoyantly perks the grapes as

he makes his way up the aisle, still debonair in his white shirt and elastic armbands. How are you? We've missed you. I did some clearing at your place last summer. George said something about Blaine. Are you teaching down there? You look well. We *do* have pitted dates, he says to a customer. Tea's here. Nabob? He tucks a parcel into the customer's cart, nods her on her way.

How are you, Frederick?

I'm fine. Harriet died, of course. It was a long sickness but Evvie's been a help to me. You know Isabelle's married? To that nice Jack Long fellow, although he's... not the same... since he came back from overseas. They're in Point Roberts. I'm sorry I never managed to arrange a light on your island. You'll be back next summer? Oh good. Maybe we can still do it. Excuse me, this is one of my regulars.

It'd been a long trip from Vancouver to Prince George where Takumi and Shima changed trains for the coast; when they began their descent from Terrace to Prince Rupert, the Skeena opened into a broad estuary between the wide vista of coast mountain and the sea. They thought the long thin striations in the mountains were cracks of snow but, as they came closer, realized they were waterfalls.

Prince Rupert is a cannery town built above the railway tracks in the deep natural port of Tuck Inlet. The smell of fish permeates the harbour. Thin lines of masts maze the gill netters lining the docks of Cow Bay. Men on top of railway carriages break huge blocks of ice and drop them in the cars. Takumi found a warehouse at 8th St. and 1st Avenue that would only need a kitchen and a bit of wiring before he and Shima could move in. Below it, someone had broken a trail and set up an old

gill netter drum for a picnic table. Creeks cascade through deep
ravines over gravel and through wet cedar. Wooden stairs rise
on an angle, take a break, find their way up another face.

Once they're settled and find a school for Shima, Takumi
gets more work on a fishing boat, makes long runs up the coast
past Metlakatla and Port Simpson as far as the entrance to the
Khutzeymateen. The man he works for knows from years of experience where the rocks are, the channels he can or cannot go
through. Stuck with a rented boat when he'd saved so long for
the one he'd bought and lost, he tells Takumi and Shima that
in the old days skiffs were hooked onto a tow line, hauled out
to the fishing grounds by a tug and let go one after the other.
Long oars and a few boards to sleep under. He was working on
his boat when the armed navy guys marched in as if he and his
fellow workers had broken some kind of law. They had to put
down their tools and go. You weren't allowed to go back for food
and clothes. Nobody had done anything wrong but the officials
issued warning shots if you fell behind.

One day when Takumi and his boss Senji are headed for the
area of sand bar near Kennedy Island known as the Glory Hole,
neck and neck with other boats racing to get to the spot where
masses of sockeye gather, they find themselves so crowded they're
almost bumping off each other like play cars at a fairground.
Ready to manoeuvre into what they call the hot spot when the
opening cannon goes off like a starting gun. The fishery closes
on the weekend so the fish would have adequate escapement to
the spawning grounds. Senji's double take is so violent it's as if
a rocket has exploded: the boat beside them might be from a
different cannery but he'd be able to pick her out a mile away.
That's my goddamn boat, he cries. It's so much an extension of

himself he wants to turn the wheel and smash it, better that it's at the bottom of the sea than in someone else's hands.

A few days later he shows Takumi and Shima a photograph of scores of Japanese fishing boats that were confiscated in Vancouver. If I'd known, I would have come down and sunk them, Takumi says equally bitterly.

After that, Shima wants all the creatures they make in the studio to have gills. They pour concrete into careful molds, combinations of boats and fish; since the sculptures would be destroyed if they sink them in water shallow enough for the keel of a boat to hit them, Takumi hires a barge and sinks them a ways down the coast.

Later, father and daughter rent a trailer on a lake in the Kispiox Valley north of Hazelton. When her father goes out to ski on his own, Shima watches him come back across the lake, a dot that grows larger and more variegated around the edges as he comes closer. On their way into town to get groceries, she skis behind him, the blue shadow of a twisted spruce lengthening as they glide. The straight path of a jet draws a line between the clouds. At the end of the lake they ride their snowmobile as far as the highway, the back of Takumi's jacket blowing in Shima's face. Duck snow-covered branches, leaning to the side to keep the machine level as he widens the trail. She thinks she sees a lynx disappear into the spruce. He tells her they have big loose prints and they stop the snowmobile to check.

Approaching the Hagwilget bridge that crosses the deep canyon before Hazelton, they marvel at the power of Stegyawden, the mountain at the junction of the Bulkley and the Skeena. They're stopped in a highway repair line-up when Shima sees a cross by the side of the road.

That's to say there's been an accident there, Takumi explains. It's a custom in Mexico. I guess someone brought the idea here. So family and friends will think about the person who died whenever they pass.

Did my mother have an accident?

Yes, Shima. She had a serious accident.

He looks so sad she doesn't ask any more questions.

32.

October, 1956.

Back on the island, Lottie takes it upon herself to visit Scarborough where she finds her brother admiring the view from the comfortable wicker chair on the verandah; pride of place brightens his face like the expanse of the Sound under the sun. He looks so at home he could be whittling a stick.

Too bad all you've got to look at is that brick wall, Lottie says.

Being needed here matters, eh? he says smugly. Flora'd said the other day she didn't know how she'd ever repay me for my help. The place was beginning to feel as much mine as hers. Oh, and did I tell you the new management at the hotel gave me work? I got the contract to tear down the picnic tables near the cottages on the Point. Put up a few gates to separate the riffraff from the hoi polloi sort of thing. You can't dock your boat in the Cove any more if you're not going to have dinner at the hotel. It's a new era, Lottie.

So I noticed, she says.

They'd raised the rents so high she'd had to take a smaller

cottage in the Orchard.

D'you know, asks George. Turns out that Japanese Yoshito kid survived the war in the bush. Showed up here trying to claim his house. You have to hand it to him.

Yes, you do.

Of course we (*we?*) had to give him the bad news. Don't know where he went after he was here.

And now look. Here's Lily Killam coming up the path with her clear, clear skin and yard-length wavy hair. A golden retriever called Roxy has taken Molly's place. Shy with people, Lily's nonplussed when it comes to knocking on a neighbour's door and asking if Duke or Max could come out for a walk. Roxy haunches on the top step as Lily folds herself over her dog, draping her long limbs over the animal's gorgeous fur.

Roxy's the nicest person I know, she says.

You can still take the Black Ball ferry from Horseshoe Bay to Bowen Island but the end of the steamship era put an end to the picnics. The dancehall closed down. Half the cottages are torn down. Get out of here, the summer kids are told when they go to the hotel desk to ask for ping-pong bats or putting green clubs. Are you guests? Whoever heard of having to be guests?

When Lottie's coming up the entrance path to the hotel – even the hotel is closing and she's volunteered to help with auctioning of the hotel's furniture and linens—who should be standing in the window done up in his bowling whites but Frederick Gallagher. In the summer, he always attends the fortnightly management meetings; today he's planning to bring up the question of the light on Lottie Fenn's island. Now that he's retired, he can concentrate on projects like this and his gardening. Come to the window, he says to the new manager, so I can show you where I mean. But the tide's high and they see nothing.

Never mind, he'll come back and show him later after he sees to things at the lawn bowling green. The new manager stands on one foot and then the other. We've been meaning to tell you, Mr. Gallagher, the lawn bowling is closed to the public. Since you're a cottager, you're welcome if you pay the non-guest membership fee.

I've volunteered for over a decade as the president and caretaker, you don't think…?

But they don't think. Outside, Lottie stands by the monkey tree mourning the state of the hydrangeas. When Frederick Gallagher comes out, deadheading is so much second nature to the two of them, they automatically re-assume with the hotel rhodos, not noticing the new manager frowning out the window.

It's the limit, Frederick says. I had today's tournament roster all lined up but they didn't even look at it. Had the nerve to ask me for a membership fee. I tried to bring up the subject of the light on your island but they were so high and mighty they weren't interested. High handed tone as well if I say so myself.

Thank you for trying. I know. Everything's changed for the worse. This poor azalea, says Lottie. Shinsuke would… I was going to say turn in his grave.

He would, says Frederick. Has anybody heard from them, do you know?

I don't know. It's so sad. How are your daughters, Frederick?

I told you about Isabelle… although Jack's… well, I said. Evvie might take over my job some day, she's that good at it. She misses her mother. Ada, I wish Ada would stop being anxious about everything. What am I going to do about the lawn bowling? Imagine them having the nerve to ask me to pay a fee. They can whistle for it, I'll tell you that.

Frederick and Lottie are standing on the hotel lawn with some former lawn bowlers watching the monkey tree come down. Difficult as it is for George Fenn to get under the branches with his saw, the execution takes place. The faces in the crowd are appalled, as if they're at a public hanging. The emblem of the heart of the place kicked aside by newcomers who haven't a clue about its history! When the tree's on its way down, the stump of its broken neck turned toward them, Frederick takes Lottie's hand as if to hold himself upright while his stomach lurches down with the tree.

He'd always thought Lottie looked at him for a second longer than she would have if she didn't care—sometimes he'd sit on the Point Point thinking about the way she touched the cameo at her throat as if making sure it covered the mottled skin underneath. As if that mattered. He'd hoped that his devotion to Harriet might stand him in good stead with Lottie, realized that the mildest flirting gesture could be interpreted as an indication of how he might behave if she (Lottie) were in Harriet's place (some day) and ruin his chances if, after a respectable amount of time, he found an opportunity to openly state his intentions. Their connection could help make up for the devastating loss of the tree—she was sure to squeeze his hand back—impossible to think of courting someone whose hand didn't feel right. He knows now he'd tried to fill the gap left by Harriet's illness by manoeuvring one or other of his daughters (not Ada though, Ada was immovable) into the place his wife'd occupied the way you'd move a pot onto an already heated burner so you don't have to turn on another one.

It's too bad that Isabelle doesn't have children, he says. And Lottie, who'd been wondering for months if the right moment to tell him about his granddaughter would ever present itself, is so taken aback she withdraws her hand.

So she doesn't like him. He'd always taken pride in his white flannel bowling pants; the last time he had them taken in, he'd tried them on with only the basting stitches in place. Pointed out to his tailor that, by taking the extra fabric off one side, he'd de-centred the crease. Wouldn't it look better if he took a little off both sides? Had them re-done for this moment, he realizes, but Lottie is looking at him as if daring him to assume that the sweetness of her demeanor would ever diminish her resolute will.

She would have been the only neighbour on the Point that winter Isabelle spent on the island. Maybe Isabelle complained to Lottie—warned her?—how harsh and demanding he was. There's justice to it but in the glaring afternoon, the monkey tree flat on its back, his hopes for Lottie dashed, he feels that his days are as numbered as the designated lots in the subdivision that they're proposing to create from the dear old resort.

33.

December, 1958.

What's all this? Percy says at Blenheim St. going through the pile of mail by his plate. At Christmas he picks up each card, glances at the name, turns it over. Never heard of them. Never heard of them. That's not funny and you know it,

Ada says. Of course they bought the Blenheim St. house so the children could live at home and be close to the University. At supper what's all this turns out to be a letter from the Union Steamship Co. informing the Killams that the company is selling their shares to a firm that's interested in selling the summer cottages to the long term renters.

How could we be interested, Percy? says Ada. Where would we find five thousand dollars? You're not going out of the house in *that*, Gwen.

Gwen straightens her black jersey top, surveys her parents over the rims of her cats' eyeglasses. In case they don't know it, a few poets are coming up from San Francisco and Dr. Kerr's asked the class to join him at that new *ersatz* club up Dunbar. After dinner, she walks the few blocks up the hill to the black walled club with its orange and green paintings of broken up musical instruments. Percy said he went to visit a professor once when he was in Players Club. Guess what he served? Beer and cheese and crackers. Gwen didn't like to say but wasn't that a perfectly ordinary thing to serve? It was like the non sequitur of Great Aunt Eleanor letting her students paint pansies on the dining room walls.

At a small table, Dr. Kerr—Eugene, he says, they're to call him Eugene—is leaning on his elbows on the rickety table. The poem being read is by Robert Creely. *She was the lovely stranger who married the forest ranger, the duck and the dog and never was seen again.* She loves the way the reader sinks into the lines as if the images could slow down time itself. At the end of the event, Dr. Kerr says maybe they should go on talking over a bottle of wine at his place which turns out to be a stucco bungalow on a weedy lot in Deep Cove. Suit jackets hang on what should have been curtain rods. He opens the bottle of wine with a lethal looking corkscrew whose arms get raised when the screw gets put in like someone having a dress dropped over her head.

The next day, hoping she might see him, she sits with her books at the bus stop café, bent over a cinnamon bun, one layer of her hair teased over the nest inside. Reads the same paragraph over and over in a book about existentialism he'd mentioned in class. First time she's ever carried a book so people could see the cover. Dr. Kerr came up from Berkeley because he'd refused to sign a statement saying he was not now nor had ever been a member of the Communist Party. With his narrow face and olive skin, eyebrows slanting up to his salt and pepper hair, he strides down the mall, listing to one side with the weight of his briefcase as if his right leg is shorter than his left. Why is this place called British Columbia? he says. Why isn't it called its original name? And translations of peoples' names instead of the Salish? I mean. Moon Dancer. Stalking Deer. We don't go around calling Beethoven Beet Patch. Well, do we?

Strange combination of courses to be teaching: anthropology and theatre, but that's what he's doing. It's all she can do to find her way to her classes in the rain, learn to decipher the structure of Greek tragedy and Restoration comedy. The humanities are what keep people human, dad, she says at the dinner table.

Is that so? Is that something that, wink, wink, Dr. Kerr said by any chance?

One night when she's upstairs studying, she sees Grandma Flora coming up the walk on her father's arm. When Grandpa Lyndon died and it became clear Grandma no longer knew night from day, her parents said thank goodness for George Fenn who was willing to caretake Scarborough because Grandma wouldn't hear of selling it and they didn't want to upset her even more when they had to move her to a home that wasn't a home.

I'm in the doghouse, she says when Gwen goes down to take her coat.

Are you, Grandma?

It seems she took a taxi to the Union dock and was found waiting for a non-existent Lady Alex. The care home called Percy at the office to say his mother was missing. Locating her was what he'd call an educated guess. In the end, they'll have to move her far enough away she won't be able to call a taxi to anywhere she knows, like having to re-forest a cougar.

As the weeks go on, Gwen spends more and more time in the comfortable, dirty Players' Club green room above the stage of the old auditorium where she reads Allan Watts and talks with other students about expanding consciousness and becoming one with the universe. It says here that you have to submerge your life in a man's by abandoning yourself and letting the man awaken you. It's all about letting your mind go—where's it supposed to go? They must know how it's done, Lady Chatterley or whomever in For Whom. She wishes she could ask them. They'd probably tell her to read more carefully.

You're not angry enough, Gwen, Dr. Kerr says as they're rehearsing The Flies by Jean-Paul Sartre. How could she not be angry enough? Her legs are tight and strong, she's extending her wings like a giant bat so the First Fury can hurl herself diagonally across the stage to belt her wicked speech at Orestes and Electra who are sleeping innocently at the feet of what will be the statue of Zeus. (Right now a chair is standing in.) Herr director looks as if he thinks they're too young and inexperienced to be doing this play. They are. What the author's trying to say, he explains, is that everyone has an inexpiable crime. Do they, she wants to ask at home at supper, but doesn't.

At the next rehearsal, Dr. Kerr asks her to think of a time when she was exceptionally angry. She'd wanted to go night skiing up Grouse; her mother said no and she railed like a banshee. Percy cornered her in the den and hit her every time she stood up. When she finally escaped and started out the front door, he asked if she'd ever forgive him. If I say no, will you hit me again? she said.

On stage at rehearsal that night she plans to be as angry as she was at her father. Dr. Kerr rushes up the stairs to the costume room and re-appears with a pile of—is it steaming—black velvet he holds out to her like an offering. Wear this, he says, and try the speech again.

Almost, is his verdict.

After the others leave, he takes her chin in his hand, turns her head gently back and forth until her hair loosens down her back. His eyes are brown as amber, his skin warm as a Brahms sonata. When he'd touched her neck in the Green Room, her bones realigned, some moved forward, others back into a position that would fit him better. *You left the door open and felt a tightness in your loins.*

At midnight on New Year's Eve, she gets up and drives to Eugene's house. When she rings the bell, he comes to the door with the phone crouched on his hand like a toad. Three auburn dachshunds scratch up, lift their small elegant faces. The only light in, you couldn't call it a room—later on she'd call it a loft— is a theatre spotlight on wheels.

You've come, he says, taking her coat. Do you smoke? he says.

No, you don't. On the couch; he pushes up the silver paper in his cigarette box, throws the empty box across the room for the dogs. The rain pizzicatos on the roof. Then his arms are around her waist, his head buried in her stomach. If she didn't like him so much, she'd be alarmed, instead is thrilled to find she knows exactly what to do. She picks up her fingers as if she'd just discovered them, checks their tips, leans over as if picking his hair for lice. When they can't get close enough to his scalp to find the exact touch he needs, she wants to throw them over her shoulders like tools that aren't fine enough to do the job. Maybe the slight touch of her teeth at his hair roots.

There's pink insulation even in the rafters of the bedroom. When they walk there awkwardly like a four legged animal, it's not where he wants to be. His feet cross the floor so quickly on his way outside, he seems to be whirring in place like an egg beater. It's dark out; grey clouds thicken with pent up rain. When he gently bends back her dripping face as if he were looking for a second mouth in her neck, her dress opens over one wet breast as she catches her breath, loving him, loving the rain. Then his mouth is down on her; the pressure of his fingers and mouth just right, then not quite as she loses what's starting to build like getting a wrong note playing the piano but keeping going anyway. He stops as if she should go back and get it right. There's lots of time, he says. She catches, then loses it, but it's okay because no one else is meant to do this. She loves his touch so much that everything closed in her body wants to open at once. The ends of his eyebrows are broken lines. Later, he gently slips off his condom and tenderly wipes the inside of her thighs. You need a little time, he says. The dogs settle down, content that at last there are people here who know how to lie in front of a fire and breathe.

One night she and her father somehow get into a discussion of the cold war.

Dad, she says, the cold war ends up being a lot of people making a profit from the proliferation of weapons. You know that.

He doesn't even bother to say what professor are you parroting now.

What do you think kept our house afloat and gave you kids reliable meals and warm beds all through the forties, Gwen? What do you think we were making all those years down at the plant? Ploughshares?

The next night she and Eugene go to see *Hiroshima, Mon Amour* at *The Varsity*. In the film, the lovemaking is mixed up with the porous, decapitated dead. A blue flash, the bleached landscape of Hiroshima and Nagasaki. Legions of walking dead stagger in from the epicentre. People with flesh hanging off their bones, eyes puffed out of their faces. When she comes home, Percy is watching television in the den.

I just saw a film about Hiroshima, Dad. I didn't have any idea. The war was almost over, wasn't it? Why did they have to detonate two bombs? Nagasaki as well.

Hiroshima ended the war, he says coldly. You don't have the faintest idea what it was like.

You should see the film, dad.

Your mother and I don't have time to go to films. Do you have any idea how frightened and panicked everyone was, Gwen?

One night lying on Eugene's couch, she's seized into a spasm that has nothing to do with him; the intensity takes her so far away she's surprised after it's over to find herself in the same room.

So that's it? she says.

That's it. He looks as if he might congratulate her.

She can't fall asleep at his place, she has to go home. The porch light is still on and her mother is sitting in her father's chair.

Why are you waiting up like this, Mom?

We couldn't reach you, Gwen. The phone number you gave us rang and rang. It's your grandma. She managed to take a taxi to Horseshoe Bay after all, got a ride on the new launch they've started for hotel guests, said she was a guest. You won't believe it after the number of times we've said it was an accident waiting to happen, but the yacht hit the rocks on Miss Fenn's island. Quite a few were rescued, but Grandma Flora drowned.

No.

She did.

Oh Mom, I'm so sorry. Where's dad?

Over there of course.

She puts her arm around her mother's shoulders. I'm so sorry, Mom.

We should have moved her here, says Ada. We did the wrong thing.

Gwen doesn't see Dr. Kerr again until after the service. We'll rehearse around you, he says on the phone. On opening night, black-tighted legs ready to spring, she stands in the wings waiting to go on, turns to Herr Director for a good luck kiss expecting him to whisper softly even if it's break a leg but he suddenly raises the back of his hand quickly to the side of her face. He doesn't nick her, but it's that close.

Her mom and dad are in the audience. Afterwards in the lobby trying to talk to them, she finds herself looking over their heads trying to find Dr. Kerr. They say they think it's an awful play, and look at her in alarm. When everyone's gone she goes back to sit in the auditorium. He comes up the aisle.

If you ever do that again, I'll leave the play. I'll leave you.

I heard you were good. I had to do that. You weren't angry enough.

You weren't there, she says. You weren't in the audience. I could feel you not in the audience. I can't stand it if you're not there.

Why?

I don't know.

A few days later, her parents say it's time they met this man she likes so much. What if they had him over for supper? At the table, Percy looks at Eugene accusingly. *If you hurt her, we'll kill you.* Ada's put out the good silver and given him the best view of the rhododendrons. *Make it so they like each other,* Gwen thinks *Make it so my loving him is all right.*

I hear you didn't think much of the play, Eugene says.

It was different, Ada says.

There's a level people might not have understood. The play was first produced in France during the Occupation. On one level, it's an invective about the price of the citizenry going along with the Vichy government's collaboration with the Nazis. Taking advantage of an expedient situation because it's the path of least resistance. The cost of that. The punishment for that kind of thing.

Why didn't the playwright say so? asks Percy.

He couldn't. He had to say it was about ancient Greece in case he was persecuted. He had to use a code.

Did he? says Ada. Well, we wouldn't know anything about

that kind of thing.

Her dad asks if Eugene is following the Lions. Strange how he misses playing football, he says, the contact with the other players on the field. Eugene gets up, goes around behind him and picks Percy up off his feet.

He's nice, says Ada, after he leaves.

He's not as smart as the thinks he is, says Percy, drying the dishes.

Knows more than you do though, Gwen thinks. I expect you're wondering if we're going to get married, but it doesn't matter all that much.

Doesn't *matter?* Who told you that?

We probably will, Dad. We'll never leave each other if that's what you're worried about.

If there are children, it will make a heck of a difference if you have legal protection or not, my girl. But that's a long way down the line.

Actually, she says, we're thinking of going to California for the summer to a place he's rented in a canyon at Big Sur.

You certainly are not, says Ada. You're going into teacher training next year and carrying on at Jasper this summer. The years you've worked up there have paid off. We're proud that you earned all of your tuition.

I'm not going to do that, mother. I'm in love with Eugene and I want to be with him.

You try living by your feelings and see where it gets you, Gwen, says Percy.

Her parents look miserable and forlorn but there's nothing she can do about it.

BUTTONHOLE THAT MAN

34.

March, 1961.

One of her favorite parts about being at Eugene's is prowling around his heaps and shelves of books. A file of periodicals turns out to be an old record of areas around Howe Sound. She takes it home and reads late into the night, unveiling what life on the coast was like in the old days, the fog stretching to shape and re-shape the humps and islands into constantly shifting forms. There was a god who could take himself apart and put himself back together in different shapes depending on his whereabouts.

When Eugene drives them up the Sea to Sky highway to Squamish and they pass Horseshoe Bay, she regales him with the news that herring roe on cedar branches had been famous down there in what they called Ch'axhai. It takes her the whole length of Roger Curtis to Hood Point to pronounce the swallows and catches emitting from the back of her throat that name her own island, Xwlil'xhwm. Her heart pounds like the quick drumming ground which translates the name. Passage Island is Smetlmetlel'ch, how would you pronounce that? It seems Eugene's interest is more or less academic; he wants to tell her about the highway in California that stretches from Carmel to Big Sur. How, when you're driving it, the rest of the world fades to black and white compared to its Technicolor splendor. The locations in the Sound she's speaking about are so psychically fragile they fade with his lack of interest. The only reason they're taking this drive is so she can finish her paper (for him actually) so they can head out for a real city like San Francisco. He reaches for her thighs and tucks them closer to his own. His pants are different from other peoples'. Softer, more European looking. She wonders where he gets them.

What a place for a highway, he says. Aren't there avalanches?

Sure there are avalanches but people build anyway.

I see that.

They pass the gloomy foreboding wedge of Anvil and turn inland. Near Brackendale, they stop for lunch at a beaten up board and batten restaurant called Chee-kye where, the waitress tells them, a lot of black ash once swept down the mountain from Garibaldi. A few people survived the flood because they made it to the top of the extinct volcano that looms in the distance.

Sunny banks of white and pastel houses climb the hills down the coast of California from San Francisco through Daly City. Dry hills tufted with sage and pampas grass widen and deepen. At Carmel, they carve around a point of massive amber cliffs; turquoise swells in the ocean hurl themselves through holes carved in the rocks. On the horizon, spume mists as the breakers crash.

They veer down a slope of the highway and turn sharply away from the coast into a low grove of walnut trees. Later, when they go back to Carmel to shop, they splat from the overhung canyon into the blue and white seascape, eyes blinking in the bright light as if they've been sprung from a theatre. Further up the canyon behind a grove of bay leaf trees, they find the split level rental built on stilts near a stream. Gwen puts potatoes in the oven and goes out exploring, forgetting about them until they start smoking. Eugene makes sandwiches to replace the wrecked potatoes, puts one on a plate beside her but she's so entranced with the bay trees she's trying to describe in her journal, she forgets to eat, instead distractedly presses the bread with the flat of her hand until it's like dough again.

She had no idea it was possible to be this happy. The sun is a constant benediction. Above the mattress on the floor, she memorizes the lines where his limbs sketch the air. When he's up it's the opposite. He's by the sink; he's in the kitchen, leaves no trace of where he's been. One minute he's soft and adoring; the next he's leaping out of bed standing at attention like a drill sergeant.

Dear Mom and Dad, We had a glorious time in San Francisco. It pulses with light. The bells on the cable cars remind me of the milk truck that used to come down Blenheim. The hill to the square at Grace Cathedral is a steep slope with sections staired into the cement like the old ramp down to the Sannie wharf. I'm making notes about everything. You can't swim, though, there are currents and sharks. In ways San Francisco's like Vancouver because of the sea and the coast but the streets are narrower, more charming, and built up steep hills. It's as if life here is in Technicolor....

Logs flick blue streamers in the fire. Scales glow under a piece of wood lying face down, its arm stretched across the iridescent dome of a sloped ceiling. Beams burst into flames and fall.

In bed, he searches her body as if the answer to whatever he's after is hidden in a touch of her flesh he hasn't discovered yet. The pillows are god knows where. Sometimes she feels headless after making love. She doesn't like to say so but she does.

Isn't it a beautiful day? she says when she takes his coffee out to him. She's said that every day since they arrived.

Gwen, he says. It's always a beautiful day down here.

He's working on some notes for a production he has in mind he wants to propose to the Academy of the Arts back in the city. Anybody who can pay can go to this university, he says. No one's going to ask about his history with UC. While she waited for him to finish his interview, she climbed up one hill of the roller-coastered city, down another. The slopes raised and lowered their faceted white and mirrored buildings like salt crystals. He looks up wanting more coffee. She pours it. I can't quite get the curtsey down, she says.

Oh, Gwen. What are you going to do here, love? You can't just.... He runs his hand up the inside of her thigh.

Well, yes, I can. That's the trouble.

Even if what she says is true—it is—she still dreams about directing him in Artaud's *Picnic on the Battlefield*.

I don't suppose you ever act.

It's been a long time.

You wouldn't consider....

When he doesn't even look up, his silence undermines the fact she'd even thought of asking.

Dear Mom and Dad, Eugene and I went to the theatre almost every night when we were in San Francisco, but I didn't see anything that resembled the kind of theatre I want to do. The theatre I want to create will not take place inside a proscenium. It's something else but I don't know what it is.

Thanks for writing. That's great you've found the money to buy the cottage with Evvie and Isabelle. So now are you all three owners or what?

That night in bed he leaps from rock to rock in his own torn river; when he kneels close to her face, his penis gently slaps her cheek before she takes it into her mouth. She keeps expecting him to surface with a glinting rock in his hand, but he flings his hair back and dives again. When he's done, is on his feet looking in the mirror, she catches the self-absorbed look he would present when he's alone. He comes back and picks up the blanket where she's lying on the floor.

Oh, you're sitting on it.

Is there any Kleenex? Be polite, Eugene.

She feels more self-contained when she includes his name, not that she wants to be self-contained. She lives more every day for his emptying touch.

One day out on the dappled deck, the part of her that's deliriously lost in the landscape of her body is surprised to hear the part of herself that's worried about making mistakes saying she might go up to the city on her own for a few days and see some theatre.

Why would you want to do that? What's wrong with here?

Nothing's wrong with here.

It would be years before she'd understand that undertaking this trip by herself was a wake up call she didn't hear. Isn't she happy? She's as happy as the cat's meow, but please will he drive her to Monterey where she could rent a car. He looks smaller and narrower sitting in the driver's seat; maybe the confidence that seems to be inside him has something to do with her after all.

The man behind the car rental counter at the airport is reading Proust so he must be all right. Who was that bounder in was it *Vanity Fair*, something by Thackeray anyway, where the protagonist rigged up a library with classic books in the disguised wing of a brothel so the ingénue would think she was staying with her kind of people? Funny that. He has a receding hairline, a wide flushed face with something of the breadth of a frog about it. I'd like a car, she says when he looks up. Is there a way to San Francisco that's not the highway? He smells a little rancid, sweat mixed with shaving cream. An alert looking young woman with short curly black hair and white short shorts joins him. What's your name again Gwen, why are we letting Gwen pay a surcharge on this airport car, Rory? Didn't you tell her we have a dealership in town that costs half of what you've got here? Suppose they took the car Gwen's renting to their alternate franchise, she could use what was probably her hard earned money to rent the cheaper car—then they could leave Maria's car at her place and all three drive to the city. Oh I think, says Gwen. If you could give me a map that marks the back roads, I'd be fine. But no. They make arrangements, and next thing she knows they're in the middle of Monterey changing to another car with a tank of gas thrown in because they're both employees. Gwen's to drive it.

Out on the freeway, somehow her suitcase is in Maria's car so she has to follow them; she's already a few cars behind, sandwiched between two six wheelers that hoist her between them catamaran style. They haven't even said which exit they're taking. Why isn't she safely back in her own place in the canyon? Her own place now, is it? One ratty palm replaces another; the vehicles hum beside her. Her first artichoke field. She's six cars behind. They change lanes quickly, so she has to. Over there, over there, sidestep. Any minute they'll turn off to what's her name's, Maria's house. She's made the exit: they're slowing onto a side road. I have someone staying with me, Maria says as Gwen gets out of the car. She's in the shower. This carpet was pure white when I left. Looks like she's been using it as an ashtray. Don't forget Gwen's bag is in my car.

When Gwen goes down the corridor to the bathroom, she passes the open bedroom door and finds all three of them in bed waiting for her eyes; the visiting friend is out of the shower and has her legs open. Rory is fingering her, Maria looking up to watch Gwen's face. Then she turns and eats her way up her friend's thigh. Gwen averts her eyes astonished and aroused. Rory puts his fingers under his nose, smells them. Time to go, he says. You girls have a good time. In the rented car, blackheads border the edge of his grey t-shirt. Maybe if she acts blasé and tells him he has nice teeth, he'll settle down, but what if they're false?

It's good to be driving again, he says. I've been in prison for a while. For marijuana possession. He slowly unzips the fly on his jeans, and starts pulling at his penis. Good lord. His smile is triumphant and sneaky as he keeps on driving and keeps on coming. They're on the outskirts of San Francisco; there has to be a traffic light soon. He spurts all over the dashboard, smiles as if he's filling up a water pistol and starts again. He glances over to see if she's watching, aims a shot at the floor. At the first red light, she jumps out of the car and runs. She has her purse but not her suitcase.

Oh god, the car. She stands stock still on the pavement. It's in her name. What if he doesn't take it back? Maybe he never worked at Hertz. Steal a car by getting a stooge to rent it and cover your tracks by scaring her out of the car so she takes the rap. If he steals it, what then? She's liable. She catches a bus north on Van Ness along Lombard St. thinking to try to find the beaches at Golden Gate Park. A dirty curtain sags from a sliding rack in the motel she checks into; the thumping of what must be laundry machines pummels from the floor below. As long as he takes the car back, that horrible man. She should phone Hertz to make sure, instead heads toward Washington Square where the tall spires and domes of the Church of St. Peter and St. Paul rise to one side. A low stage has been set up on the grass and a group of Commedia del Arte actors in patch-work costumes are working the lunchtime crowd.

Back in the canyon—there's a bus to Monterey after all— Eugene meets her at the station, clamps her palm to his arm as if he'd known how dodgy her trip was. He doesn't say anything about a phone call asking about a missing rental car. Later she tells him how the troupe in the park suggested she come back for an audition.

They'll give you an audition but you don't want to get in-volved with that crowd, he says. Nobody gets paid. What they'd do is *use* everything you have to offer.

You know them then?

Oh sure.

So even that is his.

The drive back down the coast is as spectacular as ever. Turning into their own canyon, the bay leaf trees comfort her. She's so glad to be back, her face feels bloated from the pressure of staring at him. She finally knows the trail to their place well enough not to have to leave crumbs behind. When they get home, he hands her her first joint. She holds it between her thumb and forefinger the way she's seen him do it. Her toes hook onto the edge of a path in the forest, lever her to a standing position beside a large pine. Eugene wraps his arms around her knees, pulls himself up on her as if she's a spar tree whose tip he must lop. A tiny star falls out of his eye. She catches it in hers. He steps naked from behind a tree picking out the star like a contact lens. She clutches her skin like a coat he'd thrown over her shoulders.

It's over now. I'm here, he says.

You've found me? You're here?

I'm here.

And you won't let go?

I won't let go.

Neither will I. Ever.

Their faces peels off like masks. They stand naked, face to face, their palms turned outward.

The next day he asks her to marry him. What was that out in the woods last night? she says. Isn't that what we did? Yes, he says, but I want the formality. Look how happy it would make your parents.

So will you?

I will. Yes.

Back in San Francisco, they sit on the curb outside his apartment resting from the late summer heat. She loves the brand new light, the mass of scrabbled facets forming the roofs and terraces sloping below them. The bay windows in the living room. The striped slip covers on the armchairs. The hardwood floors. In the afternoons, she dodges upturned wooden boxes in the narrow streets of Chinatown, buys recipe books about French Provençal cooking.

Do I look all right? she asks Eugene the night they're going to Sausalito to meet his mother. Shantung sheath, hair molded into a bouffant. The dress is enough, he says. No striped scarf.

They drive across the bridge to *Ondine's*. They're early so he pulls into a bar where he orders her a black coffee with brandy which he says will put lead in her pencil. In the restaurant, his mother, René Kerr, is sitting at a table in a corner with her back to the water. Handsome salt and pepper hair like her son's. A grey silk sweater set and black skirt, eyebrows arching elegantly above the deep shadow of her brow.

Hello, mother, Eugene says kissing her on the cheek. This is Gwen.

Hello, Gwen. Mrs. Kerr leans a wine menu card against a vase. I think this must be in Russia, don't you, Eugene? They have silver forests in Russia.

Who's having what? Anyone for a Bloody Mary? says Eugene.

René doesn't look at Gwen, not even sideways. Where do you live, Gwen?

Here, actually.

She looks up. Here in the city?

So he hasn't told her. I live with Eugene, she says.

Mrs. Kerr looks shocked, as if she'd only now noticed that her son's companion has two heads.

The honey locusts on the card form a sort of groved dell; licks of new grass spring in the spotlighted area. Early lady's slippers.

You're a student of Eugene's then, are you, Gwen?

I was. All I have left for my degree now is my thesis. There's so much *on* down here, in the theatre I mean. I stumbled on some actors in the park; I'd love to work with them. They can't pay anything but they're very Brecht and....

Mrs. Kerr is not listening. She's checking today's *Chronicle* folded by her side plate. Suddenly Gwen knows it was his mother Eugene was talking to on the phone that first night she drove out to Deep Cove. Eugene pulls the paper over as if he and his mother are involved in a conversation that's been going on for years. The two of them ignore their dinners—very nice too, crab for Eugene, steak tartar for René—Gwen picks up her knife and fork and starts in on her veal scaloppini.

How's the job hunting going, Eugene? says his mother. There must be dozens of colleges who would love to get their hands on you.

He smiles at her gratefully. I'm working on it, mother.

Afterward in the car, Gwen turns to him. Your mother's beautiful. She is, isn't she? Nice too. Gwen's quiet the rest of the way home. She can tell his mother expected him to do better. Somebody who'd be on a par with him. Somebody American.

A couple of weeks later, they undertake a civil ceremony at a Justice of the Peace office and Gwen sends her parents a candid camera shot taken by a stranger. In the weeks that follow, Eugene's not home much, but getting the meals and going to the Laundromat doesn't take that much time; it's fun being at the market with a basket over her arm shaking bunches of parsley. As long as she has mornings to herself. She does have a thesis to write. She's nervous before he's due home in case she's bought the wrong thing, like the time she bought turquoise and chartreuse paisley sheets she could see in his eyes were all wrong. Evidently sheets are meant to be plain cotton with so many threads to the square inch. He'd stood by the bed, rubbing the fabric between his thumb and finger, frowning at her.

The night they climb over the juniper hills of Lafayette Park and down to Pacific Heights to visit René and her mother-in-law hands her stalks of gladioli to put in a crystal vase, she feels like the ugly duckling when it was recognized by the swans. Sometimes, after she and Eugene make love, she finds herself in tears of appreciation that his mother brought him into existence. I like Eugene, her mother'd said, the night she brought him home for dinner. Even if he is a bit out of our class. Speak for yourself, Gwen'd thought at the time. She's not so sure of herself now.

On the way back from shopping one afternoon, she sees him in a bar talking to a man who's silent when he's introduced. When the man gets up to go to the bathroom, Eugene explains he's a student in one of the new courses at the Arts Academy; they were discussing his program when she'd plunked herself down and interrupted. I'm sorry, she says and leaves. There's all kinds of protocol she doesn't understand. Half the time, she doesn't even know when she's stepped over the line.

Later that evening, she tells him that she wasn't on an ordinary walk. She'd been to the doctor and she's pregnant. Think of it. a small smile down there mirroring her own. Who cares if she puts the rug back at the wrong angle after she vacuumed? Flung pine nuts and sage into the cheese tortellini without thinking about the flavours? Soon she'll evolve into a swollen balloon with flat cardboard feet that no one can push over because it'll whap right back up.

Dear Mom and Dad, It's good to hear you two are going to the Cariboo together this year. My big news is that we're pregnant and I'm going to have a baby. We're thrilled and I bet you are too, eh? Eugene's teaching work is going well; and I still love San Francisco.

The first three months she's queasy and her breasts hurt. The fourth month she feels better and suggests maybe she could get a bit of subbing work to build up their coffers for later when she'll be looking after the baby. She folds back the paper. Eugene, did you know that immediately after the Japanese surrendered in World War II, Vietnam declared independence? They had no idea the French would try to take over. She looks up. Well, why wouldn't they? There was all that rubber.

One day she's called in to teach at Mission High School, a white spacious building with a domed tower, lots of black and Hispanic kids. Her class—a double block of English and Socials—saunter in nonchalantly as if they don't mind going through the motions of being students. Is she the sub? She walks around the room looking at their work. These look interesting, she says. Book reviews, eh?

Eh? Are you Canadian? Yeah, we have to do our good copy, eh?

Good copy? Isn't that the routine of writing the same paper in better handwriting? How about an actual improvement?

Like what?

Find somewhere you've made a generalization and give us a detail. If you were writing about someone and said "she was insane" does that create a picture in your mind?

Not really.

But if you said "she plucked at her hair as if she heard something in it"? A light bulb goes on in the reader's mind, ah, she's a bit bonkers.

A bit bonkers. Is that Canadian?

Flannery O'Conner wrote that I think, someone like that. Sometimes you can't remember where you read things. Everyone's talking about Vietnam these days, aren't they? She sits on top of a desk in front of the room, surprisingly at home. Why are we over there anyway?

We already did this in world affairs, Mrs. Kerr. Let's do something fun, a boy in the back row says belligerently. The U.S. has to fight in Vietnam to keep communism from spreading, he goes on. Otherwise, Russia and Communist China are going to get the power and nuke us. The North Vietnamese are controlled by Russia and China and they give the Vietcong lots of munitions. He says this measure by measure as if parodying what another teacher said. Then he laughs nervously and looks around.

Do both the U.S. and Russia have nuclear weapons now? Gwen asks.

They think so.

So Russia could set off a bomb whether we're in Vietnam or not?

It could.

Someone else says it would be better to pull out, find a way to keep the peace. And they're off: hands up all over the place. People turn in their seats to look at those answering from the back. They look at each other for acknowledgement, and she realizes that any moment the discussion could collapse into their own agenda of trying to ascertain who likes who and all the rest of it. Keep it going, she says to herself. This is the hard part. She leaps in again. Did you know that Vietnam's been at war since the French occupation, back to 1890 actually? Why would the French want to be in Vietnam in the first place, class? Why would one country want to control another? Go to war over things?

Economics, power, says the same boy in the back. Why was she bothering, his look says.

She persists anyway. Say we're in that country, and we're flying over. A lot of bombing noises, rrrrraaaattttt—boys still make those noises even if they're fifteen? There would have been village after village and endless rice fields, right? During the French colonization period, the French and a few privileged Vietnamese replaced miles of jungle with rubber trees. Maybe there's a French businessman here who has an idea about how to make a lot of money. Does he make *a lot* of money? says the same boy from the back swaggering down the aisle. I'll be that guy. He plunks himself in the teacher's chair, puts his feet up on the desk. She steps to the side of the room.

What's your plan, Sir? What's your business plan?

I'm going to import a lot of rubber and sell it at a profit. I'll get a bunch of peasants to work for me cheap. I'm going to be a rich man and buy me a Cadillac.

What about the people here working the rubber plantations? How do they feel? Are there workers here? A few hands go up.

How much are you people being paid?

Practically nothing.

It'll be interesting to see what happens tomorrow when your plan goes into effect, she says. I wonder what kinds of conflicts might arise? And what about all that cheap offshore gas in Vietnam people would like to get their hands on? They say Japan pays a lot of money for it.

At home, she finds a few carrots and some broccoli in the bottom of the fridge. She'll make a stir fry, whatever. When Eugene comes in, he keeps his coat on, peers over her shoulder. Are you going to caramelize those onions?

It went well, she tells him. They actually *discussed* things. I figure—she hands him the spatula, grabs some paper and starts scribbling—a person could use this kind of drama to teach conflict of interest. Say a person set up a high level government meeting, Eugene, say I did. You could have one individual who already had shares in a rubber company and stood to make a lot of money if they acquired property in Vietnam. Then you'd say, what should that person do when it comes to voting about entering into a war?

Eugene hovers over the pot of rice tossing granules with a fork. Keep it simple, babe. You don't want to take on too much.

Maybe if you hadn't bailed from my thesis committee, you'd be taking more interest, Eugene.

He turns, raises his eyebrows.

Oh right, she says. I should be saying I rest my case. You did have a conflict of interest there. Anyway....

The next day the kids get straight into it. Let's get these desks out of the way, she says. Half the class should be reporters, half citizens. After the interviews, they decide it would be a good idea to circulate a petition, maybe over the whole of France, to see if people would be willing to share tires, drop their standard of living until the Vietnamese sort out the way they want to operate their own rubber plantations. One car between every three neighbours sort of thing. In the end, the students are the ones who suggest that people in the west are living too high off the hog and making fortunes in the arms trade. Their homework is write about what they, as individuals, would be prepared to give up seeing that the west has such a disproportionate standard of living.

At home, she's making a lesson plan for the next day when the phone rings. It's the school office saying that the regular teacher will be back the next day and they won't need her. She'd forgotten all about the regular teacher. *You need to get your teacher training, Gwen. You never know when you'll need something to fall back on.*

I want to go to some workshops so I can learn more about this stuff, she says to Eugene.

Well, he says smiling at her. It looks as if you're going to have that baby first.

She looks down. There is that.

He's brought some lumber to build a waterbed to help her aching back. He measures the length he wants to cut and saws it. Bless his heart for thinking of it.

The following weeks she feels exiled from the classroom and walks the streets after school hours staring in schoolroom windows. One day she wanders back to Washington Square thinking of the actors she met there as a kind of lost tribe. They'd be people who might be sharing a house where she'd be so welcome that, if she had no place to go, even if it were two in the morning, it would be okay to go in and find a bed.

Dear Mom and Dad, Jenny's grown a lot since I last wrote you. The nighties that were long when she was born are up to her knees and the long sleeves look like short sleeves. I'm glad to have the stretchy suits you sent, Mom, because they grow with her. As I sit writing to you, she's doing her favourite thing with her feet, putting them in her mouth. I can't wait for you to meet her.

What's the news from Leo? I sure hope he gets his tenure. Jenny's eyes are dark grey with more brown flecks in them every day. Eugene says the organization of her hair is a lot like his. Hope to hear from you soon.

It's not long before the days of the early marches when they thought the war would be over soon seem like cheerful picnics compared to the street action they're practising now. People are hauled off from sit-ins, their eyes and noses smarting from tear gas. Heading out on the front lines with Jenny in her stroller, Gwen tries to stay in the safe parts of the demonstrations where the police aren't likely to take a swipe at you if they don't like the cut of your jib. She finds herself endlessly typing and phoning at the Movement office. When they ask if she could come in and help, she can get everything done at home in half the time. The latest plan involves flying a plane low over the Bay area and dropping anti-war leaflets. Flying low is deemed a misdemeanor and the pilot and his team are arrested.

The morning a demonstration is planned to block the arrival of buses designated to pick up service men at the Clay St. induction centre in Oakland, she fixes her hair in a careful beehive, gets out her shortie coat, purse and heels, puts Jenny and her sign in the stroller and heads for the site. The night before she'd been to a street theatre company meeting and helped draw up a manifesto declaring their decision to abandon theatre in favour of resistance action on the larger world stage.

She's standing in the street calculating a safe position when police in hard helmets line up twenty abreast across the street, batons ready and waiting. National Guard officers in back up positions behind them. When the police start herding the demonstrators toward city hall, the white and gilt columns shine like beacons. The top section of the building looks like a giant wedding cake. When those on the flanks realize the manoeuver is designed to stop them blocking the intersections where the recruitment buses will be arriving, they look around for something to use for barricades. Lend us your car to block this street, someone hollers to a driver. When he shakes his head, a group of marchers start rocking the car until the driver panics, gets out and runs. Then they jam it into an intersection. The police surround them and begin to club and tear-gas. One policeman lifts Gwen up from behind by the elbows; another picks up the stroller and deposits it on the sidewalk.

I planned to stay in the safe area but there wasn't one, she tells Eugene at home.

You can't use a stroller as armor for heaven's sake I don't want you going on those marches anymore. He gathers Jenny up and turns away.

A morning comes when Gwen wakes up with aching ovaries. This time when she's on the table, the doctor stands with one hand inside her and one on her belly, explaining that her IUD's acted like a lightening rod. It's conducted bacteria into her ovaries and given her a low grade infection. Not to worry, once it's out—IUD devices are foreign objects after all—antibiotics will clear it up. Her husband should take some as well to be on the safe side. Once she's better, they'll have to figure out something else for birth control. They mean to, but, waking up groggy in the middle of the night, they turn to each other half asleep forgetting which body parts belong to whom let alone a condom the second time. So it's no surprise when her breasts start to ache and she wakes up nauseated in the mornings. All she wants to do is sleep.

A last push, a wall of unconscionable pain and then Maya's out squirming on the cord. When Gwen can't pee and they make her wait too long, the nurses scold that she could at least have waited for the bedpan. Swollen with tears and pain and relief that the birth is over and Eugene's there loving her. You, me, Maya and here's Jenny, he says one hand top of the other so a nurse can take their picture.

At home, life is a sea of milk and stitches. They put the TV at the foot of the bed. Marilyn Monroe gets up and puts her underwear in the fridge, so Gwen gets up and puts her underwear in the fridge. Blodged on the waterbed, she aches from her waist to her knees. Spokes pull milk down to the hub of her breasts as she jiggles her nipple trying to hit the moving target of Maya's mouth. The first few sucks are the worst. Half asleep, it's Eugene who unbuttons Gwen's nightie and props the baby on his hand to nurse as if he's staking a plant. Moving her to the other side so her mother can grab a few more winks, the three of them huddle together smelling like milk and flannel and skin. Diaper off, the baby squirts a line of bright yellow feces like toothpaste from a tube. Her legs churn. Warm cells multiply like incremental bubbles when a pot starts to boil. By the time Gwen gets the diapers washed, nurses, plays with Jenny while Maya's down, nurses again, fixes Jenny's lunch and gets the baby up, buys a few things at the store, her whole body aches and her day is done. This is what love is, Eugene says. This is what we do.

When the phone rings a few weeks later, it's Mission High asking if she could sub again. It's a *gig*, Eugene. It's only for a few days. I'll express some milk to leave. Maybe René would come over.

It's too soon, he says.

But they want me now. It's just for a few days.

I don't think mother will want to come. But maybe we can find a temporary nanny.

In the end, they find a temp agency; some of the kids remember Mrs. Kerr as she prowls up and down the aisles looking at papers on peoples' desks.

Hey, Mrs. Kerr. You've had your baby.

I have. This book? Have you people started it yet?

It's *The Chrysalids* by John Wyndham.

Our teacher says we'll read it when he gets back. I tried to start but I don't get it.

It's set in the future, somebody else says. Way in the future.

There's been a war. A nuclear war, Gwen says.

After a war, Mrs. Kerr.

So, it's happened, has it? Which side set it off? I guess the earth would be devastated whichever side set it off.

After this particular war, it seems that nothing will grow for thousands of miles. North America is a wasteland: raw, cold and in perpetual twilight. The students wander around the classroom in strips of black plastic. Survivors who manage to reach a precariously habitable area have no materials to make shelter. They live under piles of old junk and debris. The side of one house is a pretend smashed car yarded from a radioactive free zone.

What should we do about food? she asks. Should only the people who grow it be allowed to eat it?

No way. Everyone is doing a job. The food has to be put in storage and divided equally.

Does everyone agree with that?

Everyone agrees with that.

Later at home, when she's sitting on the closed toilet nursing Maya and reading the novel, Eugene kneels beside the bathtub pushing Jenny up and down in the water. If I can find a way to get the kids to explore the concerns in the novel *before* they read it, they'll experience the characters' situations more immediately, right? The excitement she felt outlining her ideas before he'd give her the go ahead on a paper has returned. He lifts Jenny into a towel. Maybe you shouldn't be getting involved with this right now, babe, he says. Couldn't it wait? Hasn't Maya been on that side for way too long?

Oh god, I guess she has. She changes breasts. I need a way to bring the kids in and out of role, so they can get some distance. I don't want them to get carried away and be upset.

I do see what you mean, he says. It sounds interesting, it really does.

The next day she meets individual students at the classroom door and presses a single uncontaminated seed into each hand. Keep this somewhere safe, she says. Each person should think of one important thing to do. Freeze into position so that, if you were turned to wax in a museum, people would know what you're doing. I see here a person who has a tool in his hand. What's in your mind?

I'm digging in the ground for a root.

I see here a person who has a hand on somebody's brow. What's in your mind?

I'm healing this sick woman.

I see here a person who has a weapon over his shoulder. What are you doing?

I'm guarding this village.

If the land around their enclave is mined with death, and cultivation has been achieved at considerable cost, what do the village people need to protect their progress? Would they need some laws? At the town meeting it's decided that each person is to get one litre of water a day. If anyone feels ill, they have to go to the hospital. No one will harvest the crops except for the agricultural workers.

At home, expressing milk into a bowl for the next day's bottles, it strikes her that her students may be working their way toward a collective agreement. When the question of communism comes up, she doesn't want to define it mechanically. Idealizing it would be a mistake as well. They should grow into the need for it. As she's talking, Eugene's picking up dirty stretch suits from the backs of chairs.

It sounds good, Gwen, but do you think Maya is getting her fair share? Of you I mean. The way Jenny did.

It's just a few more days. I'm only a sub. She fastens the flap of her nursing bra.

I know it's only a few more days, but then there'll be something else. Jenny's hanging onto his knees so he picks her up and plops her in the highchair.

Couldn't *you* get a sub and take some time off? Gwen says. Come the revolution, there'll be such a thing as paid paternity leave. What if an employer had to issue two cheques—same salary, two cheques—once there were children. If you're going to re-define the workforce properly, it's got to include whoever's doing the home job, right?

Eugene shrugs. Didn't I hear your dad say he always handed over his cheque to your mother?

The point is he had the power to do that or not do that.

He stirs cereal. Have you considered that politicizing our situation only camouflages the compatibility problem we're having?

Have you considered that sometimes you're a pompous asshole?

Well, I know that, darling, but is it relevant? They laugh then, especially when the lampshade chooses that moment to lop off its perch and slide down the stand to the floor.

Now we're really getting somewhere, she says.

Well, maybe we are. Who knows?

Look, I just want to finish this drama. The kids are into it which thrills me. There's something here that might relate to my thesis. And then I'll put the work on hold for a while.

Okay. I'll take a couple of days off.

I love you.

I love you too.

The next day at school she asks the students what they'll do if the crop they've prepared for winter ends gets destroyed by the weather. They could leave, they say. But they can't because there are still unexploded mines that might go off. What else, she asks, do people need besides food and shelter? TLC they say. That's it, people need a supportive family and community life. If survival is dodgy, the way people get along would matter, wouldn't it? In the novel you're going to read, the people have made a law. Because of the inherited deformities as a result of radiation, all humans are required to have one head, two eyes, one nose, two ears, two legs, two arms, ten fingers and ten toes. Anyone not having those body parts is not allowed to live. They're a small community and deformities might be passed on. What would happen in our village if the people tried to enforce that?

It'll have to go to a vote, someone says.

What if you vote against it, but it goes through anyway? What's a person supposed to do then?

You have to go along with it.

What if a large proportion of people don't like what happens when a government votes a law in?

Well, they'd have to form a party and run on their ideas. Or if there isn't time and it's something serious, I guess they go on marches.

Guess so, she says pointedly. They get it. Hallelujah.

That night she lies awake worrying about how to get the class to understand the possible results of the law they've made about deviants. It would be wrong to manipulate their piece, rob them of experiencing the consequences of their choices. She tosses and turns.

Gwen, you've got to get some sleep. Maybe you'll know in the morning.

The next day is Eugene's short day. He'll be home before her so would he be able to pay the nanny?

I thought you were going to pay her from your subbing cheque.

I don't have it yet. I need money to get groceries on the way home. Why don't we have a joint account, Eugene? I feel like a child, having to ask for house keeping money.

You're not making any for a start.

I'm doing the house. The kids.

How well, he has to ask.

Oh thanks.

He takes fifty dollars from his wallet and hands it to her.

The next day the phone rings as she's pulling up Jenny's tights. If she were in a TV ad, she'd be in a short skirt and high heels kneeling beside her child, not still laced with painful stitches. It's one of Eugene's colleagues. Why's she talking as if she doesn't know him, says the voice on the other end, they met at lunch the other day. Doesn't she work for that new antiques magazine? Another call to the nanny who hasn't arrived yet. Why's she still at home? She's not coming. He didn't pay her? Oh God. Nothing to do but take Maya to school with her. When she lifts the carry cot onto her desk, the boy who appointed himself inspector says it's clear to him the fingers on this child are exceptionally—he looks at the vocabulary word written on the board—deviant. He lifts a tiny finger and lets it fall back. Webbing is what we have here between what are supposed to be her fingers, folks. They look at their teacher to see how she's going to respond. Belief is everything, she'd said to them yesterday.

I was afraid something like this might happen, she says in role as the nurse in the village. I didn't vote for the law. Her fingers look normal to me.

Well, they would, wouldn't they? says the inspector. Maybe you have a vested interest in seeing things that way.

Wicked stroke of learning there, kiddo. She takes Maya from the girl who's holding her. Should they have thought more about the consequences of where some of these laws might take them? There's no way this baby should be sent out to die, she says. She's a little different, that's all.

Time to move over to where they talk about the play out of role; it's dangerous to let them get mixed up between reality and pretend. If laws are too rigid, might people rebel because of individual differences? She has Maya under one arm while she writes on the board. You've done a good job, people, she says. I'd like you to come out of role and return to the classroom. Please go to your seats and think about the play. Here are some possibilities. 1) Write an outline of a scenario for the play from here on. Or 2) Sometimes people make laws and become victims of the laws they create. Agree or disagree.

Wonderfully, there's a small office at the front of the room with a window placed at a level where she can see the students' bent heads and nurse the baby without anyone seeing. When everyone's settled, the principal comes in. He looks shocked when he sees her doing up her blouse and the baby in her arms. I'd like to talk to you after school, he says quietly. The kids look up and then down again.

After school, the secretary looks equally surprised to see Maya in Gwen's arms, but volunteers to look after her while Gwen's in with the principal. In the office, four parents are sitting on the other side of his desk.

Sit down, Mrs. Kerr.

I should have explained to you about the baby, she says. My sitter didn't turn up.

It's not that, Mrs. Kerr, although I must say I was taken aback. These parents are here because their children told them you've been teaching communism in your classroom.

That's not it, she says. I was trying to use drama as a technique for exploring themes in a novel on their curriculum.

I've explained you're only a sub, Mrs. Kerr. The regular teacher will be back tomorrow. Don't worry, he says to the parents. There won't be any more of these controversial methods in your children's classroom.

When she gets home, she stands by the sink and cries. Finishing the project mattered so much. René's coming for dinner. They're having roast lamb. We like it so rare it's walking around, she says sitting on the kitchen stool as Eugene parboils the potatoes and marinates them in olive oil before putting them around the roast. He has Maya in one arm as if she'd grown there.

After supper, Gwen takes a scarf *that doesn't go* from the hook at the door and sets out for a walk. When she comes back she sits at the bottom of the stairs, She's having a hard time, Eugene's saying as he sees René out the door. It's not working, mother. She's trying but….

Maybe she needs to be with her own people for a while, says René.

She's upset about not being able to finish what she was doing at that school.

I'm here, dear, whenever you need me.

Later, Eugene says he's been having a hard time talking to her lately.

You haven't been able to talk to *me*? You think I've been able to talk to you?

I know it's difficult finding a place for yourself here, thrashing around wondering where you fit in.

Thrashing? He wouldn't be saying any of this if his mother

hadn't been there.

It seems like there's something personal in all this.

Of course there's something personal in all this. I'm a person.

It might be good for you to take a break, Gwen, go home and see your parents.

Why's he saying that? In one appalled moment, she realizes why he's been so candid lately. Couples cut each other a lot of slack when they only have each other to accommodate. When one of them has found someone else and has a backup position, reckless truths get flung about like sprung garden hoses. He'd never be suggesting that she goes to visit her parents if he hadn't met someone else. *Don't you work for that new antiques magazine?* She can't bear to know so she doesn't ask.

After that, when he gets ready to leave in the morning, she sits at the window convinced if she doesn't keep her eyes on the spot on the building around which he'll disappear, he'll never come back. At first, he's kind. Gwen, he says. Does Maya have to be left alone in the bedroom?

She could come in here if she wants, she says distractedly. It's all cleaning and feeding, isn't it?

What happened to all the writing you were doing? You could get a job. We could get a permanent nanny.

Yes, let's do that. Her voice is completely flat.

I hate seeing you like this. What's happened to you? You're searching for me out there and I haven't even left yet.

At the supermarket, she pulls a shopping cart from the rack, puts Maya in the child container tray, takes Jenny by the hand and makes her way down through the produce section. Rumour has it some people actually begin at detergents and go backwards down and up the aisles. When she takes a tin of tomatoes from a shelf, an outline of three women appears in silhouette on the wall behind the tin. Odd. When she puts the tin back and takes it out again, they're still there. Now they seem to be on the other side of a river talking to each other but she can't hear what they're saying.

In the cashier line-up, a neighbour says I was talking to your husband the other day. He sounds charming.

Well, says Gwen. He's not.

It's not the same, is it? Eugene says that night in bed.

How could it be the same? It's going to take a while to get back to what we had.

Too long she could hear him thinking.

In the bath she's so distracted, she reaches into a bowl of bath lozenges and starts to eat them. She looks up at him shaving.

I'm afraid you've met someone else.

Of course not.

But one night, after she says that, he turns to the wall. There's no one who could be what you are to me.

Who *is it?*

It doesn't matter.

She hurls herself at him pounding his chest; he lifts her two wrists with one hand and pushes them down on the mattress. When he lets go, she pulls over to the other side of the bed, never to return.

If you hadn't started the whole thing, he says. That man you went to San Francisco with. I was trying to get even.

I didn't go to San Francisco with any man. We're *in* San Francisco.

Then why didn't you tell me you'd lost your suitcase? It was returned to me. By a woman in white shorts.

Oh Jesus. Not her.

I'd seen her before, in Monterey. Fancied her, actually. But it wasn't until she told me.

Told you what?

That you'd taken off with him. That he returned the car. You'd forgotten your bag so she brought it over.

That *man*, she says. They both offered a ride to San Francisco and she bailed. I was stuck with *that man*. *That man* turned out to be a wanker. I was terrified.

Why didn't you say anything?

I didn't want to worry you. Why didn't you say anything about the bag?

I was waiting for an explanation.

They both say what a comedy of errors, it's ridiculous, we'll look back and laugh at this. But the freezing no man's land between them has opened like a crevice in a glacier. She'll fall in if she moves over half an inch. She can't bear to have him touch her and she can't bear not to have him touch her.

It's not only this, Gwen. It's not working, is it?

You're the one who said this is love. This is what we do. We'll get through it. We have to. We have children.

35.

October, 1970.

Fine, take the car and go. No, no. Wait a minute. You don't know the way.

I'll get a map.

It'll be cold.

It's only the end of September.

It's the beginning of October. Be accurate for once, Gwen.

Are you angry at me?

Gwen, if I were angry at you, the *paint* would be blistering on the walls. *Is it?*

There's no toll heading north if you're on the highway: aiming for the 101, she takes the wrong turn, ends up heading past the Civic Centre and has to circle back, the sea passing behind them and under the span as Jenny hunches beside her. Maya is in her car seat in the back. So you're not coming home? I'll stay at the Ramada. She calls the Ramada. No Mr. Kerr is registered here. Careening around a curve, she drives up a street in Marin County, pulls over and sits with the car door open, Jenny on the ground leaning against her leg. Back on the road, the cars driving south appear to be heading directly at her, the ones behind are chasing her. The wind sweeps the pine in the opposite direction from the way it blew on their way down. Eugene started down to the cabin in Big Sur with Maya under his arm; he wants to buy it but insists it be in his name. Great. Had to come back because he'd forgotten the baby hadn't nursed, came in, arms around Maya like a log grate. Came in again, Maya in his mouth like a rabbit. The car stalls. The man in the next lane leans on his horn. What d'ya mean it won't go forward or back lady? You've got it in neutral. Wide brown hills, dark splodges of green like patches on cows. Let's talk about what we see, girls. There's some horses in a horse camp. Leaving the fog behind, they pass San Raphael and the hills begin to stretch longer across the valleys. At the next rest stop there's no bathroom; Jenny doesn't want to go down the slope by herself so they all go with her. Back on the highway, Maya starts crying and won't stop.

Look for a place for us to stay, Jenny, will you do that? A motel called the Skylark, curvy tiles on the roof, oh, they've passed that. The waves in the sea stiffen like black eggwhites. She pulls a piece of hair under her nose. One minute she's on fire, the next minute she's ice. A gantry crane rears like a dinosaur. The steering wheel melts. The steering wheel hardens. Eugene's heart is a cage where she's trapped shaking the bars. She's a thin chicken prancing its knees as if someone is hitting their backs with a towel. If she saw him on the sidewalk, she'd wrestle him to the pavement, kneel on his chest, draw a circle around his nipple with her pen knife, lift the piece of flesh like a manhole cover, remove his heart. When she tries to give his heart to a passerby, the passerby doesn't want it. The man whose heart she extracted is the wrong one. Crows caw trying to pull the carcass off the ground. She wants him on his knees with his arms around her waist; she wants to be eating him until her saliva and the tip of his penis are one. In her ear her eyes her navel, twitch it on her clitoris, between her toes. She wants him to come like a fountain until she's coated from head to foot in semen. She wants to go to his office, rip out the telephone and sit on his face. She wants him to bite her, drown in his own tears and beg for her forgiveness. If you take animals away from their wilderness and put them in a zoo, they do nothing but copulate until exhaustion. When he doesn't want to do it, it makes him feel like a machine when he's past having any interest in it. Before she left, she dragged cardboard boxes into the living room, opened them like giant flowers, sweaters and toys as centres. Carried bowlfuls of water from the waterbed to empty in the sink. Never mind, she only took her half of the water.

Here, Mom. Here's a motel, says Jenny.

How'd that happen? They seem to be in Oregon. A vacancy sign flashes on the highway. She manages the check-in, settles the two of them in the second double bed. The cheap bedside light won't turn off so she gives it a swat and it behaves.

When they get to Vancouver and Blenheim St., piles of leaves are darkening in the gutter. Dead chrysanthemums blow against the curb. Jenny runs down the laurel path straight into her grandmother's arms. Gwen drags in plastic bags of dirty laundry.

Hello, dear. You look, well you look…. *What's happened? Who's died?*

Sorry I phoned so late in the trip. I hope I haven't….

Of course you haven't, says Ada.

Sitting at the table, Percy anxiously exchanges the salt and pepper shakers with each other. He and Ada look much older because they've both gone grey. Maya's fallen back asleep but what can you do?

Your room's ready Gwen. The girls are in the small room at the head of the stairs.

Thanks, Mom. We won't stay long.

You stay as long as you like. This is your home whenever you need it.

She looks terrible, she hears her father saying as she's getting the girls to bed. I'm going down there, buttonhole that man, and say what have you done to my daughter?

She goes downstairs, picks up a dish towel. I'm sorry to be arriving like this. It's not him, it's me. I'm a terrible wife.

Is that what he said to you?

She nods miserably.

Maybe to someone else you'd be a perfect wife.

I doubt it. I couldn't keep up the, oh, I don't know. I didn't know what was what. And I'm jealous. *These are his problems, not mine, Percy's look says. I've fallen over enough tricycles. We're just getting our lives back.* We're not going to stay and cramp your style, dad. I don't want you to think....Give me a day or two to get the laundry done. I'll take the children over to the cottage for a while.

Oh, you can't do that, Gwen, says Ada in alarm.

Why not? It would give me a chance to get my bearings.

The cottage is closed for the season. The water's turned off. You can't go near the place. It's not ours for the asking.

But you bought it. You and Evvie and Isabelle bought it. You wrote to me.

We're doing a time share on it. This is Isabelle's time.

Isabelle's? Is she up there?

I don't think she goes. She can't leave Jack. He won't leave Birch Bay. They've moved down there, Stateside. She wants it left as it is.

Why?

It's complicated. You don't want to know.

I do, actually.

We don't see Isabelle, says Percy slowly. She and Jack have a store.

Gwen puts away a plate. Why didn't we see Auntie when I was growing up? I've never understood that.

You're not to go near the place, young lady. Ada pushes the cupboard door under the sink closed. After our visit, you need to go back and find a way to make your marriage work. Your girls need their father.

Of course they need their father, Gwen says. The last thing I want to do is separate. But what if you beg and plead and say we have children, we have to work this out, and he says don't think he doesn't know that but he wants out.

Then, says Ada, you're sunk.

That night in bed, when she phones Eugene to say they've arrived, she finds herself sitting over a five dollar silence, so exhausted she falls asleep with the phone line open. In the morning, is there breathing at the other end? Maybe he fell asleep too. She'll have to say the phone bill's hers, maybe the phone company will understand. Downstairs, she spoons apple sauce into Maya.

So how are you both? she manages.

We're fine.

How's Leo?

I think he's well, don't you, Perce? He's at York. I hope he gets his tenure.

I hope he gets his tenure too.

She'd watched Leo lecture once; he followed the theorem he was outlining along the front blackboards and then down the sides, rubbing off his calculations and starting again as if he were afraid to turn and face the class. He'd written her that he and his colleagues were trying to find out why the atmosphere of Venus moves in the opposite direction from its slow rotation. Why the craters are so uniform. There's a dark substance between observable heavenly bodies, but they don't know what it is.

Percy's head looks smaller, beaky around the nose. Pouring over a portfolio of maps and charts, he doesn't look at all faded.

One exciting thing, he says. I got my pilot's license.

You *did?* Why didn't you tell me?

I wrote you but my letter must have crossed with your trip.

She reaches for his hand. Do you love it?

I sure do.

At last he'll get to fly up and over the north shore mountains like he's always wanted. People on Jericho don't know they're only looking at the fronts, he used to say when they were sitting on the beach.. No idea we have mountains all the way to the North Pole. Up there he'd re-connect with the freedom he used to know on The Prairies, now that he didn't have the responsibility of *them.*

Only problem is, he says—Ada stiffens her back—your mother won't have anything to do with flying. When she was sixteen, a callow youth whose name has long been forgotten, had taken her topside in an airplane with an open cockpit and turned the plane over. She said to herself that if she ever got back to solid ground, she'd never fly in another airplane as long as she lived. When Percy gets up from the table to go to Pitt Meadows, he comes to kiss Ada's cheek.

You can go anywhere up there, Gwen, he says. You know that joke about rich people looking down from their carriage and saying I wonder how the *poor* people are doing? Up there I wonder what the poor *people* are doing,

You're gods, eh?

Yep.

He loves it that she gets it.

If you want to go with Dad, Mom, we're fine, Gwen says. For the drive anyway.

I'd like to but I can't, Ada replies. That's a good thing to say, Gwen, when you don't want to hurt someone's feelings. I'd like to but I can't.

I don't understand about the cottage, Mom. If Isabelle's not using it, couldn't I get in touch with her and see if I could stay there?

No, you could not, Gwen. You haven't shown the slightest interest in the cottage and what's been going on around here. All we've heard about are goings-on in San Francisco that, frankly, sound much too complicated for school children.

I was trying to keep in touch, mother, but if that's the way you see it.

I don't see it any particular way, we're just upset to see you like this.

I know. I'm sorry.

If you want to go to camp, you should go and see your sister at Scarborough. Lily would be the first person to help you if you were in trouble. You know that.

Oh, that's right, she's living there now. You said about Grandma Flora leaving half the place to her. With Derek Sycamore, right? What brought him back here? And Annabelle, there's a little girl…?

I guess so, Gwen. She's your niece. What's the matter with you two? You haven't been writing each other?

I heard from her once, something about some otters she said I should keep an eye on in Big Sur. You and dad own the other half, right?

That's right. I don't know all what they've got going on over there. Some kind of what did Lily call it, gestalt workshops? Do you know what that is?

Gestalt's a kind of therapy, says Gwen, picking up a dish towel. I heard about it in California.

The girls could get to know their cousin, says Ada.

How's Grandpa Gallagher, Mom?

Old.

He's still at Laburnum St., is he?

Just.

Gwen could call Isabelle and ask, says Percy at the door. As long as you leave the place the way you found it.

Of course I'd leave it the way I found it.

No, she could not, Perce. It's not winterized. You could stay here. We could look after the children and you could get your teacher training.

Percy looks as if she'd announced that she was going to burn the house down.

And the children would have no mother, says Gwen. I can't do that. I couldn't ask you.

What about child support? he says. Alimony? This with his hand on the front doorknob, grave and disappointed.

It hasn't come to that. I can't even call him right now without the telephone wires shorting out. Our clothes are on fire.

Don't be dramatic, Gwen, says Ada.

This all sounds terrible to me, Percy says. I don't know what you're going to do, but what I'm going to do is get in an airplane and fly due north.

BOOK IV

THE BONES OF MY WEDDING DRESS

36.

October, 1970.

Over at Scarborough, a waterlogged sofa and boxes of rose-hips sag on the back porch of the peeling farm house; a driftwood railing replaces the old verandah rail and a mess of morning glory trails over a mound of sacks. Between the house and beach, several tiers of gardens and pens are held in place by wedges of upended rock. There's a shed with the chalked sign: ALWAYS SECURE DOORS AGAINST BABIES PLEASE. The chickens live in a kind of adventure playground: their shingled house has round doors, turrets, and a bird bath. Masses of marigold border the vegetable garden on the next level. Tall pieces of driftwood, worn and humped as gargoyles, support the fish net protecting the garden from deer. A man in a flannel shirt, blonde beard and sloped moustache whips a glance up and down the beach to see how much seaweed the storm's brought in as two year old Annabelle waddles out on the back deck; her stiff plastic bib has a turned up lip that's supposed to catch porridge but hers hasn't. A ring of white hair circles her head like a nimbus. Derek hoists her into a pack on his back, clumps toward the shore with a sack hooked on his thumb like a jacket.

Sitting back in the classic *tai chi* position, he stops at the herb garden planted in the shape of a zodiac to kick straw over the thyme. Pushes a few sticks of wood under a small outhouse of a building where the hams and bacon are smoking. The waves are almost big enough to crash over the piles of sea lettuce, unusual for the protected Sound. He piles mounds of dulse into the wheelbarrow before heading back to the house where he dumps the seaweed in the compost, stands his daughter on a chair and together they pour rosehips onto cookie sheets, slide them into a dryer lit by an electric bulb.

This time of year the kitchen is crammed with food on the way to storage. A person needs to have six hands: two to hang the cheesecloth plum pulp bag on a doorknob to drip, two more to carry the canner over to the sink to drain the salt mixture from the piccalilli—the sour of the pickles infusing the sweet of the simmering plum—two more to heap mounds of blackberries into a pot. The berries ripen in waves across the farm from east to west; in June, the strawberries in the fields near cedars marching down the hill, the loganberries before the raspberries up by the cornfield, then the blueberries on a sunny spot over in the meadow. Finally, the hedge of blackberries in the west where boards are thrown to break a path. He's put paper collars around the bases of the cabbages to stop them getting root maggots; the ones that survived the attack are enormous and the Samson has certainly lived up to its name. For a buck, visitors to the fair in the old number four picnic grounds up by the falls can guess the weight and win the cabbage. He hates cabbage.

He grabs a wrench from an outline on the wall of the shed and goes out to bleed the brakes on his truck. Flapping onto a dolly, he slides under the vehicle head first, legs akimbo like a crab's. The wrench is the wrong size. He won't be able to deliver the vegetables over to the fairgrounds if he can't get some goddam brake pressure. The second wrench is the right size but the cap sticks. Out again for the liquid penetrant.

A lot of apples have fallen on the roof of the house and turned black; the orchard floor is covered with them. Lily sashays down through the orchard from the bus, her waist so narrow he wants to pick up the end of her skirt sash, and twirl her out across the yard. The school bus in the back field is an a eyesore, even if Lily insists on letting old George Fenn park it there for the duration. The old man figured he'd have the bus on hand when the resident population got beefed up now that there's a ferry: a bit of a bus service to supplement his taxi business, but what with one thing and another, the moss and mildew took over, Lily started using the bus as an office, then extra sleeping space and well he didn't want to think about the rest.

What was it, three years ago he'd seen her in front of the Shack café bulletin board sign fingering a phone number fringe? You interested in that job, too? he'd asked, stirring his coffee.

It's my notice. I was looking to see if any numbers had been taken. I'm looking for a caretaker.

He held up the slip he'd torn off.

She peered at him through her rimless glasses. Are you *Derek?* It *is* you.

When he expanded the distance between his eyebrows and his nose, his tapered moustache fit even more deftly from his nostrils to the corners of his mouth.

I'm Lily. You came when it was the war and slept upstairs with my brother.

She reminded him of a woman in a war poster he'd seen: a

graceful young mother sitting under a tree with a ghost out-line of Hitler whispering in her ear. *Don't do it, Mother. Leave the children where they are.* Far be it for the mothers to leave the children in London or wherever else they belonged. Instead, he'd been billeted with a family near Blackpool where the sheets smelled wrong, barbed wire lined the beach and encircled the Ferris wheel. On the beach, he'd found a piece of blubbery human flesh.

Lily needed a caretaker, she said, because she was totally involved with a raft of sea otters that were about to be shipped down from Alaska into B.C. waters. Without otters, the population of sea urchins gets out of hand because guess who eats the urchins? No more sea otters and the sea floor is a mass of spiky shell doorknobs.

Lily'd written to her sister—Gwen, did he remember Gwen—turned out lucky that Gwen was living in Big Sur, California, where she could observe one of the only living groups of sea otters in the world! They're listed as nearly extinct, but a few have survived and reproduced up north away from the eyes and ears of the rest of the world. There's a new sanctuary in the Aleutian Islands. Gwen had written to ask if she knew there'd been a nuclear test under the sea floor near Amchitka Island in the Aleutians and a much larger one planned for the near future, so the sanctuary was hardly safe. Well, of course she knew. That's why they're planning the Checleset Bay re-location. She was about to join the group of biologists heading to the west side of Vancouver Island to try to find a put-in place for the, well, raft, in a word.

Derek tried not to show his irritation at the compulsive way she talked, as if she were over compensating for something and had no idea what. When he tried to change the subject—he'd heard some gestalt therapy people were looking for a place to do group and shouldn't they consider the possible rental money—she made an effort to take an interest in what he was saying—that made him like her again—but kept slipping down the interference of the new topic, grabbing at words like roots to hand herself back up to stable ground.

Did he know the most common cause of death in sea otters? Life? he'd said.

Tooth decay. You'd think hypothermia but no. They're one of the few mammals that chew their food. Have to groom themselves to get the air back in their fur every time they dive down for a bite. They crunch so many shells their teeth give out. No fat on their bodies to speak of. Not like all that blubber you've got your seal population. A layer of air trapped in their fur is all they have to keep them warm.

In the kitchen, where greasy wallpaper peeled into a faded pattern of pineapples and cherries, she sat sadly with her arms wrapped around herself.

Whatever, he felt like saying but didn't. Later, when they were no longer roomates, he'd call her from Vancouver and ask her to say blueberries because he loved the way her lips moved when she said the word.

She arrived home from that first expedition discouraged because, in spite of the great location of the Bunsby Islands— you've got your shallow waters, seafood smorgasbord spread on the sea floor—the animals had arrived in piss poor shape, and they'd found them huddled in a corner matted in their own excrement. They must have kept them too long on the airport tarmac or something, she said, in tears, baseball cap pulled down over her eyes.

Have some pigs' feet, Lily, Derek said. She thought he said ears, pigs' ears and didn't take any.

There's never anything to eat in this place, she complained. Except kale and millet.

If you want something else to eat, grow it for christsake. We've got rakes. We've got shovels.

Instead, she sat down on the beach turning her hands over and over like a piano player who'd broken them.

Now here she comes down through the orchard, her long skirt brushing the apple trees. You'd think she'd pick a few to put through the cider press but no. Want to go get the new porkers with me, Annabelle? Derek says, carrying his little girl to the truck. He rolls down the window as Lily sways up to it and touches Annabelle on the tip of her nose. Hello, tiddlywink, she says.

You going to do some apples today, Lil? Derek's glance never lingers when you have business with him. He never flirts. Instead, he lowers his gaze as soon as you're listening, looks away. If he were a gas station attendant, he'd pluck your credit card from your hand without looking at you. People mistake his shyness for brusqueness. He is brusque in a way, but not cold.

Don't keep her long, okay? Lily says. I've made arrangements for Will to see her at the fair. I've got to head back to Checleset to try to locate any survivors. You're tied up on that Tunstall Bay job.

I can't believe this, Lily.

It's not otters she cares about, Derek thinks as he guns the truck up the driveway, it's getting her own way. It hadn't taken long to see that she wasn't interested in him any more *that way* as people said. They'd given it the old college try (she said), but it was more the place and Annabelle binding them together than anything else. They were mainly *friends*. It's been months since she started sleeping in the school bus again, himself in the goddam upstairs front bedroom.

If you ever end up going to bed with someone else, he said when they first got together, I don't want to know. Instead, she insisted on being *out front*, giving him a blow by blow about how lonely she'd been after she moved up to the bus, the rain dropping every day in sheets. She lifted her arm in front of the mirror, convinced moss had started to grow in her armpits. She'd only had a couple of one nights stands with Will; her bond with Derek was worth its weight in gold compared. Did he think of Scarborough as almost their child the way she did?

He did not. And with Kayak Will of all people. He hated the show-offy way he walked around with his fiberglass kayak on his arm like a lobster claw so he could pop his boat in the water any time. Did odd jobs to keep body and soul together like a lot of other men on the Rock. Spent hours at the dump going over items people brought in for the used goods shelf, turned product around at the Saturday market. Lives god knows where. Something about his house getting struck by lightning, which he took as a sign he wasn't supposed to have a house, so he moved into a hollow tree. That's the myth anyway.

He can just see the way their long white limbs would fit one another's. That's the trouble. The more Kayak Will's features and pale colouring surface in Annabelle's face like a photograph emerging from a rinse bath, the more determined he's been not to say a word. How could she not see the implications of letting him assume pride of place?

The stronger the evidence grew the harder it was to bring up the subject. Either we're a family or I work for eighteen dollars an hour, he said. Fair enough, she'd said. I get it. But she didn't. Can't she hear how hackneyed her point of view is, spoken without inflection no matter who she's talking to, the way she sweeps critical elements under the rug, and makes a federal case out of the trivial. An earth shaking fuss about whether Annabelle gets commercial cream of wheat rather than seven grain organic for breakfast but prepared to endorse an out and out betrayal like this. Lots of kids have two fathers these days, she says. How could he have allowed himself the luxury of believing his construct had significance to anyone but himself? That if Will got involved, he himself would be in a position where he would be over-compensating in even his smallest gesture. What's she going to call Will? he asks.

We'll have to see what she calls you both.

Oh *fuck that.*

None of this stops him from loving Annabelle. Night after night when she'd been colicky, he'd draped her over his shoulder, slept on his feet even when she wouldn't. Stiff as a board, she'd scream and wail while Lily slept on behind her custom made ear plugs. In desperation, he'd put her in the truck and driven her up and down the Government Road. Washed her diapers in the wringer washer because he didn't want her in plastic pampers. Lily hadn't objected one iota when he said he was going to write his parents and tell them they had a grandchild. The three of them called on Percy and Ada *wouldn't it be grand to be young enough to be able to sleep like that,* he and Lily lecturing them about how proud they were to be able to live off what other people threw away. Percy and Ada sat there astonished. Wasn't progress that people didn't have to do that any more?

What he needs is a lake up north where no one could find them. Set out for Hope one day and keep going. On the Government Road, the telephone poles lock behind him like the teeth of a zipper. He pulls over to let the ferry traffic pass. Someone might not see his turn signal; he's not taking chances with Annabelle in the car. Ever. She wails her blue-skinned cry, wispy pale hair so thin her skull doesn't have any protection. He himself looks as if he's been in an accident. Someone should get a blanket and cover him up.

Later that afternoon, strips of late sunlight shimmer between cedar branches where the waterfall splashes under the remains of the white picket bridge over Bridal Falls. Pick-ups park behind the old hotel site where the greenhouse used to stand. Stalls are set on makeshift platforms resting on the cement foundations that used to support the curved alder fence on the Bridal Path up the side of the falls. Half of today's profits are going to augment the LIP grant for the fish ladder fund: the hope is to build steps up the side of the lagoon causeway and the balcony side of the falls. Once the new fry are released from the new nursery, the islanders may yet see a coho return.

Derek sets up his annual tequila and haircut bar behind a rock halfway down the falls and tries to ignore the way Lily's able to wrap her head in a scarf so her high cheekbones reflect the light from the falls, dammit. Annabelle climbs down from her mother's hip, up the ladder of a slide made from a hollow log carved to look like a dragon, pulls herself out its mouth, goes around, climbs up and slides down again. When Kayak

Will arrives, their two heads blend like dandelion puffs. Derek lets the tequila burn a slow line into his stomach when the only person in the world who belongs to him goes off with his enemy. Maybe she'll start screaming and he'll have to rescue her, but no, she trundles off with *her biological father*, holding his hand without a backward glance.

37.

When Gwen shows up at Scarborough, she has Maya on her back and Jenny by the hand. Derek's in the yard chopping wood. Good to see you, Gwen. Jenny, Maya. He pushes his toque onto the back of his head.

The house is even more run down than when Flora and Lyndon lived there. At least the wallpaper's been stripped and one wall of tongue and groove restored. The table's a door laid on sawhorses. The cuckoo clock is still there. Derek pushes a brain of sausage around in the frying pan. Want some? he says. Jenny nibbles a piece, heads off for the beach, comes back with a jar of shells as Lily flies in, Annabelle a expressionless burl on her hip. What's that, a rabbit or a plastic bag? she says. That white thing flapping over by the bathtub. Gwen. Good to see you. Jenny. Are you some kind of grown-up niece or *what?*

I'm going out to harvest some onions, says Derek. He always leaves the room when Lily comes in, but Gwen doesn't know that yet.

Later, Gwen makes up foamies for Maya and Jenny on the floor of what used to be the dining room. The way Annabelle reminds her of someone but she can't think who is like having a word on the tip of her tongue. There's still enough light to see the slanted trail to Pebbley so she takes a walk to the beach and up the road up to find the hotel pulled out like a massive tooth, a split level ranch house in the middle of the tennis court. The old corner Deluxe moulders at the edge of the overgrown lawn bowling green. Where's the monkey tree?

She climbs the rickety stairs of the Deluxe and finds the floor littered with beer bottles. If they don't want her to go to the cottage, maybe if she put in an airtight, she could fix it up and bring the girls here. Then she could still be part of things at Scarborough, whatever things are. If she rented a house in Vancouver she'd have to get a job to cover the overhead. Then what? If the girls are only going to have one parent, they'll need more of her, not less.

At the village office they admit they plan to demolish the last cottages but not right away. She could rent one but there's no question of a lease. A few days later she's in overalls stirring gallons of white latex, listening to Morningside on CBC. It can't be all bad if you've got Peter Gzowski to listen to in the morning. Someone said if you want to put in a window, you have to tap along the wall with a hammer until you hear a thud.

As autumn turns into winter, puddles fill up with fir needles and rain. The mountains and the sea blend into the same dull grey. She stirs more latex, sets more mouse traps. Hammers two by fours to build bunk beds.

Let's say we have a cabin in the forest, she says to Jenny.

We're not going to sleep here? There aren't any beds.

I'm building some.

Are we camping?

That's it. We're camping.

I don't like camping.

Fine, let's say the old lawn bowling green is our house. The cottage is our bedroom. The sky's the ceiling.

That's not funny.

They hang framed prints from the thrift store on the cedars lining the path to the outhouse. What's this supposed to be, a corridor to the bathroom? Jenny says morosely.

You're supposed to hang pictures at eye level, did you know that?

Whose eye level? Jenny says with her adult frown.

Yours. We can move them up next year.

We're not going to be here next year My dad *misses* me.

He *does* miss you. Come here, sweetheart.

Dad wouldn't like those boots, Jenny says.

I think they're funny. Gwen pulls up the zipper on the knock-off rubber Cuban heeled version with pretend buttons up the side.

I don't.

In the mornings, she wakes up in the bunkhouse hoping she'll have worked her way back to solid ground, but outside the mud shifts under her feet like a loosened bank lipping over a river. Before she left Blenheim St., she told her mother that she needs to find herself as a person. I can't help you there, her mother said. I've never thought of myself as a person. I'm just somebody making a custard.

Painting the Deluxe walls the next day with Maya playing in the yard, Gwen caves into her loneliness, lies down and pulls back the edge of her panties. At the crucial moment, the silence is too silent. Races out to where Maya's playing and she's not there. A voice whispers *now he'll have to come*. She couldn't have thought that but she did. Then, there's her baby under a plum tree across the wrecked lawn bowling green. *I lost you once at the Bay and they found you outside sitting on the curb. What was I doing? Looking around.* Only when she hears the guilt in her mother's voice does Maya start to cry.

When she goes back to paint, the door of the Deluxe is open—she's sure she'd closed it---the lamp's knocked over —lucky it hadn't been lit—flour spilled all over the floor. Maybe some animals got in here, Jenny. There aren't any bears on the island, are there?

If only she could stop the night voices. Eugene. Her. Eugene. Jenny. Eugene. Maya. Eugene. Her husband's dark eyes sit in his daughters' narrow olive faces like those of his dachshunds. When she has the phone put in, he calls, asks to speak to Jenny. Darling, she says to him down the wire, then catches herself. She's right here, Eugene.

Jenny sits on the paint can. We're sort of living in the woods, dad. It's good. There's lots of kids my age. Want to speak to Mom again? Mom takes the phone wiping her face with the paint rag. Jenny hangs on her every word.

We're fine but we need money, Eugene.

Why should I send money? he says. I want the girls back where they belong in their own apartment with a decent standard of living. You've taken them out of the country. I could make a legal issue of this. I'll take the children. You could get a job and take care of yourself; that would sort it.

She changes the phone to the other ear. Eugene, this is making me sick. I couldn't be away from the children. You know that. Why do you want them back and not me? What have I done?

You haven't done anything. It's just not working. You know that as well as I do.

Gwen closes her eyes miserably. That's what you say, but I want to come back. I feel like we're camping here. She doesn't say but Jenny has her thumb in her mouth and is curled in foetal position on the floor.

A few days later he calls back and apologizes for being harsh. He'll send money soon.

How much? He doesn't say. Maybe he should come for a visit but she's not to make too much of it. Of course she'll make too much of it. She'll make hay of it. The work she's done on the cabin fades like the moon in the face of the rising sun.

The next morning in the big house voices murmur from the living room they call the group room when the gestalt people are there. Jenny's at school; Maya and Annabelle are playing in the playpen. Derek said everyone is invited so she opens the door and slips in. No one's supposed to break the silence unless they have something *real* to say. You know those people in your head who shake their finger at you every time you turn around? The ones who stop whispering when you come into the room? The soldier with the gun who chases you all night? They're all parts of ourselves we give away apparently. When people let themselves far enough into their bruised areas, the bruised areas begin to speak for themselves. You put the person who's upsetting you or someone from last night's dream in a chair across from you, change over and take that person's part. When you start to listen to the parts you've disowned, your whole self is supposed to re-convene.

Outsized pillows line the walls. Derek is kneeling in the centre of the circle in the spot they call the hot seat. (Sometimes they do it with chairs.) Working on a dream, he picks at the carpet tufts searching for Annabelle who's turned into a contact lens. Why's she turned into a contact lens when I just had her *safe?* he cries. He turns the lens concave side up on his index finger like a miniature pool, crying she's so tiny she can't hear him. Someone who used to sleep in the room above the kitchen is still there, he says. Whoever he is, he's as sad as I am. Derek looks so miserable Gwen crawls into the center of the circle and reaches out to hold him. What's wrong with you people? she says. You can't leave somebody out here alone like this. Afterwards in the kitchen, she's chastised by the others for enabling, interfering, rescuing: all of the above.

38.

September, 1970.

Takumi is still fishing out of Prince Rupert but the catch is nothing like it used to be. The day he's heading out early for the one day sockeye opening so he won't have to lump around later, the tide is high enough to navigate through the narrow channel at the entrance to Union Inlet and he makes good time up past Fort Simpson to the entrance to the Khutzeymateen. Back when they fished out of Blaine, they had so little ice, the packer would come by three or four times a day, sort everything at the canneries—steelhead, chum, coho—but now masses of bi-catch are thrown back, half dead and unlikely to live. The damage done to the unwanted fish on the decks of the huge drift netters means they'll never make it to the spawning ground.

Turns out they're paying four dollars a pound in Vancouver for fish that are kept alive in tanks until the night before they're sold. It's a lot more work bringing in the net every half hour than it was back when it didn't matter whether or not the fish were dead, but this way he can get anything out by hand that isn't sockeye. He watches the net carefully as it's rolled out; he doesn't want it to fold back on itself and tear. It shimmers green when it's turned on the drum; the pink buoys roll over and over like regulated decoys of the fish themselves. At the same time, he yards in his never ending worrying about Shima; it's been months since he's heard from her. Longer than months. She used to call every few weeks even if it was only to badger him about her grandparents. You'd remember where they lived if you tried hard enough, Dad. When he was young, he'd tuned out his parents' voices when they talked about the old country. Somehow he was certain they'd returned to Japan, sent letters to the family registries in as many areas as he could think of, but found no trace.

Quick hand work to pull in the net. He yanks off the kelp and tosses the seaweed out to sea. Carries the fish to the trough and hoses water into its mouth to help it recover from the shock of being caught. The eye is too still. When he returns with a couple more, the eye of the first fish is turning so that's good. He sets one aside for his lunch, lets it go through rigor mortis before he cooks it. If you throw a fresh fish full of lactic acid into the pan, the blood runs to the muscle and it curls up

For the next set, he heads closer to the kelp beds where the sockeye like to swim. Out goes the net, over the roller between the pins. The sea water is running steadily through the side checkers; when he opens them to insert another fish, the ones in the bottom swim up, take a bite of air, head back down. When the lid's closed, they lie recovering on the bottom of the tanks. The net gets spooled out. The net gets spooled in. It describes one arc, then another. He unhooks the buoys with his pole, patrols the line. Untangles a black bass—only the mouth is caught—throws it back. Flings out more kelp, more seaweed. A kelp bulb gets caught in the net; he stops the roller and bites the long whiplash, winding the stem around his hand and elbow as if rolling it up for future use. Another set over, only three fish this time. He only has twenty-five sockeye, but at least they're all alive and swimming as he heads back down Chatham Sound. Tomorrow he'll butcher them, pack them, and send them out on the plane.

39.

Before they head for the airport on the day Eugene's coming, Gwen and the girls have lunch in the city at McDonald's. Well, she and Eugene and the children have lunch at McDonald's since he's with them in every bite she takes. He's the man in the green mackinaw riding his bike down the street. Now he's put on a black vest and leans on the wall at the rink where she takes the girls to skate. Later, he's balded, changed into a jean jacket and walks down Granville St. She'd lined up the children's socks like small clenched fists in the drawer of their thrift shop bureau in the Deluxe.

At the airport, Eugene's legs are kid magnets. How long until night? How are you? he says. Okay now, Gwen says, smiling as Jenny tugs at his hand. Nothing can separate flesh from flesh.

Not really. We're going to ride in the ferry that looks like a birthday cake, dad. At Horseshoe Bay, Jenny drags him down the ferry dock to look at the weird stuff you can see when the tide's out. You can pop those yellow things, dad. I'll show you. Is the car in this row? *Nooooo.* Dad automatically starts to get in the driver's seat, changes his mind, lets Gwen drive onto the ferry. Jenny'd taken her boots off to get a stone out, so intent on looking at her father she put them back on the wrong feet. They're the last car on, yay. She runs bow legged to hold the button which slowly whooshes open the door to the stairs.

Dad has a new ski jacket, short hair compared to most people here. He takes one look at the homespun shirts and heavy sweaters, asks if he looks like a stranger who doesn't know how to dress. No, Gwen says even if she knows he's alluding to the way he thought about her clothes in the States. Jenny pulls out a slate with carbon-backed plastic and shows him the adding she can do. When he takes them to *Fantasia* she'll lean forward in the darkened theatre to watch his face watch her favourite parts. When he comes back from getting hot chocolate, he takes Jenny's boots off, lines them up the right way, but she crosses her legs so she can put them back on the wrong feet. Maya crawls all over him. He pulls an issue of *Harper's* from his briefcase to show Gwen an article he wants her to read, hands her some material that came for her from the Movement office. *All passengers should return to the car deck and prepare to disembark.* Gwen will always remember that ferry crossing, will dole moments out to herself spoonful by spoonful over a series of long winters. Her mother said that, in the overall scheme of things, the time when your children are young will seem short compared to the rest of your life. That's impossible.

At Scarborough, Gwen and her family stand at the kitchen door for inspection, all of them visitors now that her husband is there. Derek comes over to shake hands with Eugene. Annabelle's in her booster seat at the table, white hair puffed out around her narrow face. Eugene picks up her small limp hand and shakes it. Lily is popping cubes of frozen lemonade from the ice cube tray that they bought when lemons were on special.

We shouldn't have come empty-handed, Eugene says to Gwen quietly. There's a store, she replies standing there married. Her eyes are over bright, cheeks a spreading pink.

So this was your grandparents' place, Eugene says to Lily. It's a wonderful old house.

It is, isn't it? she says.

Derek gives him the tour, tells him how they boarded the toilets in the bathroom because the septic field was dodgy. Built composting toilets out back because there wasn't enough riparian zone left between the house and the ocean. Good idea. Both of them look and look again, the way men go over work together, the one who hasn't done it not saying anything about the way he would have done it. The bathtub by the cider press has a trough underneath, firewood piled beside it.

You fill it with a hose and wash yourself before getting in like they do in Japan, Jenny explains.

Gwen and Eugene are to have the bedroom above the kitchen. Probably Eugene doesn't say anything about wanting to sleep alone to be polite. You know what Dad? says Jenny at supper. If I've got a chocolate bar at school and my friend, Fred, finishes his first he makes me give him some of mine *and* my silver paper.

Maybe you should make a deal where you both get to eat to a midway line and whoever gets there first waits for the other.

It's not a question of logic her look says.

Eugene stays downstairs reading to the children in their makeshift bedroom, visits much too long with Lily who, Gwen now knows, spends her nights in the renovated school bus. Upstairs, she lights candles and puts on Zen music. Oh, a seduction scene, Eugene says indifferently when he finally comes up. Never ask your husband if he's sleeping with someone else. If he doesn't say anything, it will mean he is. He sits down on the edge of the bed, pats her back absently.

Don't do that. I'm not a baby.

Sorry. He moves to the window, keeping his back to her. Jenny's down there feeding a crow, he says. I thought I'd tucked her in.

It's her pet, says Gwen. She probably forgot she hadn't fed it.

Honestly now, in your heart of hearts wouldn't you like to sleep with other men once in a while? he'd said once. Not at all, she'd said which was true. *It's a lonely place if what you're doing isn't working. Clockwise. Counter clockwise.* Show me how you do it, he said then. Then I'll do it how you like.

That's private. It's trickier now... since the children. It's harder to concentrate.

Well, fine, I'll never get it.

No, sometimes you're emotionally excited and it's a whole other thing. It's not that cut and dried. If you're in love with someone, there's an emotional kind of coming that can mean more than the technical kind.

Do you ever get caught up in your own rhetoric, Gwen? I mean....

He's left his journal open on their dresser. On purpose? *Came across Lily lying in the bath today. Couldn't help admiring her handsome bush. People who read other people's diaries deserve what they get.*

Maybe if something happens to me you should marry Lily, she says to his back at the window.

Okay, he says much too quickly. You asked for that, he says.

When he comes to bed he leaves his underwear on, *so there is someone else.* He holds her stiffly, only coming into her so that she'll stop pawing at him. A few minutes of manufactured hoist holding himself still for a different second from what she's used to, waiting for his fantasy of whoever he's sleeping with now to kick in. *Whoever she is probably has a convenient low clitoris.* He moves his finger faster than she's used to, the way someone else likes it. He rolls over. Actually, love, I don't think we should be doing this. I should have left you to sort yourself out.

Oh thanks.

I don't even know why I'm here.

The children, isn't it?

You're playing your strongest card when you talk about the children, Gwen. I'm as worried about them as you are. I want them with me at least half the time. But there's something else you have to do. You know it and I know it. It's not working, you trying to live my life. You don't belong in my culture.

She rolls over to face the wall. That's all very well for you to say now. Is it still her? That Maria character?

No, he says with a snorting breath, as if how could it possibly be. It's as if no matter how much I give you, it will never be enough. I thought the separation might have made a difference but it hasn't.

His lips are swollen as if she'd beaten him. She can't put names to any of the shadows pressing her from behind. Doesn't he understand she won't be able to breathe if he stops touching her? Being entered, it seems as if the whole person comes into you and stays. Maybe for a man, she thinks, it's only part of you.

There's something wrong with me, she says. I feel like I've been struggling up a ragged stream since I met you but, when I get to the spawning ground, it's the wrong one. I wasn't born there after all.

I'm what's wrong with you, Gwen. I don't know why it's so hard.

He turns his back and falls asleep, leaving her out in the cold night. Their former selves call from his Deep Cove house like their own lost children. If she moves a millimeter closer to him, she'll beg forever. She tries to stitch herself back together, sews a finger to her heel, a breast on her head. The fingers of her other hand are basted down the side of her body like a fringe. Her cells drip into him all night at the spot where their ankles touch.

Worse, there *is* someone else in the room. The rush of two rivers meet under a mountain whose striations slant diagonally to a peak. The only way into the wooded valley at its base is by tongue. It's impossible to sleep; she's rigid with tension and desire, is still awake when the watery sun softens the window. *Look, Mommy, the dark is all better.* Eugene gets up as if it's the easiest thing in the world, stands by the window twirling her last cell on his finger like a hula hoop.

Aren't you going to get up? he says.

She's up already. He's up, so she's up. He knows it too. He comes back and sits on the edge of the bed looking out the window at the ragged cedars.

There's something wrong with this place, Gwen. I thought it was the pressure of the mountains and being at sea level but it's not that.

It's just the rain.

No, it's not just the rain.

She sits up, holds her face between her hands. I'm going to take a shower, she manages.

I'll check on the girls, he says.

The girls are all right. They're down on the beach.

They're not all right you know, Gwen.

I'll look after the girls, she hisses between her teeth.

She will too. You watch.

In the shower, she stands at an angle she's never stood at before. If she goes back into the bedroom without a plan, her fingers will end up as a begging bowl. Her tongue is a stone. She turns off the water and stands under it anyway. They're *not* going to be half and half anywhere by the way, she'll tell him later. They need a home base. All she would have to do is never touch him again. Is that all? *What I want the most, I can't have. Are you sure?*

Finally, she has to go back to the room because she's cold. The only way to stop herself clinging to him is to think of a way she won't be able to bear his seeing her. No make-up. Not clean her teeth. Keep on the ugly nightie that shows the remains of her pregnancy bulge. If she concedes one particle to her instinct to fluff her plumage, she'll end up clamping her toothless gums on his neck and hang forever like a person with no arms. Do other people need like she does? She has no idea. Tell you what. If she makes it across the room to the cupboard and outside without losing her dignity, she'll get to interpret whatever she sees when she steps into the yard as a touchstone to remember whenever she needs courage.

There's an old tweed coat hanging in the closet. She puts it on, takes a deep breath that she holds until she's across the room and down in the kitchen. Outside, a tall hollyhock has climbed the shed and is turning black. Strips of cloud split the early morning moon. Wherever she might end up settling, remind her to plant some hollyhock.

Dad?

A scrunch of feet on the gravel. Dad?

40.

Later, Eugene is walking Maya up and down the driveway holding her upraised hands. When Gwen comes out with dark circles under her eyes, he goes over he goes to sit beside her at the outside table. I know this sounds self-serving, he says. But I think what you need to do is put down roots here and really, I mean really, hang on.

She pushes a dead maple leaf around with her toe. It'd be a whole different thing if you'd said that when you wanted me to be with you.

I know.

You're only saying that to get rid of me. Is she sleeping in my bed? I can't stand it if she's sleeping in my bed.

She's not sleeping in your bed.

So there is someone! She shoots bolt upright as if she'd surfaced in her starry bathing suit and her parents weren't there after all. People didn't say cheating in those days; strong attraction was more often spoken of as undeniable.

You've got to settle down, Gwen. The kids shouldn't see you this upset. She wants to fling herself at him and hang on for dear life. But she doesn't do that. She does not do that.

Instead, she tears down the road past her pathetic attempts at refurbishing the Deluxe, hurls herself across the causeway over to her own concrete stairs above Sandy. For years to come, the mistakes she's made with him will be soft craters on the inside of her lip she'll keep biting down on by accident. Until the children are grown up, she'll dream of him almost every night, trek endlessly up the narrow hall of their apartment to find him in bed with someone else. Hauling herself back from repeating the endless ways she wants to connect with him will be like holding back a child from crossing a busy street because there's ice cream on the other side. Sometimes she'll give up trying and let her mind jerk back and back to what he might be doing, the way you'd let an encrusted pot soak for a few days before you tried to scour it.

When she goes back to the house, Eugene's in his sports jacket and is packing. Jenny's lined up the kitchen chairs beside Annabelle who's sitting on a tarp filling an egg carton with dirt. I'm going to put you in jail, Jenny says, lifting a chair over her cousin's head. But kids don't go to jail. They go to Courtney. It's a long way and you have to go on a road that makes you car sick. Then she bursts into tears. Don't *go*, Daddy. Eugene crouches so their eyes are at the same level. It's only for a little while, Jen. I love you so much. I have to go to work. You can come on the plane, or I'll come back on the plane. Annabelle sits under her chair, dead calm and stony eyed.

Is there something I can do? says Lily.

You could drive me to the ferry.

Why doesn't he ask Gwen to drive him to the ferry? She plain can't bear it.

As Lily and Eugene head up the driveway, the pain in Gwen's ovaries and uterus clenches and releases. Blood pours from her as if her waters have broken. She rushes to the toiletless bathroom, aching from her waist to her knees, bleeds through a thick sanitary pad in ten minutes. She's not menstruating, she's hemorrhaging. Back in the kitchen, old George Fenn, who's come with a load of firewood, picks up Annabelle whose weight sinks into his chest as his face softens with belonging.

It's all right, I'm here, George says as if he'll never move again.

Ready for lunch, sweetheart? Gwen asks Jenny who's huddled on the kitchen couch. We have airplanes, honey. It's a short trip to see your dad. Let's set the table for lunch. We should wash these knives and forks. She pulls up a stool, runs water and squirts detergent. Jenny sticks her hands angrily in the suds. These man knives are at the beach, she says furiously. Looking after the lady forks. The *dad* dives in the water and swims to the *mom*. She picks up two teaspoons. These are their children who are almost drownded.

They're not drowning, Gwen says matter of factly. They're here lying on the beach.

Do you know to play Chinese checkers, Jenny? asks George. I'll have a game with you.

When Gwen goes to the garden to pick spinach for an omelette, she finds herself squatting on the ground, stuffing leaves into her mouth the way pregnant women with calcium deficiency lick plaster walls. A last few Brussels sprouts knot on their bolted stalks. The firs careen as if someone's holding them at the base and swinging them like a bouquet. *Your skin is so soft.*

How do you keep it like that? You don't have to answer.

Then Lily's back from the ferry standing at the edge of the garden. Why are you holding your stomach like that, Gwen? She takes her sister's elbow and helps her up. I don't know what's going on. You'd better tell me.

It's over. My marriage is over.

Are you sure?

I've been told that. He's gone.

I'm sorry I've been so preoccupied, I....

He's gone for good. Gwen's jaw drops and she can't stop crying.

Back in the kitchen, George has Jenny and Maya and Annabelle on pillows and booster seats at the trestle table jumping marbles on the game board. Lily touches his shoulder, leads Gwen into the group room where she helps her up on the massage table.

Is it here where you're hurting? She places her palm on her belly.

From my waist to my knees but mostly there.

Lily circles her fingers around the ankle bone, feels for the acupuncture point where the ovaries meet the instep. Presses as if taking a pulse. The ache deepens into bruised tenderness.

Crying is good, she says. It's all right.

But it's not all right. Crying makes her bleed harder.

41.

Thanksgiving is awfully darn early in Canada.

Twist those cranberries through the grinder while I'm getting dressed, will you Lil? says Gwen. Zest the orange. The spinach only takes a minute to wilt if you use the last clean rinse water.

I know it only takes a moment to wilt. I live here.

Fine.

It's all a commotion, though, because it's Kayak Will's day to do the wheat run: a group of them have negotiated the franchise to clean out the bottoms of the box cars at the downtown station which gives them free flour for a bit. There's one truck between them so they take turns. Sometimes it seems there's one twenty dollar bill that gets passed around the Cove all winter. Derek's looking for the keys to go fetch Ada from the four.

Will's got them, says Lily. He's doing the wheat run.

Oh shit, and you didn't bother telling me! I'll have to get George to pick up your mother and he's getting too old for all of this.

Worse, it looks like the turkey's done too soon. The vegetables should not be ready, but they are. They'll have to keep pans of hot water under them. Poke the sweet potatoes. Thaw the frozen pesto. Grate the precious expensive Romano.. Changing upstairs, Gwen hears Ada arrive. That loose Afghan tunic thing should be pretty enough for dinner but comfortable enough to cook in. Her mother will be in her camel-hair coat, her face powder pale. It's a good coat, she'll be thinking, too good for this place. George Fenn has been such a help he's staying for dinner too.

Let's see if we can wiggle this leg, Jenny, Gwen says. Stick a fork in the breast, see if the juices run clear. Do men call women birds, she wonders, because they think of their own palms supporting curved feathered vaginas? The wetted brown paper covering the bird has started to smoke and the roasting pan has gritty handles, the sides full of dents.

Dad should be here to make the gravy, says Jenny. Dad always makes the gravy.

You let the flour soak up the fat and start adding milk, honey. It's not hard.

Jenny whisks fiercely like a propeller on an outboard.

Slowly, dear. Gently.

Fine, gently.

You should have phoned me, Gwen, says Ada, looking at the chair as if wondering whether she should put her napkin down and sit on that.. I would have brought the good roasting pan. Her look of tired disappointment says it all. *I'm willing to look after the children so you can go back to school, Gwen. I've said so a thousand times. That condemned Deluxe you're planning to have your daughters sleep in? It's a fire trap. You people don't have to live like paupers over here. Derek could find a job.* Ada's never liked coming over to camp after Labour Day. She's told them that.

The gravy's good. Everyone says so, even if the zucchini relish is served in a saucer whose cup is broken. Jenny climbs into her grandmother's lap and pats her face.

Look at this. A lovely granddaughter in my lap. How lucky can you get?

I don't know, says Jenny.

Why are they having Thanksgiving in the kitchen again? Oh right, the girls are still sleeping in the dining room. An hour ago the greying tongue and groove walls looked comfortable to Gwen but, as soon as Ada came in, they looked dirty and dismal. Gwen bends protectively over the bird as she carries it to the table. Platters pass from stove to hand. Ada smiles at Derek as he crisscrosses the carving knife with the sharpener.

So, you children? she says. What's new and different?

Where's dad? says Lily.

He's at home.

Why's he at home? He's supposed to be flying. Why didn't he come here if he didn't go flying?

You know how he gets when he's depressed. He sits in his chair and stares. He's lost his pilot's license.

No. When? Lily stops chewing.

Oh *no*, says Gwen.

He's got a bit of a heart murmur, high blood pressure. It's not serious, Ada says to their alarmed looks. It'll be all right. They won't give him a clean bill of health, though, which he says is like being a little bit pregnant. Flying up north is what's kept him going this last while.

Good dinner or not, Gwen feels as if she's going to faint. Suddenly she can't bear her shapeless dress with a button missing. The blanched tomato skin of her own appearance slips from her shoulders useless as peoples' clothes when they take them off to make love. What's going on? It seems like her outfit was chosen by someone she liked yesterday but doesn't today. The afghan print is a book brought along to get through a night in a strange hotel but, when she opens it, it's one she's already read.

A truck whooshes down the hill. The door opens and Kayak Will comes in. Grey hair mixed with premature white—his face longer, teeth more feral. Suddenly the person Annabelle reminds Gwen of is no longer on the tip of her tongue.

Jesus, man. The truck's in the ditch. You kids leave the pig pen gate open? The porkers raced right across my path. I had to slam on the brakes but there weren't any. God damn truck, excuse me ma'am. I thought you fixed the brakes, man.

I did fix them, Derek says. It must be the master cylinder.

When Will passes behind Annabelle's chair, he cups his palm over her head but she ducks as if his hand is a hat she doesn't want to wear.

You remember Billy Fenn, mother? says Lily.

Of course I remember you, Billy. Will now is it? You've changed.

Haven't we all, says Billy Will, as he sits down and pours himself a glass of blackberry wine.

42.

Later, Lily's gone out to do a massage and Derek's in the kitchen playing solitaire. After Gwen gets the children down, she sits across from him. He's drinking too much, has puffy pouches under his eyes, broken blood vessels around his nose. She picks up a placemat and puts it down.

I don't think Lily knows how hurtful she can be, Derek, she says. She smashes a lot of corn stalks trying to pick more ears than anyone else if you know what I mean.

I do know what you mean, he says, But it's not going to get me anywhere. *Who else but George Fenn would have put the old school bus up in the orchard come to think of it? Maybe it was bait for his grandson.* At dinner, a cruel glint had flashed in Will's eyes as he pointedly rolled up one of Annabelle's sleeves while Lily rolled up the other.

Derek's glance acknowledges he knows Gwen's figured out what's going on, the same way he understood what was up that time in the lanes pool at Sandy when he hit up against the pretend net she'd woven trying to protect Leo.

Annabelle loves you, she says.
Lily told you, did she?
No, I saw.

Jenny needs something to get her mind off her loss so Gwen signs her up for soccer even though her daughter says she doesn't like doing things where she has to change her clothes. If she *has* to go to soccer, alright she'll try out for goalie. That way, she can kick away anything she doesn't like coming across the field.

When there's a break in the rain, they head to the waterfalls picnic grounds, now a soccer field. Gwen'd gone to Park Royal and spent her last fifteen dollars on goalie shin pads. Applied for welfare for a couple of months to tide her over. These Americans, coming up here and going on our welfare system, said someone in the mail queue. I won't dignify *that* with a response, she thinks. Kneeling in front of Jenny, she fastens the Velcro on her goalie shin pads as if girding her for battle.

When we go back to San Francisco, I want you and dad to see each other every day, Jenny says as she heads out to the field.

Maybe Gwen's stood up too quickly because she's so dizzy her pad's soaked through; when she makes a dash for the outhouse built from the shack that used to house the generator, canoes spin like clock hands. Inmates in grey hospital gowns and paper slippers shuffle down the hall. *Yarding out words and words like a net. She has him. She has him. He gets away.* Maybe if she turns with the spinning rather than standing still, she and the numbers on the clock will stay in the same place. The game's just started. The game is over. Discharging gobs of coalesced blood thick as chocolate pudding, she manages to get back to the field to help Jenny takes off her goalie padding.

Homesick is when you want to be somewhere else, Jenny says.

The next thing she remembers is waking up in a clinic, a queasy nurse lifting blood soaked pads from her crotch as if pulling prints. Your blood count's gone from fifteen down to seven. We're giving you a transfusion now. Strange blood seeps into her body like oil that doesn't mix with water. Whose blood is this? she calls out. I don't like this blood.

It's this blood or dying, mother.

Oh well then.

Derek waits out in the corridor until they let him in to see her.

Where're the girls?

I have them. Don't worry.

I don't have any money, Derek, she says. I don't know what to do. Maybe I could start a daycare, take on a few more kids. I could do that.

You relax and get better, Gwen. Don't worry about anything right now.

Back in the room, a doctor in a white lab coat is standing by her bed. Unfortunately, he tells her, you're going to need a hysterectomy. Nowadays we can reverse uteruses back through the vagina but you have too much scar tissue and leakage from your womb to sustain that procedure. Likely we'll have to perform the operation the old-fashioned way but at least the cut will be on your bikini line. You'll have part of an ovary and your own hormones.

Small mercies, she mutters.

Out the window of the hospital—UBC actually—there's a swimming pool to the north, lights on the Grouse Mountain chair lift to the east. How are you today, Mrs. Killam? the doctor says the day after the operation.

Ms. Killam, Gwen says. Mrs. Killam is my mother. Achy. Not great.

Down on all fours are you? He smiles. A hysterectomy *is* major surgery. If you rest for the next six weeks, your pelvic floor will build a foundation to support you for the rest of your life. Otherwise.... He makes a steeple with his fingers, collapses them.

How can I do that? I have two little kids.

I understood your parents live nearby.

They do, but I don't want to impose on them.

Do you have a choice?

Of course I have a choice. I'll go back to Scarborough.

Maybe, when you're stronger, but, in the meantime, there's a colleague of mine I'd like you to have a word with.

A few days later, a resident shows her into an interview room in another part of the hospital. At least they've given back her jeans and sweater so she doesn't have to shuffle down the hall in paper slippers. Inside the small room, the wall to her right is a mirror. Is this a one way mirror? she asks.

It's not for you to see, says the resident. Yourself I mean. The psychiatrist needs to see how I'm doing.

Don't you know what you're doing either? I can't stay. I have to go and get the children.

I'll take you around behind and show you.

They're about to investigate – she's expecting a booth like a technician's sound studio—when a tall balding man who must have been behind the mirror joins them. Solemn, with a slow candor, the sort of person who might take a long time to answer a question, but his answer would be worth listening to.

This is Dr. Merrick, says the resident.

Why are you here? the psychiatrist asks once he's sitting down.

I had a hysterectomy.

No, I mean. Why did you agree to come to see me?

I don't know what's wrong with me. I'm hallucinating. They thought the blood transfusion would help but it hasn't. I have to get back. Derek can't cope with the children by himself and Lily's gone back to Checleset.

Who's Derek? Who's Lily?

When she explains, he and the resident get up and leave. Is this where you go out of the room and vote? she asks.

It's okay, he says. I'll be back.

Why does it make such a difference, his saying that? But it does. When they come back, they say they think she should stay in the hospital for a bit.

So you think I'm crazy?

We think you're a very tired human being. It's going to be okay, the doctor says softly and she hears him in a spot at the base of her brain that hasn't been touched for a long time. *The water wants to hold you up. There's nothing else for it to do.*

43.

January, 1972.

At Gwen's second interview, this one in Dr. Merrick's comforting oak office, he says he'd be willing to "work with her" if she's prepared to give up intimate relationships. Ones that count.

I don't mean for a month or two either. I mean for a long time. He sounds as if he's draping sheets to expose a surgical site.

Why? she says alarmed.

You're all over the map. He doesn't mean to sound patronizing but any gardener worth his salt would start with a bit of pruning. If you want to strengthen your base, that is. Get back to where we can take a good look at the roots of the problem.

I'm a woman not a garden.

Still, he says. It shouldn't be this bad. If you want to deal with this, we'll have to go a long way back. A very long way back indeed.

The truth is I'd do almost anything to have my husband back in my bed.

You'd pick up the phone and call him at a moment's notice, wouldn't you?

Oh yes.

She also considers the doctor's unspoken point that she's at liberty to say she's not up for this approach, in which case he would probably refer her. I'm sorry that psychology falls into jargon so quickly, he says, as if he's about to pronounce *relationships* the way Jenny would later in a snide parody of anything psychological. An ironic smile cuts briefly across his neither open nor closed face. There are other rewards, he says.

Already, she's curious as to what those might be. Slowly, as she gets physically stronger, she's more able to concentrate but the more she refuses to let herself call Eugene, the weepier she gets. Sometimes at night she makes babysitting arrangements, gets in the car, heads down to a dancehall in Point Roberts, dances blindly with whomever she picks up, heads back to strange motels.

It's a bit self indulgent, isn't it? the doctor says when she tells him.

You want me to be totally celibate? she says. I don't know if I can do that.

Slave, he says.

What did they do before *Oshkosh* overalls? You've got your striped pair, your worn jean pair. Maybe she should mount them, gild them like baby shoes. Tries to understand that throwing a fit about wanting to play with the yellow truck is a way of insisting on your right to be yourself. If somebody's got something of yours, use your words. You need to look for your hat. It's where you aren't. Keep your leg to your own body please.

At Blenheim St. when they're visiting, Grandpa makes breakfast and asks Jenny what she'd like. I'd just like a little breakfast, she says. When she comes to the table, he presents her with a crouton on a plate, a thimbleful of orange juice, and a doll's dish with a piece of scrambled egg and a crumb of bacon. Funny Grandpa. At supper, Jenny reads them a write-up on the planets she's doing for school. If Earth's a grape seed, Jupiter would be an orange. The sun is several watermelons. Percy takes an orange from the fruit bowl and places it near the ketchup bottle.

Don't put it on the bird's face, Maya cries. You'll get it in its eye. It won't be able to fly out in the planets where it wants to go. See, it's here. And it was, patterned in the grain of the table.

A few days later, Ada unties her apron in the middle of a thunderstorm, plucks her cardigan from a hook, walks down to the low corner of the lot where she used to be able to see the Fraser, but the cedar has grown so high she no longer has a view. Arrows of lightening jag across the sky. Gwen wants to call her in, but her shoulders are set against being disturbed.

I don't think I'm afraid after all, she says when she comes back.

Of what, mother? Gwen's so astonished by the flood of warm pleasure that the raised blind over her mother's face gives her—*your mother's not what you'd call accessible, is she?*—she steps up close, not in her arms exactly, but not that far away either. Her mother reaches up for her glasses but her fingers pinch the corners of her eyes because she's already taken them off.

Embrace your fears, Gwen, she says.

All of them?

Don't make any appointments for Wednesday afternoons. I go out Wednesday afternoons.

Where, Gwen wants to say, but doesn't.

Eugene calls to see what Jenny wants for her birthday.

A sheep for my bed, I guess.

When his gift arrives, it's a length of brightly patterned cloth. Orange and yellow tigers skulk in a dark green jungle. He'd thought she said a sheet for her bed.

Oh dear.

Dr. Merrick's office is low-lit; he wears tweed jackets and sober colours. What are you doing for bucks? he asks.

It's a problem.

What about formalizing the child support?

I can't talk to him, she says. I've said it and said it. Knowing a cheque's going to be there at the beginning of the month is more important than the amount. I don't know why he doesn't send me post-dated cheques.

Have his salary garnisheed.

It's not reciprocal between here and the States. I can't work full time with the girls so young and, with no father, they need more of me not less.

Call him from here, he says. He picks up the phone and hands it to her.

I owe you for the call.

He doesn't say anything.

You really think I should do this?

Silence.

She swivels the chair away. Eugene, it's me. How are you? That's good. Listen, the child support cheque's not here. How can you say that? I would have kept in touch anyway.

She hangs up. I'm glad I'm here. He said if I have to call about the cheque, that way he knows I'll keep in touch. That's a terrible thing to say.

He should be coming forward with this money, says the doctor. It should be at least $600 a month. Get a lawyer.

They'll make me take the children back. They were born there. He'll get a lawyer who'll make me do that. Why does he do this?

Control?

Why would he bother? He doesn't want me.

I'm not talking about you.

He kindly doesn't say for once.

Part of it was my fault too. I couldn't adjust and, in the end, I couldn't even do the basics I was feeling so terrible.

I know that, lassie.

Your problem, he says, is that you let need interfere with judgment. You distort situations for the sake of gratification. When I asked if there was still anything between you and

Eugene, besides the children, when you said yes it was a knee jerk reaction. You didn't ask yourself why's he asking me that question. It's the same impulse that makes you act out sexually. The trouble with school for someone like you was that it was a ball. You didn't learn to tolerate frustration.

Really? It's expensive, isn't it? says Gwen. Sex is so bonding. Did you learn that at your father's knee? That love and sex are dangerous.

Yes, I did. Darn rights it's expensive. I'm not trying to take the agony out of your life, you do realize that? So you're uncomfortable, he says looking discreetly at his desk top. No one ever died of it. I guess you're going to have to get used to a leaner diet.

How long am I supposed to go on like this, keeping the brakes on? she says. Are we nearly done?

It's good you feel like that, but no. Channeling it would be another possibility. It's an age-old technique after all. Instead of sexualizing your energy, why don't you use it to write down some of your early memories? As I said, it shouldn't be this bad, your having to separate. It's a loss. You're worried about the consequences for the girls. But you go on feeling that he's you, walking around down there. Why is that? That time he came up to see the children? Should you have had him stay with you? Isn't that what hotels are for?

He's my children's father.

Still. It doesn't *have* to work you know. You can't always make things work by putting energy into them.

When he comes up here....

I know. Nothing goes right. It's the irresistible force and the immovable object all over again but, if you learn to tolerate the frustration, a space of regard and self respect will begin to open in many aspects of your life.

A few months later on Percy's birthday at Blenheim St., there's an envelope with his name on it propped against his glass. As a joke, he holds it up to the light to see if there's a cheque inside. Unbelievably, it turns out to be a pilot's license made out to Ada Killam. He replaces it, hurt and insulted.

This is not funny, Ada.

It's not a joke.

Everyone's forks are halfway to their mouths, profiles whapped to Ada's end of the table.

I've been taking lessons. I got my license.

Percy's face is going to fall on the table if someone doesn't catch it.

You have to put a plane in free fall to get a pilot's license.

I did that.

You did the navigation school? You did the weather exam?

I did the navigation school. I did the weather exam. Ada gets up and comes back with the car keys in her hand. Let's go.

Where?

For a ride in an airplane.

I can't believe this.

Percy looks at all of them as if to say, you've witnessed this. Don't ever forget it. As if they could. I had to, Ada said later. Dad was so unhappy.

Children and grandchildren are waiting when Ada and Percy return, Jenny perched on the bottom stair as if the doors to Christmas haven't been opened yet. Percy is radiant. Would you believe my wife, you children? Now I'll be able to fly again because there'll be another qualified pilot at the dual controls.

As if they could ever forget it.

44.

Imagine my mother doing that, Gwen says to Dr. Merrick. I didn't know she had anything like that kind of courage.

You must be proud of her.

I am.

He smiles gently, letting the atmosphere settle. His consistent reliable presence sends a message that with time, hard work and a touch of grace, the patient might at last begin to integrate the fragments of her life. When she feels emotionally drawn into a situation, he says, she might try taking a step back and asking who is this person, what is he or she about? It takes a lot of practice, but it's worth a try. That way you widen the space where you can look at situations objectively. It's as if he has to take the chance of entering the place in her psyche where she's loneliest without giving her the wrong idea. Any indelicate gesture would provide an inappropriate crutch and she'd be back to square one. It's as if he knows she has to conserve her energy for an ordeal they haven't discovered yet.

I miss the closeness, she says.

Of course you do.

It's so lonely. Is this it then, is this forever?

As I said, the compensation for that is supposed to be a growing sense of inner strength.

Oh, she says sadly. When's that supposed to start?

When she goes to put on her coat hanging by one of the bookcases, she sees a clear bottle of sea stones filled with water on the green carpet.

Has that been there the whole time?

The whole time.

Why are you smiling?

Because you're smiling.

He says he brought the bottle over for the architects when they were building the hospital. He wanted the walls and floor to be the colours of stones under water.

You did a great job. This room is an oasis.

Good. You don't like things to change much, do you?

No, I like them to stay the same.

She thought he'd smiled because he was amused, but walking back to the car, she realizes it's important not to mistake analysis for social conversation. He always has a reason for what he says and does. That night, she looks at a love poem of Eugene's she'd found in the apartment and brought with her as a keepsake. Now, reading it in the driver's seat, she realizes it had been written to somebody else.

A few days later, a noisy ruckus starts up in the yard where Jenny and Annabelle are in the bath. They've been told the bath water's only for rinsing, not soaping, but a shivering Annabelle stands in the tub sluicing sudsy bubbles from her narrow body. Jenny's sitting in the tub nonchalantly soaping herself, one knee over the other like Bugs Bunny on the lam.

Tell Annabelle that Kayak Will's her dad, she says. Everybody at school says so.

Derek's her main dad, Jen, Gwen says picking up a facecloth and wiping her niece's face. You girls know there's not supposed to be soap in this bathtub.

He's not my maindajen, Annabelle cries flailing in the towel as if it's a straitjacket. He's my *Dad*.

Yes, honey, he's your dad.

A SOFT NO

45.

March, 1975.

Neither Gwen nor Derek will remember who first came up with the idea of restoring the dancehall. Maybe the pavilion itself called out to them, empty and unused as it's been all these years. Moss coats the roof, the central columns are covered in mildew and the walls are so damp they're about to collapse into the forest floor. The two of them decide that, if they prepare a strong enough application, they might be able to persuade the organizers of Habitat Forum in Vancouver to feature the Bowen pavilion as a recycled heritage building. People could take an excursion to the island and have a look see. Recycle the hall into a community centre after the conference maybe.

Don't let them touch the dancehall floor, Ada says when she hears about the project.

When the grant comes through, Derek manages to get his hands on a portable sawmill which they erect in a covered picnic table area that hasn't been torn down yet. A beachcombing gopher opens its claws on Miss Fenn's Rocky, lifts logs to drag to the dancehall to replace the moldering Corinthian columns. Peeled and varnished, they'll be erected in the centre of the hall before the originals are removed. Horizontal beams lie on the floor ready to lift into place to form the new centre octagon.

The concession stand area of the pavilion has been set aside as a child care centre: the plan is to exchange the special dance-hall window for a door so the daycare can have its own access. Gwen's stripping recycled wainscoting when Jenny shows up cranky because she had to stay behind after school and clean out her desk.

They'd better not take Will's log, she says, looking at the logs on the floor.

Billy doesn't really live in a log, Jen. It's just a way of speaking.

When he came in to help earlier, Billy Will crossed the hall to the special window where a huge huckleberry bush and a thin cedar grow from the old stump.

I'd like to have Annabelle overnight soon, Gwen. Lily and I agreed on that before she left.

She didn't say anything to me, says Gwen.

I do have some rights here, he says more humbly than she ever thought possible.

It's up to Derek, Gwen says. But he's in town.

At Jericho Beach in Vancouver where the Habitat Forum conference is to be held, the plan is to build seats in the hangars that housed the planes which patrolled the coast during the war. The results could be monitored over the years for shrinking and duration. Plus, everyone's getting paid which is very cool. Jobs for people coming out their ears, Derek tells the crowd at the pub when he gets back from the mainland. Including me, part time.

He draws a picture for the girls of the west gate logs they're going to insert into one another in the shape of a Ferris wheel. A fork lift will deposit a huge piece of driftwood to be carved into a whale.

It should be called a lifting fork, Jenny says. Is there going to be stuff for kids?

Sure there's going to be stuff for kids.

An unseasonable gale blows straight off the Sound and the wind roars through the huge doorways in the old airplane hangars, freezing the Jericho crew. Derek comes home cold and wet.

Lily told Billy he could have Annabelle overnight, Gwen says when he comes in. I've held him off so far but....

Absolutely not. I'll take her to town with me if he's bothering you. How're things at the hall?

Okay. It feels like we'll be sanding forever though. We don't mind the seating being rough, but not splintery, right?

Right.

At least she's starting to pay better attention on the home front, noticing the way Derek spends more and more time wandering around the place, half-heartedly pulling deadhead from the bush and leaving it to chop for firewood but never getting back to it. Cooking Brussels sprouts, he moans there's no reason they have to take so long. When she suggests a lid, it seems like the end of the world when he can't find it. We *had* a wok lid. Working on the truck or raking the garden, it's as if the position he's standing in refuses to jibe with the position he's used to standing in. She checks these observations off like the numbers the doctor gets her to add up to help mobilize her matter-of-fact side which got obliterated in the course of her growing up. *I know it's boring.* Maybe you were stopped mid-action so many times, it was difficult for you to figure out how you wanted to do things, he says.

Sometimes I was hit, she says. *Why do women always do things the hard way? How can you be so stupid?* Percy yelled when she tried to wind the hose on her arm instead of using the curved rack nailed to the wall. And she froze.

Leo was the one who was good with numbers so I wasn't supposed to be, she says.

I understand that, but you need a matter-of-fact side to develop a self-observing ego, he tells her. A person usually acquires one by hearing the adults make empathetic matter of fact observations. *You handled that well. What would your options be, do you suppose?*

What's a self-observing ego?

The part of a person that's looking down and observing the whole circus.

I didn't hear much in the way of that kind of voice, she says. My mother was *busy.* She did her best.

I'm not saying she didn't. Maybe you didn't like the way they handled you. What's Derek doing do you suppose? Dr. Merrick asks when she tells him about the way he's wandering aimlessly around Scarborough. Her blank look says beats me. Looking for himself? he asks.

Later, she lies awake in the bunkhouse staring at the ceiling wondering why putting herself forward to support Derek starts up her own physical yearning. If burning *down there* is a symptom of being separated from a part of herself that never grew, maybe it's true, as Dr. Merrick says, that all her "love" relationships so far have been narcissistic. Maybe if she ignores being aroused, it'll die down.

Where's the turning point in all this? How long is she going to go on rotating in space, as Dr. Merrick puts it? How long will he have to model matter-of fact behaviour before she gains some traction?

Do you have any idea how difficult this is? she asks.

I do, he says gently, and takes off his glasses which he never does. For a moment it seems that his soul steps across his desk and touches hers. The winter tide finally rises high enough to reach the driest place on the beach.

After that, she begins to see her projections slide up the body of the person she's idealizing the way paper outfits slipped up over her cardboard dolls. You idealize everybody, he'd said. The way, when anyone criticizes her, her self-respect is given over to whomever she imagines never makes mistakes. Could she permit herself the hope that Dr. Merrick trusts her a little to risk reaching out to her with nothing but his soul? That wasn't projection. She loves him when she thinks about it—she does too—but is she partly loving the fact that she feels seen and heard by him? That he treats her with respect and her mother doesn't?

If no one acknowledges your secrets as a child, it makes sense that part of you ends up sitting beside yourself feeling abandoned, Dr. Merrick says on her next visit. Maybe she's also projected that lost part of herself onto the men she's known and expected them to make up for it.. They look up phone numbers. They call mechanics. They call lawyers. The desert of celibacy exhausts her, but he keeps repeating that resisting there is the best place for her to practise tolerating frustration so her objective matter of fact side can develop. Even when she's blamming off the walls of his office, she knows he'll stay with her in no-man's land where she's perched on the end of a branch that might snap any minute. Knowing he's there makes all the difference. I'm trying to get you to care about you, he says. There are places she can feel they're skipping; places they look in but can't see anything even though he keeps going back, asking the same questions. *Straight from pre-teen to her disguise as an adult?* That pretty well says it. The unidentified pain they're not going near as long as her daily reality is difficult stays in place like a bookmark.

She could feel that he'll go the distance until she could see *what?* Something neither of them knows, but she does know that, whatever it is, when she does find out, he'll care.

One evening spring has settled in with such certainty Gwen and Derek find themselves down on the beach after the kids are asleep. The rhodos and azalea are almost out. The smell of the sea lettuce is pungent, the long grass whispers in the meadow. It isn't fair they get along so well. If he leans toward her, his soft beard would stroke her breast. And his moustache. There has to be a moustache. That *frisson,* eh? If she weren't attracted to him, it would be no contest, but in the same way the planet goes on turning away from its star, everything at that moment feels so exactly right she wants to cry. Is it part of getting older that everything has to be exactly right? Say he reached out and put his hand on her hair. (I really do try to live up to all the hard work you're putting into me, she said to the doctor.) If he did, she'd put his hand carefully back on the sand and tell him the opposite of what she wants to say. And then he does touch her hair. And then she does put his hand carefully back on the sand.

I'd better get over to the hall and help with the sanding, she says.

Oh leave it. Tomorrow. His eyes beg.

I'd like to but I can't, she says. Look what might happen to what we've got going here. It would confuse the kids even more than they are.

The kids don't have to know.

That's how it always is at the beginning.

I want you.

You think I don't want you?

Well, then.

You wouldn't think a simple thing like not acting on an inappropriate attraction would be a personal triumph, but it is. Those moments, eh, that only you know are so difficult. The leaner diet Dr. Merrick suggested means that the moment she and Derek just had could be cherished for the rest of her life. It's true they're better suited to each other than to the partners they've been with, but maybe it's impossible to abandon a marriage once there are children. It will stalk you one way or another. She's not going to crow about it to the doctor either. He'd talked about private sorrows. Well, this can be a private joy.

46.

Lily arrives at the dancehall to find Gwen sanding the walls of the concession stand counter. Where's Annabelle? she asks.

In town with Derek.

What's she doing over there?

It was Derek's decision, Gwen says. This is between you two, not me. I wish you'd figure it out.

Have you told Jenny and Maya they're not going back to San Francisco? says Lily.

Never mind what's going on with me, Lil. What kind of a set-up is going on with you? I mean who's minding the store?

We're all minding the store. That's what community is about.

Oh come on. It's so obvious about Annabelle. I mean it really is.

She's going to have two fathers.

Even if Derek's doing all the fathering? Don't talk to me about my children's confusion when you're being so wrong-headed about Billy. He had the nerve to show up here and say he was taking Annabelle overnight, that's why Derek took her to town. Look at the position you left me in.

You get yourself so cranked up about this, Gwen. You're so *tense* about it. I don't think it's good for Annabelle to be around you. Maybe we can do some co-counseling on it, all three of her parents.

I don't think Derek wants that, Gwen says carefully.

So he's talking to you now is he?

You do know that Billy tormented the life out of our brother? I don't trust him one bit. He's mellowed a little, but you never know what he's going to get up to.

Annabelle does him good, says Lily. And George has been like a grandfather to me. I have no intention of leaving either of them out of the picture.

A few days later Gwen tells Dr. Merrick that the complications at Scarborough are getting too much for her. If he notices the projection split he doesn't say anything, maybe because he sees she's figured it out for herself. He does ask her if she's noticed that it's when her self-respect gets deflated that she idealizes people.

How's your mother? he says.

We can forget about her.

We can't actually.

She shifts and wonders if to him she's in shadow. Doing far more than her share actually, she says.

It's too bad there isn't somewhere else on the island you could go seeing the girls are settled there.

Well, she says. There's the cottage.

What cottage is that?

We have a family cottage in the Cove.

He looks at her astonished. You mean to tell me you've been coming here all this time and haven't told me you have a family place over there besides that other place whatever it's called?

I can't go there. It's closed down. The water's turned off.

Well turn it on.

It's not our time.

Whose time is it?

Isabelle's.

They look at each other. *The one time I saw your mother? I've never seen anyone with such a rigid but fragile construct. And I see a lot of people.*

Who's Isabelle?

My aunt.

Is she there?

She doesn't go up. She's moved to Birch Bay in the States. With her husband. She and my Mom and Aunt Evvie do a time-share. I haven't seen her for years. We don't see her.

Why?

I don't know. She doesn't want anyone there.

How do you know that?

My mom.

Your mother's trying to be loyal to her family of origin it looks like. What would happen if you went anyway?

I'm more afraid to do that than I was to go to the hospital to have the children.

That bad, eh?

He scribbles a few notes on a pad. You have to go, he says.

A few days later, Billy saunters into the daycare and stands watching Annabelle playing jacks on the edge of the old stage. Lily told you it's okay if I take her overnight, right? he says to Gwen.

Right.

When he tries to pick her up, big girl that she is, Annabelle turns stiff as a board and begins to cry.

Worse, when Gwen goes to the store and sees the communal truck coming up the Government Road with Billy driving, Annabelle is sitting like an iron rod in the seat beside him. Derek's outside the post office checking his mail. When he sees the truck, the lines from his nostrils down the sides of his moustache deepen and his face collapses. When he sees Gwen, he looks momentarily comforted, then wrenches his face away.

That afternoon Gwen finds herself standing on the resting rock thinking about the way you're supposed to point your skis straight down the hill instead of hanging onto the side of the mountain. Their cottage at the end of the Point looks frozen; when she finally makes it down the hill, the walls seem miserably thin. The light switches don't work, maybe there's no hydro. She'll have to light a candle when it gets dark, shade it with her palm so no one will know she's there.

In the living room, magazines are piled neatly on the chairs so people won't sit on them. A scroll with the moon painted on it is laid out on a card table. A few pieces of porcelain dinner ware with a bird of paradise pattern. It's not a house, it's a memorial. But to what? The telephone rings and she jumps. Maybe a neighbour has called her mother to say a stranger's broken in. She finds a piece of paper and draws a diagram of the way the wood is arranged in the wood box. Makes a few notes about the position of the pile of ashes in the fireplace so she can re-create the layout when she leaves. In the front bedroom, the mattress is covered with an old chenille bedspread, the top edge turned back diagonally as if waiting for a guest. It's raining again, the damp air chills through the cedars. She manages to get a fire going by blowing through a hollow brass stick, picks pieces of ash from her lips. The first couple of times she tries to light the gas furnace, the flame goes out when she releases the pilot light. The third time it works.

She dozes off in Grandpa Gallagher's old chair in front of the fireplace. Dreams she's on a ladder in the dancehall trying to tie a rope around a tarp she's flung over the pillars, manages to get it stretched over the thumb and first two fingers but it's windy and there isn't enough fabric for the third. A bat darts into her sleeping bag; she jumps both hands on it like a cat after a mouse. A thudding that sounds like a body being dragged along the side of the house wakes her up from her nap. She leaps to attention beside the shaking gas furnace. A new voice— her own—replaces the doctor's for the first time. Listen to it. *Really* listen to it. Maybe the furnace can't function properly on high. Maybe it would do better on medium.

So this is what they call a therapeutic moment, lying on your stomach on a cold linoleum floor in a deserted cabin, scraping cobwebs with a flashlight so you can read a scummy dial. When she slowly turns the dial to medium, the furnace settles down. Percy is *not* standing above her with his hand raised. Neither is Grandpa Gallagher. Everything's not going to blow up because she's there. She's there with whoever's waiting for someone who's supposed to be there and isn't.

Maybe she'll bring all three girls over one day soon and spend the night since the furnace is humming along so nicely. It looks as if someone's loosened the fuses so there wouldn't be a fire. She tightens them and the switches work. Yay. Brings her journal up to date, washes the dishes in the old chipped dishpan, and goes down to reacquaint herself with Miss Fenn's Rocky.

47.

When she returns to Scarborough, fork and shovel handles stick out of the ground with no one attached to them. Derek's toque hangs on a wheelbarrow handle, one of his shirts spread out on a lilac bush as if to dry. It's raining so hard she stumbles and slips on a bunch of apples spilled from a box. Why's the bathtub pushed over? Inside the house there's a miserable empty feeling as if someone she doesn't care about is sick. The clock ticks. She calls; no answer. No one's in the shed, no one up in the pens. Climbing up through the orchard, she sees Derek's chainsaw stuck into the ground outside the barn door. *Enabler,* someone hissed the morning she held him in the group room. Inside, the large barn walls vault into a wide roof with a loft. Below it, Derek's feet are swinging back and forth like a pendulum. When she sees him, her own feet jump off the floor with shock. Maybe he was leaping from the loft and miscalculated; she rushes over and tries to push a bale of hay under him but, above her, his head lolls to the side, squeezed through the noose as if his neck'd been wrung. The rest of him points straight down. When she climbs up to chop the rope and he tumbles down, she tries to breathe into him but his lips won't stay open. Hooking his dental partial out like a wishbone, she tries to spread his mouth with her thumb and middle finger but it won't stay. Flipping him over, she straddles his back, presses and releases with her palms as if he'd drowned. Turns him face front, pushes hard on his chest. Nothing. *Don't let this be happening.* Hauls him up, leans his back against her chest, tucks her knees around his hips. But he won't come back, he won't ever come back, and down at the house, the truck's pulling into the driveway.

Are you all right, Gwen? You don't look too good, Billy says standing by the truck holding Annabelle's hand. She didn't want to stay overnight this time. I've brought her back. The little girl's stricken eyes follow the line of Derek's markers up through the orchard as if she knew something terrible would happen if she was ever in the truck when Will was driving instead of Derek. When Roxy jumps up on her, instead of telling her to get down, she takes her paws and walks her stiffly into the house. Gwen gets through to Lily on the phone at the Jericho site. You need to come home, Lily. Right away.

Are the children okay?

Yes, but you need to come home. I'll tell you when you get here.

What have I done? says Lily at the door.

You haven't done anything.

When the school bus arrives, Jenny and Maya charge in, smash the fridge door open, smear peanut butter on bread.

I need to talk to you, Lil. Gwen takes her sister's arm into the living room, closes the door. Sit down, she says.

Lily does.

It's Derek. It's terrible, it's so terrible but he's dead. He hung himself in the barn.

Oh god. No. Lily shakes her head over and over again. It can't be true. Is he still…?

Up there, yes. I tried everything. She starts to cry.

I have to go to him.

Rushing past the children up through the orchard, she disappears into the barn. Gwen stays in the living room staring at the wall, then Lily's back at the picnic table staring at the ground, lips and eyes tight and thin.

I can't believe this. What are we going to tell the children? she says when Gwen comes out.

It's too late to tell them anything tonight, Gwen says. Let's get them to bed. *If you take a step back you'll fall off the loft.* I called the police and the coroner when you were in the barn.

Annabelle comes out and climbs into her mother's lap. Lily stretches out her daughter's arm, touches the Band-aid. What's this?

It's an owie.

An owie. You're too big a girl to say that. Lily looks up at her sister. It looks like she's had some kind of a needle.

Has she had all her vaccinations? says Gwen. Billy wouldn't have taken her for a booster?

Of course she has. Derek took care of that. Where did this owie come from, Annabelle?

Annabelle doesn't answer.

Are you going to tell me?

She shakes her head.

When the police and coroner arrive, Gwen heads them off at the driveway, herds them up the hill. As they're approaching the building containing Derek's body, her view expands to include the old logged in pool at Sandy where, as a visitor, Derek'd flipped over and turned back to the diving tower end after encountering her imaginary net, but this time when he returns to where he'd pushed off, he reaches out to pick up the tooth retainer he'd left behind.

When she and Lily tell the children the next day, Jenny starts picking at her fingernails, alarmingly mature as she tells Maya and Annabelle it's the same as when they found the dead bird in the garden and buried it in the lane.

We'll have to bury him, Jenny says. Like the bird. In the living room, she lies on the sofa with her head on her mother's knee wanting to have her hair stroked back over and over again.

Poor Derek, says Jenny as if he were a whippoorwill.

The place feels so bereft of him, littered with unfinished jobs, his outline standing at the ready. Lily keeps telling the kids things they already know. When Jenny takes leftover porridge out to feed the dogs, her aunt informs her she should put the porridge in the dish, not give it to the dog in the pot.

I know that, says Jenny.

Annabelle stops talking. She doesn't open her mouth except to eat. When they ask her about the owie again, she tightens her lips and turns her head from side to side the way Lily used to when they were trying to feed her.

He wouldn't have taken her for a blood test thinking of a paternity suit or something? Gwen says.

Would he have, without saying anything to me? says Lily.

I don't know.

Now it's Lily's turn to wander around staring at the places she and Derek had been together as if it's taken this unerring silence for her to know how unhappy he was. She goes quietly around picking up after him. At least she's stopped in her tracks for once. She has to call Derek's parents in England and that's just awful. She puts down the phone. They said they're going to come over to see Annabelle. I didn't know what to say.

Well, what are you going to say?

I don't know.

The adage about the children in your neighbourhood being everyone's children Gwen kept touting to Eugene? If you ever find yourself trying to live in that never-never land, he said, count me out.

THREE WAY SPLIT

48.

August, 1975.

Isabelle? This is Gwen.

Gwen. How good to hear your voice. Where are you?

I've been spending time at the cottage actually.

I've phoned a few times. I had the feeling someone was there.

So it was you calling. I was wondering if I could come and see you?

Of course you can come and see me.

I was thinking of tomorrow.

Tomorrow it is. Will you come on the bus?

I'll come on the bus.

I'll meet you at the station in Blaine.

And there she is, still tall and gaunt as a heron, her long neck creviced as if by a potter's thumbs. Dressed thinly in gabardine slacks and a fake leather jacket, her protruding eyes look watery, but she still has that amused ironic smile playing around her mouth as if she'll always find life strange and amusing. It's been a freak spring, yesterday cold as winter; today the sun's melting the tarred centre line. They climb into her old Pontiac, find themselves held up by a circus parade of all things.

Everyone's been looking forward to having a parade with an elephant in it, Isabelle says. An official stops the car, leans in the window. It's the elephants, he says. They're being watered. It's such a hot day the pavement is hurting their feet. We're going to hose the streets down now.

Isabelle's smile shows a couple of gold-rimmed teeth. She lifts her rhinestone cornered glasses from her face, dabs at her eyes with a hanky. Laughs in that old way of not caring whether anyone's going to join in. They could have made shoes for them out of cardboard, she says. How's your mother?

Fine. She has her gardening, and she's learned to fly.

No.

It's true. The planes she and dad fly are too small to take any luggage. When they go anywhere, she has to wear the same out-fit the whole time. She has one sleeveless dress, wears a viyella blouse under it if it's cool.

That's the most astonishing news I've ever heard, says Isabelle. I tried to get up to see her once, but the line-up at the border was too long and I gave up. Tell me about your girls.

My girls are the cat's meow.

Are they? And how are you?

I'm getting there.

When the parade starts up, and the elephants pass the in-tersection, the thick leather of their twitching skin crisscrosses with lines. Glittery chains drape their foreheads and their ears are like wide floppy sleeves. They keep picking up their feet and replacing them.

I don't know why they didn't spray the streets with the fire hose. It's good to see you, Gwen.

It's good to see you too.

When they get to Birch Bay, Isabelle parks the car at the beach. The tide flats stretch to the water's edge; wide striations of blown sand banded with pale pink and dusty blue reflect in the tidal pools. Dungeness crabs bracket their way along the sea floor. The local road passes in front of their weather-beaten board and batten store leached to pale grey blue by the salt wind. Their house, *Bide-a-Wile*, is joined to the store by a wooden boardwalk leading to the beach. When people visit, they park their cars on the hosts' front lawns, knock on car fenders to announce their arrival. Both the store and the house are clean and decrepit with the same worn scraped look. A few ancient looking tins of sardines and canned milk that look as if they're long past their *better before* dates line the store shelves.

Gwen's offered a milkshake from a machine so old-fashioned it could have been recycled from the tearoom. She drinks it sitting on one of the swivel stools, excuses herself to go to the bathroom. The toilet walls are scrubbed and chipped, a mop and a bucket in one corner and a limp Evergreen air freshener. Back in the café part of the store, Isabelle's pouring coffee, talking to a couple of customers.

Jack's crabbing again, is he?

Every day. It's his life.

A series of what look like varnished cupboard handles lie on the arborite counter. Jack makes them for people to take out on the tide flats to measure their crabs, Isabelle says. Gwen picks one up, holds it to an invisible cupboard, puts it back down.

The tide's retreated so far Jack is a distant speck on the horizon. Even at this distance, you can see he has a life of his own out there. He comes slowly up from the beach in hip waders and an old suede jacket so soft and patched it's more mend than fabric. Looks carefully both ways before he crosses the street.

Morning, Jack, says a passer-by. See you've been crabbing. Catch anything?

Five, actually. We'll all eat today. He dumps the contents of his galvanized buckets into a tub of salt water on the café floor. A claw surfaces and grabs the stick.

His forehead is tight as if something behind him is trying to pull back his head. He sits on a stool, reaches over and puts his hand on his wife's waist. His hair is thin and grey red.

This is Gwen, Jack. I've told you about Gwen.

He looks at his niece blankly. His face is frightened, as if he doesn't want anyone to know how high the stakes are. One minute he's dignified and fine; the next it's taking everything he has to remember he's meant to shake hands. He reaches out but misses and, to his own amazement, finds himself at the end of one of the rows of shelves. It seems someone's stolen some of the ham tins. Who would have walked off with them? They're all the rations we have, Isabelle.

When he looks at his wife in despair, she puts down the coffee pot and starts toward him, but when he sees her coming, he races down between the next two rows, and she returns to the counter. Then he's back peering at them as if he'd never run away in the first place. When's the last time you had a crab omelette for lunch, Gwen? he asks. He hasn't moved; he hasn't run away. He's been there the whole time. Why are they looking at him like that?

He starts back to the beach. Once out the door it's as if he's being disassembled and re-assembled by a force beyond his control. He looks wildly around the unweeded front yard as if wondering whether he can get out, but when he glances back and sees Isabelle through the window, his face relaxes as if no time has passed because the last time he was alive was when he saw her.

He crosses the street, glancing back as if being chased, runs out to the flats again. He's never still, says Isabelle. He'd be lost without the tide flats. If you go out with him in the morning, Gwen, crabbing I mean.... She sits on the customer side of the counter slipping specials inserts into the menus as she talks. Be patient, she says.

I understand now, Gwen says. It isn't right the family shunned Uncle Jack and we didn't see you all those years. Was it the war did this to him? Isabelle looks at her, as if allowing her to surmise the wrong reason she's been out of touch with the family while she makes up her mind about trusting her.

As I say, if he asks you to go crabbing with him, it'd be nice if you go, but you have to understand. He was in prison camp in Japan in the war. His head was injured. He has brain damage. Know the way we have various trains of thought and we choose which one to communicate? For Jack, the choosing part of his mind is destroyed; the wrong wires have been connected up, so he tells you contradicting things one after the other. You have to get to know him.

How do you manage all this, Auntie?

I'm alright. I'm used to it.

The next morning dawns bright and clear; the shore is deserted and the tide flats, with their variations in slope and terrain, seem a country unto themselves. Tiny coils of wet sand pass through the bodies of periwinkles dotting the beach. Small sea streams define new areas at the turn of each tide. Isabelle sits in a worn lazy boy chair by the café window smoking and drinking coffee. The water is shallow a long way out, the tide flats much older than Rocky or even the dark heaps on Sandy. The sky is long and pale, the far away sections of beach banded by light turquoise ribbons of water. When Gwen arrives on the long stretch, Jack doesn't recognize her. Hi, he says shame-facedly as if he should remember who she is but can't. Lunges after a crab scurrying from the tall grasses to colder water. A few people trail burlap bags in the early dawn, the odd claw pricking through. He hands out varnished handles as if they're batons at the start of a relay race.

You'll be okay if you have one of these, he says. They won't take you away.

People seem to accept his measuring sticks as if they're part of daily life. He comes over to check Gwen's catch. It's a large male but its shell is soft. It has to go back, he says. Sorry.

The further away they get from the boardwalk, the less he seems to realize she's with him. If they'd been children and she'd left, he'd instantly have forgotten her existence. He hands her a measuring stick as if he has no idea he'd given her one ten minutes before. Gives her another sack, tells her to be careful where she's stepping. She copies the way he pushes the water away with his stomach, drags the grass slowly aside with her forked stick. They walk for an hour and catch nothing. He doesn't seem to be aware of how far they've walked, or that her stick keeps getting caught in the grass. All that matters is that they keep going. When she scoops, the crab's claws frantically scrape the sides. Then Jack's behind her backing her stick with his, tossing the crab and catching it with the flat of his own. He takes a measuring handle from his pocket.

This one looks pretty good. Not quite. Back it goes.

This one, Jack. This one's big enough. She reaches for it.

No. It's a female.

She's beginning to get seaweed burns across her shins. Maybe she should go back and get some socks she says, but he doesn't hear or turn around because he hasn't found his kill yet. He won't stop, no matter what, until he has what's going to let them survive for a day. Every day would be the same for him. If he looked back and said you look tired, it wouldn't be with the follow-up logic that she should go back. If he was out in the bush with someone and wanted to be alone, he would walk away. If the person made it back to the parked vehicle and didn't have enough gas to get to town, he wouldn't care. Of course they can't leave. It would be dangerous.

Do you ever go crabbing with him, she asks Isabelle as the two of them sit outside the *Bide-a-Wile* breaking off the ends of green beans.

No, he likes to go alone. He feels he has to provide.

As if on cue, he walks up to them, standing stock still on over alert. Hyper vigilant as always. Later, when Isabelle needs help lifting the steamer, she hands him a ceramic onion but doesn't say anything. Maybe it's good for his mind to figure out what she needs, or maybe she's tired of explaining. Maybe he likes the game. He stands there like a blind person waiting to be noticed so someone will let him know in which direction to move. After he puts the pot on the stove, he hands the onion back to her and she puts it in an egg cup.

After supper they make a fire on the beach. Every fire's a good fire, he says feeding it pieces of alder. When he walks over to his rowboat to go check his nets, Isabelle's forehead seems attached to his by a string. When he pulls away, it jerks hers as well.

Auntie, are you okay?

I'm just feeling my age, Gwen.

You're not old, Auntie.

I know but it all passes so quickly. Everything goes along for a while, for quite a while sometimes, and then something you knew was going to happen finally happens. Your coming here I mean. I knew you'd come one day. You look sad. What about *your* husband? Where is he?

Back in San Francisco, she says. I got dumped actually.

Do you feel like talking about it?

Not now. Maybe later.

(Maybe, just maybe, Dr. Merrick said once, standing up to show her out. It wasn't *all* your fault.)

Isabelle takes a long time to say anything further. For a moment the fire seems to be made of discarded shoes. She leans over and kisses Gwen on the cheek, leaves a lipstick mark that she blends with her thumb. I'd better kiss the other side as well. Even things up. The light from the Cherry Point oil refinery blinks on and off.

I want my girls to meet you.

I want to meet them. Where are you living now?

Mainly at Scarborough. Did you know that Grandma Flora left her half of Scarborough to Lily? I remember it used to be the Yoshitos'. Your friends, right? Whatever happened to them? I remember they moved.

They were evacuated, Gwen. With everyone else. Sent to the interior to camps they couldn't leave.

I didn't know that.

How could you not know that? It was all over the papers.

I was a child. They kept grown-up things from children in those days. We didn't have it at school either. I remember mother saying they'd gone to another camp. I thought maybe it was a camp at Sechelt. It was all British and American history and literature at high school and university. A brief look, one course in First Nations history and well, then I married the teacher. After that, I was so caught up the politics down in the States I didn't… I'm embarrassed.

You should be, says Isabelle. It's a shocking gap.

Strange how Isabelle can say that without humiliating her. Even after all this time and separation, she knows her aunt loves her.

I tried to get your father to help me buy the Scarborough house from the Yoshitos so I could sell it back to them after the war, Isabelle says. Instead he bought it for himself and his parents. War is war, he said. Property gets appropriated.

He *did*? So the spoils of war were involved? Gwen's quiet for a few minutes, poking the fire. No wonder it feels sad over there, she says. Nothing ever goes right. Does Lily know?

I assume so, says Isabelle. The Yoshitos might come back and have nowhere to go. That's why I keep the cottage set up as a beacon for them. If they came back and saw other people in their own house, they might come looking for me at the cottage. Maybe they'd look through the window and see their things. They know where the key's hidden.

If they did come back, perhaps we could sort something about Scarborough, Gwen says.

I don't know. Let's go to bed, says Isabelle. It's been quite a day.

The next day Isabelle tells Gwen that she's been going through some of her papers. I don't know what to keep. What to burn. They get down boxes of file folders, spend hours writing dates and names on the backs of old photographs. She holds up a bunch of letters tied with ribbon. I'd like you to have a look at these, Gwen. So someone in the family knows the history. I only got this first letter from Jack. The rest he managed to keep folded in his hat band all the way through his time in prison camp. Here's one written by his mother when she was informed he was alive. *Dear Jack, We just had the wonderful news. Words cannot express what we feel. It's the grandest thing that ever happened. Dad and I will be at the station to meet you. Let us know what boat you'll be arriving on. Love, Mother.* And on the envelope stamped to return. *It is regrettable that this letter could not be forwarded in time to connect with the ship or aircraft on which the addressee was repatriated.*

The reason I don't see Ada and Percy, Isabelle says, isn't to do with Jack. It's because I can't forgive your father.

Gwen remembers the forced smiles on her parents' faces as they came back into the dining room that long ago Christmas night. Then Isabelle herself in the winter field at Scarborough, eyes blank and unblinking as if the dearest part of her soul had been obliterated.

49.

Returning from Birch Bay, Gwen drives straight to her parents' house. Percy turns his book face down on the arm of his chair. He likes reading too. How's tricks? he says.

Not bad, father. It's going to be sad at the farm for a long time though. She sits on the piano bench. We miss Derek.

We miss him too.

I've been spending time at the cottage, she says. To get away. And to do a little

writing.

Her mother comes in from the kitchen looking distant and angry, sits down opposite her daughter. You went to the cottage when I told you not to, Gwen? I'll sell it. I really will.

Gwen looks up. Auntie said it was all right for me to be there.

Isabelle? She's supposed to ask me. We don't let other people go over without asking the others.

I'm not other people. I'm your daughter. I went to see her. We might as well get straight to it. She explained about Scarborough being stolen property.

Her mother looks frightened. It is not stolen property, she says. Dad went through all the procedures, paid what was asked. What's she doing telling you that?

Which was next to nothing, right dad? says Gwen. Does anybody know what happened to the Yoshitos? I'm trying to understand more.

Nobody thought any of those people would come back, Isabelle I mean Gwen, says Ada.

Why wouldn't they come back? Those were their houses, all those years of work. Nobody had gardens that compared to the hotel gardens, I remember people saying that.

It was Indian fishing territory before the Yoshitos came along, Percy says slowly.

That's a dodge, dad. It's not part of any land claim as far as I know.

It could be though.

There wasn't a midden anyone had left there. There wasn't years of work.

Bad things happen in war, he says.

There wasn't one proven case of a Japanese Canadian being accused of spying.

That's because they were all in the interior, says Percy. As I said, you have no idea what it was like at the time, Gwen. All this bleeding heart liberal hindsight.

Nobody's been able to settle there or make things go right. Derek's suicide seems like part of it. Maybe the place isn't working because it's not ours.

Of course it's ours, says Ada. People have to make the best of things and carry on.

Well, of course they do but weren't those people citizens, some of whom tried to volunteer and weren't considered?

Ada stands up briskly as if seeing her out. It's pie in the sky, Gwen. It's too long ago to think anything different can be done. Most of those people have probably cut their losses and moved on the way you should be.

I don't know about that. It seems like a pretty complicated situation to me.

Later, back on the island Gwen sits on the rock under the tree house on Miss Fenn's Rocky watching small waves lap pits that were once bubbles in a volcano. Thinking, of all things, about what the men she knows would be like in a war. Derek would be stoic. Leo? Leo couldn't go. He'd have a medical excuse. Uncle Jack? He'd be in there helping everybody. At least the old Jack who wrote these letters would. Eugene would be capable and brave.

50.

October, 1975.

Amemorial was the last thing any of them thought they were preparing the dancehall for. Gwen and Lily set chairs in front of the stage and Annabelle silently positions her storybook and Barbie dolls like flower pots down the back stairs. The eyes of the china one that open and shut are pressed closed.

Quite a few come over from Jericho. People shake hands and exchange hugs. Someone tells about the time Derek passed along the twenty-dollar bill that did the rounds of the Cove all winter when he was the one who needed it most. The night he'd sat up with someone who was afraid to go to sleep after group.

Frances and Jeanette stand at the back, older now of course. The other week, Derek had posted a snapshot on the fridge door of the two of them holding pumpkin pies they'd made in the crooks of their arms. Frances is dressed in a flowing tunic. When she comes to the front to speak, she takes off her glasses and polishes them on her hem. Tells the gathering how Derek was one of the children who came from Britain during the war and how they were meant to—her voice breaks—keep him safe. When he left, he said he was going home to visit his other parents but didn't think he would be able to live without the forest and the sea. She and Jeanette didn't know how they would live without *him*. They don't know how they'll live without him now. Jeanette comes up through the crowd and stands proudly beside her partner.

Ada, Percy and Grandpa Frederick Gallagher sit quietly on one of the benches. As Miss Fenn passes through the formal line, Ada gets up and crosses the hall to get the men pieces of zucchini cake.

Miss Fenn, I haven't seen you in ages, Frances says. Do you remember me, I used to be the lifeguard in the olden days. Isabelle introduced us years ago. It was so sad that her baby died.

I do remember you, Frances, says Lottie. (So that's what they told Isabelle. No wonder she's never heard from her.) I'm feeling terrible about this. I was planning on going to Scarborough to get some gardening advice from Derek and didn't get there in time.

Coming back across the floor Ada hears Frances's *faux pas* and glares at her. Maybe nobody but Lottie heard. She hasn't seen or heard from Lottie since that long ago day in Blaine. There's so much being held at bay in this room; wonder how many people here know about Annabelle for instance. She herself only realized what was going on the night of that Thanksgiving dinner, talked about it with Percy and they decided it was best to wait until Lily came forward. But she never has come forward.

We're sorry about losing Derek, says George Fenn when he and Billy Will put in an appearance at Scarborough later that afternoon. Lily won't look at Billy, then finally blurts out. So did you ever prove what you were after, Billy? You had no right. What doctor would…?

Annabelle and I have the same blood type, he says quietly.

Well, there you are, says Lily. As if it's not obvious. Don't ever do anything like that again without my permission.

The way George seems to take Lily's words as an acknowledgement of Billy's paternity and thus his own status as Annabelle's grandfather is like someone taking an item they've given as a gift back into their own keeping when the owner dies.

Well, George says as if the meeting's over. The last thing Derek and I agreed was that the roof needed replacing so we'd better get on with it.

51.

The next spring, on the day the first Habitat delegates are due to arrive, Gwen and Lily unfold tables in the hall, lay out before and after pictures of the dancehall restoration. Old brochures from the Union days and mimeographed sheets explain how they'd retained the octagonal structure of the original hall and replaced the pillars with beachcombed logs.

As Gwen shows a group of visitors around, she notices a young Japanese-Canadian woman staring at the brochure featuring a hollyhock sided Scarborough. She's so thin she's almost not there, but the wiry way she carries herself skewers you into noticing she certainly is. In a vivid turquoise t-shirt that contrasts her hair into matte black, she stands alone for a few minutes, then turns and walks out the front door.

Lottie's sitting on the wharf at the taco bar filling in a questionnaire about what would make the Cove more elder friendly. Part of the Habitat shenanigans it looks like. Benches, that's what we need, she'd written. More benches. When she looks up, a young woman in a bright turquoise shirt is making her way into the old corrugated shed (now a consignment shop) where her father'd once slept to guide in the Sannies. She comes out with a few postcards, heads to the ferry ramp.

Lottie would know her anywhere, can still feel the delicate bone structure of her small face in her hands when she kissed her good-bye. She's kept all the letters Takumi had written about their life in Prince Rupert. But she doesn't approach her, looks away quickly so the young woman won't see her, knowing that right moment isn't here yet.

The alternative conference at Jericho Beach is in full swing when Gwen goes to pick up Derek's tools. The old hangars look festive decked out in appliquéd banners. A Bill Reid mural covers an entire outside wall. She stops to listen to a chamber music group in one of the carved arcades; when they finish, the same thin young woman, this time in maroon velvet pants and a tailored black jacket with dark beading on the lapels, opens the lid of her flute case and puts away her instrument.

Hello, says Gwen. Do you remember me? I spoke to you the other day at the pavilion opening on Bowen.

Shima closes the lid. I do, she says.

When they go for a drink in what's billed as the longest bar in the world, Shima tells her she's come to Habitat as a conference delegate. Thinking of moving here actually, she says. From Toronto where she practices law. When she talks, she stalls in unexpected places as if keeping particular notes in her mind while she scans ahead in the music. The wild locked rain is over; the pale blue mountains extend along the horizon.

My family used to live on Bowen, she says. Shima's the name. Shima Yoshito.

You're part of the family who originally owned Scarborough?

That's right. Takumi Yoshito is my father.

Oh, for goodness sake. Takumi was my swimming teacher. I missed him. You must come over soon. We've had a death in the family though, everything's a bit sad....

Oh, I wouldn't want to....

You wouldn't be. Is there a number where I could reach you?

There is.

Back at the farm, it's even sadder and lonelier than it was before the memorial. Gwen hates the way Billy's shouldering in, not even trying to hide his satisfaction at the chance to fill the empty role. Annabelle won't look up at him when he calls down to her from the roof where he's fastening rows of asphalt shingles. Tools are scattered all over the back porch. George is making pork chops. What better time to work on the place than when there's nobody here, eh? George says as if he's the one on the roof.

The day she comes to visit, Shima sits quietly at the kitchen table, patting their new golden retriever. Nice dog you've got here, she says, making a point of not noticing too much about the place, as if it would be beneath her dignity to ask to be shown around.

Hello, she says, when Jenny comes home from school. I'm Shima.

Hi Shima.

And who's that? Shima says looking out the kitchen window at Annabelle who's standing on the back porch where she always waited for Derek to come up from the beach. She still hasn't spoken.

That's Annabelle, says Gwen. Derek was her father. She hasn't spoken since he died. We don't know what to do.

Shima watches her for a while, then goes out, gently takes her hand and leads her to the driveway where she heels a marker line in the dirt. Let's race, she says. One two three GO, They run and come back, run and come back. Then, when Shima leaves out the GO, Annabelle says it without thinking. The strategy makes Gwen think of a trick Isabelle would do with Jack. Later, when Gwen's taking her to the ferry, Shima asks if George is one of the owners. No, but he's done quite a bit of work around here over the years, Gwen says.

The next day Shima calls to say she's definitely decided to stay on the coast, has moved into the Buchan Hotel in the west end for a while. Had a swim this morning in that cove near the park. It wasn't a long swim but, hey, it was a very wet one. She wonders if Gwen would like to join her at a preliminary redress meeting in the classrooms below Robson Square, it's exploratory, but if she's interested? Gwen *is* interested – she takes the bus in from Horseshoe Bay, and the two of them listen to a speaker explain that, when they finally do manage to open the wartime archives, it may be made clear that the Japanese community was not seen as a threat by all the military people. What's needed is common sense justice for wrongs that have to be made right.

Later, she and Gwen sit leaning against a log in English Bay. Gwen rakes the sand with her hand, picks up a piece of seaweed and puts it down. It's terrible that your family had to leave their home, Shima. I'm ashamed that my father bought it from the war office and deeded it to himself and my grandmother.

The waves lap quietly.

No one expects to get their homes back, Shima says. The deeds of sale will hold. But some kind of compensation. Our people had to pay for their own incarceration, did you know that? Taken out of the sale of their properties.

No, I didn't know that.

My dad didn't go with his parents, Shima says. He spent the

war up the coast in the bush. He's a sculptor, and a fisherman. He's taken up deep sea diving. My mother died.

Oh, says Gwen. I'm sorry.

52.

The next night Gwen goes up to talk to Lily who's in Derek's old bedroom fitting up a new electric radiator to keep on at night in the fall. She has it upside down screwing on the wheels. Nuts, bolts and washers all over the floor. It's lucky for whoever's talking to Lily that her glasses camouflage her cheek bones a little. Otherwise you keep thinking why does she have to be so darn pretty? I'm trying to concentrate on what I'm saying.

They've shorted me a set of wheels, Lily says. Oh no, there they are.

You're trying to screw the wheel gizmos on the wrong attachments, Gwen says, handing her sister the parts one after the other. Are you going to sleep in this room now? Is that the plan?

For a bit, says Lily.

Remember that woman I told you I met at Habitat? The one who was playing in the chamber music group. Turns out her name is Shima and the incredible news is that Takumi Yoshito, the son of the people who used to live here, is her father.

That's interesting, Lily says mildly. Oh this is better.

You know about the Yoshitos then?

It was war. Dad told me. But it's cool she's turned up.

Did you tell Derek?

Nope.

Why?

It's long gone, isn't it? People have to move on.

Gwen hands her sister another part. What do you think of the idea of asking Shima to come and live here with us? she says. Formally becoming an owner without putting in any money? I know you and Derek talked about buying mom and dad out, but with him... gone, maybe we can find an alternative. Maybe I could buy our parents out instead. Then you and I could change the deed to a three way split, all three of our names on it.

How are you going to find the money for that? says Lily.

I have some ideas.

I can see that it's fair. I can hardly stand being here myself. I want to take Annabelle and move closer to Checleset. Maybe Port Renfrew. We've finally figured out a transport box for the otters that looks as if it will work.

What about Billy? says Gwen.

Since when did you care about Billy?

I've always had to one way or another.

Lily sits back on her haunches, job complete. It's terrible that Derek killed himself, she says. Don't think I don't feel that. But somehow, awful as it is to say, it's made the situation simpler.

Annabelle doesn't think so.

She'll get used to it.

Will she?

Billy can come and visit, Lily says. George is happy because I've written a will and made Annabelle my beneficiary.

So it's okay with you if I approach Mom and Dad?

It's okay with me.

Lottie's in the habit of taking a long walk in the summer evenings down past her old cottage, then on to the point. When she passes what she still thinks of as her place, the local real estate agent is showing a couple about her age around. They all say hello; the clients inform her they've come over from England. Used to visit Bowen in the old hotel days. Sycamore's the name. They're wanting to buy a house. They have a grandchild here and want her to have a nice place to come to. Maybe she knows her. Her name is Annabelle Sycamore.

Nice name, says Lottie.

Gwen asks Shima, without telling her why, if she would recommend a legal aid lawyer who could arrange an attorney for her in the States. By now, maybe they wouldn't make her take the children back seeing they'd established a life here. Might there be something like a statute of limitations? A lawyer is found; a court date set in San Francisco. Plane and hotel reservations put in place. Lily agrees it's her turn to look after the children.

I've been meaning to put it to you, Lil, Billy says when he comes in. For future reference, I think we should change the birth certificate. It means a lot to dad that Annabelle will always have a home here. I don't want her to have problems further down the line.

Later, Billy. The Sycamores are here, Lily says, as their rented car appears in the driveway. I told you Derek told his parents they have a grandchild. They've been in the loop way too long to just.... They already love her from the pictures we've sent.

It could be Christmas Eve, the Sycamores are that embracing when they're ushered in, their coats taken. They've wanted to meet Lily for a long time; Derek told them so much about her. And Annabelle. What an angel with that cloud of fair hair.

This is Billy Fenn, says Lily. He's fixing the roof.

Oh roofs, says Mr. Sycamore. Aren't they the limit?

Annabelle's already tugging at their hands, wanting to show them the apple orchard and the beach. They're torn, thinking they should talk to their granddaughter's mother, but wanting to have Annabelle to themselves like someone who wants to be lovers with the host but an unwanted guest won't leave.

Once they're out the door, Billy pounds his fist on the table. Fuck, Lily. What do you think you're doing? Why do you think we're over here repairing the roof, bringing the bloody garden in?

You'd better go.

I'm not going anywhere. I'm going to sleep in the goddam bus.

The Sycamores come again the next day. They've rented a car, plan to take Annabelle over to Tunstall Bay for lunch. Billy's in the yard, not exactly trimming hedges but he could be. Could he get a ride with them as far as Evergreen Hall? He has to see to the indoor shuffle board equipment. The hotel's gone, of course, but they keep up the hall near the site of the old greenhouse for rainy days.

Sad, isn't it? says Mrs. Sycamore. About the hotel. Looking back over the seat to commiserate, she's suddenly aware that their passenger's eyes are identical to Annabelle's and that his hair blends exactly with her continuous blonde-white puffs. Mrs. Sycamore is like someone who's been taken to identify a body whose description fits one they're ready to mourn, but when they get there, it's someone else. After a confusing lunch, they return Annabelle to her mother as if they tried her on and she's the wrong size.

Would you like to come in? Maybe see some of Derek's gardens?

They would if they had more time, they say, but they'd better go if they're going to catch the next ferry. They'll be in touch.

53.

September, 1976.

In the San Francisco YWCA, Gwen puts on a simple dress, takes a taxi to the courthouse, waits for an hour on a bench outside the assigned courtroom with a file containing copies of her household accounts. Sitting there calming her nerves by adding up columns of figures and reading the notes she's taken about their lives, she feels like she's attending her orals for a degree in family management. The lawyers have scheduled a preliminary meeting to see if they can settle out of court.

Strange how much easier it is to act on someone else's behalf, especially if the action has political merit. She re-reads the list of arguments she's outlined for keeping Scarborough as an established home for the girls: family nearby, steady routines. As for money, it's not so much the amount as the predictability. Alternate Christmases and Easters with their dad. Summer vacations.

When she hears Eugene's voice down the corridor announcing that he has to be out of here by noon, it's as if he's arriving at one of his rehearsals. Maybe he kept walking west around the earth from the concrete stairs at Sandy that fateful day in order to be able to approach her correctly from the east.

Hi, he says.

If she stands up to greet him, will he hold her more tenderly now because she's a better person? You don't even have to have eye contact, the lawyer said yesterday when she told him how scared she was. Eugene has a hand woven strap tied on the ear pieces of his glasses. She stills feels he could yard her in with a single glance and has to fight the transference. I like your glasses strap, she says.

Jenny sent it to me for my birthday. How're the girls?

They're well, she says.

The two of them are led off by their separate lawyers. Why do all their visits feel like prison visits?

She makes it to the pew on the other side of the empty courtroom. I'll be all right in a minute, she says to her lawyer. You feel completely comfortable here, don't you?

Oh sure, he says surprised.

It's lucky we're good at different things. I'd last two minutes in a courtroom but I'm okay with kids.

Good, he says. Let's get a floor under yours then.

When the lawyers go into the judge's chambers for a conference, it's as if Eugene's on the groom's side of the church. He gets up and comes over. Please tell me about the girls, he says. *Maya used to say she's kishered instead of finished when she was on the toilet. Annabelle stopped talking when Derek died but Shima got her speaking again. Jenny will never forgive me for drowning the newborn kittens in the rain barrel. Their eyes weren't open, she said. They couldn't even see themselves drown.*

I'm not meant to talk to you right now, she says.

He goes back to his pew and picks up his book. What's he reading?

In the chambers, the judge sits at the head of the table, Eugene on one side with his lawyer, herself on the other with hers. She expects a thorough grilling, but instead the judge asks her a surprising question.

What do you plan to do after the children grow up?

She astonishes herself by saying that she wants to teach high school.

Good for you. How much money a month do you need right now?

Money, I've sent money, says Eugene angrily.

I'm not saying you haven't, says the judge. Eugene backs down. Enough? he asks.

He rears again. The way they live, their expenses aren't much. I don't want my daughters living on a half-assed piece of land in a shambles of a house. There are better schools here. No one knows who's with whom. God knows who's looking after them now.

The fact is, the judge says. They've been with their mother for the last several years and she's kept the ship afloat.

I'm losing precious years of my daughters' lives, Eugene fumes.

So you want them to come home?

I want my *daughters* to come home. Their mother was, probably still is, a mess.

Well, they're going to stay with her for now, with organized and predictable access and visits. I'm going to order a lump sum payment unless you can give the court a series of certified post dated cheques. I have read the file.

Oh, the file! scoffs Eugene.

In the end, he agrees to twelve post-dated monthly cheques for five hundred dollars and a lump sum for an additional back payment. As soon as the money's settled, Gwen wants to cry. Don't think I don't know how much they need you, she says she hopes with dignity. I want them to have predictable times with you to look forward to. I want them to have a steady routine.

That'll be the day.

Does she want to settle, her lawyer asks when the two of them are back in the hall, or does she want to go to court and try for more?

What about what I owe you?

Dribs and drabs are okay for that, he says. If your ship comes in one day, you could send a catch-up amount.

Thank you very much, she says. We'll settle.

When she gets home, Jenny runs up holding a Rubik's cube she's completed to surprise her. I didn't take off the plastic pieces and paste them back on, she says.

Why would I think that, Jenny?

I don't know, she says miserably.

HARD WEST

54.

Christmas, 1976.

Christmas is at Evvie's this year. Isn't it great that everybody's coming? Even Isabelle and Jack are travelling up from Birch Bay. Well, everybody except Lily and Annabelle who are at Checleset and don't want to face the holiday ferries. Oh, and Grandpa Gallagher who's not up to it because he tired himself out taking one of his unpopular trips to Bowen so he could visit his old fireplace and wants his dinner brought to Laburnum St. on a tray.

Evvie's apartment is several floors up in a high rise near the sea wall at the edge of Stanley Park. If you lean out her side balcony, you can glimpse the sea. Wonderful view of the tennis courts. The blonde streaks in her pelt of hair are white now; the sequins on the scalloped neck of her sweater glint as she squares her handsome shoulders and peers around Gwen's shoulder at the bathroom mirror. Do you think my capped teeth look too young in my old face? she asks, clenching her teeth and stretching her lips so her gums show. When you do that, they do. Gwen laughs with her, not at her.

When Jack and Isabelle arrive, Jack stands behind his wife in the vestibule hanging onto the lapels of his coat. If he takes it off, someone might steal it. He streaks for the balcony door as if trying to gage the distance he'd have to vault if he jumped over the railing. Isabelle's been persuaded by Gwen to start seeing the family again, at least on formal occasions when there'd be enough structure to keep everyone polite.

On the balcony—it's mild enough to step outside—Evvie crouches, a touch stiffly, to clear away a heap of nuts piled in the corner. The rainy cedars are dark green. The squirrels scramble up the side of the building but what can you do? Jenny cocks her old young face and peers sideways down the wall. They must think the apartments are trees, she says. And the balconies are holes in the trees. Exactly, says Evvie. Living alone is all very well, but it's nice to have someone take an interest. Maya has small round glasses now and looks like Grandpa Percy. She's in burgundy velveteen with a lace collar, Jenny in forest green. White tights and patent leather flats. Wonders will never cease.

Talking to Evvie in a flat abstract voice as if he's just met her even if he's known her all his life, Leo, home for Christmas, allows as to how the west end must be a nice place for her to live. He always tries, bless his heart, as if he'd like to be appropriately present in a room and how can people think he's not? He spent the summer near Princeton working in microwave technology, part of a team that discovered a hum they thought might be in the machinery was actually an echo of the big bang. Jenny listens, fascinated. If the universe is expanding faster and faster, it has to be moving away from some starting point, he explains, helping Evvie pile acorns. Does Evvie have a long piece of elastic he could borrow? Even though Venus is almost a sister planet to Earth, do they have any idea how dry and barren it is? There's a runaway greenhouse effect, he says. (Maya sees a glass house with arms and legs running along the seawall.) You'd think when galaxies move away from each other, they'd slow down, but they don't because there's some kind of dark matter pushing them apart but they still don't know what it is. He tries to thread acorns on the circle of elastic Evvie finds for him, but ends up using ping pong balls instead to demonstrate how the planets gain distance when they move with the stretch.

Ada still looks like a queen-sized version of her son. Her beige camel hair coat never seems to wear out. I like your jigsaw puzzles, Ev, she says. Evvie does them to keep her brain from atrophying now that she's retired from Woodward's, hangs them on her living rooms walls. With Ada, it's crossword puzzles.

Jenny's been seconded to pass around a tray of appetizers. Guess what they are? Oysters? Dates wrapped in bacon, actually. Jack nibbles one, perched tensely on the arm of the sofa as if terrified by the Christmas crackers on the table.

Nothing like being near a tennis court, Evvie says.

You're going to play to the bitter end, are you? Leo asks.

The bitter end, she says.

Maybe Evvie should open one of her leftover presents under the tree while they wait for the Cornish game hens she's made to give people a change from turkey. She pushes aside a place setting on the table, unwraps the new puzzle. How the sam hill is she supposed to put this together? It's too difficult, all yellow pieces with no pattern. Gwen turns the lid over. Yellow Peril it's called. Who'd give somebody a thing like this? she says. In this day and age? If Shima were here, she'd put down her napkin and go. Her departing hand would leave a print on the table like a glove.

Isabelle looks so stricken, Gwen takes her hand. When Evvie spreads out the jigsaw, Leo picks up a corner piece of the puzzle with two wings and a marking as if for a bird's eye, lets it land it near the edge of the table. People better be careful running on the seawall, he says. A man on the radio said he got his scalp pecked by an owl when he was jogging at dawn. The owls think peoples' heads of hair running below them are squirrels so they swoop down and attack them. Of course, from high up, that's how it *would* look.

I had friends whose table had a pattern in it like that puzzle piece, Isabelle says quietly.

When Percy sits down across from Isabelle, she manages a nod.

At dinner, Jack's barely sitting down before he's up on his feet tipping over his chair. Glancing over the balcony railing, he spots a sandy path stretching to the edge of the low tide. I can go there, he says dashing for the door.

He's not well, Isabelle says getting up to go after him. Another chair pushed back. The two empty spots at the table gape like missing teeth.

Shall we eat, Ada says, reaching for the platter. Put your hand against the thigh, Perce, it should be soft.

I think it's soft, he says.

Are the juices running clear? Twirl the legs.

They twirl.

Napkins are shaken into laps, plates passed to receive the small plucked birds. The relish is that fresh ground cranberry and orange everyone likes. Leo eats fixedly, staring at his plate as if trying to put layers of food between himself and whatever it is he's trying to keep at bay. Dessert is lime sorbet—nice to have something different for a change.

When everyone's finished dessert, Ada says she has an an-

nouncement to make. She wants to tell everyone that she and
Percy have decided to put their share of the Scarborough property up for sale.

Mother, no, Gwen says. I want to talk to you and dad about
that.

It's not your decision, Gwen, says Ada. Who wants more
coffee?

Please, Mom. Lily owns half, right? She'd have to agree to
sell too. Right Leo?

The deed is tenants-in-common; either side can sell, he insists. We need to get market value, Gwen.

We, what is this we? But family has first option? she asks.

Not officially. Mom and Dad need every bit of money they
can raise to invest and live on the interest. It's expensive to retire.

Why does she always feel that Leo wants to make things
difficult for her?

We do have our eye on a small plane, admits Percy.

You could mortgage Blenheim St., says Gwen.

How could you suggest such a thing, Gwen? Ada says. I can't
believe you'd say that.

Are they coming back? says Jenny and everyone looks at her.
They've forgotten who she means. Don't forget to take Grandpa
Gallagher his dinner, she says.

The next day, Gwen walks up Denman and along Haro to the
small brownstone canopied hotel with wisteria vines twisting
up the front posts. Shima's in her room practising her flute
when the desk clerk comes to the door. Is she making too much
noise? Aren't the rooms either side of her empty? It's not that.
There's someone downstairs to see her.

Two sofas face each other in front of the gas fire in the lobby. In the last few days, Gwen's researched what she could find out about tenants-in-common law. What's clear is that a half owner is not required to take a discount if he or she wants to sell. Her parents are under no obligation to sell to her at a lower price than they could get elsewhere; they're entitled to sell their half to someone outside the family, but, if a family member were to come up with the money, the case would likely be settled in her favour.

Shima, I've come to ask if you'd like to live with us at Scarborough as an owner of a full third without any money changing hands, Gwen says. My parents are willing to be bought out—I hope to be the one to do that—Lily and I have agreed to change the deed so the three of us would own the place. Actually, I should be paying your parents. We owe the money to *your* parents and grandparents, but at least this way you'd be getting a share.

But you aren't a co-owner, says Shima.

I'm working on it. My parents wouldn't sell to a stranger if I can come up with close to the market value.

Thank you, Gwen. I'll certainly think about it. Your father did pay the government even if it was token. And some day, there'll be the compensation.

You think that?

I'm dedicating my life to it.

Ada's taking the Christmas lights and cedar from around the front door when Gwen drives up. Her daughter looks officious with that briefcase; she's not sure that she didn't like her better when she was more undone. She's been trying not to say too much when her daughters are in crisis which is pretty much all the time.

About the other night, Mom.

At least let me get these lights down, Gwen.

Sorry, Gwen says, helping dismantle the string. Mom, could we sit down a minute. No, Mom, listen. About Scarborough. As I said on the phone, I'm trying to raise the money to buy you and dad out. Lily doesn't want to live there any more. She owns half as it stands now, right? I have some extraordinary news. Takumi Yoshito's daughter has shown up out of the blue; I met her at Habitat. It's so sad what happened to her grandparents, and her mother's dead. If I owned half, we could change the title and bring her in for a third with no money changing hands as a way of making it up to her. Lily agrees with my idea and says it's okay if I approach you on her behalf. So what do you think?

Ada looks like someone who's prepared a virulent divorce petition and submitted it to her lawyer before realizing that her husband would be reading it as well.

I don't understand why you're being Lily's messenger, Gwen, she says, slowly circling the lights into their box. Why isn't she talking to me herself?

She's on her way back to Checleset to find a place for her and Annabelle to live in Port Renfrew. I guess it doesn't mean that much to her.

It's too complicated, Ada says.

Will you at least approach dad about it? You have to admit the idea has merit.

Gwen, the purchase was Dad's idea. I didn't know about the transaction, but he was the one who got the cheque for his work, if you see what I mean.

Oh I do, mother. I do. But get back to me, will you? This is important.

Frankly, Percy says walking with Gwen on the flats below Marine Drive, I didn't know your mother was going to present our decision so undiplomatically at Evvie's like that. They stop to give sugar cubes to a horse who rolls his lips in their palms. He'd been thinking. Oh no, not thinking! Their old running joke. He does have some money put aside. He didn't spend all their savings on flying. The golfers on the other side of the bushes swish the grass with their irons. But he didn't tell her mother about his secret fund. How much has she managed to raise from her daycare work?

The daycare almost breaks even, Dad. I'm not doing it full time. I got a bit of a settlement from Eugene. I'm good for five at this point. The judge ordered a lump sum payment and since it's going to shelter for the kids.... If you could front another five, maybe I could take out a loan for the rest if the interest were cheaper than that on a mortgage. I could pay you back the way I'd pay a mortgage back. I have monthly post-dated cheques now and I could budget....

So I'd be loaning you money to help buy half the place from me so you could deal in this Yoshito girl?

I know it sounds complicated.

Well, I never did think it was fair that Mother left her half only to Lily.

She takes his arm. It didn't feel right to me over there from the start, dad. I knew something was wrong. I didn't want to go there, remember? I think Grandma Flora thought I didn't like her, but it wasn't that. Would it be fair to Mom, though, not leveling with her about the extra money? She's only thinking of you when it comes to the plane. (Dad deserves his retirement, she'd said coldly as if Gwen was sure to be thinking otherwise.)

Let me worry about that, Percy says. Things were different in the war and the Depression, Gwen. I don't know how much you're going to need: the market value might have changed by the time you get the paperwork done, but I'll trust you to sort it. We're leaving on our trip to Mexico in a small borrowed plane. He gives her a blank cheque; that way she can fill in the amount when she knows how much she'll need from him.

She drives away. Even if the new set-up would mean more heirs with each generation, it's a big place and they can divide it up and build lots of houses. Derek would want Annabelle to inherit as well so maybe it's all to the good. Wonder how these cousins will get along when all is said and done?

When she gets back to Scarborough, the phone rings. It's Shima saying she's thinking of coming over. It's a go, Shima, she says. My dad's on side. Maybe you'd like to stay for a night or two, see how you feel about the place? Get a chance to walk around, find out the lay of the land. Shima says she would.

Gwen decides to take the girls to town overnight to check her parents' place and give her new friend a chance to be alone. The next day it turns seriously cold. Strolling close to the house on her first round, Shima notices that most of the pipes are on the outside. It's mild here, but not that mild. It's getting cold—really cold—what about the water? Anyone who's grown up in the north is used to worrying about pipes. She gets a shovel to see how far down the pipes are laid: way too close to the surface in her opinion. The barometer in the kitchen is falling. There's an iron rod sticking up from the ground that must be the water lever; she finds a wrench on a painted outline on the shed wall above an old clay urn. Thrashes away at the dead burdock. Tries to pick burrs off her cord trousers as she works, but they stick to her gloves and clump on her boots. Dead pea vines trail over the garden fence behind the mountain ash. She turns the lever hard west; back in the house, the twist seems to have done the trick. When the taps are open, after a brief trickle, there's no water coming out. Kitchen sink taps open. Bathroom sink taps. Upstairs bathroom taps. Basement laundry sinks. Done. Finishing the chore feels good: she likes Gwen and the place certainly needs people. And work. She heard people on the ferry talking about commuting. So maybe it's a possibility. She locks up the house and heads for the three.

Later that afternoon, a three-wheeler howls to a stop at the bottom of the driveway. Billy's relieved to find nobody home; that way, he can get on with his search for Annabelle's birth certificate. Now that he has proof of biological paternity, he's going to take up the matter with the birth registrar. If he can get legal access, he won't have future ownership problems with the likes of the Sycamores or those lesbians Derek'd been so crazy about. He hates it that Annabelle's last name is Sycamore. The document is easier to find upstairs in Lily's desk than the money had ever been, even though that quest turned into a joke. It's turning colder; he'd better make sure the water's off so those outside pipes don't freeze. He grabs the wrench from its outline on the shed wall, gives the lever a hard turn east to make sure it's fast against the stopping place, then races off. As soon as he leaves, water starts pouring from every tap in the house.

55.

Gwen hears the water before she sees it flowing under the door frames where it rises high enough to float the plastic toys left in the kitchen. The Donnacona ceiling has disintegrated so the upstairs taps must be on as well. She wades through the kitchen in her gumboots, manages to turn off the downstairs ones.

She's on the phone to Shima when Billy pulls up with a godawful roar. You turned the water off? she's saying to her new friend. Well then, how…? Straddling his ATV, Billy stands listening to the conversation, throws his head back and laughs. It was me. I thought the water was on.

Oh god.

It's not your fault, she says to Shima. It was Billy. He thought the water was on.

Except that it was turned off, she says to Billy. In the southern hemisphere, they say water circles down the drain in the opposite direction from the way it coils in the north. You skin burn somebody's arm by encircling the victim's skin with both hands and wringing it. The dancers on the outside circle move clockwise; the ones on the inside move counter-clockwise. When the music stops, you dance with the person across from you.

At least he'd rescued the birth certificate.

Gwen calls Leo to ask him to go over to Blenheim St. and look through the den desk for the insurance policy. That's terrible, he says. Why wouldn't our parents have left us an address or phone number? It's irresponsible of them. *The trouble with raising children, Percy said to Ada drying the dishes. Is they never leave.*

I'll look. It's got to be here somewhere.

Gwen changes the phone to her other ear. Lily's still got most of her things here, and Annabelle's. Some of it is upstairs. Lucky a lot of our stuff is over at the Deluxe. It's a *mess.*

She pulls the truck up to the general store, rushes in to ask if anybody knows where to get flood pumps. When she comes out, Billy's pulling away in the truck. I know where to pick some up, Gwen. Hang on.

She sits on the curb to wait for him. *What was I doing? Looking around.* Oh no. Her purse is in the glove compartment. The blank cheque. Oh Jesus. The flood distracted her from depositing it. Percy and Ada are halfway across Nevada with a piece of folded plastic in the plane in case they have to make a crash landing. In the morning, they'll spread it out and have a nice glass of water. What bank's it written on? She hadn't thought to notice. Anyone could fill in the amount and present fake ID. They wouldn't even have to do that. Her ID is in her purse. All Billy has to do is open the glove compartment.

When Leo comes, he and Gwen stand on the rim of the sunken kitchen. What's going to happen when Billy and Leo see each other?

I have to tell you, Leo. Billy Fenn, you remember Billy, he's gone to Tunstall to get flood pumps. He's been doing some work around here.

Leo backs away from the floor edge as if someone were about to push him in. Here's the insurance stuff, Gwen. I'd better leave.

What if you stayed? What if you faced him? she says. Her brother's heavier than he used to be, and his trousers aren't quite long enough. The way you did at Killarney that day when he was out on the dam? You were brave that day.

You saw that? I thought I was alone. He never bothered me after that.

Well there you go.

When Billy shows up with a water vacuum and flood pumps— the wiring's too messed up to take a chance so he's brought a generator as well—Gwen steps outside, gets in the truck, pushes the button on the glove compartment which opens slowly as if on a timer. *Let my purse be there. I'll never ask for anything else.* It's there. The warm leather safe in her hand. The cheque is there. Hallelujah. Even though Billy doesn't know anything about it, she feels as if he's returned her down payment.

Down in the basement, Leo's trying to cope with the twisted hoses. I can put those to the side, Leo, says Billy meeting Gwen's level gaze when she comes in. Later, after they've got the pumps going and are sitting out at the old picnic table, Billy tells them he doesn't think the house is salvageable. Leo is dying beside her, steeling himself to stay because he told her he would.

I'm sorry about what I did to you when we were kids, Leo, says Billy. I've started to understand a lot more since I've had a child of my own. Thinking about what I wouldn't want to happen to her.

Leo nods, but doesn't say anything. When Billy leaves, Leo says what does he mean he has a child?

Annabelle, says Gwen.

Annabelle? But she's Derek's.

Lily was living with Derek but she had an affair with Billy.

She did? So he's Annabelle's real father?

He is. You probably heard how George Fenn's family used to own Scarborough. It was given to the Yoshitos way back and the whole time we were kids, George was beating up on Billy because he was angry about being disinherited.

So my torturer is the father of my niece?

Yes.

The next time Leo sees Billy, he's reminded of the way a house you've lived in as a child seems shrunk when you go back to it as an adult. Maybe because Gwen is beside him, for the first time he notices how shifty Billy looks. Still, his torturer turns his head to the side with the same touching, brave expression that Annabelle offered when she pushed aside her last bottle. I'm too big, she'd said valiantly.

56.

As for Lottie, she still walks by her old cottage almost every night to see if it's for sale even if she'll never be able to afford it. All she has is her old age pension and the bit of money Takumi still sends her every month. She'd heard that the Sycamores decided not to buy it. And then the poor Scarborough house. Everyone at the store's talking about it. Even that Shima'd shown up and been invited to live there. It's not only for their sakes she needs to bring Isabelle and Takumi and Shima together; the three of them are the closest to family she has.

Odd, there's a light in the front bedroom of the Gallagher cottage. Maybe Ada's up. At Derek's memorial, when Ada realized Lottie had heard, she looked as if she'd caught a shockingly aged reflection of herself in a mirror. She knocks on the door and goes in. Ada? Is that you? It's Lottie. But it's not, it's Frederick's voice that sounds from the front bedroom. In here....

When she opens the door, he's sitting on the bed in front of an open bureau drawer, a white infant's hand knit dress laid out on his knees.

Do you have any idea who put this here? I was looking for some old things of Harriet's.

When Lottie sits down on the bed beside him, he hands her a note he'd found inside the box. *This was the dress I made for you if only you had lived. Love, Mother.* She reaches out, touches the dress, takes his hand.

I have to tell you, Frederick. Isabelle had a baby the winter Harriet died. She left her in White Rock at the hospital where she was born. Only, I know now, because she thought the baby died. It was the war; the baby was part Japanese. She spent her first three years with me. Her name is Shima. She's a young woman now and she's here.

Here on the island?

Not at the moment. But she's here.

Isabelle had a *baby*? You looked after her for three years and didn't tell anyone?

I did.

Would you mind keeping an eye on things at our place over the winter? Frederick puts the dress back in its box and tucks the tissue paper around it like a blanket. That's what was wrong with her when she came to Laburnum St. that Christmas all those years ago, he says slowly. And I didn't even see it. If only Harriet hadn't been so sick. He looks as if he's been blindfolded, turned around. When they take the blindfold off, he doesn't recognize anything he sees. Before Lottie leaves, she takes the silver whistle from her purse and slips it under the lidded cavity in the fireplace.

BLUEBERRIES

57.

Have I told you about my great idea for a TV phone-in programme, Mom? At their new rented house in Vancouver, layers of magazines are glued to the bedroom floor with stale juice and dust. Jenny crawls up to the TV, switches it on, squirms back on her bed. It's called phone-in-for-death, she says. What you've got is someone hanging onto a window ledge by their teeth. She picks up the remote, flicks it. People get to phone in. They have three minutes to save the person. If they don't, they lose their washer and dryer.

Late the night before, Gwen heard her daughter rocketing off the walls on her way down the corridor to the bathroom. Twitching as if ferrets were nipping her heels. What are you doing home at this hour, Jenny, it's way too late for you to be out.

What are you doing at home at this hour, it's way too late for you to be out, she mocks.

You do realize I've got other people in this house to be thinking about besides you.

You do realize I've got other people in this house to be thinking about besides you.

I'm going to haul off and deck you one of these days.

You just try.

Never talk to anyone between the hours of three and eight, Dr. Merrick'd said. It's mankind's darkest hour. Say get to bed.

Get some sleep. We'll talk in the morning.

Get to bed, Gwen says. Get some. sleep. We'll talk in the morning.

In the morning, she stands by the kitchen stool, scissors in hand, waiting to cut Jenny's hair. The air smells like dippity-do, the bloop she uses to keep her dyed blonde points on end. She crosses one orange-tighted leg over the other, fastens a second outsized safety pin in her plaid mini skirt. It's got to be more *spiky*, Mom. More off here. I gotta TV, you gotta TV, they've all got a TV. It's not easy getting your hair to defy gravity every day. She leaps up, grabs the dictionary, as if it's Gwen's job to get the scissors to whatever spot in the room she deigns to anoint. Back on the stool humming. Gnawing a hunk of lettuce. Safety pinning the clipping to her shirt. Big black letters. Pontiff. Turns the pages. Right, she says.It's either a shade of purple or the pope. *Let her have her adolescence. If people try to mature too soon, they end up having their adolescence when they're middle aged. (Pointed glance.)*It's all so cosmic and groovy, isn't it, mom? You and your granola freak friends. Oh, and by the way I'm not going to University Hill School next semester. All they'll expect is for me to be a liberal young adult. I've been a liberal young adult all my life. I'm going to be a teen-ager and I'm going to be bad. The worst part is I know why I have to do this. Why can't I just do it?

Why do you have to do this? says Gwen.

Because you want me to be fine all the time. I'm not always fine. You're such a flaming ding bat.

Don't talk to me like that, Jenny. I'm your mother.

Really? Because half the time I feel like I'm supposed to be the mother.

Great. She's probably been transferring her need for a matter of fact caring voice, onto Jenny as well. No wonder she's angry. No dad's voice and a mother's needing re-assurance. Apparently you don't get a rehearsal in this child raising business. Maybe she's been mistaking precociousness for maturity, that's the trouble. *Whatever you do, it's wrong.* One thing she does know: if she tries to hold Jenny back, she'll leave in a huff like the odds and sods she brings home to hunker in their black plastic bags along the hall corridor. Maybe she'll strip for a while, Jenny says now. Save some money, go traveling.

Right and all the money you make would be used to survive.

Just kidding, mom.

A few more bits of hair on the floor, the phone rings, and she's up and out of the room. Oh, it's you, she says shutting her bedroom door. You is probably the boy who called the other night. Jenny's not in, Gwen'd said. Do you want the phone number where she's babysitting?

Excuse me, Jenny's mom, did you say four, six, eight...? I don't have enough paper for eight. I'm in a phone booth. No pen. I'm making piles of pieces for each number. I can do four but don't know as I can handle eight.

Couldn't you remember it?

I'm drunk. What's after the eight?

Nine, I'm afraid.

Maya comes and leans against her mother. Jenny's back on the stool, swiping at the air around her face. I can't believe this. He hung up on me. *Be an anchor to windward. The future's a black box.*

Maybe you got cut off.

The phone didn't snap. It clunked.

Keep your voice neutral. Stay in the adult role. Steady her no matter what.

He's probably wondering what happened too. Maybe you could call back.

Okay, I'll have to sit on your knee to do it, though. As soon as she re-connects, she's back in her bedroom. The hair will wait.

Gwen picks up Jenny's fanzine. It says here there might be a world where a thimble full of matter weighs as much as Mt. Everest.

What's a thimbleful? asks Maya.

You know what a thimble is. Well, a full one.

I've got nothing to do, says Maya.

Don't tell me you've got nothing to do. I'll give you a job.

For Jenny it'd all started when those eighteen somethings moved into the basement apartment across the street. The day she saw the group of them strut up the basement steps in their black clothes, she sprang from her bed as if she'd been waiting an eternity for her cue. Threw on the old gabardine raincoat she'd found in the alley and headed out.

The night Gwen tracked her down at the Smiling Buddha on Hastings St., Jenny tenderly reached out to help her mother navigate the bodies leaping up and down in the mosh pit. When everyone else had been trying to clean up and salvage what they could from Scarborough, Jenny trailed a scarf around what was left of the living room. Cracked like a live wire if anyone said anything to her. Insisted on starting a second dispute while the first was still in progress.

Down in Birch Bay, Isabelle's sliding dampened labels off

ketchup bottles when Leo phones to ask if they happen to have a beach down there with a long, flat horizon because there's an important astronomical conjunction he wants to observe. Only one chance every eight years to see the morning star and the evening star on the same day. You have to have a long low horizon to see it.

So a few days later it's Leo sitting at the *Bide-a-Wile* counter drinking a milkshake, telling Jack how they used to think that, because Venus was seen west of the sun the morning of the day it's also seen east of the sun, the sighting to the east of the sun must be another celestial body. But it's not, it's Venus itself. You know that first bright star you see at night because it's so near us, Jack? We're going to see it in the morning and then we're going to see it again at night.

Is that so?

Would you help me find the best viewing spot?

You betcha.

Jack sets his shoulders back, confident he's the one they count on to know what's what on the tide flats.

But in the morning when Leo knocks on their bedroom door, Jack mistakes him for a guard who's come to take him to a new camp—further north and cooler maybe. Traveling north through Thailand, he'd crouched in a box car holding another prisoner out the door to defecate, the car shaking so badly he almost dropped him. The man babbled about a snake that bit him the time he'd tried to escape through the jungle. Tied himself to a tree to stay upright hoping gravity would draw down the poison, but the guard found him, cut him down, and put him in a hole in the ground.

Out on the flats behind a dune waiting for dawn as if for

an ambush, Jack tells his nephew he'd better try to keep that maggoty soup down, otherwise he'll starve. Touches what he sees as an ulcer pushing out Leo's lower lip. The one on his leg has pulled away so much flesh the bone and tendon are exposed. See here? They have to sharpen the spoons he's brought so he can dig out the ulcerated flesh. I don't want to cut into you without anesthetic, but we can't save this leg.

It's okay, says Leo. I can manage with the leg for now. Remember the planet sighting we're waiting for, the one we're going to see again tonight? That's what we want to concentrate on.

It's all very well for Leo, but in case his nephew doesn't know, Jack has more important things to do: he has to plant the nest of termites in the bridge trestle before the guards pull up the rope cradle. His letters to Isabelle are safe in his hat band; he's late being ready. As a punishment, the guard pushes him back over the bridge where he falls fifteen feet and lands on his head.

But now here's someone holding him up, telling him all he has to do is look up and he's going to see the morning star that's also the evening star. Come on, look up now, Jack, over there, if you look up, you're going to see the morning star.

And there it is, shining and beautiful.

In the afternoon, on one of his expeditions to the end of the shelves in the store, Jack stops short and flips up the lid of their steamer trunk. What's the termite nest doing in there? Ash inside instead of termites? *You hold me like a vase. I do that?*

Where was this, Jack? Isabelle says.

In our trunk back there. If I push it under a beam on the bridge, the termites will go to work and that'll slow the enemy down for a while.

That's not a termite nest, dear. It's a cremation urn and it doesn't belong here. I'd forgotten all about it.

Gwen is fixing up the spare room in the basement of their 20th Avenue rental; she wants it nice so Isabelle can come for a visit and meet Shima, the Yoshitos being her friends and all. The girls rabbit around as their mother tries to manoeuver a futon frame through the basement door.

For once, plain let me give you jobs, Gwen says, tacking up a couple of posters.

Have you noticed how Impressionist posters are everywhere now, Mom? says Jenny pulling at one end of the futon. Placemats in restaurants, you name it. Like Blue Boy and Pinky at Grandma's when you were young. As long as you don't wear that bedspread skirt when dad comes to visit. They are so lame.

Couple of days ago, Jenny and a couple of her friends had gone to Kitsilano beach done up in long dresses and hats with veils. People were offended, she said. I don't plan to look like I'm a prune when I'm sixty, not that there's any way I want to live as old as sixty.

After they finish making the bed, well, that's a diplomatic way of putting it—the girls resentfully bear witness is more like it—Maya leans listlessly against the kitchen wall. Summer in the city has possibilities for adults; you can go to a patio and drink sangria after a swim, but for children used to the coastal beaches, nothing compares to the forest and the dark green water. Maya holds herself back when she wants something, Jenny pushes forward.

When Eugene comes, they'll sit at the table with their youngest between them. *Do they regress at Christmas?* She understands now how Eugene felt about her being a bottomless pit. Will he notice she's changed? That she sometimes manages to mobilize her abandoned and unrecognized self? Hope so.

58.

It's a hot afternoon when Gwen and the girls head downtown to pick up Isabelle. An ice cream truck plays *Greensleeves* over and over as it wheels down the street. No one comes out to buy revels. The tar strips on the road soften to glue as drivers squeeze more heat waves from their car horns.

At the bus station, Gwen, Jenny and Maya make their way along the bay of Greyhounds until they locate the one from Blaine. They're late; the other passengers are all off and Auntie is waiting in the door. Her ankles are swollen from the trip but the rest of her is the same, all long bones and angles, her thin mouth smaller and tighter with lines fanning out from her lips. Same old leatherette coat and gabardine slacks, a hat crocheted from the sides of beer tins—is it a joke—the girls stare as she hands down a hat box and a series of plastic bags. Her hair is shorter and drier, frizzed wiry ends perk from the sides of her alarming hat. Electrolysis it looks like for her faint moustache. Don't anybody lose *that,* she says pointing at the hat box. Maya's still in the fluorescent green bathing suit she put on to run in the sprinkler. Isabelle grabs the hat box, makes a staccato turn and heads for the terminal. They practically have to lasso her to angle her in the direction of the car.

Oh, she says when Gwen puts the car in reverse, steadying herself with one hand on the dashboard. Maya fingers the curved discs on her great aunt's hat to see if they're aluminum or pretend. They're aluminum. Isabelle's breath pops as if from a squeezed bladderwrack as she leans against the head rest, then smacks her foot on the floor as if there were a brake on her side. Stop the car. Stop it right now, she says. There's something wrong with the girls.

When she'd turned around, they were smiling like Cheshire cats but their teeth were bright blue.

It's okay, Auntie. They've just been eating blueberries.

Oh. I didn't know what to think.

See that parachute over there? Jenny says as they drive onto the Cambie St. bridge. Kind of a half parachute? Black straps are tied over the curve of the ceiling dome. It's the new stadium. Mom says it looks like a diaphragm in bondage.

What's a diaphragm? says Maya.

A thing for stopping babies, Jenny says looking out the opposite window.

At Christmas, she and Maya count houses with outdoor lights and argue about whether you're allowed to include ones on streets that angle off the street they're driving on.

How's Jack? says Gwen.

Maintaining, I think that's the word. He's given up smoking praise the lord. He thinks I don't know he's planning to run the lunch counter by himself while I'm away. You go, Isabelle, he said. I'll make out fine. Dusty white face powder works its way in splotches down the sides of her nose. Did I tell you Leo came down to visit? He was good with Jack. He took him out to see the morning star.

I'm glad to hear that, Gwen says, looking over her shoulder to check the next lane—the girls' mouths really are startling. Auntie reaches into one of the shopping bags and lifts out a large round zucchini, its eyes and nose cut in triangles, mouth carved in a zigzag pattern like a jack-o-lantern. Places it on the armrest so it's staring back at the girls. I've grown so many of these I thought I could get rid of one by getting it confiscated at the border, she says. Give the customs officers a laugh at the same time. They laughed all right and let it through. Now what're we going to do with it?

This is more like the Auntie they've heard about. The one everybody said was a riot. Even Jenny's reluctantly interested, not that anything the adults do these days is worth her attention.

Let's stop at Baskin Robbins, says Maya. You get free tastes of three kinds of ice cream before you have to pick. Mom, stop.

No. Maybe after supper.

The sun's glinting off the triangular panes of the domed greenhouse on the top of Queen Elizabeth Park as they drive up the Cambie St. hill. It won't be long until the sunsets will have more purple in them because of the volcano in Washington. Isabelle's hand rests on the swollen zucchini. The ash from Mt. St. Helen will turn the moon blue. Blueberries floating in milk have tiny furled mouths.

Maybe it could be a summer Jack-o'-lantern, says Maya.

Sure it could, says Isabelle. Why not?

Jenny stares out the window as if having to wait for her own life to start is unendurable. When they pull up in front of the house, she bolts ahead without taking anything in. Jenny would you just.... Gwen says. Jenny snarls and doesn't come back. Isabelle flashes her niece a commiserating look (oh, it's like *that*), passes the zucchini to Maya who levers it up the stairs on her hip and tips it onto the wide porch railing. Those petunias should not be in the shade, says Isabelle. They're all stems.

Forgive the mess. The hall is full of bikes and soccer balls. A ring around the living room at kid level. Someday, when she's alone again, Gwen will have nothing in her front hall but a slim table with a perfectly centred vase of gladioli.

The house is arts and crafts style with the dining room split from the living room by a sliding door. A foundation of handsome stone work. Maya tugs Isabelle down the back stairs and into the garden to show her the zucchini plants they have growing over the fence, thick stems that Gwen tied up so the wide leaves drape down the boards. When the flowers dry and the green tubes engorge, she lifts the baby squashes onto the ledge to thicken. More leaves trail over a net hung on four corner posts to make a shady grapevine arbour with a bench inside that Gwen hopes will take Isabelle back.

Coals to Newcastle, I'd say, says Isabelle.

What does that mean? says Maya.

It means I brought you something you already had lots of.

But none of these can *see*.

That's true.

Later, unpacking, Isabelle centres the hat box on the shelf above her bed. Jenny brings a pair of tennis shoes blotched with white shoe polish into the kitchen that Isabelle'd pushed through her door as if mailing them.

What're these supposed to be?

Isabelle's just trying to help, Jenny.

They're not *supposed* to be clean.

Besides her temp secretarial work out at the university, Gwen's signed up to take some courses in the Education Dept. Jenny's due home by the time Maya gets back from day camp the afternoon Auntie decides to head over to Bowen. At the Horseshoe Bay terminal, black loops hold the dark pilings together. Isabelle walks off the ferry with the other passengers, carrying the hat box with the Yoshito urn inside. The freshly painted restored dancehall community centre assumes pride of place on the rise above the wharf. The shadow of the bluff darkens the road as she crosses the causeway; a lot of concrete on the cement bridge has worn away. The lagoon is lower than she's ever seen it. Not a swan in sight. The honeysuckle and wild rose arbor trail is blocked off by a no trespassing sign, the demolished hotel replaced with a nearby luxury home. The corner Deluxe is gone. She has to detour around the area where the greenhouse used to stand. The tide is out so she takes the beach way along the slanted path up from Pebbley to meet the upper road past Millers Landing

She's tired and hot when she finally stands on the edge of the Scarborough house pit formed by the scooped out mass of water logged rubble. Over at the sheds – at least they're still standing—she pulls back the grape vine growing through the paneless frame. Once inside, she takes the urn from the hat box and lifts it to a shelf where she finds an identical urn standing in the spot where she was intending to leave hers. She leaves the two of them side by side, stops for tea at an upgraded version of The Shack Café, then starts back for the ferry.

No one's at home when Maya gets back from day camp. Small carved zucchini statues line up on the kitchen table like finger puppets; she sits down forlornly and changes them from place to place as if arranging soldiers for a parade. Tags her hand down the row of dresses in her mother's closet like rat-a-tatting a stick along a garden fence. A seagull shimmies its wings closed on top of a street lamp as the sun rolls over the tall elm, shining like a hot penny. Falls asleep on the couch, stripes of light between the venetian blinds slanting down the wall.

Eugene's rented corvette pulls up at the curb. He comes up the stairs relaxed in his tan chinos and a polo shirt with an alligator over his heart. Maya leaps up and rushes into his arms. Even if it's too babyish a thing to do, she stands on his shoes so he can't take a step without taking her with him.

Where's your mother?

At work.

Dad! Jenny comes pounding up the stairs and hugs him around the waist.

Lucky I came a day early, eh? I tried to phone but there was no answer. Isn't that what you say here, eh? Eh?

Very funny, dad, says Jenny.

Half an hour later, Isabelle's yoo-hooing at the door and Maya's dragging her down the hall to meet her dad.

So you're the famous Auntie who knew how to make island paradises for small girls? he says.

I did?

That's what I heard.

When Gwen comes in, Eugene kisses her cheek. He's thinner, the same only different. Narrower neck with wrinkles. It's necks that give people away. Eyes stay the same. Browner, even. She's not going to say Jenny was supposed to be covering in case Isabelle's ferry and bus didn't connect. What could be more important than saving face in front of your dad? This is nice, Eugene says, admiring the panel work in the living room and the fireplace. She thought he'd like it. At the kitchen table, Maya leans her chin on folded hands, and refuses to take her eyes off him. Jenny's at the mirror in the hall pulling at her hair. It's all matted, that's the problem, dad. I keep my tension in my hair. I still can't hear out of this ear.

It's dangerous that loud music. Don't you wear ear-plugs?

Mad Dog was lonely, she says. If he wants us to lay our heads on the stage, we lay our heads on the stage.

At supper, when Eugene picks up the pepper mill, Maya tells him he has to turn the handle to get the pepper to come out. All weekend, the girls will announce what they're doing or about to do and watch to make sure he's paying attention. Isabelle says she's going down to Cambie to buy some impatiens to replace the petunias.

I want to study about birds, says Maya.

Do you? Eugene says, and she lays her head on his shoulder. I love you, Maya.

I love you too, dad.

When Auntie gets back from Cambie St. and is kneeling besides the front stairs troweling in the impatiens, Shima drives up in her Volvo. She gets out and comes around the fender, smart and trim in a seer sucker suit. Says hello to Isabelle as if she's the gardener, then starts up the scuffed stairs.

Inside, she slips off her jacket, lets her strapped wedgies fall on the floor as she flops into an arm chair. Gwen can feel Eugene thinking who do we have here? When Gwen introduces them, Shima leans back and stretches her arms along the top of the sofa. Hello Eugene. Has anybody ever told you you look a lot like Jenny Kerr?

Rumour has it. How do you do, Shima?

I do very well, she says. That is, if someone would pour me a drink.

He obliges too quickly but never mind, *never mind,* sits down as casually as if he lived there, holding the bottle between his knees to pull the cork. The girls punch each other in the hall, arguing about a circle skirt with a poodle Maya found on the floor in Jenny's room. The waist is too big, it's dropped to Maya's hips.

I didn't say you could wear that, says Jenny.

Shima's a lawyer, Gwen says proudly. She's working on the redress issue for Japanese Canadians who lost their property during the war.

How much has Gwen told him about Scarborough after that one time he was there? Precious little, actually. She wasn't expecting Shima tonight, not that she always phones when she drops over. She's been waiting for the right moment to tell Auntie about her – she'll be thrilled that the first of the long lost Yoshitos has turned up. When Shima stands up, she's so thin that from the side she's almost a silhouette.

Do you know, she says, opening her briefcase. We've finally managed to get the government files opened and found out that some of the RCMP didn't think the evacuation was necessary. She passes the document to Gwen who's helping build a filing system for her.

It was pretty bad in the States too, Eugene says, setting out a checkerboard to play with Maya.

Shima sits up at attention on the couch. Your citizens didn't have their property sold and confiscated to pay for their own internment, she says. Removing citizens' rights was legal because of the War Measures Act. After the War Measures Act, do you know what we had? The National Emergency Transitional Powers Act, you didn't have that in the States. Then the Continuation of the National Emergency Transitional Powers Act. People weren't allowed to come back to the coast for half a decade after the war was over.

I didn't know that, says Eugene. I thought it was the same as in the States. Jenny strums her fingers on the table and beseeches the ceiling. *My dad's here. Shut up about it for once.*

Eugene's face brightens when he looks at Shima, the way it always does when he's attracted to someone. No more politics, Jenny shouts like a newsboy hollering a headline. Did you know that Johnny Rotten really loves his parents, dad? Well, he does. She pushes her dad down the back steps into the garden, thrusts a croquet mallet at him, another at Shima who's changed into short shorts of all things. As Shima whacks balls through the wickets down the stretch of lawn, a sheet whips up and blows over the upper wire of the clothesline and jams on top of the new arbour. Shima and Eugene declare the game a tie and retire to the grapevine arbour while Jenny resets the wickets. The sheet blocks their view of Isabelle who's come up the back steps to flip the sheet back. A lot of people want to forget about the internment because they don't think they have a prayer of restitution, Shima's saying. Take my father. He never talks about it. He's given up, suppressed all of it. Imagine rowing all night and sleeping in the bush during the day so you can get far enough up the coast that no one's going to find you. If someone hadn't shown up and told him the war was over, who knows when he would have found out. He wasn't allowed back in B.C. so he went to Blaine and that's where he found me with Lottie Fenn.

And your mother?

My mother's dead.

Back inside the house Jenny, resplendent in tulle and logging shirt plaid, is ready to take her parents—together at last—down to the Smiling Buddha. Before they leave, Gwen goes down to Isabelle's room thinking her aunt's probably come in the basement door. When she knocks, there's no answer. Opens the door but she's not there.

Has anyone seen Auntie? she says coming back up the stairs.

Who? says Shima.

My aunt was here. I want you to meet her. She was in the garden. She was supposed to be keeping Maya company tonight.

It's okay. I'll hang out with Maya, says Shima. You people have a good time.

On Hastings, a gloating Jenny insists Eugene's hand into hers as they pass a pawn shop and are about to turn into the club. Her father asks her to hold still, crouches and places his palms either side of her calf to straighten the seams in her stockings. It's all right, dad, she says. It doesn't matter if they're straight. Inside the unbelievably seedy club, Jenny shows her parents to a rickety ice cream parlour table on the edge of the mosh pit, seats them as politely as a *maître d'*, smiles back at them as she joins her friends. The band lands with a crash of scraped brakes. Eugene shouts over the violence of the music. What's she doing here, Gwen? For christ sake, she's one step away from the heroin addicts on the street. Half of these kids are on something. Do they know she's under age? Is she on drugs?

You try asking her, Eugene. She's got some smart ass reply every time. Well, we're not smoking *pot* if that's what you mean.

She's getting far too much freedom, he says.

I don't want her to run with this crowd but I don't know what to do. If I try to ground her, she'll leave. I can't have that.

You took them here his look says, but they both know how the fight will go if they start so they stop.

Gwen's gaze snags on a young man and woman who spot each other across the floor, open their arms and fold into each other with such certainty and tenderness it's as if they've been meeting forever and for the first time all at once. He whispers something in her ear that appeals to her so much she rises to him with a smile that wants to spread past the corners of her mouth, but her mouth can't stretch any further so she buries her face in his collar bone. Her narrow hand caresses the back of his limp khaki shirt. That girl, whoever she is, Gwen thinks, is capable of serious and abiding love. She looks again and realizes it's Jenny.

She's too young, Gwen, says Eugene. She's way too young.

At home, Shima's sleepy but still awake, kisses each of them goodnight and leaves. Point me to a bed, Eugene says and Gwen opens her hand at the couch. When she manages not to turn her face toward his, she sees instantly where she left the good scarf she'd been looking for earlier.

Still no Auntie. Where could she be?

59.

When Ada sees Isabelle coming down the street, she stands up from her gardening pad and brushes off the knees of her slacks. Looks at the bulbs she's planting as if she wants to eat them. Isabelle stalks through the gap in the laurel hedge, so upset you'd think she'd seen her beloved ahead of her on the street, was comforted by the fact he'd looked back, then realized he was checking to make sure she wasn't following him.

I've been at Gwen's, Ada. I can't believe what you did. I cannot *believe* it. My *daughter* was there. I overheard her talking about her father. She thinks I'm dead. For god's sake, she thinks I'm dead.

The chairs on the Blenheim St. lawn beg for conversation. Come and sit down, Isabelle, please. Isabelle stands as if turned to a pillar of salt, then screams at her sister. Can you imagine how you'd feel? Can you *imagine?*

I did the wrong thing. I know that now. I thought it was for the best.

For God's sake, you didn't tell me about my only chance at happiness in this world? Don't come near me. Just answer my questions. Does Gwen know?

You've forgotten what it was like, Isabelle. They would have taken the baby away and sent her to a camp somewhere. If not, both of you would have had to live with people shaming you all the time.

You mean *you* would have had to live with people shaming you all the time. It... should... have... been... my... decision. It's unbelievable. I've had to live with YOUR lie all this time. I will never ever forgive you! What exactly does Gwen know?

Ada wipes off her trowel. Only that Takumi is Shima's father which is why she was angling to bring Shima into the Scarborough house as an equal partner for free.

Good for Gwen, says Isabelle. And what's this about Lottie Fenn looking after her in Blaine?

I don't know anything about that.

Oh come on.

I really don't. Lottie was going to take care of adoption arrangements. Shima *knows* her?

Lottie helped *raise* her.

I had no idea. Ada sits on the front stairs.

When did Takumi find Shima? How old was she?

I don't know, Isabelle. If you'd come down off your high horse and try for one moment to see one iota of how other people might have been feeling…

You didn't respect me enough to discuss this with me?

You wouldn't have listened.

Why would I have listened? You did a terrible thing. It's going to take me the rest of my life to put it to rights.

At least you know Shima and her father are both alive.

You'd do anything to save face wouldn't you, Ada? All I know is that how Shima finds out is everything. Don't you dare say one word to Shima or Gwen. Or to Lottie Fenn. You're not to have anything more to do with Lottie Fenn. How could she have gone along with this?

She didn't know I told you the baby was dead. I haven't even met Shima.

Does Dad know? asks Isabelle.

Not as far as I know. Where are you going, Isabelle?

Everyone was asleep when she got back to 20ᵗʰ Ave. She packed her bag, called a taxi, and left a note for Gwen saying she'd call. Something's come up, she wrote. If she said anything more, she'd be putting Gwen in the position of asking her not to say anything to Shima. At least the set-up in the cottage worked. It brought her daughter here. She'll know where her father is.

Maybe she even knows where her grandparents are. She's alive, that's all she can think about. Astonishingly, Laburnum St. is the only place she feels she can cope and she wants to be with her father.

Frederick's in the same bed he was in when Isabelle came to him from White Rock that long ago Christmas. He's too old to get up; someone comes in every day. When Isabelle calls up the stairs,,he thinks it's the homemaker. When he turns to her, his pale eyes leak.

You know, he says.

She looks at him. So do you.

Just be with me a while, he says. Can you do that?

I can do that, dad.

I was at the cottage, he says. Lottie came by. Do you know, she was in Blaine the whole time we were wondering about her place. I wanted to wait until you came to see me, not push myself at you. Not push myself at you ever again.

Did Lottie tell you about Shima, Dad? Have you met her?

No. I want to.

She's beautiful. I don't want to do anything to startle her if she thinks I'm dead. I've been dead. I'm not now.

I didn't mean not to have faith in you. I just worried....

I know, dad. It's okay.

60.

Lottie's uninsulated orchard cottage is as cold as her old place; it stays damp and clammy all year round. She's chopping kindling when Isabelle comes up the path. The two of them pick up the firewood, sit in the kitchen on low stools and feed the stove even though it's still summer.

I've found out about Shima, Lottie, Isabelle says. They told me she was dead. She saw me at Gwen's place but didn't know who I was. I overheard her telling Gwen's ex that Takumi survived the war hiding out up Narrows Inlet. She said she lived with you when she was little.

I kept expecting to hear from you, Isabelle. Ada told me she was going to tell you I'd be taking care of adoption arrangements. I didn't know until Derek's memorial that you'd been told the baby died.

I don't know how I'll be able to be in the same room with Ada ever again, Isabelle says. Takumi was so upset and angry that I'd let myself be followed. He didn't know how hard I'd tried to cover my tracks. Maybe he told her I'd died to protect her, stop her from trying to find me if he thought I'd abandoned her. Oh god, he thought I abandoned her. He must have. She starts to cry. It wasn't you who told the police officers then?

Lottie shakes her head. No. It might have been my brother. When Shima was little, I came to the city to find you but heard you were married and I didn't know whether you'd left the baby on purpose. Then Frederick and I found the dress you made for her.

I am married, says Isabelle. But this is about Shima. You're telling me that Takumi came to Blaine? Right near where I've been living all this time?

Yes. Lottie goes to the sideboard, gets out a picture of Takumi and Shima holding ping pong bats.

Oh, I love this. Is she in touch with you? May I borrow this and get it copied?

Of course you can. Takumi keeps in touch; he's been good to me. For some reason, he feels as if he has to guess something to win Shima back.

Where is he?

In Prince Rupert. He's a fisherman. Has had some success as a sculptor, actually.

Has he? Is he well?

He says he's fine. I don't really know.

What was she like? The baby? Shima?

Tender, and always, I don't know, can you say level-headed about a baby, but she was.

But what can I say to her?

What about the dress in the drawer in the cottage? Frederick and I found it. What if we showed it to her?

Isabelle looks surprised, then relieved, as if coming to a fork in the road she hadn't recognized until she was standing at the crossroads. I didn't know I knew what I was doing but I guess I did.

Do you want my help?

Of course I want your help. You're part of my family now.

SILVERDALE

61.

September, 1979.

Back at 20th Ave., Jenny's living with one leg hanging out the window. Doesn't even want eye contact in the mornings. Gwen's on the phone to her mother when her daughter comes downstairs and sidles past, muttering that she's going to Oakridge to buy clothes to take to San Francisco.

I know you and Auntie are still on the outs, Mom, says Gwen, but I don't know where she is. I'm worried. She was here, now she's gone. I don't like to call and worry Jack in case she hasn't come back there.

Is Eugene still there? says Ada.

No, he's gone.

Isabelle will be in touch when she's ready. She has a lot on her plate.

She *wanted* to see me, Mom, says Gwen. She even gave me Jack's letters from prison camp to read. Hang on a minute. There's someone on the other line. Maybe it's her.

But it's not. It's an agent about some extra film work. They want her to come down at Hastings and Nanaimo for a night shoot. Would Ada take the girls? Of course Ada will take the girls. When has she not taken the girls?

That afternoon, Isabelle's over at the Gallagher cottage walking around plumping cushions, wrapping and unwrapping the
white knitted dress. Is that a mildew smell? She finds some old
Ivory Snow under the sink, washes the dress and spreads it on a
towel in front of the fire. The phone rings.

There you are, Auntie, Gwen says.

Here I am.

What are you doing at Bowen? Your note says something's
come up.

I have something to tell you, Gwen, but it may take a little
time. I need you to trust me and wait.

But I wanted you to meet Shima, Auntie. She's Takumi
Yoshito's daughter. I was about to call you in from the garden
and you'd gone. I need to know what's going on.

You will. I promise.

At Nanaimo St., the street signs have been replaced with the
names of New York streets and the restaurants converted to del-
icatessens. Good, they say, when Gwen arrives. They've finally sent someone middle aged. They must be talking about the
woman in the line behind her, but no, she's handed a frumpy
polyester blouse, thick tweed skirt, and told to walk down
Hastings to Nanaimo and drop plums from a shopping bag as
she goes. When she hears a gunshot, she's to run into a nearby
grocery store.

After that section of the shoot, she and the other extras
spread their sleeping bags on the community centre floor where
she lies studying Blume's taxonomy with a flashlight. The shoot
continues deep into the night. At three a.m. they wake her
up and tell her to drive her car around the block; the section

of script they're working on occurs at six p.m. and at six p.m. there'd be street traffic. A traffic monitor in a fluorescent vest motions her car into the line-up; when her head starts to nod on her chest, she slaps her face to stay awake, but keeps falling asleep again. Nothing to do but park for a minute to sort herself out. The next thing she knows the traffic monitor is knocking at the window.

Gwen Killam! What are you doing here ? It's Jeanette of all people, dressed in a suit jacket, her grey hair in a crew cut. Bending over her car window as if to give her a ticket, she motions the cars in the lineup behind her to pass. If this isn't just…, she says.

I'm too old for this. I should be home in bed.

You're too old? Where do you live now?

Twentieth Ave. just east of Cambie.

For heaven sake, we're at Main and 32nd.

Gwen should visit; why don't they set a date? Once the time is jotted down on Jeanette's wrist, she suggests they wrap her. Gwen sticks the envelope of cash in her hatband and goes home to bed.

When Isabelle gets back to Birch Bay, Jack is out on the tide flats. So it's done, he says to her when he comes in. You've planted it. Wonder how long it will take for the termites to chew through the bridge trestle?

That's not where I was, says Isabelle. That was back when you were a prisoner of war. We live here now.

That girl who came here that day. Who was she?

Gwen. Our niece. Jack, I have some good news. I had a daughter a long time ago and I've found her. I thought she was dead.

Am I her father?

No, she says softly.

When she came here, did she think I was her father?

She hasn't been here yet, sweetheart. It was before we were married, when you were overseas.

So someone lived inside you before I went there? I thought so. Isabelle, if we get enough food on the other side of the bridge, it won't matter if it collapses, the enemy won't reach us. Soon you'll be leaving, he adds.

I won't be leaving. I love you too. But she's the only daughter I have. We have to find a way to bring her into our lives.

That's all to the good then, isn't it?

It's all to the good.

She smiles with a deep glow he's never seen before.

Frances and Jeanette's house is a grey shingled affair on a narrow shady lot near Little Mountain. It has a romantic garden with white iron garden furniture and a magnolia tree. Varied brightly coloured walls inside, newly painted as if they'd come back from Mexico and said, the way people do, we really must get some colour in this place.

Frances is in the garden sitting at a table covered in a flowered cloth. Chintz curtains at the window. Rose bushes. Lemonade all round.

I love your magnolia tree, Gwen says.

Turns out they have something to tell her. They're going to get married as soon as it's legal which won't be too long from now. When they do tie the knot, guess where they want to have the wedding?

Beats me, says Gwen.

In the dancehall. That way Derek can be with us.

It's not until they're sitting on the bed where Shima was conceived that Lottie opens the bottom drawer and hands the young woman the box with the dress inside. Of course I remember you, Shima'd said when Lottie called. How could you think I wouldn't? Shima unfastens the satin bow, holds the dress up by its shoulders. Picks up the card.

It's a present for you, says Lottie. From your mother.

I don't have a mother.

You do. You've even seen her. And it's not her fault. They told her *you* were dead as well.

Where did I see her?

At Gwen's. At 20th Avenue. She was planting flowers she said.

Oh *her!* Does she know I'm me?

She does.

62.

On sunny days when the pressure is high on the Prince Rupert shore, out flow winds start up suddenly because the ground warms up faster than the sea. Until last year, Takumi'd spent the winters fishing the sea urchin beds: demand for urchins in the sushi restaurants in Vancouver and Prince Rupert meant that it'd been worth his while to hire divers to unscrew the spiked globes and fill outsized net bags. But now that the otters have begun to re-populate, the pickings are so slim it's not worth it.

What is it about having an old letter from Shima tacked to his bulletin board the way his father used to pin seed envelopes above his desk in the greenhouse that gives him his clue? He's in his studio molding unrefined silver, pushing his grey hair under a bandana as he blows hot air through the *fuigo*. Reaching up, he flaps the envelope with his finger. Even as he blows—the oxides of lead are absorbed by the bone and pine needle ash and the silver remains on top—he sees his father asking his mother to stretch her mouth over her teeth, worried that the blue line along her gums might be a symptom of lead poisoning caused by the contamination from the silver mine that leeched into the village ground water back home in Japan. Miracle boy, tell me again where you live. If you're ever lost, you tell the person who finds you that you live over the hill past Millers Landing at the Scarborough farm. The announcers in the cuckoo clock that Noriko brought with her from the village, a present from a Dutch trading company her family had done business with, will chime out that he's home. Tapping the envelope again, he looks up at his daughter's signature, Shima Yoshito. His mother's hand is on his shoulder again until he repeats what she said because that was what her mother said to her. If she's ever lost, her mother instructed her, say you live in the Shimane district, in the town of Omori. All along Noriko's location was in her name. Shima. Shimane. Her name's been staring him in the face since he found her.

Dad?

Shima. I'm so glad you called. I need to come and talk to you.

I want to talk to you too, she says. I'm on the island in the Gallagher cottage. Lottie brought me here and says I should stay until you get here.

I'll be there as soon as I can.

Dad, says Shima as Takumi comes up the verandah stairs. Dad, she says pulling back the blanket she'd hung along the beam to block the wind. Dad, she says sliding open the glass door, passing him the box with the knitted baby dress and note. He reads it, looks up astonished. She didn't know, he says.

They told her I was dead, Shima says. I saw her at Gwen's but she didn't know who I was. She overheard me saying my mother was dead. What're we going to do? She knows who I am, but she hasn't come to me.

Yes, she has, he says. He touches the dress tenderly. It's going to be okay. I was so hurt because I thought she'd abandoned you, saying she was dead was a way of speaking but it was wrong of me.

Yes, it was. Very wrong.

I can't believe this but the name of the area where my parents lived was in your name the whole time. It's where they probably returned. They talked about a row of village houses built for the workers who made the Iwami silver. We can write to them together.

He reaches over and slides the family jewels stone lid from its basin. In it lies the silver lifeguard whistle his mother'd brought from Japan. He holds it in his hand like a talisman while he anxiously makes the phone call.

Isabelle? This is Takumi.

No.

I'm here.

I can't believe you're here. Where's here?

On the island. With Shima. We found, she found, the dress. May we see you?

Is that what she wants?

He covers the mouthpiece. Shima's sitting on one of the old cots by the window. She wants to know if you want to see her. Shima nods. Yes, she does. Where? The Sylvia Hotel?

Isabelle? Mom?

Oh Shima. Are you really there? With your father?

I'm really here with my father.

I can't wait to see you both.

When they get to the hotel, Isabelle's sitting nervously in the lounge. She stands up when they come in and reaches out a hand for each of them. Her eyes meet Takumi's at last. When Shima steps forward her perimeter is sharper as if the person she stepped from is nobody's business. Coats are flung over chairs and they're all three in each other's arms crying too much to worry whether they're standing up or sitting down. They can hardly stop holding each others' hands to even breathe.

63.

Over at 20th Ave. Jenny's on the line from San Francisco. Her mother's not to be upset but dad wonders, well she wonders. She and Maya both wonder. They're having a good time in California. They'd like to stay on. She can start college there and... do you want to speak to Dad?

I would like to speak to dad.

Life goes on, Mom.

Life does, does it?

Gwen? How are you? Good. The girls say, well they say

they'd like to spend next year here, then see how it goes.

Do you think you can help Jenny settle down?

I do. Do you want to speak to Maya?

I want to speak to Maya.

Dad wants us to stay here for a while, Mommy.

That's okay if you want to, honey. Do you like it there?

I do, but I miss you.

I sure miss you too, but there are holidays. Let's talk about it some more and then see how everybody feels.

Okay.

After she hangs up, she goes into each of their rooms and starts packing. Seeing their clothes the way Eugene would, everything looks scruffy, as if the play is over and the house lights are back up. He wouldn't want any of this stuff.

When she looks out the window, she sees Isabelle coming up the path by the impatiens. She goes down to her in tears. I'm glad to see you, Auntie.

What is it, sweetheart?

It's the girls. They say they want to stay in San Francisco with their dad. Guess he's got more to offer when you come right down to it. Expensive private schools for a start. They're going to be so far away. How'll I keep in touch?

You'll stay in touch, says Isabelle taking her in her arms. When she sees Shima pulling up to the curb, she smiles like someone rejoicing that the sun is arcing higher on the horizon when all winter she thought it might never come back. This time when Shima comes around the fender in her seersucker suit, the same narrow amused smile plays around both their eyes.

Oh god, says Gwen. How couldn't I have seen this before? It's right here in front of me. You're her mother.

It was a mistake. It was a terrible mistake, says Shima. My dad was so bitter he lied to me. But now that you see us together...?

I see the obvious. It's wonderful, a miracle. Does mother know?

I think you'd better talk to her about that, says Isabelle.

64.

Ada's washed her long grey-white hair, has it spread over a towel around her shoulders. Set the waves with bobby pins. A pile of large hair pins ready to fasten her French roll. These are gold, Gwen, she says holding one up. If you ever see any, buy them.

Mom, she says kissing her. I have more news. How couldn't I have seen it before? I've found out Isabelle is Shima's *mother*. Takumi thought Auntie had abandoned her and was so angry when he found Shima in Blaine with Lottie Fenn, he told Shima her mother had died. Did you know he spent the war way up the coast in the bush? Isabelle wasn't married and had to have her adopted, right? You'd have known about that.

Ada twists up her hair and fastens a hair pin. The skin on her hand is thinner, papery. Finger prints would stay in place longer. People kept things like that secret in those days, Gwen. Have they met each other, then?

They've all three met each other. You and Auntie will make up now, right? You have a new niece. Auntie will forgive you about the Scarborough house. She's so happy, I'm sure she'll let it go. You should call her.

Ada straightens her placemat and looks out the window at her garden. I'll think I'll wait for her to call me, she says.

65.

Are you married? Takumi asks Isabelle when they're walking on the seawall.

I am, she says. We live in Birch Bay; we have a store and a café.

She looks so thin to him, so deadened.

I want the two of you to stay in the cottage for a bit, she says. It's my time over there and I have the say.

That night, Shima sleeps in the front room of the Gallagher cottage, her father in the back bedroom where the flaw still runs down the mirror. In the morning, he climbs the south slope of the Cove up and over the hill to the abandoned September Morn shack—George has moved to the new Seniors home—where he hopes to find some of his old drawings, at least the one of himself and Isabelle lying in the meadow so that he can give it to her, but there's nothing there except an old bedstead and some cutlery.

Dear Mr. and Ms. Yoshito,
As requested, we conducted a search here at the Family Registry Office of Omori under the names Mr. & Mrs. Shinsuke and Noriko Yoshito. Unfortunately, our records show that both Yoshitos are deceased, Mrs. Yoshito on April 26th, 1977 and Mr. Yoshito, July 9th, 1978. They repatriated here after WWII. Please find enclosed a copy of the page of the family registry that includes their names.
Regretfully yours,

Shoji Matano
Town Clerk, Omori Town Hall

66.

The next time the phone rings at 20th Ave. it's a school superintendent from the Central Interior calling to tell Gwen she's been recommended by the Vancouver supervisor who'd overseen her practicum. They're offering her a long term sub position teaching English and Humanities in a mining town up near Smithers. She should think half way between Prince George and Prince Rupert.

How do you mean long term? she asks.

Six months for a start. Maybe longer.

As soon as she's hung up the phone she knows she's going. *I'm going to get in an airplane and fly due north.* In the next couple of weeks she manages to sublet the house, get books and school materials off to the girls, and buy herself some teaching clothes. On a clear fall morning she flies up and over miles and miles of uninhabited peaks, then so many isolated lakes and rivers appear below the plane she's taken aback to see the small settlement of Silverdale scrabbled on the land under the wing. The four corners of the unfolding valley are held into place by paperweights of cut edged mountains, the Telkwa range all slanted ledges, lines cutting the sky with ice daggers and wedges that cross the slopes' expanse diagonal by diagonal. Deep blue hills shoulder the pale sky as the Babine range fastens down another corner. Across from Smithers airport, a huge griz claw swipes ski runs down a slope on Hudson Bay mountain.

She hires a car and starts down a long stretch of highway past a curve, another curve, then more sweeping fields that alternate with stands of lodgepole pine. Between the time she's sighted a house on the horizon and arrived alongside it, she's passed a small lake, another field or two, a stand of trembling aspen, and yet another field as a roll of hay disappears out the back window. A shadow of cloud sweeps over a meadow above tree line, flies past, and wings flat up against a ridge. The hay in the fields rolls into silage, long packages covered with white plastic like gigantic cut up cigarettes. Puffs of low-hanging clouds darken one hill, cast a shadow over another. In the summer and early fall, even the clear cuts look like golf courses. At one rest stop, a hitch-hiker is sound asleep among the magenta shafts of fireweed. Flat on his back on the pavement, his head rests on his backpack, wild baby's breath in the background.

A truck roars past, a streak of rushing logs is her sky. From further away, logs on a truck taper like dreadlocks. Another plywood sided house. You'll get your siding one day, she'll hear people say. At least the two people on the motorcycles in front of her have something going: one rider passes the other and holds out a low hand that appears to be a signal until the second rider touches it as she passes.

The entrance to the town of Silverdale is monumented by a bulldozer down on its knees on a plinth like a young dinosaur doing yoga. The mill yards spread in back: pile upon pile of stems beside the outsize beehive burners that look like massive shuttlecocks. The burners were supposed to have been closed down years ago but have some kind of special dispensation. A hedge of new trucks for sale. The creek running into the Bulkley River is dead, killed long ago by seepage from the silver mine. The tailings have to be monitored in perpetuity. Perpetuity is a long time.

She drives up a small hill to the high school which sits on a plateau, compact and alone like something that's landed from outer space. In the staff room, with its soft view up Mt. Abelard, the conversation revolves around an iron stove which somebody should drag up the mountain before the snow flies so they can ski in in the winter. The way to deal with the portage at Kid Price Lake is to take the cart hidden behind a particular tree and load your supplies in it.

The school is all on one level with floor to ceiling windows and halls radiating out from the library, the hub of the wheel of classrooms, centred and skylighted and inviting. I'm a stranger here, she says to her first group of students, pushing back the chairs and tables. If there was one thing I should know about you people that might help me to get on, what might it be? When she asks them to write, there's nothing else going on in their eyes. *Today we had the dandelion storms.* Wishes float to the floor like petals. Paper cutouts angle like seagulls, feathers clipped to the bone. *The lurking darkness in my chilling room. Alcohol poisoning can't hurt you when it's money from the mill.* She hangs a long scroll of paper from one of the bookshelves, pastes their lines at random. *Now we'll never see him sun himself amongst the bald of hell.* Who wrote that? Whoever wrote that line, contact me so I can give you credit. It's for marks.

If a place like this were to have a crisis, what kind of a crisis might it be? she asks.

We had one, Ms. Killam. The Norwegian Burn. Some tourists from Norway forgot to put out their camp fire. It was only because the wind changed at the last minute that we're even here now.

Was there a lot of damage?

There was *a lot* of damage. Two and a half million dollars of timber was burned, maybe more.

What if it was still going on?

People would be crying.

Maybe they are, she says. Maybe there's a television crew here, and the interviewers want to talk to the people who've been impacted. Let's see if the television people can find the locals they want to interview. Who wants to be crew? The rest of you are residents. What you do is find out who, what, where, why when. That's what journalists do.

This here is Elmer P. Smythe, says one student. He got booted out of his trailer. He's a bucker and has nothing to fall back on. This one is Glen Timber who owned eight thousand hectares and had a small business; he had insurance but forgot to read the small print and his policy had already foreclosed.

Oh no.

Oh no is right.

One of the elevens, a solid straight forward young man called Garth Vandermere, wants to be on the camcorder telling everyone how the fire is still raging through the valley burning everything in its way. Thick black clouds push through the trees. Scorched trunks side a once green mountain that's now covered in ash. His father is alone in their house out on the Silvermine road. Smoke from the other side of the hill darkens the skyline. When night approaches in a roar, he pulls himself up a hill tree by tree and buries his face in his hands. When he opens them to stare between his fingers, a violent hem of fire spreads as far as he can see, twisting rows of trees that explode into writhing sticks of kicking black lace. Sprung red arteries whip out, tentacle the tops of the closer trees. Deer and moose parka the border at the bottom, running in front of the flames.

You think we have a province? she says to the kids the next day after spending the night in a bleak motel in the wall to wall cement block town below. Flying up here in the plane, it looked like a patchwork quilt down below. A man in the café last night—what's that restaurant called, *The Valley Café, oh The Valley Café*—even he, and he looked pretty much like a logger, said it looked more patch than quilt. I don't know what they're going to do fifty years from now, he said. Pick rocks, I guess. Can they plant as fast as they're cutting? Can a tree grow as fast as it's cut? Only one percent of a wood lot is supposed to go out each year, but it looks like way more than that. Trees and more trees transmuted into overpriced groceries, cocaine, cars you spend six hundred dollars a wheel on because the hubcaps shine. Reams of paper tug-o'-warred through the hands of teachers reaching into their staff room boxes deciding where to tear for a good wipe. Oh yes, and the same logging industry has given her a job, by the way.

All she'd have to do is drive a few miles further east and the same lodge pole pines would become a front for acres of plucked wide mounds of stiff black hairs rising on curved hills one behind the other, the results of the Norwegian Burn. If you turn around quickly and take off your blindfold, way up there above the slope, Mt. Abelard is barely able to hold down her soft skirts of grass.

Up here in the north, nobody sidelines you—they don't appear to even notice—if you find yourself in the middle of your classroom in your best pumps, a run in your stocking, a dab of mustard on the corner of your mouth and you've forgotten to take off your hat. That's not true about the hats. There's a no hats rule in the school. Not being able to wear baseball hats for men north of Hope is like hitting below the belt. They're embarrassed to go out in public without their beaks. They feel humiliated and naked without them, as if they've been asked to kiss somebody without brushing their teeth.

A few days later when she's crossing the parking lot she sees a man she's been told is Garth's father, Nils Vandermere, looking up at the gutters of the school.

Bats, he says, skin stretched tight over his face, maybe from being outside so much. He wears a jersey and fleece and has a shy habit of looking away whenever you speak to him directly. The bats look like frayed pieces of black parchment, huddled tight under the eaves.

Aren't they okay where they are? Don't they only come out at night?

That's what I thought but it's the droppings, the guano.

At recess and noon hour, arms, heads and legs flick from doors at the end of the school corridors, wave around like flares on the edge of the sun. Crows twist and careen over the playing field. There's a computer program in the library that demonstrates the movement of daylight and darkness across the planet. You can see where and when darkness will strike at any time of the day or year.

I've been thinking, Nils says, tense and relaxed at the same time. If I came to class while we're waiting for the new mine to open, I could help Garth, and improve my English at the same time.

Sure, she says. Why not?

Once he joins the group, the kids treat him like any other person in the class. If he's older, they're not going to say as to how they've noticed. He sits reined in like a good traveler trying not to take up too much space, a touching quality in someone who says he can't live without tracts of bush stretched out either side. When he came from Holland, he stayed in Canada because there was so much bush. One day, he says, he'll take her out the Silvermine Road and show her around the old mine site.

Looking for a place to rent after school, she asks the realtor to stop at a housing unit on the same hill as the school. Built for the workers in the defunct silver mine, the rows of joined townhouses slope in ramshackle curves down the hill. Not bad on the inside though. Door frames extend almost to the ceiling, saving her from architectural starvation as do the long windows in the classrooms at school. No trees in the yard, no shrubbery. Raze everything they told the bulldozer and evidently it did. Maybe plant some juniper in the front yard to screen the truck traffic around the curved bend that already feels like her shoulder. The neighbouring streets are all vinyl-siding split levels with two car garages.

She buys a second hand station wagon at a local garage and, on the weekend, drives out to nearby Taylor Lake, backdropped by pale grey and pink clouds that cover and uncover the top of Mt. Abelard. The reflections of spruce trees corkscrew the still water. Across the lake, half way up what she thinks of as the first foothill, there's a small warming hut on the rough path around the lake. A dock once extended into the lake but it's been burnt by *some hoodlums*—no kids she teaches—and continues life as a charred black inversion of itself. All it would take to collapse it would be the flick of a middle logger finger on a logger thumb. The remains would scatter and float away like the curved black tire fragments that litter the highway. A boy and his parents come wading along the edge of the lake collecting mint. He opens his hand to show her a tiny frog on his palm. They can't go over their heads, or they drown, he says.

The road into Taylor Lake might double as her own drive-way if she starts to think of it that way. Groups of picnic tables cluster in the disused campsites. She tucks parboiled spuds wrapped in aluminum foil into the fire, backs her tent onto the lake edge. Places a sharp knife by her sleeping bag in case a bear appears at her door and she has to slit the back wall and beaver herself into the water. When she upgrades her tent, she'll buy one with two doors. As a precaution, she tramps the lakeshore wetlands to hide a dry jogging suit in a plastic bag behind a stump at the end of a nearby promontory. A clean slice, slip into the water and swim to her clothes. Bears can swim but would they bother?

The moon is out like a fingernail. Not my fingernail, Isabelle used to say.

Whose then?

On Sunday, Nils calls to see if he could take her for a drive and she takes a couple of hours off. The road out of town has no shade trees to protect the gritty industrial expanse. The distance goes on and on, the view of pine and spruce either side of the road replaces itself with the same view of more pine and spruce. They're there on your left. They're there on your right. They never stop. They pass her pretend driveway into Taylor Lake, stare at the silence of the Norwegian Burn which marks the beginning of what he seems to think of as his territory. Waist high trees stand bravely beside their charred parents. The Burn isn't so bad, he says, looking at her stricken face. At least there's more light. The raptors are starting to come back. The owls and foxes and squirrels.

Once they're out of town he relaxes into his element. It's almost as if he's embarrassed to be in town. He pulls over to make way for a thundering logging truck smashing down the road toward them. There's no shoulder so they have to pull over and hunker in a ditch.

I drive out here all the time, she says. Maybe I shouldn't. I don't have a radio.

It's okay, he says. They know where you are. The first truck that comes your way will be saying what it is you're driving, Honda unloaded.

So they know I'm here?

They know you're here.

He tells her he did a lot of truck driving before he started working at the processing plant at the mine, drove loads of silver ore concentrate to Rupert to ship to Japan. They took the un-leached concentrate and treated it over there. She doesn't like to say because he seems proud, but to her even the forest feels in-dustrial. At least they're starting to contour the clearcuts along the slopes of the hills. A feller buncher lifts its grapple iron, raises the tall trees like pick-up sticks and shakes them.

More long roads, more trees. It won't be long before the pine begins to turn red, scourged by the mountain pine beetle. Auburn spikes will take over an area the size of Greece, moving westward through the valley like a tide. You'll almost expect tourists to turn up and marvel at the fall colours. The mature trees get hit first: thousands of insects in one tree travel through a maze of galleries. Pitch, the life blood, drains out until the pine dies. Pink when it comes out, turns to gum later. They'll pull the bug kill out as fast as they can but won't be able to keep up with it. Nothing to do but feature it as blue wood. Denim wood they'll call it. Good for whoever thinks up that name.

It's almost sinister coming over the hill and down yet another stretch to see what looks like a huge inviting lake at the end of the road. But no, it's the tailings pond from the expired mine where millions of tons of waste rock have to be kept under a meter and a half of water forever so they won't produce acid mine drainage. It's being held, contained and treated with lime. Otherwise, bacteria acts on sulphide bearing minerals in the waste rock and then you have all that sulphuric acid. *Like Venus.* They get out and view a vast manufactured landscape, the piles of orange rocks oxidizing along the sides of what used to be a stream. Three tons of ore are needed to produce enough silver for one engagement ring.

His house is on a slope down by the river, set in the middle of yellowing grasslands and occasional scrub pine. It's a serviceable and roomy pre-fab affair—the log house he'd built years ago was destroyed in the Burn. He doesn't ask her in that day; instead they make their way down the slope and onto the lip of the river bed. She's already used to slipping the point of her new canoe into Taylor Lake where it's so calm the water looks shellacked. The weeds in the bottom of the river are jelled, sunlight edging the Corinthian ridges on the rushes. The cupped round yellow lilies like an enlargement of buttercups. Back at her lake, her lake now is it, the wind would be blowing the silver aspen leaves back in spatterdock. He pushes the canoe off the bank with his foot. You're going to have to be a passenger this time, he says. I've lost the other paddle.

All kinds of plants she's never seen before grow at the bottom of the river. She peers over to enquire about a tree that seems to be growing from the bottom of the river bed. There's a beaver dam a hundred yards up river. We could climb over it, he says. They know how to build.

How could it make them so happy to be looking at a beaver dam together, knowing they were two people who could enjoy doing everything together for the rest of their lives. They get out, pull the canoe over the dam, lower it slowly over the other side. Get back in. Can't stop smiling. Beavers only build dams when the water is getting shallow, he says. They can't take the shallow water. They'd be too exposed to their enemies.

He starts to paddle backward when he doesn't want to disturb a nest of geese. I had to stay here, he says. After the fire. No one would buy the place. That's why I'm like I am, he says. Shattered, it looks like he's thinking. Then he brightens. The forest really is coming back. I don't feel too barren here any more.

Good.

He places his paddle carefully on the ribbed floor of the canoe. The canoe seems to propel itself for a moment, as if it had a sail. All that was left of his house were charred posts sticking out of the ground, he says cupping his fingers. We had to live for a while in the units you're in now, he says. This is the first time he's mentioned his absent wife, the "we" with its own exclusion. Oh, that seat's taken. In one way it's a relief. Garth told her she's gone to Mexico for a while.

Now he wants to show her his special trees—the last ones that hadn't been touched by the fire. He visits them regularly. When they park the canoe and walk in, he holds the branches up for her one by one. When the kids go tree planting, they compete to see how many hundred trees a day they can plant.

They do it at a run: a hot and sweating two steps, shovel in, bend it forward, tree seedling in, close the flap, step step dig. Foresters are paying more attention to variety now; the hazards of one species plantations have become all too apparent. And then there's the top soil and the microbiotic level to worry about. Does she know that, in a greenhouse, the microbes can start multiplying at an uncontrollable rate and everything crashes. I've forgotten where I left the canoe, he says. They're sitting under a spruce in his grove of magic trees. They look like ordinary trees to her but what does she know. He keeps looking at her as if trying to ascertain the stitch that started her body.

I haven't forgotten, she says. I might have though. I didn't know I was supposed to be remembering. I didn't know that was my job.

Well, it is.

She hates to leave all that expanse and privacy, shadows casting a different pattern on the hills every minute. To think a person could sit beside him and know you were both looking at the same shadow passing across the same hill. Watch it lift and light up a new slope. That you would be there together doing that tomorrow.

So you've never stood on top of Mt. Abelard? he says.

Not yet.

Driving back, she envies his wife, whoever she is. Are all marriages as expensive as hers? Sexual jealousy is the worst pain she's ever known. Not if you'd been tortured, of course, or your children. What about that photograph someone took of a German soldier who'd been ignited in front of his tank and lay smoldering but still able to cry for his mother? The photographer hadn't even covered him with a soaked blanket before he took his picture. Remember how quickly it happens? You have your focus, if you fall for him, a few days later there you are waiting for the sound of his footsteps. Maybe it's in our genes that survival depended on his coming back with food. You're lying there lost in the landscape of your body and he's already gone hunting.

I never worry about being abandoned, he says. Do you?

Oh yes.

Nevertheless, something passed between the two of them on the river that was permanent. It was as if they'd exchanged keepsakes that could never be returned. There's probably a mysterious story about his life like there is about many people in this valley, but you don't ask. Part of his being here was that he would be left alone; people wouldn't pry. She certainly wouldn't.

She'll make herself forget about this day. She can do that now. Meeting him was one of those things, but it's not going anywhere. *Withdraw further inland, build a new inner chamber.*

67.

At Thanksgiving, she heads for Vancouver but the Smithers airport is fogged in and she ends up taking a lugubrious bus trip to Prince George which is socked in as well but at least they have a beam so the plane can climb up it and over the fog.

It's misty at Blenheim St., the dark cedar waves in the yard. The rhododendron and laurel have taken over the sunken garden. Lovely to see all that green. Annabelle's staying with Percy and Ada now; here she is crisp as all get-out in a neat A-line skirt and tucked in gingham shirt. Quiet, almost too quiet, Ada says, the way she reads for hours in the window seat beside the leaded glass windows. She *likes* the leaded glass windows, the neat begonia borders alongside the laurel hedge. It's a comfort that she loves everything about the house and, well, them, in a word. Is glad they have poached eggs on toast for breakfast every single morning.

Ada's watching a re-run of an old TV cooking program, well, a gardening program that's sometimes a cooking program. Winter pansies in a bowl with dried hydrangeas, a pink silk peony. On the screen, a chef is preparing pizza, the dough stretched between his hands like a concertina. Cuts black olives for Halloween. It's a ruse. Fill the kids up on pizza which they love before they go trick or treating.

Good idea, says Ada.

I'm sorry I couldn't get back for Grandpa Gallagher's service, Mom.

He wouldn't have wanted you to leave your students, Gwen. Especially since you were starting out at a new job. We knew you were there in spirit.

I was. He had a good long life. I like your French roll, says Gwen. If you cut your hair, the thinness on top would show.

That's because I've had my hair piled on top. Don't make a mistake and do what I did—it didn't get any air. If I sat outside for an hour a day and let the top of my head air, it would start growing again.

You sound like you're talking about grass.

I am. She moves to her place at the dining room table, picks up a book of coupons. I've saved these for you. Mayonnaise for two-fifty. That's a good price. How are your classes going?

I'm enjoying teaching, Mom.

Notice I'm not saying I told you so, Gwen.

Have you heard from Isabelle, Mom? Have you met Shima?

Not yet. I'm sorry to have to tell you this because I don't want to worry you, but Dad's not well. Nothing serious, but he's acting tired.

How do you mean tired?

In bed a lot. That's where he is now.

When Gwen goes upstairs, Percy tells her he's miserable because his flying days might be over. His breath comes in short spurts.

Don't breathe so shallowly, Dad. Take slow deep breaths.

When I do that my lungs hurt.

Have you seen the doctor?

Evidently I'm going to.

He's lined up all the books he wants to read in retirement but is too sick to read any of them. It can't be cancer, he says, because he quit smoking. Remember when he put out his last cigarette and said he'd never smoke again? He's never stopped missing the ritual of opening the package, undoing the silver paper. On his death bed, he's going to say I made it.

After the medical tests are finished—Gwen has to go back to work before they get the results—it turns out, to everyone's shock and misery, that he does have cancer. Lung cancer. And here they thought the worry was a heart condition. She can't bear to think how far along his illness is, that he's going to die. Nothing to do when she gets back to Silverdale but phone every night and plan to get down again as soon as she can arrange an alternate sub for a few days.

A troop of girls sits on the floor outside the staffroom every morning. You move them on, they creep back like cats into a garden. Crouch practising sign language for a Directed Studies assignment, singing with their fingers as if they're stringed.

Why *here* you kids? We keep falling over you.

We like it here.

Oh well then.

These look good, Gwen says taking in her first class's writing assignments. They're well typed and turned out. I hope they read as well. It's better to have something serious that's a little messy—I'm not saying I want them messy—than a tidy page saying nothing. Kind of like preferring to eat at a greasy spoon where the food is good rather than in a restaurant with a fancy decor and bad food.

I'd just ask them to bring me a clean spoon, says Garth, looking around for laughs which he gets.

A few broken seats are stashed in the back of the classroom. Everyone take your seats, she says. Garth picks one up from the stash and carries it like a tray to the front of the class. Ha ha. After school he wants to talk to Gwen about his marks. He won't be allowed to play basketball unless he's done all his make-up assignments whether he gets credit for them or not.

You always have interesting things to say, Garth, I wish you'd write some of them down. We were talking about gifts. You had a story about Raven. But then you had to get up and walk up and down the foyer. Didn't you have something written on the screen?

I lost that.

You forgot to save that?

I forgot to save that.

For a moment, she walks in a meadow on the mountain, then turns to see the next class coming in. By the end of the day, a hundred kids will have passed through these desks with barely enough time to unpack their backpacks, let alone settle into a lesson. Next year, if they switch to the semester system, maybe her students will be disposed to settle down and get involved with whatever they're studying instead of faking it while they wait for the bell. Why do I have to go and talk about theorems? Scalpel poised. I'm just getting into the fish.

What are you doing, Ms. Killam? *Tripping out?* Were you at Woodstock, Ms. Killam? They ask her that again and again.

In spirit, I was, she says.

This period it's the *Aggressors, Victims, Bullies* bunch. Jenny said on the phone the other night it sounded useless to her; if anyone lets a teacher know she's being bullied, she's asking for a double whammy after school. She should know.

Was it that bad?

It was hell. You took us to that *horrible* commune and you never even apologized. At least you're not running around in the woods in ethnic clothes any longer being a witch or was it a *lady?*

I was anemic. I was hemorrhaging.

Oh I *know.*

It was terrible for you, Jen. Leaving San Francisco and the apartment and your dad.

Yes, well. It says here, what does it say here? Maybe she'll find the right things to say and do for this lot. Hope so. If there's a way to help prevent what Leo went through, she'll try it. Define aggressors, victims and bystanders; talk about how a bystander might turn into a problem solver. It's not that teachers don't care at recess when a lot of the bullying takes place; it's just that they're desperate for a few quiet minutes to set up the next class. But kids have a right to come to school and feel safe. The issue has to be front and centre in a way it hasn't been before. She writes the word *conflict* on the board. Talk about what it means to different people, teach them to understand that it's a normal part of life.

Violence. What is it anyway? she asks.

Fighting.

Do you think people can disagree without fighting?

Sure.

What should they do?

Talk.

Would that help?

Sometimes.

(Do you think it's possible to be in love with the *idea* of someone? she said once when she was writing with the kids. Garth looked up from his work.

Yes.

Why do you say that?

It's safer. You can keep it to yourself.

He looked back down.)

She's stored magazine pictures of potentially confrontational situations in the back room; she'll break the kids into groups and get them to describe possible hot and cold outcomes. Hand in her pocket. No keys. Great. Anybody seen my keys?

They were right here. We've got a problem, people.

You do, Ms. Killam.

No, we do. I've got some pictures in the back room to help you learn about handling people who are being mean, and my keys are gone. What'll we do?

Search everybody, Garth suggests.

She picks up the chalk. Writes on the board. *One. Search everybody.*

Keep everyone in at recess.

Two. Detention for the whole class at recess.

Maybe they'll show up.

Three. Wait for them to show up.

Any other suggestions? Let's vote.

No hands for the first or second. Everyone votes for the third.

Fine. We'll try the third. If that doesn't work, we'll pick one of the others.

What'll we do while we wait?

Theatre sports, they call out.

They love theatre sports. Maybe it's because they're so social. That could have been the plan all along. Trick the teacher into doing theatre sports. The difficult part is the deepening, the follow-up that will make the students think about what happened in their improvisations. They always want to charge on. Sometimes staying in the same place and going deeper is the hardest part of all.

Does doing drama help? she asks. I mean about feelings. We're trying to look at what happens when people get into conflict.

Everybody has feelings, Ms. Killam. Being mad and stuff.

Should I be mad right now?

You could be.

Maybe we could do a theatre sport that helps us understand a way for people to get out of conflict without using violence. Or is violence okay?

Yah, fighting's great.

No, it's not, someone else says. People get hurt and killed.

Suppose it was your Mom or your brother?

Daybook note. An improv where we only show the results on the family, the deed itself off stage.

There's that one *Emotions* she says. We need a big square on the floor for that one. Guess we'd better go to the foyer.

Out in the foyer, she chalks an outsized cross on the floor with a circle around it and writes a word up in each corner where the lines intersect. Anger. Pity. Kindness. Forgiveness. We need four people. Who are they?

A beautician, a farmer, a bagpipe player, a nurse.

Where are they?

On a cruise to Alaska.

They must be having the time of their lives.

No, they're not because the bagpipe player insists on walking up and down the deck at night playing his music to the waves.

I want to be the beautician, you saw my binder, Ms. Killam. I'm doing a make-up study for Directed Studies and I've got every type and every colour chart.

The beautician's mad because she's losing her beauty sleep?

That's it. She's really mad.

What about the farmer? He's saved for this cruise his whole life. He doesn't want to be woken up at night by some bagpipe player squeezing plaid bags at those passing sky rats known as seagulls. Do you know what Malcolm Lowry called a seagull? 'A hook-nosed angel that walks like a sailor.'? That's pretty good, eh?

Not bad.

The players have to move around the circle from segment to segment. The minute they step into the next quadrant, they have to play the situation according to the emotion written up where the lines intersect.

Can we choose our feelings?

Sort of.

Not when they're really strong.

The bagpipe player blares his music and the other passengers are furious. He gets turfed overboard. So do the bagpipes. The beautician and farmer go back to their cabins brushing off their hands. *Note for tomorrow: the bagpipe players' family gets the phone call, the visit from the police officer.*

The bell rings. Don't forget where we were. They will so don't you. *Daybook note: We have not, repeat not, tackled the subject yet. Get serious.* One crowd rushes out; another rushes in. What was wrong with the last one? The vice principal stops her in the hall on the way back to her classroom, says he wants to see her after school.

I'm sorry my class is so noisy. I don't seem to be able to convince them my class isn't a party.

It's not that. He touches her arm.

It *is* a party, says a passing student, giving the thumb up sign.

The door of her room is open. The keys are on the rug. Small mercies.

After school, the vice principal is sitting behind his desk. Her life has been about men sitting behind desks. He says he doesn't mean to complain about a room that has so much laughter coming from it, but he needs to talk to her about the chalk writing on the foyer floor. He's worried they might be giving the kids a message that it's okay to write on school property. Maybe she could write on paper instead and tape it to the floor. He wasn't going to say anything. He didn't want her to think she had a repressive administration. She's so grateful to him she could cry. With colleagues like him, she'll stay.

At Blenheim St. on Gwen's next visit, Ada's hung a long sheet of paper over the bedroom mirror so Percy won't have to watch himself die. They hover over his bed watching the home nurse inject morphine. Ada gets in bed and props her back against his, looking at Gwen defiantly as if to say this is how it's always been between us but it was none of you children's business.

I thought only people who had TB spit blood, Gwen says.

Percy checks his watch as if it were a navigating instrument on his plane. If he can get the timing right, he can line himself up to meet his own death.

They eat somehow. Gwen's so distracted she buys stewing chicken by mistake, sautés it for the usual hour. When it's too tough to eat, Ada bursts into tears. He doesn't want to leave, she cries. He plain doesn't want to leave.

The house will never be the same. How could ordinary life go on here after this? Upstairs, Annabelle lies crying on her bed. Ada goes in and takes her in her arms. Gwen's standing by the door. I won't have anybody if Grandpa dies, she cries. No grandpa. No Derek.

You'll have me. You'll have your cousins, says Ada.

They're not even here. I want to see Shima.

It's not the right time for visitors, dear, with Grandpa so sick.

Mom, what's going on? Your prejudices are still making themselves felt, I see, says Gwen back downstairs, folding flannel pads to cushion Percy's mattress so he won't get bedsores. If Annabelle wants Shima to come over, why shouldn't she come? She's the one who helped her when Derek died. If she feels Shima could comfort her now, why shouldn't she? I'm going to call Isabelle. Shima, as well.

Please don't. It's an awful time, Gwen, please.

As Percy's laboured breathing becomes shallower, his skin clarifies and his body grows gaunt. Gwen's sitting beside him when the fish jaw shape takes hold of his face. Who knew that human noses could tip down and their jaws turn up when they die? His breath becomes more and more spaced until it holds itself into silence. She wants to say breathe, Dad, breathe, get to the surface and breathe but he's gone.

Leo arrives to supervise the attendants from the crematorium whose burner Percy once fixed; they pick up either end of the sheet as if it's a hammock. Leo insists they respect the way Percy spoke scathingly about funeral services: accepting his own less than miniscule place in the universe was his way of respecting reality. He took offense that anyone could think the physical universe Leo was dedicated to studying was anything less than miraculous in itself. The girls want to come up from San Francisco service or no service, but Leo persuades them their grandfather would rather they say goodbye to him from there.

68.

Back in Silverdale, the work on the asphalt road outside Gwen's unit never stops. Intermittent beeps herald yet another sander or grader, snow plough or gravel mixer. Month after month the snow shovel clashes on the gravel. Living alone, at least you can come home and put on something really ugly. Kiss the pictures of your children on the fridge if you're feeling lonely. Play your answering machine message and imagine how it would sound to someone else. Talk to your poor dead father while you're doing the laundry. You get: concentration, the dry pleasure of predictability. Comfort in routine. On Saturdays you can make some time for writing instead of marking. Write when your students are writing the way you nap when the baby's napping. Her manners go down the tube, so used to double dipping at home she does it when she goes out. It's Friday, she's exhausted, maybe there's a decent Masterpiece Theatre even if the Gainsborough landscapes and period dress are all starting to look the same. Fractals. Leo'd be interested in this. Another channel shows a herb farm down south where a few pairs of women's hands dart in and out preparing a salad. Wonder why they're using sage? Sage is too strong for a salad. Oh it's just the flower.

Outside her unit, a sand truck hammers down the street, giant bee wings flapping either side. The kids arrive at her door in their t-shirts for homework help. They should freeze, but they don't. She takes a brisk cold walk around the subdivision and heads up to bed.

The next time she goes out to Taylor Lake, she finds junk piled all over the floor of the lakeside warming cabin. The stuffing pulled out of the sofa, the hinge with the padlock yanked out of the door. Empty butane canisters line the fire pit; the picnic table at her campsite is smashed and burned. A black bear scuttles across the trail. It's late in the season; he should be down. She starts to sing the way she's been told, expecting him to run into the bush but instead, he turns around and pads back. She backs slowly toward the cabin, her heart beating high in her chest like a trapped bird. Would it go for the back of your neck and put you out of your misery quickly? There's a tape doing the rounds

right now of a poor soul getting killed by a griz and the screaming goes on for over ten minutes.

After the bear turns and leaves, she strikes the tent—she'll
sleep in the cabin tonight—is spreading it out on one of the
leftover picnic tables when Garth pulls up in his truck. Feels
him—Garth, not the bear—large and solid in the dusk. They
each take one end of the tent and walk toward the other as if
they'd laundered it. Maybe he liked your song, he says matching
tent sides with her, stepping back and forward as low backhand
scripted clouds spread to let in a flight of geese. The east ridge
pales as if it's dawn. The geese honks grow faint as they fly farther away until they look like a swarm of no see-ums above the
flank of the mountain.

What an awesome hunting week we had, me and my dad,
Garth says. We were up at the tree line on the mountain. Came
up the Caledonia Road the other way. Know how male elk can
get their antlers locked at mating season? This particular elk
must have got tangled up with another elk. Maybe a cougar got
one, but ours must have got free because he was dragging part
of the other one's carcass from his antlers. We did him a favour
putting him out of his misery. My dog here? He pulls the black
lab's head against his knees. Know what he did? Took sections
of the hide where we'd skinned that particular elk, brought us
each a piece and dropped it at our feet.

Sharing with the pack, eh? Gwen asks.

Sounds like a bit of a stretch but what does she know? When
she tries to lift the package of broccoli from the ashes, the pot
holder catches fire. She sticks it in a can of water where it flares
and dies. The high dark sky is pricked by stars.

I know the kids who trashed this cabin, Ms. Killam, Garth

says. Maybe we could get them out here and my dad and some of the other people who helped build it and do one of those, what do you call them things?

Those? she asks gently.

Right, those.

Conflict resolutions?

Yeah, them. He sketches two overlapping circles in the snow, says the middle of the Venn diagram could be used to record common ground.

A few days later, following up on Garth's idea, she takes her Elevens and Twelves out to the lake where they sit on stumps and folding chairs. The trashed cabin is with them as well, undisturbed evidence like the scene of a crime investigation. The consensus at the hardware store was that there's no point re-paning the windows, they'd only get broken again. Might as well put plywood over them and be done with it. This time it's the grown-ups who built the cabin who are being bullied, eh? she says to the group. Nils sits quietly with his lean face and square gold rimmed glasses. The place was a mess, he says. Dirty dishes, no wood brought in. That's why I put a lock on the door.

That's the way we liked it, the kids say. We felt hurt because it's *our* place too. It made us mad when there was a lock on the door. The lock did it. It's the lock's fault.

Do you have anything in common? Mutual interest? Gwen asks. What do you want, Nils?

I want the cabin to be used properly and respected.

What do you people want?

We want to be trusted with the place and people stop being so fussy.

So everyone wants to see the cabin enjoyed, right?

Right.

Is it because of the fire and losing everything you'd worked for all those years that made you want to make sure this place was secure, Nils?

He looks up, nods slowly. It was, you know. That was part of it.

They're good kids. They hear him. There's the teaching window. A touch of understanding filters through the air that seems to free something in Nils. She doesn't know what but something. He doesn't look so alone for a moment.

If you both want the same thing, what might some solutions to the problem be? she asks.

The first suggestion is that they remove the lock; everyone helps clean up and they promise to leave it in better condition from now on. Two, give them a key. Three. No teen-agers. Everyone votes for the first. Nils leans over with his arms between his knees. Maybe there'll be other kids who'll do the same thing, he says.

There won't be, they say. They'll tell the others.

Cleaning up, there's talk about a raffle or bake sale to raise money for the windows. When they're finished, the other side of the lake seems a touch less shadowed.

69.

A few days later, Lily calls to say she's in Terrace doing some research and wants to stop by Silverdale on her way back to Port Renfrew.

Okay, says Gwen. You won't like it, though. It's not charming.

How to tell her sister she's hopeless company when she's teaching; that when she's not at school, she has to rehearse ways to change her strategy every twenty minutes so the kids won't get bored.

Lily says she's not expecting charming.

When she arrives, Lily sits on a stool in the kitchen and unhooks a dangling earring. Her cheekbones are still there. Where else would they be? Her skin is perfect, her hair cropped short and curly around her ears.

Mom's doing well, don't you think? she says. Considering.

I do. I think she's brave.

Dad didn't deserve to be wiped out like that. He was looking forward to his retirement.

I guess most people don't, eh?

I miss him, Lily says. This is nice, she says looking around the galley kitchen. You've done a lot with it. Remember last summer when I had a hard time getting Mom to wear a hat in the garden. There's nothing wrong with the sun, she kept saying. How can there be anything wrong with the sun?

Lily, I didn't want to get into it when we were trying to help Dad, but has Isabelle been in touch with you?

No. Why do you ask?

And Mother hasn't said anything?

About what?

About the fact that Isabelle has found her long lost daughter. She didn't even know she was alive until recently.

I didn't know Isabelle had a daughter.

None of us did. And you know her as well.

I do?

It's Shima.

Shima? But she's Japanese.

Only half.

Oh, I get it. What's with Mom then? Why hasn't she invited her over?

I hate to say it, but I'm afraid she's being racist.

When the phone rings, it's Nils calling her at home for the first time, his voice casual and intimate at the same time. When Gwen presses the phone to her cheek, and turns away, Lily sits up straight and alert.

My sister's here, Gwen says, looking at her. We're going out to Taylor Lake for a picnic. Do you want to come?

Who was that? says Lily.

A friend. A dad, actually. Lives way the heck out in the bush. He started coming to my Grade 12 class for his English. He's a back country trekker, walks miles and miles out there.

An hour later the doorbell rings. Nils comes softly down the corridor, shakes hands with Lily. Why does she keep wanting to put her hands on either side of Nils' face, close her eyes over it and pray? When they get to the lake—Nils follows in his truck—a tall aspen speared by lightning has folded in half at the entrance to her campsite. Nils has brought his own plate, some dried moose meat that he shish kabobs on a long stick. They've forgotten the forks so he carves some. Gwen throws the aluminum wrapped seared chicken into a steel bowl blackened from earlier fires, lets it sit in the flames while the wood burns down. The reflection of Mt. Abelard grows darker in the water. If you're in the bush and don't have a fire, Nils tells them, you have to hurry if you're going to have something to eat before night.

Lily goes down and stands by the shore. Comes back to the

fire subdued for the first time since she arrived. Don't you get lonely out here, Gwen? she says.

Not with all this beauty.

It's only when the four wheelers arrive, even if it is the school kids, that the lake spirits get scared away. Nils would understand; she likes their bond being unspoken, that they know they both belong to the same place. Sometimes people don't have to be together to be together.

I hear you spend a lot of time in the local mountains, Lily says. I was hoping to have a look at the foraging range of the threatened caribou herd. They've been tracking radio collared individuals for quite a while but the numbers go on declining.

Yes they do, Nils says. Their predators can travel down the network of logging roads. It's even worse in Alberta where the caribou have more supposed habitat and more roads.

I'm pretty involved with the fish farm problem these days, Lily says. Salmon don't have scales when they're young. Sea lice implant on their skin and sometimes they don't make it to the sea. I've been thinking if you had some kind of a flowing sea water tank on a boat, the salmon could be ferried a few kilometers past the lice. But then you'd have to worry about whether they'd still have their route back to their home river imprinted or if the interruption would blank them out.

Are you cold, Nils? Gwen asks. He's only wearing a fleece.

When he nods, Gwen goes over to her car, pulls her camp overcoat from the back, an ancient tweed affair she'd found in the bedroom above the kitchen at Scarborough. Wearing it, he looks contentedly homeless.

In the car, Lily stares ahead with a serene air as if the lake now belongs to her as well. Stretches up to check her face in the rear view mirror. What a nice man, she says, settling back. At home, Gwen opens the fridge to put away the leftovers. I need to tell you, Lil. I might have made a friend here. I mean really a friend. And if his wife wants him, I wish she'd come back.

Maybe he already has someone else, says Lily.

Why did you say that?

I don't know.

If there's a chance to throw her off balance, Lily will take it. If she were trying to walk a tight rope, her sister would pick up the end and shake it.

The only time Gwen goes down to the basement is to ar-range and re-arrange class place cards, sorting out who she wants to work with whom. There's a bed down there where she sleeps when it's hot or she needs to ground herself. In Dr. Merrick days, she'd marked the occasion of giving up lovers by taking the loop out of the G in her signature. Has never again telephoned anyone while she was sitting in bed. But now she drags the phone cord into the basement, curls up on the bed, and dials Nils.

He picks up right away. Did you get home okay? he says softly, as if he knew she'd call.

I did. Did you?

Just.

Just is a lot.

She hears him smile over the phone. I know this is a per-sonal question, Nils, but I have to ask. Did your wife leave you because you have someone else?

My wife hasn't left me.

Oh well, then.

I want *you* to tell *me* why you're living like you are, he says.

Like a nun. You're not built to live like that.

No one has spoken to her that way for so long she wants to weep. It's a long story, she says. It would take too long to explain.

Could you try?

Maybe someday, she says. But not now.

Lily calls down the stairs that she wants to use the phone. She should call Annabelle. Gwen comes back upstairs, hands it over. She's still upset about Dad, Lily says, punching numbers. Hello sweetheart she says when she reaches her daughter. I know you're sad, Annabelle, but I have to say. You have all of us and you have Billy Will,. He loves you. More than loves you. I did tell Grandma but she said she knew already from looking at you.

Was it too delicate a subject to talk about over the phone maybe? Gwen says when her sister hangs up.

Could be.

Maybe Lily should stick to otters.

The next morning, Lily has made coffee and is having her breakfast when Gwen comes down.

What are you going to do today, Lil? Gwen says gathering up her school stuff.

I think I'll call Nils and take him up on his offer to show me the mountain.

He offered to do that? When was that?

Out at the lake.

I guess you'll need his phone number then.

Those moments, eh? She manages to write it down and hand it over. Thank goodness for school. Once more into the breach, she says to herself in the staff room and heads to her first class. Nils isn't there so Lily must have reached him. Garth notices right away that the subject-verb agreement tests marked out of forty were supposed to have been out of twenty. She apologizes and collects them to mark again. Circulates, checking homework.

Dilemma. What does that word mean again, Ms. Killam?

No matter which way you turn you're going to lose something.

She asks the class to spend a few minutes reading possible organizational plans and models for ways to put an essay together, decide whether they want to try a cause and effect or a persuasive. A few minutes later, Garth has his computer science binder open to a photograph of a huge tire half stuck in the ground. Through the arch you can see a whole building in the distance.

Interesting photo, Garth. Got any thoughts about how you want to shape your next essay?

Yeah, I've got it figured.

You've read the models?

I've read them.

It's only been five minutes.

Oh, so I'm stupid, am I? As if a person couldn't have read them while you were going over instructions.

The intercom announces that it's skittles, licorice and cake on sale in the foyer at recess. In the hall, Garth loops his self-esteem and waves it in front of himself like a lasso. I'm going to make her apologize, he says. I had read it. Who does she think she is?

Back in class, she goes up to his desk. I'm sorry, Garth. I over-reacted. I apologize.

That's all I wanted. I wanted you to apologize.

Do I seem a bit edgy today?

You sure do.

After school, she sits in her car bracing herself to face her sister, the way in Dr. Merrick days she used to struggle to compose herself before going into Blenheim St. Fifth position, she called it, the most difficult one in ballet where you bend your right foot directly in front of your left so they're facing opposite directions. Last night, Lily asked if she knew that northern seals have to spend all winter nibbling at their breathing holes in the sea ice to keep them open. No, she said. She didn't.

At home, her sister meets her at the door quivering with excitement. She and Nils had driven quite a ways up the mountain. Up the Caledonia Road, then onto a sort of trail. They didn't find any caribou but they did see a couple of elk and a group of deer. She took a picture of Nils. A good one, she thinks. He looks a lot like dad, doesn't he?

Oh, please.

She's never thought of words as plumage before, but maybe she can read something particularly beautiful in class tomorrow. Maybe even something of her own. The next day Nils arrives early and sits in the back of the classroom, forehead resting on the tips of his fingers. She goes up to his desk.

Thanks for showing Lily around, she says.

I did it so you could get some breathing space. I want to take *you* up the mountain.

Tears pull into her nose, her knuckles push her lips to one side. Before the kids come in, he holds the back of her hand to his cheek.

That night Lily says she thinks the two of them have a lot to offer each other.

You mean me and Nils?

Of course I mean you and Nils.

Find a recovering alcoholic, any recovering alcoholic, offer her a drink. A family member's approbation is such a powerful green light her sister's seal of approval immediately affirms what she's been trying to deny for weeks. Talk about accelerating the situation. This is where she has to fight for it. Who is this woman, what is she about? Okay. Lily's probably trying to make amends because she feels guilty for moving in on her. She did say once that she doesn't intend to take a back seat to her sister. Ever. *Well done.*

What I'm saying is that I don't want you to miss out, Lily says as she gets in her car to leave.

I'm not missing out, Lil. I like my life.

That evening, after she's gone, Nils calls. Are we seeing each other on Sunday, he asks. Are we going up the mountain?

I don't know, Nils.

What if she ends up on the other side of the river and someone's moved all the trees? She packs for the hike with him anyway. In September, when she'd gone to school at the day of the equinox, her Twelves were coming out the front door.

Where are you going, people? We have a class.

Did you forget to turn your clock back, Ms. Killam?

When she opened the door to the classroom, every piece of furniture in the room had been reversed; the desks were switched to face north instead of south. Her desk as well. Even the filing cabinet and the lectern had done an about face. There's a door from the classroom to the outside, but the kids must have stayed and prepared this stunt instead. She left it and still hasn't said anything. Probably Nils put them up to it. One day she'll ask.

Later, she tramps around the lake, a stick of bear mace in her back pocket. When she was out at his place that first day, he told her how moose sometimes stumble onto the track in front of the train when it's hurtling through the valley. They think it's a corridor for travelling. One driver had to quit because there was nothing else for the train to do but bear down on the panic stricken animal.

For her, it feels like the end of a drought, a soft rain begins to fall. All she's doing is going over and over the content so she won't have to take responsibility for the decision she knows is the wrong one. She can't go up the mountain with Nils. There's too much between them already even if nothing's happened.

At home, she drags her back pack into the basement. Puts the fruit back in the bowl. The brandy back in its snifter. The Kahlúa back on the shelf. When she starts to sort some of her papers as a way of re-occupying the space, she finds herself going through the letters her mother wrote during their trip to Mexico. *Dear Gwen, We're having quite a time. Dad has the airports marked all the way down through the States. We can only fly each day as far as the fuel will hold out. At the airport where we landed in the Yucatan we didn't see anybody. We had no idea where we were going to sleep so we started down a road in the jungle and came to a village where people offered us a bed. In the morning light, we could see the road better which made it easier to walk back to the plane. It's fun to be adventurers again the way we were on our sailing honeymoon. Did I tell you Dad and I raced each other up the Sound in separate boats and how exciting it was because we didn't know whether we would meet up at night or not? We always did.*

The phone rings in the middle of the night. Are you sleeping? Nils asks.

Not very well. It's a long night. Are you?

No, I'm waking up every two hours thinking about you.

He phones again about noon.

We can't go up the mountain, she says. It's too late. We'd have to stay over and that'd be too much to ask of ourselves.

Sounds like we have an agreement, he says.

In another letter her mother wrote about staying in Melaque where a tidal wave from an earthquake sucked out a whole bay before it crashed back over the town and the people had to flee into the hills. Some people were so traumatized they were sleeping in the streets months after the event. The trip to Mexico changed them; they weren't nearly as upset about the Scarborough disaster as she'd expected they'd be.

Do you swim in the pool? Nils asked. In Smithers?

I'm getting old. I swim alone now.

So do I.

He says he's coming over, even if they're not going up the mountain. Maybe they could drive to K'san in Hazelton. A person goes to the store, finishes one list and the minute she gets home, has to start another. Baking soda. No way she's going to give him tea in a stained cup. He'll think she doesn't know how to clean teacups. Life as a middle aged adolescent. Oh well. How can she have so many black socks that don't match? She leaves a note on the door telling him to come in. When she gets back from her second trip, he's standing in her living room looking at her books. Will they do?

How come you've got so much food? he says taking the plastic bags from her by the necks one by one, like slaughtered chickens.

I'm feeding the masses next week. It's my day to bring food

to school for the staff meeting.

He sits on the stool where Lily sat. After the war, I heard my mother say if only I had a piece of butter, he says. Then all you Canadians came and freed us. That's why we're here in this valley, us Dutch. I nearly starved to death in the war.

You were hungry?

I was very hungry.

Do you want one of these wrap things? They're like tortillas. I'll put it around some cheese.

She's spread an array of items on the counter as if offering her credentials. He peers at a photograph of her mother on the swing between the Douglas firs above Miss Fenn's Rocky.

Your mother's lovely, he says. I'd like to see those trees. If I came there and asked for you, would people tell me where to go?

I don't know.

What's this spirulina? St. John's Wort? I don't eat anything green.

It's anti-depression food.

I'll eat it.

When he chews, he still keeps the food in the front of his mouth for a long time to make it last.

It's a beautiful day. They should get going. She's put the foamie and tent in the car and taken them out again four times. The encased tent sits beside the car like an outsized boot. She carries it back to the basement. This is being dressed for the bush? he asks. She has on a flattering ribbed t-shirt with a scooped neck.

I keep lots of clothes in the car, she says.

Tents too?

He sits beside her, not wanting to drive. Her right wrist

hurts from all the writing and marking she's been doing. She rests it in his palm.

How far out of town do we have to get before you take off that terrible hat? she says.

Not far.

He lets go her wrist, tosses his baseball hat in the back seat, picks up her wrist again, circling it with his thumb and forefinger like a bracelet. He'll hold it all the way to Kiyah-wiget, immobilized between his two hands like a newborn kitten. When they get to the other side of the blue bridge that isn't a blue bridge, she pulls off the road. I forgot the wine, she says.

They sit there. We'll get some in Smithers.

It's Sunday. I forgot the food too.

We'll go back for it. It doesn't matter what we do.

On the second try, they make it up and over the hill. The mountains take on more distance and the valley spreads below them. Sections of torn truck tires are wrenched to the side of the road like giant ravens' wings. An asphalt paving machine sputters and belches, a chain gang hanging onto the sides. What happens to the vehicles that get their tires shredded off? she asks. Isn't it dangerous? My truck would capsize if it lost a chunk of its tire.

It's from the big rigs, it's only one layer. They get, is the word re-furbished, those tires? Re-constituted? Re-juvenated?

The mist on the river makes it look as if it's on fire. She's never seen the mountains so beautiful; spoons of wind blow off the peaks. Crater Lake is a deep ache a few miles up Hudson Bay mountain, the glacier a perfect white filling. They sail by. The crevices take on new diamonds minute by minute. As they pass Kiyah-wiget, the river flips alongside the station wagon like a long silver tail.

Am I old? Do I seem old to you? he asks.

No, she says softly.

One of them keeps saying it's going to be all right, as if the one who isn't speaking is being rushed to emergency. A life can be born and lived and end in half an hour. *I think about you every time I cut flowers under running water.* She said the same thing to me, he says when she tells him about Lily saying they had a lot to offer each other. In a flash, the years of fleshing out the voice she found mewing in the corner of the cottage would count for nothing. She can't let that happen. They turn off the highway past a statue of a logger lassoing a tree, round a few more curves past Hagwilget, then stop at the bridge to wait for their turn to cross.

Hello, my beauty, my love she says to the most stunning mountain of all.

As soon as I saw that mountain, I knew I was staying, he says.

Me too.

From the front, Stegyawden does seem to stand as alone as its name suggests, a pyramid of multiple crags and crevices that look impossible to climb. Coming upon its magnificence changes everything, as if its power seduced them there.

There must be a way up, he says.

If you climbed it, I'd watch you.

They walk out on the bridge to look down at the Widzin'kwa rushing through the deep canyon to join the Skeena. The floor is open steel work. Don't look down, she says placing the strap of Percy's old binoculars around his neck.

The Skeena is wide and deep; on Stegyawden point, brushed campsites are separated from each other by cottonwoods. When the river's running low, there's a long walk over smooth stones to the water. When it's high, the point is a narrow foot path. Snarled pieces of river debris wrap themselves in the trees like birds' nests.

Yesterday she was old. Today, she angles the collar on her jacket to a chicer angle. In the summer, the cottonwood storms thicken like eagle down. She could have slate streaks in her hair by the weekend. At the camp site, an attendant wants fifteen dollars. The last time Gwen was here, the same woman said her house land is along the other side of the river.

We're not staying. We're just here for a picnic.

Come and get some wood if you want.

We're all right. There's lots of dead fall.

When stones begin to cascade down the opposite slope, desire strikes them like lightning. She leans against the car fender as he sucks his tongue into a tiny point and pushes it between her teeth. No one's kissed her like that before. She instantly loses five pounds. He stands bolt upright as if the tourists coming down the campsite path are walking straight into his head.

They won't come here. I won't let them.

Can you do that? How do you do it, Gwen? It's what I wanted to ask you the whole time.

She takes his face in her hands. Do what?

Live like you do. The way you're so self contained. I wanted to be with you to see how you do it. I find it hard, and I've sworn....

Sworn what?

To be faithful. I need to be with someone who knows how to do that.

It's a strange drive home. She's tired and wants him to drive but he doesn't offer. It's better she's been put in her place. In a way, it's easier. Just before Round Lake, the sky darkens with that eerie blowing light when the sun sneaks in and lights the hills and trees from the side.

Tomorrow he'll be on Mt. Abelard by himself. When he phoned the other night, he didn't like hearing noises other than her voice.

Is there someone in your house?

It's the news. I've got the radio on.

Can you cook and talk on the phone at the same time?

I was a single mother for a long time. Where would we be if I hadn't been able to do at least two things at once?

How's the food?

It gets exhausting, all this sublimation.

The next morning her carefully constructed inner armature lies smashed on the floor beside her bed. Wedges of frozen flesh heave inside her like ice breaking on the river. Something vast has happened inside her. An enormous hand lays itself on the mountain which rises to it like bread. The car surfed back on the cool wind above the river.

At recess she walks around the track, her hands feeling softly at the silence behind her. She passes the science room where Mr. Parkinson is explaining how the contents of a cell expand faster than the membrane containing it, so what's it going to do? Stop taking in nourishment? He doesn't think so. Hey, it says to itself, there'll be more surface area if I divide.

Back in her room, Garth is standing by her desk. She wants

to reach out and take his hand, but she doesn't.

Your marks are up, Garth. I know you'll get accepted at UNBC.

I would go but… he says. It's my dad. I can't leave him.

Why can't you leave him?

I promised my mother I wouldn't leave him until she came back.

Should you think about whether that's fair to yourself, Garth? Your dad will be all right. He's a survivor.

70.

On her next visit, helpful notes are pinned up all over Blenheim St. The one on the front door says not to open it to any stranger who doesn't have identification.

What does this one say? Ada says.

Don't take a bath unless someone is in the house.

You're in the house.

Their neighbours are having their large cedar cut down; a couple of men are lopping off an enormous branch that careens wildly before it crashes. There goes a big section, Ada says from her dining room chair. You haven't got any kind of view from where you're sitting, Gwen. The best seat in the house is what I have. All I can say is they have my admiration. Oh, did I tell you? I do not want any homemakers in.

Is it right for us to be depending on neighbours?

You're not depending on anyone.

We've made an appointment for Dr. Enright to see you this afternoon.

I'm not going anywhere.

You don't have to. He's coming here.

If you're wondering where I am for the next ten minutes, I'm taking out the garbage. Can you hear the doorbell? Tidy the living room, will you, Gwen? And go over the downstairs bathroom. Dr. Enright might go in there to wash his hands. All right for you.

The first thing Ada does the next morning is place a candle in the window on a tin of peanut butter so her neighbour will know she's up. You can't have your cereal box there, Gwen. Jean will get mixed up. Oh, she's blown me a kiss. I'll blow one back. It's payback time, she says sitting down with her toast. It's because of what we did to Grandma Flora that you're after me to have someone in. We should have let her stay at the Scarborough house until she died.

How would you have arranged for her to be safe, Mom?

It doesn't matter about being safe. You're going to die anyway. I did the wrong thing and now they're punishing me.

You mean because of Scarborough?

Oh more than that, Gwen. Way more than that. I didn't want to have to tell you, but I'm afraid I have to. Those kids came again in the night. If you go down the basement, you'll see the Christmas ornaments are smashed on the playroom floor. Even that skater with the red dress that Percy always hung beside the sugar cookie moose. Oh, I meant to tell you. If I ever sell Blenheim St., Lily gets the grandfather clock.

May I have the dining room table?

Why would you want the dining room table? It's gone to rack and ruin.

I've always thought it was special.

Down in the playroom, the decorations are where they've always been, wrapped in tissue paper and packed in a box. The tinsel ends are tied with string like long soft presents. The Honey Bunch books are still there. Little Men. The Water Babies. The Just Mary Stories. Uncle Wiggley's Travels. She finds a tiny Barbie boot in the bottom drawer of a doll's bureau.

The boy must have brought them back when I wasn't looking, Ada says when she goes back upstairs. The one who keeps coming to my door. Where's Leo? I haven't seen Leo for ages.

Leo came out and looked after you these last few weeks, Mom. He bought you a microwave.

It's not there now. Did you cancel the homemaker?

I did because you made a dentist appointment the day she was coming over to meet you.

When Dr. Enright comes in, she strikes her Sweetheart of Sigma Chi pose, bright and pretty. Of course if I get really old, she says. I can move to somewhere smaller.

Do you think you'll do that?

Only if I can't manage. I'm managing fine now.

Perhaps, he says gently, kneeling to examine her swollen knees, your children have a point. Isn't it because Leo's been looking after you this last while that it's been safe for you to be here?

I could still be on my own if they can't come.

I don't think you could get up and walk to the store now.

I could if I had to.

The doctor puts down her leg. In the night, by the time your neighbour sees that your candle is not in the window, it might be too late, he says. You could be in trouble from three a.m. on. I wouldn't want you to have heart failure or anything of that nature because no one's here. I've seen that happen time and again.

Ada grits her teeth, but her knees are so swollen it's all she can do to get up. Try and design a thing like a body, Percy said once. Imagine trying to invent tendons and muscles. A central nervous system. Now erect it and propel it forward. She grabs the arm rails of both stairs, pulls herself back like a slingshot and aims for the first stair. Whoever designed this house must have known someone was going to get old in it, she says. Putting railings on both sides like this. I go up and down these at least ten times a day. How else do you think I've kept my figure?

This time, though, she can't do it. It's terrible for her, out there by herself, intruders behind her and she has to turn and see they know she won't make it. They shouldn't even be in her house, let alone watch her do something so private.

After the doctor leaves, she sits down to write her cheques. The first is for a hundred dollars to B.C. Hydro but she writes ninety in her account book.

Is there a bit of a discrepancy there, Mom?

Give that back.

Maybe you could be kinder to people who are trying to help you, mother.

You're used to the school kids, Gwen. Don't tell me what to do.

Right.

Still, she gives in and admits it might be best if the door isn't locked when she's in her bath. Sitting on her dad's bed where her mother sleeps now, Gwen leafs through a magazine. There's a long silence without a splash. I guess you're going to have to come and help me. I'm sorry to say I don't have any clothes on. She's managed to swing her feet into the tub but is sitting on the lip. Can I stay here? It's nice here.

It'll be a long night.

What do we do now?

Gwen sits on the toilet seat behind her. Her mother's hips form a curved heart from the small of her back to the tips of her buttocks. Gravity pulls furrows of dry skin toward her knees. How about stretching your arms along the sides, shuffling your feet forward and sliding down the slope? she says.

It's too steep, Ada says. She tries but can't bend her knees, lands hard on her tail bone.

Oh dear, they both say.

The only way to get her out is to have her manage to kneel, one hand on the tub edge, the other on the soap container handle. One foot in get set position, the other on the no-slip mat. Gwen puts her arms around her waist and heaves. Wouldn't dad think we were having a time of it?

You can say that again.

The next night she lets Gwen hold her from behind to ease her body down the tub. I'll never get there, she says. From behind her shoulder, Gwen can look at her mother's deep breasts as long as she wants because she can't see her and ask what she's staring at. Keep going, Gwen says. I've got you.

I'll never get there.

Yes, you will.

When she's washed herself, she reaches her hand to be steadied out—she hates it—but maybe because she's tired and discouraged she lets Gwen dry her. She doesn't turn away, not wanting to be touched; she simply stands there, a woman in her own body. This is the way her dad must have felt when he looked at his wife naked. She'd like to have stood where her mother stands now and touch the side of her father's face. She'd like to have kissed him when he wasn't angry. With the towel wrapped around her,

Ada bends one knee into the slight curve of the other the way she does when she's having her picture taken.

Oh Mom, Gwen says softly. You're so pretty.

Thank you, her mother says matter of factly, as if used to being told her whole life she has a lovely figure. She does have a lovely figure. If someone seems to think she's getting old, she hasn't noticed.

Don't any of you take my money. You can have it when I'm dead.

We won't.

There's a door from the bathroom to the master bedroom, another from the hall. If her door's been left open in the night, she wakes up and says anxiously, Is that you, Gwen? As if anybody who could be there in the night couldn't possibly belong.

Worrying her own breathing might be keeping her mother awake, the silence in the house frightens her into thinking it's her mother's lack of breathing that's alerted her. Striding across the hall, turning on lights as she goes, slow motion now—running, lurching, falling her way into her parents' bedroom, she almost stumbles over her mother lying on the floor, mouth opening and closing. Eyes wide open. When Gwen slips her arms under her knees and shoulders, and lifts her into bed, her mother tightens her arms around her daughter's neck as Gwen dials 911 with the one hand, strokes her forehead with the other until the ambulance's siren is the only sound for miles in a deafeningly silent Kerrisdale.

71.

What's wrong exactly? says Leo when she calls him from the hospital corridor.

The doctors say she's lost all her potassium which she says is impossible because she eats a banana every day. Would you call her? There's a phone by her bed. She thinks you're stuck in an elevator full of water. She says Isabelle's here to see her and the nurses won't let either of you in.

Before she'd left Blenheim St., Gwen'd ironed a couple of her mother's blouses that were the same size as Jenny's when she was eleven. As well as the dementia and potassium loss, her mother's likely had a small stroke, they say, and can't possibly be on her own.

I'm glad we're together, Gwen says when she goes back in the room. It means a lot to me.

It means a lot to me too.

They're saying that maybe you should be thinking about going to Brighton Manor for a while, Mom, with all of us working out of town. Lily's completely set up in Port Renfrew now. She has clients.

What kind of clients? She's not a lawyer.

Massage. Massage therapy clients.

Ada turns and looks at the wall. You have to have clothes to go to a place like Brighton Manor, Gwen. You have to have money. You wait until you're old and your daughter wants to move you to a home.

Dad would want you to be safe.

I don't care if I'm safe. I want to die in my own home.

Would you like to come back up north with me, Mom? My

place isn't much but we could manage. I don't know if you'd like it though.

No. They're not moving Isabelle to a home.

Isabelle has Jack.

You mean Jack has Isabelle. She came out here to get mad at me again but they wouldn't let her in. I can't afford a place like that.

Leo thinks you can, Mom.

What's Leo got to do with it?

You gave him power of attorney.

Well, I'm taking it back.

The next day Gwen arranges a conference call with Leo and Lily, tells them about the dementia diagnosis. Poor Mom, says Lily.

What do you think about Brighton Manor? Gwen says.

Blenheim St. and mother's share of the Scarborough property are her equity, says Leo. The best available care is what we should spend it on.

I'll talk to a financial adviser, should I? says Gwen.

Absolutely, says Lily.

The financial adviser suggests that, if they were to invest the money from the sale of Blenheim St. into something safe and reasonable, the interest alone would pay for Brighton Manor. We're out of here, Gwen thinks. But how's she going to work it so her mother will think it's her own idea?

Back at Blenheim St. a few days later, Gwen stands at the stove stirring mushroom soup. Never mind me, Ada says at her elbow. I'm just getting warm. That afternoon, Gwen picks up some of her mother's clothes from the cleaners, and a strawberry milkshake as a treat. Hangs the cleaning bags in Leo's old room so her mother won't find her dresses and get upset. She finds them anyway. Comes downstairs with her purple shirt-waist and turquoise polka dot slung over her arm.

I can't wear any of these, Gwen. They're covered in dust from hanging in the back of the closet.

I had them cleaned.

No, you didn't. Why are we in such a hurry? The toaster's not working. Maybe it's not plugged in. Maybe it's the wrong cord. You can't unplug the clock one. In case you kids are thinking of selling this place to pay for me to go to prison, you can forget that idea. I've put a lien on the property. All you have to do is read my will. It's in the desk drawer. Blenheim St. is yours but not until Annabelle's graduated. She has the right to live here until then.

We'll figure out something else then, Mom, if you decide you want to go to Brighton Manor. We'll all chip in or something.

On the phone that night when she reads Leo the will, he points out that, if dementia has rendered their mother incompetent, she won't be able to revoke power of attorney. He doesn't think much of the add-on about Annabelle's tenure which likely won't stand up anyway.

Even if she forgets about this tomorrow, I think we should respect her wishes, Leo. I would hate her to be desperately trying to remember what she intended. It should be Brighton Manor if she goes anywhere. She deserves to stay in her own neighbourhood. We're lucky a place is available, period.

All right, Ada says finally. I'll go but only for the afternoon. I go in the spring anyway, when I'm dividing my perennials. They like perennials over there. I'm not staying the night though. Off off off off, she says to the stove when they go out the front

door. What about the rhodos? I want to see them open this year.
Gwen helps her into the car and does up her seat belt.

This is so difficult, Mom.

I don't even know where my cheque book and bank book are.

They're in your purse. She opens the clasp for her. Right
there. And I'm here. I'm with you.

Fat lot of good that will do. You're enjoying this, aren't you?

No, mother, I'm not enjoying this.

Why do I have this tooth in my purse?

You've been to the dentist. It must have been the one he
pulled out and gave to you.

Oh, that one. Ada puts it back and clips the lock shut. I'll
never see this place again, she says in the same brave tone as
Annabelle's declaration that she was too big for her last bottle.
They're both brave. Courageous, actually.

At Brighton Manor, she refuses Gwen's arm up the driveway
to the entrance and insists on walking alone. Inside the lobby,
the residents struggle along on their walkers.

They're never going to catch me on one of those things, she
says tightening her stomach muscles and setting her shoulders
back.

No one's going to make you, Mom.

The staff has arranged for them to have a look at one of the
vacant garden rooms; the walls are pale peach and there's an
unlocked door to a patio garden. The handsome easy chair has a
grey silk shantung slip cover. I need a new chair, she says sitting
down with her coat still on, purse in her lap as if she's at the
airport. It's a lovely room, Gwen. I can see you like it. An edition
of the same boxed square calendar she was using at home lies
on the side table.

There's choral singing on Wednesday night, she says picking it up. Do you want to go to that?

I sure do.

By night, she likes the colour of the walls. When they come to announce supper, she asks if it's all right if she brings her daughter. Which number is our room again? she says as they go down the hall.

Gwen'd put a suitcase with a few night things in the trunk of the car in case: a new dusky green cotton pants suit with a quilted yoke and mandarin collar, dressy enough for the dining room but comfortable enough to lounge in. Oh, that's nice, her mother says. But it's going to be too small. When she goes into the bathroom to try it on, it's fine.

Mandarin collars don't have buttons on them, she says. Please take it off.

You bet.

Would you buy me a new dressing gown? There's money in my purse. This one won't do.

Astonishingly, Ada never mentions Blenheim St. again. Is she pretending to go along as a strategy so they'll see she deserves to be in her own home? It doesn't seem that way. Her unstated relief reminds Gwen of the way Maya used to run around insisting she wasn't going to bed until you held her firmly and told her she *was* going to bed.

Being in the moment is part of dementia they tell Gwen at the supervisor's office when she goes in to get their advice; they're not surprised to hear her mother's settling in better than expected. They'll proceed as if it's a given that she's going to have a bath. In the stainless steel bathroom, they back the wheelchair into the outsized tub; the door closes in front like the stern of the ferry.

You'll see how the water comes up around your feet, the attendant says. It goes into the channels right along there.

It's quite a deal. Will the water come right up?

Oh yes.

Why did I jump?

You jumped because the nurse put her face cloth on your back, Gwen says.

She doesn't seem to notice when the attendant lifts her breasts to wash under them.

Do you want to wash your privates or do you want me to do it? asks the nurse.

I don't mind.

Unbelievable. Her mottled swollen legs float in the tub that's high enough for the nurse to work comfortably like a raised garden bed.

Do you want to try the jets? The Jacuzzi? she asks.

Why not? I'll try anything once. *She laughs.*

That night at Blenheim St., the only light in the kitchen is from the open fridge. Gwen moves the various candle holders to one end of the table. The only light in Percy's painting comes from a small window in the cabin. You know it's an oil lamp. The horse is tied up outside on the wild plain and it seems that it's him sitting in that cabin having his supper. She must be doing something right if he's finally made it.

72.

Back at the town house, there's a Christmas card and letter from Isabelle. Where to read it? On the mountain, of course. At the helicopter office in a trailer by the highway, they say they'll charge her $350 for the round trip to the Alpine cabin unless she wants to take a chance on hitchhiking if they're heading out to a logging show. I'm a teacher, she says. I only have a few days. In that case, she should get herself over to Reach Communications, and rent a radio phone or a cell. A cell might not work up there. She should get a radio phone.

Glasses' cords, hot pockets in red packets like ketchup, extra sweaters, extreme weather mitts, her notebooks, even a bunch of spruce twigs for kindling; the snow will be deep and it might be hard to get at the undersides of the trees. Someone said there's no such thing as bad weather, only bad clothing. She piles the items by the front door the way Percy used to prepare for his hunting trips, not caring two hoots whether they'd trip over his stuff or not.

Before she leaves, she calls her mother to tell her she'll be away from her usual phone for a few days and not to worry. That Leo and Lily will be there for Christmas.

I won't, she says. Why didn't someone think to bring some clothes out to wherever I am now? The last thing I remember was grabbing the bedroom door knob, then I woke up in the hospital.

You're not in the hospital any more, Mom. You're in Brighton Manor.

I am?

You're going to have people to talk to. It's going to be better.

It is?

What about the turquoise polka dot?

Dear knows where the turquoise polka dot has got to.

It's probably in your cupboard. Why don't you look?

I could do that. Hang on a minute.

While Gwen's waiting, the van with the dining room table arrives. Leo's taking care of selling Blenheim St. and had the table shipped up to her. The moving men unload it, leave the chairs in the yard while they set up the table in the front room as a desk.

Thank you, Gwen says.

Finally her mother comes back on the line. I'm wearing it, she says.

What's that?

The turquoise polka dot.

That would explain it. I love you, Mom.

I love you too.

The table is wonky on its central pedestal; it must have been damaged in transit. A few evenings later, she looks up to see Nils standing at the door. I can't stand to see you writing on that table, he says. I'll take it to my place and fix it for you. She already knows that he'll return with it hoisted on his shoulder, kneel to lay it at her feet like an outsized wooden bouquet. His head against her hip, her hand in his hair. She'll close her eyes and touch his shoulder as if changing film under a heavy cloth. He'll leave, bent over his erection as if he's been shot.

When she has everything packed, she calls Great Northern Helicopters to confirm. Who took this booking? they ask.

Geoff he said his name was.

We've never heard of any Geoff. No one here would have given you that low a price.

I'm a teacher you know. I'm not a prankster.

Well, you be here with bells on at eight o'clock tomorrow morning and we'll get you up there.

At school finishing her marks, she can't remember whether her comment *Garth is a talented student but his casual approach to turning in assignments has lowered his grade* was supposed to be moved from Word into Classroom Manager or the other way around. Whoever Geoff was, he told her that the Alpine cabin at the tree line on Mt. Abelard had been built a few summers ago. What's his name who lives out on Silvermine Road was one of them.

Nils Vandermere?

Right.

So you know it's not going to fall down.

Off off off off she says to the stove at six in the morning the day she's scheduled to head out. When she arrives at the helicopter station, Geoff-who-turns-out-to-be-Ivan says he'd been so excited about going on vacation, he decided to fool around and give out a different name.

The trip only takes fifteen minutes once they're clacking in the air; the land tips in as they veer into the meadow beside the cabin, wait for a moment after they've landed while the blashing blades slow their rotation. Ivan-Geoff offers to dig a path to the latrine before he leaves. The pilot light on the stove doesn't catch even when the gas has been turned on. Looks as if the tank's empty. She tromps around the back to switch to the other one, makes a note to herself to leave a message in the information book at base camp that the next person up will need to bring a replacement.

Before you go, let me test the phone, she says to the pilot.

At Reach Communications, someone at the other end is saying hello over and over even when she responds. The louder she shouts the more the clerk doesn't hear her.

I can hear her but she can't hear me, she says to Ivan-Geoff.

If you climbed up on that ridge it would probably work.

If I have a broken leg, that's not going help. When you get back to town, would you tell them that if they get a series of three repeat calls and no one's there, that it'll be me and please send help.

Good idea, he says and leaves.

Once he's gone, it's so still you can hear the snow thaw and freeze again. When the mist pulls away, the ledges and crags pronounce themselves before the shroud closes back in. A ptarmigan darts white on white like a blown piece of snow. The snow she loads into a pot on the stove to melt for drinking water has to be cut into smaller pieces with the egg lifter. A moose plods down one of the corridors across the meadow, turns sideways as if to show off his profile. He carries his wide spread antlers like a tray. Lift, lope. Lift, lope. Stops and raises his ears when she calls. Stares her in the face as if he knows she's there even though she's a hundred yards away. A female comes into the clearing but doesn't stay; she stands around for a few minutes, turns and walks back the way she came.

She's brought napkins with a Christmas fruit and berry pattern to leave for the people coming after her. A whole family fell out of the sky from a helicopter on their way up here not long ago. There's a bottle of wine with their name on it no one has the heart to throw away.

When she stands below the porch lifting firewood onto the high deck, she turns her head to the side to protect her eyes from slivers. Checking out the lofts, she places both feet on one step before climbing the next. If she fell, she'd be lying there for days. If you were up here with someone but wanted to sleep alone, you could have your own ladder up to your own loft. It's so still it doesn't matter if you're dead or alive. The highest cabin yet.

People have left comments in the guest book. *This place is the Taj Mahal. The chairs are thrones. We were waist high in the snow the last hundred yards. Our snow shoes were useless. Our felts froze inside our boots.* Once she's spread her sleeping bag on the upstairs foamie, she climbs back down the ladder, sits at the table, and reads her aunt's letter.

Dearest Gwen,

How are you getting on up there? Well, I hope. Sorry it's taken me such a long time to write to you. You must be wondering why I haven't been in touch with you or your mother. When you and I met again, the Scarborough house was the only issue I had with your parents, but that was only the beginning, Gwen. I have to tell you that Ada has known all along about Shima. She was with me when the baby was born, bribed a hospital orderly to help get me back to Laburnum St. when I was still drugged from the birth. She told me that Shima died. She asked Lottie Fenn to take care of adoption arrangements but Lottie took matters into her own hands and raised Shima for the first three years of her life before Takumi found them. I didn't know any of this until I heard Shima talking to Eugene in your grape arbour. That's when I left to confront Ada. I have lived without my daughter all these years because of her.

I know this is going to come as a shock and I'd like to see you so we can talk more about it. Shima and I are going to Prince Rupert to visit Takumi and will stop by to visit you on the way home. It won't be for long because I'll have to get back to Jack, but we were hoping you might know somewhere isolated and quiet where we might have

a little time to get to know each other.
Shima sends her love. See you soon, I hope.

All my love,
Auntie.

Oh no. Poor Auntie. Poor Shima. Poor Takumi. How could her mother have done that? How? If only it weren't too late to talk with her about what happened but it is. So it *was* him in the dancehall meadow all those years ago. Nothing to do but go back to the beginning to try to make some sense of this. All those times her mother pulled that blind down over her face would have been partly to protect herself.

That afternoon, she puts on her skis and side steps carefully down the bank into the meadow, crying for all of them. The wind reddens her face as the snow eases into a low curve. It's softer down there like corn snow, wetter farther down. When she's almost at the lowest point she starts to slide sideways, not realizing the slope is a stream bed that stretches as if blown up from the inside. She edges her skis and side steps back up.

I want to explore your edges.
Not when I'm hungry.

That night when she's up in the loft, she dreams her mother is sleeping on a cot in the cottage attic with her legs open like scissors. A thunk wakes her, snow slides in chunks off the roof. A scratch on the porch, a scuttleflash. What is that? A pack rat? Pat racks aren't around in the snow. The marten probably. She bangs on the wall with the broom. Back in the dream, dirt is matted on the tongue and groove walls. We can't stay here, Mom. It's like a green house here. There are all kinds of rakes and shovels.

I like it here, she says. I hope I've done the right things, Gwen. Who do we have?

We have Evvie and Leo and Lily and Annabelle and Jenny and Maya.

That's quite a lot.

It is.

The next day when she skis out into the field again, her steps lengthen and perforate like Morse code. Every day she traverses farther down the meadow until she's marked out a large rectangle the size of a soccer field.

I had visitors.
You did?

The next day she finds snow gulleys where before there were burls. Sounds are more recognizable; the throaty glug downstairs is a heap of snow melting in a pot on the stove. The cabin log says the marten stole a skier's steak while he was out climbing the peak. The grain of the wood on the table has golden motes like sequins in the snow. Like the eyes of the ptarmigan.

After three days, the snow patterns in the lodge pole pines form tall wiry creatures like hooved and clawed Giacometti sculptures, clumps of snow sealed to their tops like hats. Their presence wakes her earlier and earlier in the dark. She takes her candle and climbs the stairs. The blue shadows above the stream form new shapes every day.

In the mornings, she sits with plastic bags inside her felt boot liners, hot pockets inside her plastic bags. When the wind comes up, the tin roof rattles and a cloud passes over the hills. When the sculpted crowd gathers, snow blows against their ankles and encrusted joints. It's so quiet you can hear candle wax dripping into the saucers. Their reflections look like candles on holders decorating the branches on the outside trees. If she lived here, each day would unfold as slowly as this one; every night the wind would sweep the snow into new shapes. Any minute, a brush will flick the black and white brambles with chartreuse. She blows out the candles as the sky lightens. The image of the candles on the tree boughs pales with the dawn.

Now her mother is dying. When she passes over, her body is still warm so she pushes down the guard rail and crawls in beside her. Takes her in her arms.

You died, Mom, she says, stroking her hair. But it's okay.

She held you when you were born, and you're holding her when she died, the nurse says.

Below, in the valley, a jagged build-up of ice floods into a brown torrent of water that cascades over the banks of Silverdale Creek, roars toward the railway bridge pushing an upended log that slants by hard and fast as the train screams down the valley. The water is so high the log smacks against the steel bridge with a force that would have sent the locomotive into the river if it'd crossed the bridge two minutes earlier. Inside, a conductor from Quesnel with a wooden hand is telling a visiting sculptor from Prince Rupert, his beloved friend and their daughter that this is his last run. All four are oblivious to the fact they've come within seconds of being smashed to pieces by an upended log.

The next day, Gwen gets up at four a.m. and begins to pack. At five a.m. it's snowing furiously so there's no way the helicopter will get in. She climbs the stairs and goes back to bed. As she turns over to sleep, there's a wild clacking overhead, *then in an instant they heard on the roof* the chopper on the ground hurling snow in all directions. The pilot rushes into the cabin, starts throwing her gear into the machine. There's a ten minute window, he shouts. Let's go.

As they lift up across the corner of the meadow sized rectangle, Gwen is fastened in her seat like the eye of the helicopter bird. They fly along Silver Creek and over the Caledonia Road. When they land in town ten minutes later, she piles her stuff in the Honda and heads out the Silverdale Road to Nils' house. He must be asleep because he doesn't answer the door. She'll ski up the river while she waits for him to wake up. Stopped short by the snow-covered beaver dam, she turns her skis to sidestep over it but it's too uneven so she takes her skis off, climbs over it on foot, puts her skis back on and continues. Up a bank, she sees a small cross planted by the side of the road. *The way they do in Mexico*. Was that what Nils meant when he said that's where his wife had gone?

He's standing on the deck watching her come back. You've been gone a while, he says. How did you get over the beaver dam?

I took off my skis.

You can't do that. Oh well, you can swim.

Under the ice?

He takes her parka and leads her into his shop where he's polishing her table.

I have to tell you something, Nils. Something I learned on

the mountain.

You were on the mountain?

That's not my table, she says. Now that it's beautiful again, it can go to the person it belongs to. She's coming to see me.

Tell me something, Gwen. Do you think I could get you to rest for a while if I thought your writing arm was getting too tired?

You'd have to do something amazing to my hand, she says.

THE END.

Thanks to my parents, Bill and Irene Haggerty; my brother and sister, Michael Haggerty and Robin Pretious; my cousins, Rosalyn Hood, Sharon Haggerty and Maureen FitzGerald; my nephew, Steve Pretious; my children, Justine Brown, Thomas Schmitt and Eli Matson.

Much appreciation to Kimyio Kamimura for her advice regarding the Yoshito family; to Lee MacKay, Heather Sosnowski and Maureen FitzGerald for their early reads; and to my invaluable editors, Erin Kelly, Pearl Luke and Mona Fertig. Robert Amussen, my former editor and publisher, supported this project from the outset. Dr. J.S. Tyhurst, and later, Dr. Tom Strong, provided much personal encouragement. Linda and Fred Hawkshaw, Jane Watson, Harm Dekker, David Mio, Hank Bull, Glenn Lewis, Tanis Layzell and Linda St. John assisted the research. Alison Spokes, Dave Stevens, Peter Haines, Erin Kelly, Kara Knight and Matthew Peeters contributed valuable technical expertise.

Many friends and associates have given me support and respite over the years. Thanks to King Anderson, bill bissett, Heather Marren-Reitsma, Paul Batley, Carole Itter, Anne and Jack Silberman, Tony and Janet Harris, Nik and Lise Karelis, Helen Truran and Elmar Plate, Linda and Gary Hanson, Richard and Shawna Audet, Nicole and Jim Tessier, Lee MacKay and Susan Douglas, Dennis and Dylan Conlan, Nancy Rothstein, Murray Hawse, Davey Gibbons, Wayne Tofsrud, Randy Buth,

Claudia MacDonald, Ingrid Klassen, Paulie Haines, Sharron McCrimmon, Susan Foran, Teresa Plowright and Kris Glen. Thanks also to everyone at the Buchan Hotel in Vancouver and to my publisher, Mona Fertig.

Several locations have inspired the creation of *The Dancehall Years*. The Bowen Inn and The Pavilion on Bowen Island, B.C., provided the initial set, backed as they were by the coastal Salish Sea. The mountains and lakes of the Bulkley Valley, particularly the peaks of Dzil Yez and Stegyawden, and the reaches of Silverthorne Lake, Round Lake, McDowell Lake and Tyhee Lake, all helped expand the novel's horizons.

Many books provided key historical facts. I am indebted to Irene Howard's *Bowen Island 1872-1972*; Gerald Rushton's *Whistle Up the Inlet: The Union Steamship Story*; Barry Broadfoot's books, *Ten Lost Years*, *Years of Sorrow, Years of Shame* and *Six War Years*. *Justice in Our Time* by Roy Miki and Cassandra Kobayashi helped me understand the aftermath of the internment years, as did *Redress: Inside the Japanese Canadian Call for Justice* by Roy Miki. *The Nature of Sea Otters* by Stephanie Paine informed the narrative, as did *Our Coast Salish Way of Life: The Squamish* by Daniel Conner and Doreen Bethune-Johnson. *Along the Number Twenty Line* by Rolf Knight revealed much about Vancouver in the 1940s. *Man Along the Shore: The Story of the Vancouver Waterfront* was written by the longshoremen who worked there. Many thanks to Betty Jane Wagner for her excellent study of a master teacher: *Dorothy Heathcote: Drama as a Learning Medium*; to John Wyndham for his novel, *The Chrysalids*, and to Jean-Paul Sarte for his play, *The Flies*. The story of *The Dancehall Years* is imaginary, and any errors or minor shifts in time sequences are mine.

Sections of this novel have appeared in slightly different form in the following magazines: *The Capilano Review*, *Herizons*, *The B.C. Monthly*, and *Western Living*.

Many thanks to all.

Joan Haggerty
Telkwa, B.C., 2016.

Photograph by Dany Couture

Joan Haggerty was born in 1940 and raised in Vancouver, B.C. From 1962 to 1972 she lived and wrote in London, England; Formentera, Spain; and New York City. Returning to the B.C. coast, she made her home in Roberts Creek and Vancouver where she taught in the Creative Writing Dept. at the University of British Columbia. She began a second career as a high school teacher in the Bulkley Valley in 1990. Her previous books are *Please, Miss, Can I Play God?*, *Daughters of the Moon*, and *The Invitation* which was nominated for the Governor General's Award in 1994. She has spent summers on Bowen Island since childhood.